JUST KILL THE HOSTAGES

JUST KILL THE HOSTAGES

HUNTING FOR KIDNAPPERS IN A WAR ZONE

JOSEPH M. NILAND

LUMINARE PRESS
WWW.LUMINAREPRESS.COM

Just Kill the Hostages: Hunting for Kidnappers in a War Zone

Printed in the United States of America

Luminare Press
442 Charnelton St.
Eugene, OR 97401
www.luminarepress.com

LCCN: 2022919204
ISBN: 979-8-88679-139-6

For the fallen hostages—military and civilian—and their still grieving families.

CONTENTS

"The only thing necessary for the triumph of evil is that good men should do nothing."

—*Edmund Burke*

"For every complex problem there is an answer that is clear, simple, and wrong."

—*H.L. Mencken*

"It is not the critic who counts; not the man who points out how the strong man stumbles, or where the doer of deeds could have done them better. The credit belongs to the man who is actually in the arena, whose face is marred by dust and sweat and blood; who strives valiantly; who errs, who comes short again and again, because there is no effort without error and shortcoming; but who does actually strive to do the deeds; who knows great enthusiasms, the great devotions; who spends himself in a worthy cause; who at the best knows in the end the triumph of high achievement, and who at the worst, if he fails, at least fails while daring greatly, so that his place shall never be with those cold and timid souls who neither know victory nor defeat."

—*Theodore Roosevelt*

BRITISH DISCLAIMER BY THE WRITER

Some remarks and thoughts in this writing might be offensive to citizens of the United Kingdom, particularly British military or other British government personnel. The writer meant the comments to be tongue in cheek. The writer has the utmost respect, appreciation, and gratitude for the British military and other government personnel. He was there—with you—in Basra.

AMERICAN DISCLAIMER BY THE WRITER

For those who might be offended in the US government, the writer urges you to evaluate how you did business and how you are doing business today.

Recognize we can always do better.

FBI/US GOVERNMENT DISCLAIMER BY THE WRITER

The opinions expressed in this book are the writer's and not that of the FBI or the US government.

INTRODUCTION

Most hostages were not greeted with parades when they returned. Only processions. Many hostages were brutally murdered in captivity. Hostage bodies came back through complicated processes in Dover, Delaware—the US government mortuary. Only a select few people in the US government had any idea what transpired during the initial kidnap event, the hostage-holding period, and the return of a hostage.

We have all been in the wrong place at the wrong time. This is the case for all hostages and for some who simply went to Iraq and experienced the war firsthand. War zones are hazardous, and terrible things happen. Being close to a rocket impact is usually detrimental to your health. Too close and you are dead. Maybe you were "lucky" or "close enough" and not shredded with shards of hot metal and debris—just an incessant ringing in your ears. Hostage casework with the federal government can existentially hold you hostage if you let it—I did. The hostage work we oversaw in Iraq never went away in my head, like the constant ringing in my ears.

I was in the wrong place at the wrong time. Maybe it was actually the right place at the right time, depending on one's perspective. I was an employee of the US government. The second time I was in Iraq I accidentally fell into a series of unanticipated events resulting in unintended consequences: hunting for hostages and their kidnappers. I went back three more times to develop hostage casework over the next few years.

CHARACTERS IN ORDER OF APPEARANCE

John McNeil – FBI agent; assigned to HWG Baghdad and to Basra

Sheryl – FBI agent; BOC; present when John found folder

Annie Caden – FBI agent; BOC; lead agent assigned to HWG Baghdad

Palash (Paul) – TCN worked at US embassy Green Beans

Frank – FBI agent; BOC; new agent; assisted in moving furniture

Buzz – FBI agent; BOC; self-named braggart who represented macho arrogance

Ryan – SF team leader

Nathan – SF Bravo; weapons

Ashton – SF Delta; medic

Mike – SF team sergeant

Sasha – Server at the British chow hall

Kyle – SF Fox; intelligence specialist

Bradley – British security officer at Brit-HQ

Donovan – NSA analyst in Basra

Jensen – GCHQ analyst and liaison to NSA in Basra

Mr. Ethan – Senior British enlisted soldier; wielded enormous influence

Cricket – Source in Basra; wore a cricket helmet

On-Scene Commander – FBI BOC; unnamed; executive level supervisory position in Baghdad

Amelia – British Foreign Office representative

Quinn – British Foreign Office representative

PROLOGUE

The US government strategy for handling hostage events in Iraq was disjointed and faced epic operational challenges. Personnel with a passion to hunt for hostages arrived at the FBI Baghdad Operations Center in Baghdad, known as the BOC. Wide-eyed agents full of the urgency and haughtiness of the moment worked seven days a week. Then, after three months, they were exchanged for someone new.

War was a difficult environment and hard on people. Constant personnel change was a necessary requirement. Government personnel under the supervision of the FBI came to Iraq in groups referred to as a *rotation*. Some came from other agencies and worked under the umbrella of the FBI. Domestic office managers who lost personnel to the temporary assignment tolerated the mandate—via the attorney general.

Over several years, a new personnel rotation would cycle through every three months, fix what was broken, and leave with war stories to tell forever. To be fair, real work did get accomplished. The mindset was straightforward and constant from rotation to rotation. Members of the new rotation were always unhappy with the physical aspects of the BOC, such as furniture configuration, file cabinet placement, paper flow, the height of computer monitors, and on and on. The mantra from rotation to rotation: *We inherited a real mess, and we are determined to hand it over to the next rotation better than we received it.*

The prospects of rescuing a hostage in Iraq were grim. There would be very few rescues, releases, or grand homecoming parades. Numerous kidnapped contractors and soldiers were brutally executed and came home through the US government mortuary in Dover, Delaware. Smart people of great character and ability understood and developed a taste for battle in the hostage arena—but the arena was larger and more complicated than most people fathomed.

US military personnel levels in Iraq peaked in 2007 with the presence of approximately 170,000 troops. An already deadly insurgency grew and evolved. US and coalition partners responded by growing the force and putting more boots on the ground. The US war machine was bigger and broader than during the invasion four years earlier. According to the Defense Casualty Analysis System, 901 troops died in Iraq in 2007 (764 hostile and 137 non-hostile), along with 6,130 wounded. More American troops died in 2007 than any other year. The US military industrial complex mobilized and presented a thirst, hunger, and level of consumption beyond most imaginations.

BEANS, BULLETS, and BANDAIDS…The life support for a large, protracted conflict required a constant supply of materials and equipment. Open highways and byways were imperative for the continued flow of goods into Iraq and around the country. The care and feeding of US troops, along with an indeterminate number of government civilian employees, coalition forces, and contractors was complicated and dangerous.

Modern warfare environments had changed with the threat.

US and coalition military members, intelligence analysts and operators, and civilian contractors were truly surrounded. Everyone lived on Forward Operating Bases (FOBs) that dotted the country in remote and urban environments. FOB perimeters usually consisted of concrete walls and barriers moved with cranes. People living in FOBs were often under siege from indirect and direct fire from random rifle rounds, rockets, and mortars. The entry and exit points and corresponding routes were dogged by homemade bombs called improvised explosive devices (IEDs). Lethal munitions were on the ground, in the ground, and in vehicles.

Supplies and equipment arrived from outside of Iraq, sometimes aboard large cargo planes, but more often moving on the ground. Convoys of cargo trucks plied the roads twenty-four hours a day.

These convoys were often escorted and protected by civilian contract security personnel, mostly men. Some had prior military or tactical training. The work was dangerous, but it paid well.

Violence continued to escalate throughout the country in 2007. International eyes scrutinized the US military, the Iraqi government, and Western civilian security contractors carrying guns in a war zone.

Inevitably, someone would be captured and held hostage.

CHAPTER 1

WHEN EVERYTHING GOES WRONG... TAKEN HOSTAGE

DAY 1: APRIL 15, 2007

The morning began like any other. Fine dust in the air acted as a prism and bent the light—the sky exhaling a dramatic multicolored sunrise. A blood red horizon was gently consumed by the rising sun. Such opulent mornings evoked a sense of serenity—maybe even hope and promise.

That was a mirage—the place was Iraq, during the troop surge—there was no fucking serenity. It had melted into the desert sand, taking hope and promise with it.

Fifty-nine US military members had already died this month—April was only half over.

The four American security contractors were preparing to escort a convoy of trucks: cleaning guns, checking radios, and topping off gas tanks. They were ready. Each carried a rifle and a pistol and drove an SUV. Ideally each SUV would also carry an armed passenger but not today—nobody was available. The contractors escorted a small convoy of trucks carrying folding chairs, air conditioners, and lettuce: random necessities of war. They safely delivered the trucks and cargo to a small British forward operating base, or FOB, in southern Iraq. The trip had been unremarkable. The four Americans lived on a compound on a British FOB in Al Muthanna and were ready to return. US FOBs in southern Iraq were sparse; the British were major coalition partners, maintaining the largest force in the south and occupying the lower third of Iraq. So far, the day was unremarkable, the conditions were hot and dry and perfect for driving fast on a desolate Iraqi highway.

The contractors were friends and got along well. As it often happens when people work together, the men had come up with nicknames for each other. The names were as original as they were cliché. The most recent addition to the group was from Austin, Texas—he was dubbed ***Tex***. The oldest member was from West Virginia and habitually hummed the state song "Take Me Home, Country Roads." He was briefly called Country Roads, which was later shortened to ***CR***. The group's prior military member was a former Marine who grew up on a farm on the Eastern Shore of Maryland and harvested crabs in the summer—he was lightheartedly called ***Shorebilly***. The youngest of the group was a surfing instructor from California—fondly given the name ***Surfboy***.

Soon after the American contractors delivered the convoy to its destined warehouse, one of their SUVs began overheating. The SUV was turned off to cool and would not restart. The contractors decided to leave it in the warehouse parking lot and deal with retrieval later. Returning to their compound with three trucks was safe and reasonable. Nobody could predict that this was the first mishap in a series of cascading life-altering events.

The driver of the lead SUV took a shortcut to the front gate and hit a piece of rebar protruding from the ground.

The thick metal rod anchored in concrete ripped through the oil pan causing the engine to shut down within a minute. Fortunately, the SUV stopped running while they were still within the perimeter and safety of the FOB.

The two remaining SUVs were in good condition. One SUV had a cracked exhaust pipe, making it very loud, but otherwise the vehicle was running well. Collectively, the four contractors agreed the best option was to get back to their compound. The hard part of their day was over. Besides, nobody was prepared to stay overnight—accommodations at this FOB were known to be terrible.

The drive was only forty minutes at high speed. Each contractor had traveled this route over 150 times—what could go wrong?

Fifteen minutes after leaving the safety of the FOB, the easy drive back to the compound went horrendously downhill. Surfboy was driving the lead SUV. He had particularly quick reflexes and liked driving fast. Surfboy saw a large hole in the pavement and tried to swerve around it—the lifeless crater showed no mercy. The SUV's left rear tire hit the edge at eighty-five miles per hour. The angle and speed snapped the wheel from the axle. The SUV rolled twice then landed back on its remaining three wheels and slid sideways—slowly grinding to a stop.

Tex was driving the second SUV. He swerved just in time to miss the hole, stopping about five yards behind the damaged SUV. Tex saw sparks flying from the edge of the damaged SUV as it scraped to a halt against the pavement—smoke billowed from its rear. The passenger in the second SUV was CR. He grabbed a fire extinguisher and ran to snuff out a small fire burning in the lead vehicle's empty rear wheel well, while Surfboy and his passenger Shorebilly clambered out of the SUV. Remarkably, Surfboy was unhurt. Shorebilly had a four-inch gash across his forehead.

Tex backed the last SUV about thirty yards away in case the fire in the damaged SUV erupted. He grabbed a first aid kit and ran to the damaged SUV.

Keeping the last SUV safe and running was critical. Tex's decision to back up and park at such a distance was smart. They could not lose their only remaining vehicle.

The four fatigued contractors gathered near the back of the damaged SUV in the sweltering sun. CR took what he needed from the first aid kit and cleaned and bandaged the gash on Shorebilly's forehead.

The four men discussed what to do next while glaring at the smoking three-wheeled SUV. The deafening roar of the still-running SUV with the broken exhaust system was almost unbearable even thirty yards behind them. The physical environment was unfriendly, as were some of the people they might meet in this part of the country. The contractors knew to get going quickly—a moving target was harder to hit or grab.

Tex tried radioing the company command center from the transmitters in both SUVs. The radio signal would not connect to the communication center or tower repeaters. Distance and terrain rendered the radios useless.

Everyone agreed not to hit the "panic-button" in either SUV since they still had one functioning vehicle. The "panic-button" triggered an emergency satellite communication with their location and need for immediate help. It was not an actual emergency—close, but not yet. They were not under fire, the injury was relatively minor, and they still had functioning transportation: one last and very loud SUV.

The satellite telephone in the console of the lead SUV was useless. The battery was dead. The phone had been left in the "on" position the day before, draining the battery. It was supposed to shut off after a period of no-use, but someone had disabled that feature...so it would be on and always ready to use. The cord for charging the satellite phone was kept at their compound taped to a computer by the front door...so it would not get lost.

Each contractor had a cellular telephone. Cell towers in this part of the country were sparse: no signal. The phones were as useless as the radios.

They needed to keep moving. An open desolate road in the middle of the desert...in a war zone...was the wrong place to be standing still—it was dangerous and an invitation for disaster.

They briefly discussed the likelihood that the broken vehicle would be stolen or set ablaze before tomorrow—nobody cared. Tex mentioned how *lucky* they were that the SUV only rolled twice, and Shorebilly responded by throwing a water bottle at him. The laceration on Shorebilly's forehead was seeping blood and mixed with sweat—running into his eyes.

The contractors focused on the damaged SUV, the unusable communication equipment, and Shorebilly's bleeding forehead—they needed to get moving. The four Americans turned around and began walking toward the last functional SUV. Only then did they see the nine vehicles streaming toward them. The blaring noise from the broken exhaust blocked the sound of the arriving trucks. The earlier decision to park the SUV in case of fire had been correct—but now their escape vehicle seemed a million miles away.

The line of vehicles skidding to a stop was more of a security motorcade than a convoy: four open-bed trucks, four SUVs, and one black van. Machine guns on improvised mounts were staffed and ready to fire in four of the open-bed trucks. Makeshift "gun trucks" were common in Iraq and usually had space for extra personnel carrying more guns. One gun truck parked behind the contractor's roaring SUV, and a second pulled in front of it. Even if the contractors could make it to their SUV, they were surrounded and boxed in. In the back of each open-bed truck, three men with rifles crouched beside the machine gunner, each dressed in black and wearing face and head coverings.

The riflemen jumped to the pavement, as additional gunmen flowed from the SUVs. The contractors were now completely cut off from their still-running SUV. The gunmen moved with efficiency and ease as though rehearsed. Rifle barrels and hand grips were wrapped with burlap to avoid burning their hands. Movement from the trucks and SUVs was tactically precise and aggressive. The contractors intuitively knew that initiating a gunfight would be suicide. The contractors were in serious trouble—immediately outgunned and outnumbered.

People who provided security rarely considered being overpowered and overwhelmed. Life-and-death scenarios evolved and shifted. Sometimes the escalation toward deadly force could be slow and incremental. And other times the deadliness of a situation could be unexpectedly violent and immediate like a brick slamming you in the face during a tornado—in the dark.

The gunmen stood within twenty feet of the contractors—yelling. A cacophony of screaming in Arabic and broken English resulted in a confusing blur of noise.

The sliding door opened on the side of the van. The gunmen stood still. It was silent except for the blaring exhaust system on the SUV. Nobody moved—the contractors barely breathing.

A deep voice from inside the van called out in Arabic.

The machine gunner in the open-bed truck nearest the contractors spun his belt-fed machine gun toward the contractors' last-loud-lifesaving-only-hope-SUV. An ear-splitting burst of machine gun fire lasted four seconds. Holes were everywhere with the engine billowing smoke. The SUV with the absurdly loud exhaust pipe was permanently and crushingly quiet.

Spent shell casings bouncing and clattering in the bed of the truck and on the pavement gave way to the rumble of gun truck engines.

Things got worse.

Gunmen pushed the contractors closer to each other. Resistance was met with the pounding of rifle butts. The contractors struggled to keep their weapons but fighting the gunmen was useless. The men were brutally beaten by the overpowering gunmen. Two contractors suffered broken fingers, and the bandage was ripped from Shorebilly's forehead by the front sight of a rifle barrel dragging across his face.

The situation was deteriorating as a voice from inside the van yelled something in Arabic. The contractors were immediately hit with rifle butts knocking them to the ground, and quickly stomped into submission. The beating continued—pushing their heads down into the flour-like dirt, which immediately mixed with blood and sweat, coating their faces with a muddy red paste.

Facedown and disoriented, they felt aggressive yanking and pulling of their feet and legs—the gunmen removing the contractors' boots. A moment later each had his hands tightly bound behind his back with his own bootlaces.

The contractors were viciously grabbed by the throat, neck, and elbows—hoisted from a prone position to their knees. A rifle barrel pressed against each forehead.

The contractors never imagined or believed they would be physically overwhelmed and disarmed. That was something that happened to someone else...not them...they had never considered or trained to be devastatingly vanquished.

The gunmen stood unmoving and menacingly on the balls of their feet—leaning forward and ready to pull the trigger or pounce on the contractors. All they needed was the command to move.

An exceptionally tall figure dressed in black stepped effortlessly out of the van's side door and silently surveyed the scene—he was unarmed. One hand gesturing toward the van, he calmy said something in Arabic.

The gunmen holding guns to the heads of the contractors stepped back while others stepped forward. The contractors were kicked and pounded to the ground, grabbed by the elbows, and dragged facedown toward the van—feet and knees scraped against the earth, raising a mirky fog of fine dirt. The boot laces securing their hands cut into their already bleeding wrists. One contractor suffered a dislocated shoulder, another a broken hand, and two were rendered unconscious when they were slammed onto the pavement near the van.

The gunmen hastily blindfolded the contractors with the burlap from their rifle barrels, then picked up the men—and literally threw them into the van. The gunmen did not attempt to hide or cover the contractors.

The contractors were now hostages.

THESE FOUR AMERICAN CONTRACTORS WOULD LATER BE referred to as the *Broken Wheel Hostages* or *BWH* by people searching for them. Multi-person hostage events were often nicknamed for easy reference. A moniker usually came from a distinguishing component of a kidnapping.

The SUV missing a wheel at the end of gouged pavement near a giant pothole made it clear what had probably happened. The SUV hit the hole, and the wheel broke. The SUVs were found the next day by a British military convoy.

CHAPTER 2

FBI BAGHDAD OPERATIONS CENTER... FIRST STEPS

DAY 72: JUNE 26, 2007

Nothing was easy in Iraq, starting with your first steps.

Ten FBI agents trudged through the heat across the gravel lot and entered a nondescript four-story building: the FBI Baghdad Operations Center, known simply as the BOC. Eight of the agents had arrived in Iraq the night before; the two senior FBI agents had been in the country only two weeks. On the same concrete step, nine of the ten agents tripped. Two agents completely fell. Water bottles scattered about the floor. A subtle first lesson. Stop thinking *American* while in Iraq—if you do not, you are destined to stumble.

US building codes gave Americans reasonable assurance that construction met safe, consistent standards. In fact, most people usually took them for granted. As a result, Americans anticipated the height of a stairway's step would be the same from step to step, and from one place to the next. Americans walked up and down steps all day and never thought about foot placement, or the rise or depth of a step. Construction at the FBI BOC was abysmal. The steps were not level and had different heights. It was easy to fall. Some people learned to avoid tripping on the steps—adapting quickly. Others tripped over the same steps every few hours throughout their entire deployment.

Late June 2007 FBI Baghdad Operations Center

John McNeil lumbered up the stairs at the BOC, sweating profusely, and drank from a bottle of water he grabbed from an open crate at the bottom of the stairs just inside the building entrance. His head pounded. John attributed the magnitude of his hangover to dehydration and extreme temperatures. Of course, the real culprit was the six hours of heavy drinking at the Saturday night FBI BOC liaison function. The Saturday night parties were infamous. He did not stumble or fall as he negotiated the malformed stairs. John was physically and mentally agile.

John stood six feet one inches weighing 195 and was in shape. He had played high school football at Eleanor Roosevelt High School in Greenbelt, Maryland, and was a walk-on outside linebacker at the University of Maryland in College Park. He suffered a broken hand in practice in his second year, which allowed for academics to become more of a priority—John permanently left the football field for the library. He earned an accounting degree with honors and was the flavor of the day for hiring by the FBI when he graduated. The FBI preferred hiring people with work experience, but it went through phases of targeting specific disciplines. Accounting degrees and law degrees were popular the year John was hired.

John was assigned to a white-collar fraud squad in Norfolk, Virginia. He hated it. Eventually transferring to a drug squad, he found his niche. He thrived when working on the street and coordinating with other agencies. John had been with the FBI for about ten years before volunteering for an FBI rotational deployment in Iraq.

He had never been married and had no kids—he liked the independence. It allowed for a variety of work assignments. The women he dated seemed to like him more when he was around less—John was fine on his own, and he lived for the job.

Shortly after arriving on his first Iraq rotation last year, John discovered how real work got done. Like in the US—relationships and trust often developed informally. Having a cup of coffee or a beer with someone opened channels never available at a conference room table.

John turned the corner near the BOC command center: a small office staffed twenty-four hours a day, seven days a week to answer phones, log phone calls, monitor random events, and funnel information to the BOC hierarchy. Watching TV and surfing the Internet were the predominant activities. Today was Sheryl's turn to occupy the center. Her eyes bloodshot and her stomach nauseous, she called out to John as he walked by. She needed a small but pressing favor.

Sheryl was another quick learner. She had an astute understanding of how life worked in Baghdad—after only one week. She was on a fraud squad in a large suburb outside of Chicago and was well-regarded by her peers. Sheryl and John got along well, and since John had been in Iraq before she trusted his guidance. This morning she was not feeling well.

"John, do you have a minute…I gotta pee. Can you watch the phones?"

"Sure, no problem," John said. "I need to catch my breath after those steps, and my brain is throbbing."

"Thanks," she said.

Her forehead was bathed in sweat even though the room was cold. Sheryl passed John as he came through the door. Sheryl was more hungover than John. Unfortunately, she had to get up early to sit in the command center. Fortunately, the bathroom was nearby, and she was in full stride. If she did not make it to the bathroom, it would not be the first time someone had puked in a trash can at the BOC after a Saturday night.

John stepped into the room, briefly recalling the furniture arrangement a year ago. Not much had changed. He had spent three months in 2006 at the BOC before returning home for ten months. In January 2007 FBI headquarters announced they needed to fill personnel positions in Baghdad. He was one of the few who volunteered to return. He had the same assignment as the year before, organizing detainee debriefing reports. This year he was two weeks into his rotation and saw that his workload would not be very time consuming. He had already started going to the gym daily.

John slumped into a misshapen black plastic-leather chair and looked around the room. He had sat in the exact chair a year earlier. It was overstuffed and comfortable. The worn seat was low to the floor, and the padded arms were shredded. Everything looked about the same. As usual, the furniture had been rearranged.

The room contained a couple of telephones, two computer monitors, a security camera monitor, two small desks along the walls, a television, a bunk bed, and a small two-seat black plastic-leather couch next to the chair where John was sitting. John stretched his back, took another pull off the water bottle, and set the bottle down. His head throbbed. The torn plastic-leather padding on the chair arms irritated his arms. John rested them outside either side of the chair, leaning forward to stretch his back again. His hand brushed against a folder that was on the floor between the chair and couch. When he picked up the folder, he had no idea that it would be one of those ridiculously random life-changing moments. But it was—and all because Sheryl had a horrendous hangover and had to pee…or puke.

"Hey John, thanks for covering the phones," Sheryl said a few minutes later as she wiped her forehead with her sleeve and took a sip of Gatorade. She sat in the chair near the desk and glanced at the camera monitor to view the BOC entrances.

She looked back to John. "These liaison bar nights here are brutal. I didn't think I could drink any more or sing 'Sweet Caroline' any louder. My throat still hurts…and I feel like a zombie."

She leaned to her right and spit into a trash can. Today was the beginning of what would be a two-day hangover for Sheryl.

John nodded then held up the folder he had found between the chair and couch, and said, "Hey, the title on this folder looks familiar for some reason." Handwritten across the top of the folder were the letters *BWH* and the word *hostages*. "Is this a kidnap case where there was something to do with contractors in a convoy or something?" John thumbed the open edge and took a drink of water.

Sheryl spit in the trash can again. "Yep, that sounds right. Annie was just in here, and she's assigned to HWG, it must have slid out of the pile of paperwork she was carrying. She's in the HWG area around the corner on this floor. She's easy to find. She's the only other woman in the building. I'm sure she's gonna be looking for that folder."

"What does HWG stand for again?" John asked.

Sheryl spit in the trash can and said, "HWG is a Hostage Working Group."

"Oh yeah," said John. He took another sip of water and heaved himself out of the chair, "I'll track her down and get this back to her." John stopped at the door and looked back at Sheryl. "Let me know if you need a break; I'll be around for a few."

"Thanks...much appreciated," she said, eking out a grateful smile before spitting in the trash can again and sipping her Gatorade.

Many government entities in Iraq were referred to by some acronym or another. The FBI Hostage Working Group or HWG was staffed with FBI BOC personnel and coordinated with HWGs at the embassy and elsewhere around Iraq. HWGs seemed to be everywhere. Discerning who was with what HWG and what their role was could be challenging.

John and many others did not know that almost every military command or area with a large, independent operational activity had some sort of Hostage Working Group. The FBI had an HWG, the US embassy in Baghdad had a multi-agency HWG, and various military commands throughout Iraq set up HWGs. Information was hoarded, redundancy was the norm, and the lack of interagency coordination was a constant battle. Kidnap events increased. More Westerners and American soldiers were kidnapped and killed.

John's current assignment kept him inside the US embassy. He was already bored. It was going to be a long three months. John went to return the file and introduce himself to Annie, not realizing he was taking the first physical steps to being reassigned to the HWG.

John walked through the makeshift conference room and across the hall to the HWG office. It was simple: Four computer stations against the wall and a long conference table in the middle strewn with junk food from thoughtfully sent care packages. File cabinets sat in one corner next to a desk that overflowed with randomly stacked files and notebooks. Flow charts adorned the walls and showed enemy organizational structure that made sense only to the person who had made them. Over one desk was a list of hostages with dates of capture.

Since the invasion in 2003, American and coalition hostage events had mixed results; from beheading to release or rescue. By the summer of 2007 there were numerous American and British hostages. John had seen the graphics and charts before and recalled that incidents involving US soldiers seemed to stay within the purview of the military.

A small office in the corner was for the HWG supervisor. The door was shut, and John heard an animated but muffled conversation. He was about to toss the folder in a pile on the conference table when the door to the small office opened and the intensity of an ongoing argument was clear. Annie marched out of the office, red faced, holding a pile of case files in one hand and a pad of paper and pen in the other. She shook her head and muttered just under her breath.

John saw her silently mouth the words "stupid fuck."

Annie walked across the room to the corner workstation, sat down, and unlocked her computer screen. It was clear this was Annie's work area. Folders and files next to her computer had sticky notes with her name on them: Annie Caden. John stood at the edge of the room for a moment and debated whether he should try to return the folder another time. Annie immediately clicked her computer mouse and watched a video of a hostage that the man's captors had made and broadcast over the Internet a month ago. She took notes while the hostage read a list of demands from a piece of paper he was holding. The hostage spoke in a quiet monotone that only Annie heard with her earbuds. She was oblivious to anything else. John decided to approach Annie and drop off the folder as she picked up a case file.

She looked toward the supervisor's office and muttered, "What a fuckin' idiot." Then she shook her head. John made sure he came into Annie's peripheral view before he got too close. Intuitively, John knew it might be a bad idea to surprise Annie.

Annie turned toward John as she saw him out of the corner of her eye, pulled out her earbuds, and nodded with a civil one syllable greeting. "Hey."

"Hi, I'm John," he said. "We're on the same rotation, but I'm not around much. They have me over at the embassy, so I haven't met everyone yet."

She looked quizzically at John, prompting him to continue. "I think this is yours," he said, handing the folder to Annie and adding, "Sheryl thought it was one of your cases. I found it in the command center."

Annie looked at the BWH folder and said, "Thanks, I'm Annie. Thanks for bringing this over. I was going through files when I covered the phones last night. It must've slid out of the pile. It's the folder with the monthly overviews and summaries."

Annie was doing the job of four people and needed help with the BWH case. In fact, she had just finished arguing with her supervisor about the need for more people. Annie knew she would have to try to find extra help on her own. Fighting with her supervisor about reassigning personnel was going nowhere.

She tapped the edge of the folder and said, "This case needs work...and at least two more people working on it... which won't happen."

She sneered in the direction of her supervisor's office glanced at the folder and looked at John. "Did you check out any of the summaries?"

John shrugged his shoulders and shook his head. "No, I didn't want to overstep or get into anyone's lane."

Annie nodded in approval at John's point of professional courtesy. Agents have boundaries, and nobody likes another agent stepping into their sandbox without asking. John had been around long enough to know a little civility and professional etiquette can remove barriers and obstacles that are immovable once in place.

To make progress on the case, Annie needed help or at the very least someone with a fresh view and innovative ideas. She pulled out the chair next to her that had been pushed tightly against the edge of the table.

She dragged a pile of case files off the seat, tossed them under her desk, and said, "Do you have a minute? You know, check out the summaries? Look, I need help, and I'm trying to recruit anyone I can." Annie had to take a chance. Besides, Sheryl spoke well of him, and he seemed...OK.

The case files contained documents and notes to be burned. Annie kept this pile of scrap paper in a case file on the chair to keep people from wandering up and taking a seat. She was a worker, she was serious, and you did not get invited into Annie's world unless Annie did the inviting. Annie appreciated John's tact and handed the BWH hostage file back to him. Another view might be productive.

Annie was smart, hardworking and fearless. She hailed from Elkhorn, Kentucky, a small town outside of Louisville. Her accent faded when she went away to college. It came back strong during the summers when mucking stables on the family horse farm. Like her charm, she could turn it on and off at will.

She had an academic scholarship to Stanford and played soccer. She graduated with honors and stayed to earn a law degree. She passed the bar on her first attempt but never practiced law. She was not sure she wanted to be a lawyer—she was building her options. She applied for the FBI. As usual they were looking for recruits with accounting and law degrees—an exemption from the work requirement. She was a fit and did well when arriving at her first office in Fresno, California, five years ago. She stood about five foot four, and weighed 110 pounds, and was into CrossFit training. She had never fired a gun before going to agent training in Quantico. Like many people without a firearms background, she excelled—never using guns meant no bad habits to break. She was the third-highest-scoring shooter in the class.

When the field office needed another firearms instructor to conduct training and qualifications, she jumped at the chance. She was the only woman in the firearms training class at Quantico and won the Best Shooter award. Annie was highly regarded by her supervisor and peers at the office. She was on a bank robbery squad and thriving professionally. For now, the job was her life.

Turning and reaching behind her computer, Annie grabbed another pile of files about four inches thick. "This is everything on BWH; if you have time, can you see what you think?" She smiled gently, "I really could use a second set of eyes. This Hostage Working Group thing is a clusterfuck."

John maintained his composure, but his pulse was racing; he was elated to have something like this to do. "Sure, my pleasure. Is there anything I should be thinking about?" He tapped gently on the top file.

Annie scratched her head, shrugged, and said, "No, just consider solutions and operational options. These kidnap cases are going nowhere fast. These four guys have been held hostage since the middle of April. We have no idea where they are or what really happened. We have a hostage video they sent to the press somehow. There are six different agents working several hostage cases each. It's a mess."

John turned and walked, then stopping at the door looked to Annie. "What are the chances some of these cases that are treated like individual events might be somehow related?"

Annie shrugged and shook her head. "Hard to say…but, right now any way you look at it, we are way behind in the game—we need to think outside the box."

Hostage Status: 72 Days in Captivity

All four hostages were held in the same location—a basement. They had no idea what day it was. The cut on Shorebilly's forehead had finally stopped bleeding but oozed pus from infection. The metal door locked from the outside. The only light came through an eight-by-twelve-inch vent high on a wall—the vent had bars. The air was stale, and the stench was overwhelming. The temperature was about one hundred degrees—at night.

Food consisted of about six ounces of crushed chickpeas and dates in the mornings. If they were *lucky*, they were fed twice per day. The frequency and quantity sometimes changed depending on which set of guards was in charge. Two sixteen-ounce bottles of water per day still left them dehydrated. They were emaciated and weak.

They relieved themselves in a five-gallon utility bucket that they called the *bathroom bucket*. The bucket always stayed in the room. Typically, a guard randomly picked one hostage for the daily rinsing of the bucket. For the last two weeks, the frequency dropped to once every two days.

Guards changed every three days. The hostages referred to one set of guards as *nice* and the other set as *mean*. The mean set was vicious—upon arriving for their three-day shift, a guard picked one hostage randomly and bound his wrists with rope. The hostage hung by the wrists for the first hour of their shift. Any hostage attempting to assist the suspended hostage was beaten. Like many buildings in Iraq, the holding cell had rebar protruding from the ceiling. The metal rods were curved and sometimes used to hold light fixtures. The short length of rebar easily held the weight of an American hostage getting lighter by the day.

The hostages were video recorded about once a week. Recording stopped after the first month as their appearance began to deteriorate. The hostages would wait outside in a courtyard while two guards recorded. The hostage was required to say their name and read a list of demands. The list of demands changed every week.

The thought of hostages overpowering their captors and

escaping was inconceivable. The hostages had no idea where they were but suspected they were in a city. Escaping without transportation and a means to defend themselves would result in death at the hands of the city dwellers; sort of like jumping from the proverbial frying pan into the fire. For now, they would have to survive where they were.

Hope was fading along with their strength and weight.

CHAPTER 3

FROM THE FBI BOC TO THE US EMBASSY... ALWAYS A CHALLENGE

DAY 72 (*CONTINUED*): JUNE 26, 2007

John packed the files in a courier bag and set off for the embassy, where he had a desk and finally something to do. The embassy was about a half mile away. John easily walked down the misshapen stairs and glanced at the courier bag. As he descended the dimly lit stairway, he fleetingly wondered about the files in the satchel and what might be in store for him. He was excited about the new challenge.

He took a few breaths of cool air to prepare himself, then crossed what once had been a kitchen, and stepped out a door into the brutal inferno of the day.

The BOC had its own covered parking lot adjacent to the main building. With space for about ten SUVs, it ran the length of the main BOC building and the FBI BOC bar. John glanced at the bar area and shook his head. Just twelve short hours ago the space had held 150 people drinking from red cups and standing on crushed pretzels and potato chips—music blaring.

He ambled across the lot through the dusty gravel, got into a yellow pickup truck, and reached under the seat for the screwdriver otherwise known as the ignition key. John shoved it into the steering column, twisted, and the engine started on the first try. He had backed into a parking spot like most others who knew how difficult the environment was in Iraq. Experienced drivers always backed into parking places in case they needed a jump-start or tow.

John pulled out of the covered area and cut the wheel hard, tires crushing into the gravel. The first gate was a twenty-foot steel door on metal wheels resting on a metal rail. He got out of the truck, walked to the edge of the steel door, which had a four-by-four-inch opening at chest level. He reached through the hole, grabbed the chain, and spun it around so he could access the combination lock. After opening the lock and hanging the loose chain back in the hole, John used all of his weight and leg-strength to slide the door on the rail far enough to drive the truck through the gap. After driving through the opening, he put the truck in park, got out, dragged the gate shut, and padlocked the chain.

He drove about thirty yards through a series of garages and storage units on either side of the street to the second gate: chain link with canvas-lined fencing. The fence had to be picked up at the edge, moved, then put back in place and locked. He passed through the fence and waved politely to the Iraqi guard who stood a post nearby. John was never sure exactly what the Iraqi was protecting, but smiling and waving to people with machine guns seemed like a polite gesture.

He drove through neighborhood streets to the main artery in Baghdad leading to the US embassy. He arrived at a large parking lot between the airfield and the embassy and stopped for the guard at the gate. John held up the pouch constantly hanging around his neck containing his identification card, and waved to the guard, who smiled and directed him through. John parked, picked up the currier bag off the front seat, and walked across the lot to the embassy fence line gate. He held up his identification card in its pouch, removing his sunglasses.

Odd courtesies *down range* made a significant difference in day-to-day life. Simple things like removing your sunglasses so the guard could see your eyes and lifting your identification card near your face made the entire process work better. Modest civilities improved the quality of life immeasurably.

John walked through the gate and passed the empty fountain with sculpted dolphins in front of the embassy. John never saw the fountain with water and wondered what it might have been like before the invasion, and before pockmarks gouged its edge. John vividly remembered when a rocket carved those gashes into the fountain. He had been walking to the front doors at the embassy the previous year for the first time. As he stepped through the door, an ear-splitting sound like thunder from a lightning strike fifty feet away reverberated through the building; the sound of a rocket crashing into the inner edge of the fountain. The embassy perimeter doors slammed shut; nobody could enter or leave. An alarm finally sounded, and everyone was directed away from windows. Nobody was killed, but several people were hurt. John kept that rocket attack in the back of his mind whenever he entered the embassy. He was not sure why, he just did.

John continued across the pavement to the embassy doors, taking off his sunglasses, and holding up his identification pouch. He nodded and smiled. John was quickly recognized and welcomed—he was polite and respectful to the guards. He walked forward as the bullet- and bombproof doors clicked and opened. He maintained his stride. Security personnel at gates and doors made life easy, or difficult.

A BURST OF FRIGID AIR RAN OVER JOHN AS HE TURNED the corner of the first embassy corridor. By 2007, over a billion dollars had been spent on the US embassy operations in Iraq. The former palace and now US embassy was one of the few structures where systems like water, sewage, air conditioning, and electricity consistently functioned. When something broke, a small army of contractors was immediately available to address the problem. Keeping the embassy personnel happy and comfortable meant large future contracts, renewals, and new business acquisition across the war-torn country indefinitely. The US war chest was fully funded, and money flowed.

John wound his way through the corridors to a huge open hall with ceilings fifty feet high. At either end of the hall, huge portraits of someone or something—likenesses of Saddam Hussein—were covered with large sheets of canvas. A station of twenty internet terminals occupied one end of the hall. The computers were always busy, and to use them one took a number like at a deli. A thirty-minute limit was in place if people were waiting. Email had replaced most letter writing.

Adjacent to the internet stations were several amazingly comfortable couches and chairs where soldiers and civilians sat, talked, read, or dozed. On the other side of the hall sat twenty circular tables that seated four to six people. Embassy personnel or visitors would eat or hold meetings, or simply connect and go elsewhere. More couches sprawled against the wall.

The hall's most important feature stood next to the tables, across from the internet stations against the wall. A Green Beans coffee kiosk. It was the closest thing in Baghdad to Starbucks and served a wide variety of coffee drinks. The kiosk was crewed by some of the hardest-working people in Iraq, known as TCNs or Third-Country Nationals. Recruited from the poorest parts of the globe, TCNs were the backbone of difficult physical labor and were paid at rates based on salaries in their home country. Contractors recruited them because they would work tirelessly for far less pay than any westerner.

The workers at the US embassy Green Beans came from India, worked sixteen-hour shifts with few breaks, and earned a pittance. They never failed or hesitated to offer a smile or kind word when they handed a fancy three-dollar coffee to a busy, self-absorbed, and oblivious embassy staffer. Often, a line of ten or more people waited for fancy coffee. John was lucky today: only two people in line. He stopped to get a quick caffeine fix.

John stepped up to the counter and said, "Hey, Paul, how are things today?"

TCNs from India often adopted a common American name that sounded like their given name. Paul's real name was Palash, but John respected his wishes and used the Americanized version. It made things easier for the Americans who bothered to learn their names, and it was part of their assimilation into the embassy arena.

Paul, with fatigued eyes, fourteen hours into his sixteen-hour shift, grinned and said, "Hello, Mr. John, how are you?"

John tried to get Paul to drop the *Mister*, but Paul would not have it. Paul's trainee just finished John's drink, even though John had not ordered yet.

"How's your afternoon going, Paul?" John asked.

"Very well as always, thank you for asking," Paul responded in his most proper English, masking fatigue and aching feet.

The trainee reverently handed the prepared coffee to Paul, so he could present it to John. Paul inspected the surface of the drink while the trainee stood anxiously awaiting the verdict. The trainee somehow had used a straw and toothpick to create a perfect smiley face out of foam in the center of the drink. Paul passed the drink to John and nodded to his assistant, who paused just a moment for John's reaction.

"Well, look at that, it's so perfect I don't know if I can drink it!" Paul and his trainee were beaming. John smiled, gave the coffee a grateful sniff, and nodded, tucking a dollar into a Styrofoam cup near the register. Everyone's day was better, for a minute or two. Small acts of kindness changed the landscape of one's life in Iraq.

John walked past the internet stations, out of the large rotunda, and on to the end of an adjoining hallway. He pushed the start button on the electronic cypher lock, touched the four-digit security code, and the door lock clicked. He opened the door and crossed the room, passing three empty computer cubicles to reach his desk in the far corner.

For the next eight hours, John pored over the case files and took notes. As he read the hostage profiles that someone from the last rotation had prepared, he saw Shorebilly was from Maryland. He wondered what the former Marine might be going through. John knew his hometown: Stevensville. He had passed through it back when he used to take long weekends and drive from Quantico, Virginia, to Maryland's Eastern Shore. He even knew the store where the guy worked before going to Iraq. The Love Point Deli, just off Route 50. It was where John had usually stopped to pick up beer and ice.

HOSTAGE PROFILES

Stephen "Surfboy" Kearney

Age/Gender: Twenty-two-year-old male

Born: Encinitas, California

Education: Homeschooled in Del Mar, California; certificate, 2005

Employment: Carlsbad Surf Academy (Instructor), 2005-2007

Military: None

Family: Southern California; unmarried/no children

Miscellaneous: Motivation for current employment—financial; curiosity to see Iraq firsthand

Denny "Shorebilly" Roland

Age/Gender: Twenty-six-year-old male

Born: Stevensville, Maryland

Education: High school graduate; Kent Island High School, 1999

Employment: From high school to USMC; post-USMC Love Point Deli, Wine and Spirits, Stevensville, Maryland, 2005-2007

Military: USMC: 1999-2005; Honorable; one-year tour in Iraq (2005)

Family: All located on Kent Island, Maryland; married with one infant daughter

Miscellaneous: Motivation for current employment—financial (recent birth of daughter and knowledge of salaries paid for contract security work in Iraq)

Ben "Tex" Devito

Age/Gender: Twenty-five-year-old male

Born: Laredo, Texas

Education: High school graduate; St. Augustine High School, 2000

Employment: Road construction surveyor, 2001 to 2006

Military: None

Family: Laredo, Texas; unmarried/no children

Miscellaneous: Motivation for current employment; financial; deferred admission for Texas A&M (enrolled for next semester); provided full-time care to parents (home hospice); mother deceased 2003 and father deceased 2007 (one month before hired by contractor)

Mitchell "CR" Engle

Age/Gender: Thirty-five-year-old male

Born: Keyser, West Virginia

Education: High school graduate; Keyser High School, 1990

Employment: Long-haul truck driver, 1990-2005

Military: None

Family: Keyser and Fort Ashby, West Virginia; married, divorced, remarried; one son from first marriage, sixteen years old; twin daughters, two years old

Miscellaneous: Motivation for current employment—financial; employed as a contract truck driver in Iraq for one year (2005) and transitioned to contract security 2006

Hostage Status: 72 Days in Captivity

Surfboy and Shorebilly were whispering—any communication between hostages was not allowed. The nice guards turned their heads ignoring quiet talk among the hostages. The mean guards were brutally intolerant. Right now, the nice guards were on duty.

Surfboy said, "Bro, waves off of Tamarack Beach in Carlsbad are always righteous...the sets are steady and amped...not like those bullshit ankle slappers on the East Coast." He was the epitome of a California surf-dude—living proof they existed beyond movie stereotyping.

Wiping the pus at the edge of the semi-healed cut on his forehead, Shorebilly smirked and defended his coast, saying, "Well, I guess our waves do suck...but we have the Chesapeake Bay...tons of cool shoreline for kayaking...and our seafood is better. We have crabs...Old Bay spice...shit like that."

They shared a muted laugh. Both knew Southern California beaches were famous for surfing and consistently great weather. The other hostages nodded off or dreamed with their eyes open.

Surfboy lightheartedly tossed a small pebble at Shore-billy and said, "When we get out of here, come on over to the left coast and we'll shred some waves and..."

Before he could finish his sentence, the metal door flew open slamming against the wall—four guards stormed in carrying three-foot pieces of hose. The hostages had lost track of time, not realizing the change in guard shifts. The mean guards were on duty.

The first guard looked around the room. "Shut the fuck up...filthy fucking Americans!"

A melee of guards swinging rubber hoses at the hostages lasted three minutes. The hostages would not talk for the next three days. Right now, the mean guards were in charge.

CHAPTER 4

BOOZE RUN . . . BAR PREP

DAY 76: JUNE 30, 2007

For the next several days John read the case files and followed up on details that caught his attention. He scoured databases and pored over intelligence reports up to the Secret level from his computer and spoke repeatedly with Annie via secure telephone. Fortunately, John's supervisor supported the hostage project. For now, John had the tacit nod to work with HWG if he was *seen* at the embassy.

The first time he called Annie with a "quick question," the conversation lasted an hour. It was clear to Annie that John took a sincere interest in the hostage casework. In subsequent calls, Annie noted that John had researched events and prepared for the conversation. By the end of the week, Annie was relying upon John as a sounding board.

Annie and John agreed to meet Saturday after the 10 a.m. rotation meeting held each week in a single-story building adjacent to the main FBI BOC building. This smaller building and surrounding courtyard were otherwise known as the FBI bar. The meeting room was the bar's largest space and doubled as a makeshift movie theater during the week.

During the weekly assembly, the BOC hierarchy praised and chastised the deployed personnel, summarized the successes of the prior week, and presented the challenges of the week ahead. Duties were assigned, such as destruction of classified documents, usually by burning them in an open fire pit in the bar's courtyard, organizing people and vehicles for a booze run, and, of course, moving furniture. For the next few hours, preparing for the Saturday night event was the true focus. The FBI hosted the bar on Saturdays, and the weekly party was infamous within the Green Zone.

John was usually assigned to the booze run because he had a pickup truck. The run required at least eight people because of the volume of booze involved. Each week, thirty cases of beer and other alcohol filled the back of a pickup truck and two armored SUVs.

After the meeting, all the furniture was dragged outside and stacked. Twelve hours from now the meeting area would consist of puddles of spilled beer, dropped drinks, crushed potato chips and pretzels, and standing room only. Often over 150 people crammed into the bar and courtyard. After the group meeting, John and Annie briefly met in the bar courtyard by the fire pit.

Annie nodded at John, and they shook hands. "Hey, what do you have? Booze run?" she asked.

John nodded and said, "Yep, it's no big deal. I could be doing worse, like cleaning the bar or something."

She grinned, shaking her head. "Or like me: I've been directed to lead the group to rearrange the fuckin' furniture in the bar courtyard, then burn documents in this stupid-ass pit... You'd think the FBI might invest in goddamn paper shredder or something."

John shrugged and said, "It is what it is..."

They agreed to meet in her workspace after lunch around 2:00 p.m.

"Pace yourselves," Annie said to two of the newer agents. It was their first Saturday in Baghdad, and they were undertaking their task of moving furniture and preparing the bar with great urgency. They sweated profusely in the brutal 112-degree heat as they moved tables and chairs out of the barroom and into a corner of the courtyard.

Annie took a deep breath and said, "Let's take a break and get in the air conditioning for the next ten or fifteen minutes."

The two new agents nodded gratefully, and Annie tossed them cold bottles of water from one of the bar refrigerators. They momentarily held the cold bottles of water on their necks. The room with the bar had two refrigerators and a large portable cooler for ice. The bar itself was unremarkable, made from plywood and pieced together with two-by-fours in an L shape. It was only about four feet long on one side and ten feet long on the other. Sometime after the bar's creation, personnel wrapping up a rotation began memorializing their time in Baghdad by signing their names on the bar with black Magic Marker pens. The graffiti-signature craze took hold and spread from the bar surface to the barroom's walls. The writing was once witty and original, but now cliché. New rotation personnel who saw the bar and barroom for the first time were enamored by the sight and could not wait to leave their mark. Most of what was written was just like graffiti through the ages…a name, a date, and—here in the FBI bar—often a rotation number.

Periodically, after a big Saturday night gathering a derogatory comment about someone or an organization, or the random graphic drawing appeared on the wall. A bucket of white paint and an old paintbrush in the adjacent room with the beer coolers was readily accessible. Anything considered unsavory was whitewashed within a day. Even faster if it was demeaning to the FBI.

In the adjacent room were two standard home refrigerators and two commercial size beverage refrigerators that were stocked with ice and booze and later locked before the crowd arrived. Annie sat with the two new guys savoring the air conditioning in the three chairs yet to be moved outside and stacked.

“I heard these Saturday night gatherings get pretty crowded,” Frank said to nobody in general. Frank, an agent who had been on the job for about two years, worked at a small office on the outskirts of Omaha, Nebraska.

Annie nodded and drank about half of the bottle of water she had just opened. Frank had been assigned to HWG and worked hostage cases. Annie took it upon herself to look out for him when she could. Annie thought he was down to earth, likable, and had a good dose of Midwest humility.

Frank, still sweating and halfway through his bottle of water, shook his head, and said, “Annie, what is that stench in the back courtyard? There's nothing but dirt and concrete, and it reeks.”

“Oh yes, I'm glad you reminded me, we have to drag the hose from inside the storage room and hose-down that section, especially the dirt area. It knocks the smell down a little and will dry in a few hours,” she added.

Frank's brow furrowed slightly, “Is there something buried out there, or something. It smells sort of wrong?”

“No,” Annie smiled and shook her head. “Consider that area a giant urinal; that's the men's restroom on Saturday nights.”

Frank gave her a perplexed look.

Annie grinned and said, "In about twelve hours from right now, there will be about 150 people right here drinking a beer or two. There's one bathroom in this building."

Frank could do the math.

Hostage Status: 76 Days in Captivity

The air was stale, and stench of the bathroom bucket was horrific. The metal door opened without warning. Two guards came in, pointed at the bucket and Shorebilly. One guard motioned to the door saying something in Arabic. Nobody understood the words—pointing and gesturing was enough.

Shorebilly wiped the pus from the edge of the still healing gash on his forehead and grabbed the bucket by the handle. The guard motioned for him to follow. Shorebilly understood and walked carefully to avoid sloshing the contents of the bucket. The guard pointed to a trench at the edge of the courtyard for dumping sewage. Shorebilly neared the trench, and the overwhelming stench. He was immediately reminded of the time he helped a friend with a septic tank in Chester, Maryland. The tank ruptured, and a deer had fallen inside and was decomposing in the contents of the septic tank. The smell was ghastly but was nothing compared to the courtyard trench.

Emptying the bucket required standing in the filth of the trench up to his ankles. Shorebilly focused on getting the bucket emptied. Several weeks ago, he had learned how to dump the contents without splashing himself.

A guard turned on the hose at the edge of the trench. Shorebilly knew he had about thirty seconds to rinse the bucket and his feet. He rinsed his feet first; trying to avoid more infections. Then he rinsed the bucket as quickly as he could—dumping the putrid remains close to the trench.

The hostages had a love-hate relationship with cleaning the rancid bathroom bucket. They were disgusted by the bucket and the trench. Yet each embraced his minute or two in the courtyard—a break from their hot fetid concrete hell.

CHAPTER 5

DON'T CALL ME HONEY

DAY 76 (*CONTINUED*): JUNE 30, 2007

After the booze run, John was ready to meet with Annie at the BOC at 2:00 p.m. He trudged up the irregular stairs to her work area. As John arrived at the edge of the door, he saw a couple of agents coming out of the room. They were wide-eyed and moved quickly. The agents had only been in-country about two days, so the look did not really surprise John. When he got to the doorway, he realized they were trying to get away from an ongoing confrontation in the room.

John turned the corner into the room and saw Annie's supervisor shutting the door to his office; he did not want to be a witness to the verbal beatdown Annie was giving one of the recently arrived agents. The agent had been with the FBI for several years and was on an FBI SWAT team in Wyoming. He was like many civilian government workers or contractors who had served in the peacetime military. Now that there was a war, they wanted to be part of it.

Many people had a genuine interest in simply "doing one's part;" however, far too often the tough-guy rhetoric, immersed in excessive testosterone with inflated egos, was overwhelming. Annie had great admiration for the quiet professional and obvious overt disdain for braggarts. The new FBI SWAT guy, self-named Buzz, because he claimed he had tactical scenarios constantly *buzzing* in his head every time he entered a room. He had poked a proverbial hornet's nest within the past few minutes—Annie was pissed, and she was about to sting.

Buzz, who had been in Iraq for two days, constantly whined and complained about security and tactical lapses he perceived around the Green Zone. From the beginning he was someone to stay away from and would eventually earn the title at the embassy of *that-guy*. Nobody ever wanted the title of *that-guy*, which was vaguely defined as someone with undesired traits who could be described by antics, personality, or other characteristics without using a name. Once identified by name during the descriptive conversation, the person being described was usually acknowledged: "Oh, yeah…*that-guy*. I know who you're talking about now." Do not be *that-guy*.

Buzz exemplified *that-guy* just now as he sat next to Annie. Buzz was assigned to HWG, but Annie had already written him off. Buzz did not want to labor through case files and navigate the complicated paths of hostage work in Iraq.

Buzz was at the war, and he wanted to have his picture taken somewhere while holding a gun.

About five minutes earlier, just before John arrived at HWG, Buzz had decided he needed to clean his rifle. And this rifle cleaning needed to happen on the table in the middle of the HWG workspace. He made sure everyone was aware of his weapons proficiency, ability to disassemble and assemble a rifle, and talk about gun stuff.

Annie sat at her workstation with her earbuds in her ears, watching and listening to a hostage video and taking notes. It was another video of one of the BWH hostages. Annie had watched the same four videos over and over—each hostage reading a list of demands. The hostages did not look good, but they did not look that bad. One hostage had a cut on his forehead that looked like it needed stitches. Based on facial hair the recordings were likely made within their first two weeks of captivity. She wondered if there were more videos.

She ignored Buzz as the man-banter continued between him and one of the other new guys.

Buzz and the other new guy told each other SWAT stories that had no beginning and certainly no end in sight. Earlier, Buzz had interrupted Annie with a loud "Hello" to get her attention. Annie entertained a few of his questions regarding the timeline of the evening's pending party. She gave curt and precise answers and went back to work.

Now Buzz waved his hand in front of Annie's face as she looked at her computer monitor to get her attention, and said, "Hey, we want to get some range time and make sure our rifles are sighted in. Do you know where we can do that?"

Buzz picked up a Gatorade bottle about one quarter full of a thick brown liquid. He took off the top, spit into the bottle, and wiped the edge of his lip with the rim of the bottle.

Annie pulled one earbud out to hear the question and simply said, "No."

Two of the newer agents pecked away on their laptops in the corner and sent personal emails to friends and family describing the hardships of war and furniture moving. They stopped typing when they heard Annie's tone and the pause that followed. The room grew quiet. Buzz was on the precipice of Annie's wrath; whether he realized it or not was unclear. If he knew, he did not care.

Buzz looked at Annie and pointed to his reassembled rifle lying on the table and with great condescension asked, "You know how to handle one of these? Are your qualifications up to speed?"

Buzz was the epitome of arrogance. He simply assumed Annie's gender made her less than proficient with a rifle. He had no idea he was talking down to the number one student in a Firearms Instructor class in Quantico.

Annie looked at him and projected clear disgust. "Who the fuck do you think you're talking to?"

"Relax, honey, it was just a question," Buzz spit into the Gatorade bottle and wiped his lip. Buzz played his man-card way too hard—Annie was about to tear it up.

"Honey?" Annie asked. "Honey? Did you just fucking call me 'honey?'"

Buzz inadvertently swallowed a little tobacco juice, paused slightly, and said, "I'm a SWAT agent, and I want to make sure people around me are up to speed."

That was when the new agents on their laptops realized the smartest thing to do was to get out immediately—and it was when John turned the corner into the room. John entered just as Annie used the length of the cord to pull the other earbud from her ear. She tossed the cord and earbuds onto the keyboard and stood.

Her voice lowered, she shrugged her shoulders, and said, "If you're here to try to impress or charm me with some bullshit SWAT story or how you saved the town of Podunk, Nowhere, from a check forger or some bullshit, don't waste your time." She stepped forward slightly and said, "If you call me *honey* again, I will break that fucking rifle off in your ass, rip your head off, and pour that bottle of spit down your goddamn throat."

John stepped around the edge of the table near Annie and said, "I have the case files to go over when you're ready." Annie glared at Buzz who had taken a half step back, looked a little pale, and spit into the bottle again.

John quickly assessed the tension in the room, looked at Buzz, and said, "They have new ammunition across the hall in the command center, if you need it."

John looked at the rifle, back to Buzz, and then nodded toward the door. Buzz took the opportunity John provided to escape any further wrath of Annie. He picked up his rifle, his Gatorade bottle of spit, and made for the door.

Annie shook her head and said, "Where do these jerkoffs come from?" She was fuming. "How about we go upstairs to one of the TV rooms and go over things there. We can spread everything out on a table, and there shouldn't be anyone there this time of day."

"That sounds great," John said.

Annie nudged a cardboard box toward John and picked up one herself about twice the size, and they walked out of the room. The other new agent who had been telling SWAT stories and cleaning guns with Buzz stood at the opposite edge of the table trying to absorb what just had happened over the past five minutes.

It occurred to the new guy that this was going to be a long three-month rotation.

Hostage Status: 76 Days in Captivity (*continued*)

The hostages were flat on their backs and unmoving on the concrete floor. The filthy, putrid air was motionless, and the temperature was above one hundred degrees. Sitting up for long periods of time was fatiguing and painful. The concrete floor was cooler providing some respite from the stifling heat. The nice guards were in charge—the hostages whispered.

While lying flat on his back and only moving his head, Surfboy looked over to CR. "Hey, what's that song you keep humming...some West Virginia-hillbilly-tunes? Is it that 'country roads' song again? You got it stuck in my head too, and I don't even know the words."

Surfboy had bursts of energy and liked to talk. He was the youngest of the group and looked up to CR, the oldest. From opposite worlds—a surfer from Southern California and a truck driver from West Virginia—they had become fast friends before they were captured.

CR barely raised a hand, grinned, and playfully gave Surfboy the finger. "Shut up hippie...go back to sleep."

Both hostages grinned. "Hey, gimme a West Coast buzz...hum some Nirvana or something, bro."

CR turned his head slightly, looking at the vent, and watched the dust wafting. He said, "Hey hippie, did you ever notice that drummer from Nirvana looks like that dude that sings in the Foo Fighters?"

In unison, the other three hostages murmured, "No shit..."

They all knew it was the same person—peculiar rituals can unify a group. About twice a week someone would have the revelation aligning the drummer with the singer. The back and forth always lightened the moment.

"Alright hillbilly...I'm going back to sleep." Surfboy smiled and crossed his arms.

CR had begun a faint, breathy humming to himself. It was the same tune over and over—inadvertently becoming a group mantra. At first, the other hostages told him to shut up—fearing a beating by the guards. He started again a few days later without realizing it. CR's faint murmur breathed wisps of sound into the air—like smoke from a campfire refusing to go out—cautiously spurning death.

The faint human sound helped. Hearing CR kept them away from the silent shroud of their own impending deaths. If they could hear CR, they were still alive.

All the hostages grinned momentarily, then thought about anyplace besides where they were.

Odd rituals bring people together.

CHAPTER 6

ANNIE AND JOHN ORGANIZE...AND COME UP WITH A PLAN

DAY 76 (*CONTINUED*): JUNE 30, 2007

Annie and John found a room upstairs usually utilized for TV viewing and cleared the junk food off a coffee table. The furniture was the typical misshapen, torn black plastic-leather cushion. They dragged the best chairs they could find to either end of the coffee table, pulled the files out of the box, and laid them out in chronological order based on the date of kidnap occurrence. Annie was only responsible for one hostage event, the Broken Wheel Hostages case with four hostages. Still, she brought copies of other case files, too. Annie suspected there was a big picture to consider.

"I'm gonna get a couple of bottles of water," John said as he walked to the mini fridge in the adjacent room.

Annie set up an easel and a two-by-three-foot pad of paper used for briefing. She did not like to have meetings for the sake of having a meeting. She was interested in tackling issues and developing solutions and results.

Annie sat down and said, "Thanks for taking a look at things over the last few days."

John nodded. “No problem. There are a lot of moving parts. I’m glad we talked through a few things over the week. It gave me a chance to think through some of these details.”

Annie grinned momentarily and sat back in her chair. “Yeah, me too. I have some thoughts, but I want to get your opinion on a few things first.”

She wanted his opinion without her own perspective coloring it.

“So, what direction do you think we can take this? How can we move it forward?”

John nodded and thought for just a moment. Her use of the term *we* was not lost on him.

He tilted his head slightly, shrugged his shoulders, and said, “Well, first we’ve gotta get out of Baghdad. This might be a bad analogy, but I think we are trying to play in the game, and we aren’t even near the field. All the potential case development is in the southern part of the country, in and around Basra.”

He tossed a pen on the writing pad. “It also seems like every rotation tries the same thing.” He looked directly at Annie and asked, “Why are we so hands-off when it comes to talking with witnesses and potential sources?”

Annie threw up her hands. “Exactly!” she said. “I asked the same fuckin’ question, and that’s one of the battles raging between me and some of the other guys working this stuff. Annie took a breath, a drink of water, sat back in her chair, and said, “Keep going, what else?”

John talked for another five minutes. Annie did not take notes. She wrote one-word reminders for topics to discuss.

John went on. “It seems to me that we are waiting for some sort of bullshit opportunity to fall out of the sky into our laps, when the reality is that we have to go out and make something happen. That will be virtually impossible to do from here in Baghdad."

Annie and John knew hostage casework was getting nowhere partly because of poor communication and lack of coordination between agencies. It was time to produce solutions. Annie stood and walked to the easel holding the large paper. She flipped through the first couple of blank pages to a page where she had previously written a list that read:

1. Baghdad v. Basra (location)
2. HWG case labor
3. Longevity/Consistency/Continuity
4. Coordination/Interagency/???

Annie stood beside the chart with a black Magic Marker and said, "Good, I think you and I are on the same page… If I can talk or badger the hierarchy to get you over to the HWG…even part time, are you in?"

John had anticipated the question and already thought it through. He was bored out of his mind at the embassy and welcomed the opportunity to delve into something he thought might be worthwhile.

John nodded. "Yep, if you can make it happen, I'm in."

A visual sense of relief passed over Annie, as her shoulders relaxed, and she took a drink of water.

She nodded and said, "OK, thanks. I really can't make anything really happen on my own. There's just too much."

As they continued to discuss the big-picture-issue list Annie had created, she added potential operational solutions under each category. They were on the same page. It was not going to be simple. They both recognized nothing was simple in Iraq.

Annie finally sat down and said, "I'm trying to lay the groundwork for a sort of exploratory trip to Basra at the end of next week. If I can convince the hierarchy to give the OK to go down there for a few days, and maybe get you on board, even part time, can you do the trip?" She already knew the answer.

"Yep, let me know what I can do to help." John paused for a moment, looked at Annie, and said, "Well, maybe between the two of us, if we really lean into this, we can make something happen. Is there any word on how the hostages are doing?"

She rubbed her forehead. "No…nothing. Can you imagine if they knew the only two people looking for them are sitting right here and aren't even close to finding them?"

Hostage Status: 76 Days in Captivity (continued)

The hostages were still flat on their backs on the concrete floor—four hours had passed since their brief bantering about the Nirvana drummer. They were awake but laid still. The oppressive heat was unending.

Tex looked toward the vent, watching the dust slowly float in the light. "Hey, do you think anyone is looking for us?" The question was not directed toward anyone.

"I fuckin' hope so." Surfboy quietly flicked a pebble toward the wall. "We're Americans...we gotta be worth a lot."

CR stayed flat on his back and turned his head toward Surfboy, whispering, "Maybe not, hippie...we ain't worth shit...not a dime. How much do you think America will pay for your surfer ass? Same as my hillbilly ass."

Tex held his palms up for a moment and dropped them back to the floor.

"We gotta be worth something."

Shorebilly wiped the pus from the edge of his scar. "Maybe... maybe not. The US won't pay ransom...and won't give in to demands...someone will just have to figure this shit out."

Surfboy looked at Shorebilly and lightheartedly asked, "Hey jarhead, what about your guys...where the fuck are they, bro?" Shorebilly had been in the US Marine Corps.

The room grew quiet. They knew the answer, but nobody was saying it aloud.

Shorebilly sat up and looked at the vent, the light slowly dimming. "The cavalry ain't coming."

CHAPTER 7

TRANSFERRED . . . GREEN BERETS GET READY FOR A VISIT

DAY 81: JULY 5, 2007

John sat at his desk doing a Secret-level word search on a computer system that maintained intelligence reports. He methodically plugged terms into the search criteria and read the associated documents. His phone rang. It was the FBI BOC deputy commander, who told John that he had been transferred part time to the HWG. John received an email saying the same thing from the on-scene commander. Everyone likes to be the first to get or give news.

John thanked the deputy commander for the call, hung up, leaned back in his chair, and looked up at the incredibly ornate yet malformed ceiling with its crooked, gold and green Greek key patterned borders. John was in the moment of a life-changing circumstance, and he knew it.

Annie came through the door behind him. He had given her the combination to the lock. He slid his feet off the desk, and his heels hit the floor as he spun in the chair. Annie ambled through the office with a searching look and saw nobody else.

She sat in the rolling chair nearest John and slid it toward him with a courier pouch on her lap. "Hey, what we talked about and you coming over to HWG, I think it might happen."

John grinned. "Yeah, I figured that out with the last call and email I just got."

Annie looked at him quizzically, shrugged, and asked, "What...what's up?"

John looked confused for a moment and realized it was the typical communication miss. Often there were gaps from bottom to top. In this case it was top to bottom.

"Well, it sounds like you got a little bit of attention," John said as he spun in his chair to face Annie.

She tossed the courier bag on the desk in front of him and said, "Yeah, I thought I might be going nowhere. What the hell are you hearing?"

John put one hand on the courier bag and said, "I just got off the phone with the deputy commander of the rotation. While I was talking with him, I received an email from the on-scene commander. They were both letting me know of the personnel reassignments, and that I was essentially assigned to you and your shop."

Annie shook her head, shrugged her shoulders, and said, "OK, good. We are making something happen. I think we put them in a position where they couldn't say no. It's so frustrating trying to get anything done...especially something new."

"Right...exactly...baby steps," he said with a grin.

Annie sat straight in the chair. "Hey, you and I are going to Basra in two days to meet and live with a Green Beret ODA for a few days."

The only sound was the faint hiss of air-conditioning. She crossed her arms—wondering why it was always so cold at the embassy.

Annie looked up. "We need to talk. Things are bad in Basra."

Basra, Iraq

(280 miles southeast of Baghdad near the Iranian border/ British Contingency Operating Base)

In a trailer next to eight-foot-tall Hesco barriers, four men dressed in civilian clothes—jeans and khaki cargo pants, T-shirts, ball caps—were immersed in conversation, calmly discussing the plans for the next few days. Their ages ranged from late twenties to mid-thirties. None were clean shaven, two had full beards, and all four spoke with one another casually but professionally. Three of the four had elaborate tattoos on both arms that traveled from the wrist up the arm and disappeared at the sleeve. All had shoulder length hair. The average onlooker might have thought they were another group of contractors in the area to fix air conditioners or plumbing. They were members of a US Army Special Forces Operational Detachment Alpha—an A-Team. Usually referred to as an ODA. They were Green Berets.

The youngest of the four had a baby face, even without shaving for the past week. He was the only one without visible tattoos and spoke the least. He listened. His name was Ryan, and he learned the critical importance of listening during his four years at West Point. After graduating with a degree in history, Ryan spent his first two years in the infantry. He completed one twelve-month combat tour in Iraq and then went through the Green Beret Q-course. He was a captain now and two months into this tour, his first experience as an ODA team leader.

Ryan leaned back in his chair and listened to the team sergeant and a team "Charlie," or engineer and explosives expert, as they discussed the coordination necessary for the care and feeding of their pending FBI visitors: Annie and John.

In the corner of the trailer, Nathan, the team "Bravo" or weapons and tactical expert, watched and listened as he took apart the lower receiver and bolt of a rifle without looking at his hands. He could take it apart, clean it, inspect the intricate pieces, and put it back together literally in the dark. Nathan kept quiet, but he was unhappy about the FBI coming to their area. *Feds* made Nathan anxious, and he did not like the idea of them being around. They were not to be trusted.

Ryan looked across the table at Ashton and said, "You're pretty quiet on this. What do you think?"

Ashton was the team "Delta" or medic and had an incredible ability to assess situations and develop solutions. Ashton had been in the Army for eight years, done one twelve-month tour in Iraq with the infantry, and was now on his second war tour with Special Forces.

Ashton shrugged. "I think this hostage stuff, you know, what they are coming here for is admirable…hostage stuff is part of our mission, and I know we can probably help, but…" Ashton shrugged.

Ryan nodded toward Ashton prodding. "But what?"

Ashton shrugged. "I think it's good they are coming here if this is where they need to be operationally. I just hope they aren't jerking around and doing the sightseeing tour of Iraq for their scrapbooks."

Everyone at the table nodded, and Nathan finally chimed in from the corner while fiddling with pieces from several disassembled guns. "I don't like *Feds*. They can't be trusted, and they are coming for our guns one day!"

Nathan was an avid hunter who grew up in Alabama and owned three gun safes. Two of the safes were in his bedroom at home, and the third was buried in a remote area where he hunted. Like many in Special Operations, Nathan harbored the mindset of a peculiar disdain for authority and unrelenting love of country.

Mike, the team sergeant, looked over to Nathan and said, "Nathan, we know you don't like the Feds. We will keep them from getting any of their *Fed* on you."

Everyone grinned and snickered. Nathan tossed an oil-soaked rag on the table, placed a piece of a trigger mechanism that only he could identify on top, and said, "I don't like them coming, but Ashton has something when it comes to them coming for a good reason. If they are real, then I can handle making sure things are handled with extra work on my side. Plus, maybe that will help keep an eye on them."

That was Nathan's way of letting team members know he was in support of the team, and the decision process. Special Forces personnel were supposed to think creatively. Green Berets were professionals and did not usually need to be "ordered" to do something.

Nathan looked over to Ryan and said, "If they are serious about this hostage thing, they could be here for a while, or go away and come back for some time. This is Basra, nothing goes well down here, and nothing is simple."

Ryan said, "Yep, this is Basra, not Baghdad. They said they wanted to evaluate things for about four days." Ryan looked up at the ceiling and to everyone at the table, then added, "We should be able to assess if they have the heart to be here after about…a day."

Mike nodded in agreement and said to Ryan, "How about you and I meet them after they get some rest...maybe in the afternoon on the day they arrive so we can see where things stand?"

Ryan nodded. "Sounds good. Nathan and Ashton, would you mind working through things to pick them up and get them settled."

Ryan was savvy when it came to leading in the Green Beret environment. Discussion, independent thought, and suggestion worked much better than barking orders. Infantry thinking and structure did not work in the unconventional world of Special Forces.

Nathan responded, "Yep, got it...We'll take care of things."

Ashton nodded. "No problem, I will email the FBI folks to find out flight details and go over to the Brit-Air terminal and figure out what the timing really looks like."

Ryan looked over at Team Sergeant Mike and said, "If you have a minute, how about we go meet with Kyle and see if he's had a chance to work up a hostage package?"

Mike nodded. "Sounds good. We can grab something to eat by Brit-HQ."

Anyone from outside of the Special Forces world would swear they had just watched anything *but* a highly specialized, astute, and critical thinking military unit work out operational details. Independent thought, mutual respect, and outside-the-box thinking is how Special Operations Forces functioned. The proverbial army-in-your-face-tough-guy-barking-orders-thing did not work here, and few outside Special Operations Command understood this. Army personnel who failed to flourish at a higher-thinking and functioning level were usually weeded out during the Green Beret selection processes; the Q-course. If someone made it through the Q-course and did not adapt to the Special Forces mentality, they were quickly identified and ended up in administrative command units in Baghdad or other places where they could do no harm.

John and Annie were due to land in Basra at 7:00 the next morning.

Hostage Status: 81 Days in Captivity

The mean guards left yesterday, so the hostages could whisper for another day if they were careful. The filth and stench of the room were staggering, but nobody complained. Even with the chance to whisper, Tex remained silent. Evening was coming, and the light in the vent was fading.

Each hostage periodically woke from bad dreams. Nightmares were to be expected. For the past two nights, Tex had woken hourly and not spoken the entire day. Earlier he had antagonized one of the nice guards bringing food. The secondary guard did not hesitate to beat him with a hose for about a minute. He did not eat the meager portion of food and only drank half his water.

Tex sat up, bringing his knees to his chest, and crossing his arms in front of his face in an upright fetal position. "I know I did this to us."

He was wracked with guilt. The decision he made to park the loud SUV at a distance was eating at him.

CR sat up and could barely see Tex in the shadows. He said, "No fuckin' way. I saw the fire in the other SUV... shit, I grabbed the fire extinguisher. You needed to keep our last ride safe."

Tex held his knees rocking back and forth. "When I close my eyes, all I can see is our last SUV...and those bastards stepping in front of us."

Surfboy lightly tossed a pebble in front of Tex and said, "Hey bro...if I didn't hit that fuckin' hole we wouldn't be here."

The room was almost dark, momentarily quiet, and Shore-billy sat up. "We can 'what if' and second-guess this all day. The fact is we had to deal with what was happening and we did. We were outnumbered and outgunned from the beginning. We never stood a chance. Don't beat yourself up with this."

Only the outlines of shadows were visible. CR said, "We all did the best we could and thought we were doing right. It was just a daylong shit show, and we had the front row seats. Stick together."

The hostages laid flat on the concrete. For the first time in a week, Tex slept through the night.

CHAPTER 8

TRAVEL FROM BAGHDAD INTERNATIONAL AIRPORT (BIAP) TO BASRA

DAY 82: JULY 6, 2007

Annie and John boarded a helicopter in the Green Zone at the US embassy flight line called LZ Washington. The helicopter touched down at the Baghdad International Airport on the military side after the seven-minute flight. It was 2:00 a.m. The embassy's US military liaison had told Annie and John to be at LZ Washington at 8:00 p.m.; they sat for six hours. This was the norm.

At the Baghdad International Airport, usually referred to as BIAP, Annie and John switched to the British military air system. They trekked from the US Army Blackhawk helicopter to the hangar at the edge of the tarmac and found the civilian flight contractor who organized military flights. Ironically, the US Army military helicopter-taxi-system in Iraq was run by civilian contractors who coordinated the most complex movement of personnel in the country. The contractor guided Annie and John to the British section of the tarmac. The British soldier inspected their picture ID at the flight line. He was quite polite.

The soldier looked Annie and John up and down, and asked, "Baghdad to Baaasra?"

The British had a different way of saying Basra, stretching out the first syllable longer than the American pronunciation.

The British soldier smirked. "Mates, sure you want to go there?" He shook his head, looked up from his clipboard, and without waiting for a response said, "…Very well, you're on the list."

Annie and John stood in front of the young yet very competent soldier. They were fatigued and dehydrated, but they focused so they could understand instructions through the British accent.

The British soldier asked, "Any grenades. If so, are they taped?"

Annie and John shook their heads as if on cue. "No, no grenades."

"Any accessible knives on your persons?"

Annie and John briefly talked over each other, but successfully relayed that knives were packed in bags loaded at cargo.

The soldier nodded. "Any torches on your person?"

Annie and John shook their heads. They figured out that "no" was the right answer, but both wondered why anyone would bring a torch onto a plane.

The British soldier nodded, thanked them for their patience, and invited them to sit on the edge of the runway until they were guided to the C-130. He was incredibly professional and polite.

As they walked to the staging area by the runway, Annie looked over at John and said, "Why in the hell would I bring a fuckin' torch on a plane?"

John shook his head, plodded along, and said, "Hell if I

know, that makes no sense to me...Maybe there's something lost in the translation."

Annie and John laid on the edge of the runway dozing with a group of the British soldiers and a few miscellaneous contractors for the next two hours. Finally, a soldier politely told them that the C-130 was two hundred meters in front of the group on the tarmac. The soldier held yellow glow sticks and led the crowd to the plane.

Annie and John were in the middle of the group—boarding the aircraft from the rear. The British flight crew was quite kind and passed around a bucket of ice with cold water bottles for the inexperienced, like Annie and John, as well as a box full of what was referred to as *squishy ear protection*. The yellow foam material was rolled with the fingertips and pushed into the ear canal to protect hearing during the flight. It made the engine noise tolerable and sleeping possible.

Baggage was loaded into the back of the plane by a fork-lift, and everyone was directed to put on their protective vests and helmets for the duration of the flight. The lights were turned off for the rest of the flight, which was about an hour and ten minutes. It was 4:30 a.m.

Hostage Status: 82 Days in Captivity

The door flew open, and four guards ran in swinging rubber hoses. The beating lasted about two minutes and ended as abruptly as it began. The hostages looked at the door to make sure it was shut—each shaking their head. As if on cue, they all gave the door the finger. The mean guards were on duty.

Two hours later the door opened, and the hostages prepared for another random beating. They got a break. It was time to empty the bathroom bucket. A lone guard pointed to Surfboy and the bucket.

Surfboy picked up the bucket by the handle and walked to the courtyard trench. He stood ankle deep in the filth, dumping the contents of the bucket. Something caught his attention at the edge of the trench—a small white index card. It was unusual to see something so clean. He bent over to pick up the hose to clean his feet and the bucket, grabbing the piece of paper with the same hand holding the hose—squeezing tightly. He had seen writing on it and wondered what it said. People in desperate situations take risks. Sometimes just out of boredom.

The guard turned off the water gesturing for Surfboy to go inside. He held the paper with the same hand as the bucket, knowing the guard did not want to get near him—the hostages were filthy and wreaked. Surfboy walked to the cell with the guard following and shutting the door. He squeezed the recently filched paper, putting it under the bucket. The guards would not get near the bucket. He waited about an hour before retrieving the paper from under the bucket.

Surfboy smoothed the index card flat and looked at the indecipherable Arabic writing. Along with Arabic writing were numbers—an obvious pattern.

Surfboy passed the paper to Shorebilly and gently murmured, "Hey bro, I think I know what this is...what do you think?"

Shorebilly knew immediately. "The fuckin' guard schedule."

The index card was passed around, and everyone agreed—the Arabic writing repeated every three days.

Between the four of them, they were able to determine the approximate date based on the rotation of guards.

One of the mean guards had thrown the schedule in the trench. It was the end of the month, and time for a new schedule. The piece of paper was trash to the guard, but treasure to the hostages—a mental gem.

The hostages finally knew today's date.

Tex looked up at the vent, and the dust swirled in the light. "I don't know why, but it feels good knowing the date. I can't believe not knowing the date makes time hopelessly endless. Weird."

Shorebilly nodded and said, "Tomorrow is my little girl's first birthday...we were gonna take her on her first boat ride on the Chesapeake..."

Nobody said anything for six hours.

CHAPTER 9

ANNIE AND JOHN ARRIVE IN BASRA... WELCOME TO ROCKETS

DAY 82 (*CONTINUED*): JULY 6, 2007

The hour and ten minutes on the plane extended to three hours due to a delay in departing Baghdad and a landing holdup in Basra. Upon arrival in Basra airspace, they flew in circles for fifteen minutes before landing. Annie and John sat facing each other in the red mesh netting seats. It was 6:30 a.m. and already hot, and everyone was uncomfortable with the netting and seat bars digging into their thighs. Nobody complained.

The back of the C-130 lowered, and a giant forklift waited to unload the stacked luggage and equipment secured with a nylon strap net. The soldiers moved equipment, luggage, and personnel very efficiently. The flight crew directed everyone to disembark. Annie and John looked at each other curiously for a moment. Between the noise of the plane and the British accent, they did not understand anything said; however, both were intuitive enough to know when to embrace the herd mentality and move with the crowd. Annie and John stood along with everyone else and faced the back of the plane. A cacophony of metal-on-metal clatter filled the air as rifles and equipment banged and clashed against seat rails.

Annie and John grabbed their backpacks from hooks on rails above their heads and followed the herd moving toward the light. Both almost fell when they inadvertently walked upon rollers on the floor used to move multi-ton loads onto and off the plane, but they stayed composed. They awkwardly stumbled to the end of the plane, stepped down off the back, and kept up with the group.

The sun was just coming up, the sky was clear, yet there was a haze from the ever-present dust in the air. Near the plane three passenger buses waited. The giant forklift full of luggage and cargo was already two hundred yards down the flight line heading to the hangar. Annie and John boarded the second bus.

The bus was remarkably clean and cool. Everyone was quiet and orderly, knew what to do, and walked to the back of the bus so it would fill from back to front in the most efficient manner.

Annie and John knew to stay quiet and moved with the crowd to figure out how things worked. A British soldier stepped onto the bus once it was loaded. He gave them their flight-line briefing.

The accent was going to take getting used to. Annie and John picked up only bits and pieces.

"Welcome to Baaasra, I am...this is your flight-line safety briefing. As we move toward the hangar...should we encounter any indirect fire, such as rockets, mortars, or otherwise, we will...Your bags and equipment will be waiting at the hangar...Thank you for your attention and have a splendid stay here in beautiful Baaasra!"

The last sentence was said with a tip of his helmet and a smirk.

It was dry British humor smoothly presented. There was a faint murmur through the bus of "Cheers." The soldier stepped off, the doors shut, and the bus ambled off. The two-minute drive to the hangar was uneventful.

The British military had taken over a section of the flight line at the Basra airport and built a temporary structure complete with a luggage conveyor belt. Annie and John flowed with the line of people into the makeshift passenger arrival area. The belt was to the right of the door, and British soldiers brought order to the chaos of baggage and equipment claim.

Annie and John looked across the large room and saw two men casually attired in jeans, T-shirts, and ball caps. The two men would have blended into the background, but as they stood near the edge of the receiving area their eyes were fixed on Annie and John.

Nathan nodded to Ashton as he saw Annie and John come through the door of the hangar. Rarely could Americans completely blend in with their surroundings, and this was no exception.

Ashton watched Annie and John, and said, "So far so good, they made the flights, and the bus ride, and they look like they are keeping up."

Nathan nodded skeptically. "Yep, they haven't fucked up anything yet. It's early."

They momentarily grinned, fixed their eyes on Annie and John, and noted that they moved well after being up all night. Nathan and Ashton wanted to see how alert and situationally aware Annie and John were, so they just watched to see if Annie and John would pick up on the visual weight of their watch.

Nathan said to Ashton, "There it is." They saw Annie and John nod in their direction, and Nathan subtly pointed toward the door they were standing nearby.

ANNIE AND JOHN COLLECTED THEIR BAGS AS THEY rolled out on the conveyer belt and shouldered their backpacks. They did not carry rifles, but their handguns were on their hips. Everyone in Iraq had guns. They walked through the door near where they had seen Nathan and Ashton, who now waited just outside with a pickup truck and an SUV positioned near the entrance.

Everybody introduced themselves, shook hands, and exchanged pleasantries. Nathan and Ashton placed the larger pieces of luggage in the back of the pickup while Annie and John slid their backpacks off their shoulders and tossed them on top of the larger bags.

Ashton looked at Annie and John and said, "How about we dump this stuff at our camp in your trailers and slide by the chow hall to grab something to eat?"

Everyone nodded in agreement. Nathan and Ashton knew Annie and John had been up all night, the fatigue factor had to be considered. The FBI agents needed to sleep.

"We didn't plan to start going over things until early afternoon," Ashton said to John and Annie. "A few hours of sleep after the all-nighter is usually a good idea, if that works for you two?"

Annie and John nodded and smiled. They were not sure how hard they were going to be tested by their hosts, but they appreciated that rest was being considered.

Annie nodded and said, "That sounds great…perfect."

John smiled. "Thanks, much appreciated, and thanks for picking us up and handling details."

Nathan simply nodded. Ashton said, "Sure, no problem…Annie how about you jump in with me, and John you ride with Nathan? The ride to the camp is only about five minutes from here. We can dump this stuff in your trailers, and it's a short walk to the Brit chow hall."

Ashton and Annie walked across the rutty gravel lot to a dirty and dented white SUV missing a back bumper. They got in without saying anything, and Nathan drove across the edge of the flight line. Nathan and John were in the front of the pickup. Nathan was about to explain to John the setup of the base when an ear-splitting crash shattered the silence of the ride. Smoke instantly rose from the runway fifty yards to their right. Another explosion immediately went off nearby, but the four Americans could not see where the rocket had struck.

Nathan and Ashton instinctively hit the gas and drove to the edge of the tarmac where several Hesco barriers had been inadvertently misaligned when they were placed. It was the least bad option. To stay still and sit out in the open was the worst. They got as close as they could to the barriers, and Nathan rolled his window down and looked back to Ashton and Annie in the SUV immediately behind them. Everyone was OK. Nathan put his arm out of the window and gestured forward. He hit the gas, drove along the edge of the flight line, then crossed onto a dirty, pockmarked asphalt road.

The indirect fire siren that warned of incoming rockets and mortar shells finally sounded. The rocket attack was over, and nobody was hurt. The siren often sounded after an attack instead of before. The alarm continued as they proceeded toward the camp gate and swerved around two British trucks in the road. British soldiers could be seen under the trucks holding their helmets on their heads as they lay on the road. Protocol for the British soldiers' response to an attack was to stop immediately, exit their armored trucks, get underneath, and wait for the siren to stop. An all-clear signal would sound over a base-wide sound system.

The Green Berets clearly did not subscribe to that protocol.

They arrived at a fork in the road at a line of Hesco barriers. To the left was an eight-by-eight-foot square guard shack surrounded by sandbags four feet high. An aboveground concrete duck-and-cover bunker sat next to the sandbag box. A British soldier sat on a milk crate inside the duck-and-cover bunker waiting for the all-clear signal. The soldier was assigned to check identification of those entering an adjacent British compound, which was across from the gate to the SF compound. They arrived at a chained gate secured with a combination lock, like the FBI BOC gate in Baghdad. They passed through the gate and drove up the gravel road to the SF compound parking lot.

Nathan and Ashton parked in the gravel lot near several misaligned Hesco barriers. A four-foot-wide brown porous plastic walkway at the opening of the Hesco barriers served as a path. The walkway interlocked from one piece to the next like Legos—easier than walking on gravel all the time and it made a substantial difference on those few occasions when it rained.

Nathan and Ashton helped move the luggage on wheels, which rolled well on the fitted plastic walkway, making a sort of earthy rumbling sound. Annie and John carried their backpacks and protective vests. They trudged to trailers about thirty yards from the edge of the parking lot.

After the backpacks, luggage, protective vests, and helmets were tossed on the floor in the trailers, John and Annie used the restrooms on either end of their trailers. Restrooms were in the center between two trailers; however, the adjoining trailers were empty. John and Annie had their own bathrooms—toilets flushed. It was a pretty good setup.

John and Annie met Nathan and Ashton near the opening in the Hesco barriers and the parking lot. Ashton explained they would walk the three to four minutes to the chow hall.

Ashton nodded to the opening in the Hesco barriers and said, "Basra is actually a British base; we don't really have all the things you might find around Baghdad. We eat at a British chow hall right next to our compound on the other side of the blast walls."

"The food isn't great," Nathan chimed in. "But it's better than packaged food, and there's plenty of it."

Ashton led the way and explained things as they went. "We will walk through the trailer area to the T-walls at the edge and go through a giant steel door."

Nathan said, "There aren't many T-walls here, but these Hesco barriers come in handy because the British artillery is on the other side. It's kind of close and really loud."

John's ears were still ringing from the rocket attack at the airport, so he took the opportunity to bring up the earlier incident. "Speaking of loud and close, how far away do you think the impact was from us at the airport?"

Nathan casually responded, "…Ummm, maybe fifty yards. It was a smaller rocket, or it would have been much louder…more smoke…and damage to the concrete probably."

Nathan was nonchalant as he described the impact and spoke of it with the same calm tempo he used when describing the British chow hall.

Annie turned and asked, "How often are you guys getting rocketed?"

Nathan shrugged, held out his palms as they got to the door at the T-wall, and said, "...Ummm, maybe two to six times a day. Sometimes they miss a day, lately they have hit us at night. That's smart. It disrupts sleep, and they know it."

John turned and looked at Nathan. "Are you talking about rocket launches or actual impacts in the perimeter?"

Nathan looked at John and shook his head. "We don't usually bother counting the launches—that's an intelligence bean-counter thing. Who cares about a rocket or an impact if it wasn't in the perimeter?" Nathan's question was rhetorical.

Ashton reached for the cypher lock near the doorknob of a ten-foot steel door set between two twelve-foot T-walls. The gap between the T-walls above the door was filled with razor wire. He manipulated the mechanical keys for the door combination and turned the knob. They walked through the door to the British side and out of the SF compound.

ON THE OTHER SIDE OF THE GIANT STEEL DOOR, THERE was no plastic path, only hard packed tan dirt. Their apparent path was straight down the slight incline in front of them for about thirty yards, then onto a dirt road to the right. Any gravel that might have been spread had been swallowed by the dirt and crushed into the ground.

One hundred yards in the distance, a constantly spinning radar dish sat next to a mechanism that looked like R2D2 from Star Wars. It was surrounded with Hesco barriers and razor wire. Annie was curious about the apparatus but would leave some questions for later.

The hardpacked dirt changed to loose, floury dust that puffed from the edges of their boots and covered everything. They walked in the already uncomfortable heat for about fifty yards and came to a prefabricated double-wide trailer. The British chow hall. The British soldier assigned to check identification recognized Nathan and Ashton, nodded, and gestured with his hand to enter. John and Annie unnecessarily reached for their identification. The soldier just shrugged and waved them into the chow hall. John and Annie were with people the soldier recognized, and the mere gesture of trying to show identification was good enough. Besides, who is going to try to sneak into a damn British chow hall in Basra?!

The British chow hall had no frills. Either side of the double-wide trailer held four tables that seated six. Through the center of the room were four tables that seated four. Getting to the food line required walking around two large trash cans. The food line was opposite the entrance and was empty. It was late in the day for breakfast and quiet. Eight British soldiers sat at the center tables and pushed remnants of food around their plates and talked.

Annie and John followed the lead of Ashton and Nathan. Two TCNs, women from Eastern Europe, stood behind the plexiglass sneeze protectors at the food line counter. They looked up to see the Americans and dutifully picked up large serving spoons. They liked the Americans because the soldiers usually smiled and would flirt with them. Plus, they were Americans.

All plates and utensils were disposable. Nathan and Ashton collected plastic plates and prewrapped packets containing a plastic spoon, fork and knife; Annie and John did the same. In addition to a plastic plate Nathan grabbed a plastic bowl. Nathan and Ashton nodded and smiled at the chow hall server and pointed to what they wanted, which was scooped and heaped upon their plates.

In their best English, the women behind the counter said, "Good morning, nice to see you again," and smiled gushingly at Nathan and Ashton.

Annie pointed to what she wanted to eat and smiled at the women behind the counter. The two women smiled curtly and spooned what Annie requested. Her helpings were significantly smaller.

On the way to a table, they passed several commercial-grade upright coolers with glass doors where they grabbed milk, juice, and water. Nathan and Ashton sat opposite each other near the wall and by a window, while John and Annie sat opposite each other near the aisle. Once everyone sat, they started eating. The food selection was limited: scrambled eggs, corned beef hash, sausage, and potatoes with gravy. The sausage had a different texture than American sausage. Nobody had a complaint, and they were grateful to have what was in front of them.

The typical small talk ensued. Annie and John were brimming with questions they had yet to ask. The recent sights and sounds—rockets at the airport—were on their minds, but they tried to appear relaxed.

Annie asked Ashton, "Why isn't there an American chow hall here?"

Ashton shrugged and said, "Well, there just aren't many Americans here, I guess. The British control the lower third of the war…and the country. Americans have their hands full with the upper two-thirds."

Nathan remarked, "Down here we are either invisible to Baghdad or just forgotten."

Ashton grinned and said, "The only people that know Americans are down in this part of the country are the insurgents." They all laughed, and he added, "There are only a few Americans here and in the US embassy or consulate, and they stay to themselves, mostly under their top-cover in their compound."

John asked, "What do you mean their top-cover…their boss…the ambassador?"

Ashton shook his head, took a sip of water, and said, "No, literally they have *top-cover*. Ashton used his hands to illustrate. "They have blast walls around their perimeter and a rocket-resistant roof made from some high-tech materials and high-speed engineering. It's supposed to be able to stop a rocket or mortar."

Annie took a spoonful of cereal and said, "I didn't see that at your camp."

"And you won't. We don't have it, and it's not coming," Ashton knocked on the wall next to him and said, "We have this…trailer walls and trailer roofs," he gestured out the window with his fork, "and a few Hesco barriers."

Nathan smiled. "And we have one other thing on our side."

"What's that?" asked John.

Nathan shrugged. "We have *random* on our side." He paused for a moment, then said, "They really are trying to kill us, but actually getting killed is random as hell." Nathan took a sip of water. "If it's coming, it's coming, and there's not really much you can do. It's random."

The table sat quiet for a moment.

Ashton shrugged, sat back in his chair, drank from a bottle of a British orange drink like American orange juice, and said, "Well, Nathan and I have a few things to handle this morning, if you two want to get settled and get some sleep, we can meet this afternoon. How about 2:00 p.m.?"

Annie and John nodded in agreement and suddenly an explosion shook the trailer. The incoming alarm sounded, and the British soldiers dove to the floor; they were immediately under the tables, and most of their chairs were turned over. Annie and John were startled and pushed themselves back from the table to do something…anything. They both wanted to join the British soldiers under the table. John and Annie looked to Ashton and Nathan. Ashton took another spoonful of cereal and chewed slowly.

Nathan shrugged. "It wasn't that close."

John said, "Should we get away from the windows or something?" He was doing all he could to keep his voice calm and level.

Ashton looked out of the window and said, "Nah, it really doesn't matter, we've already thought it through, and figured things out with these rocket attacks."

Annie shook her head and asked, "What do you mean?"

Nathan pointed to the British soldiers on the floor a few feet away, shook his head, and said, "That's just fuckin' ridiculous." Ashton glanced at the soldiers, two of whom looked up and scowled at the Americans still nonchalantly sitting at a table.

Ashton looked at Annie and John, then tilted his head toward the window, and said, "First, if there's an impact on the other side of those barriers, we are protected by the barrier itself. Second, if there's an impact within the barrier, in other words a direct hit on this trailer, laying on the floor does nothing. It will likely kill us or shred us pretty bad."

Ashton looked out of the window again and said, "Besides, most of these attacks are over before you can do anything…between one and three rockets, then it's done."

Nathan nodded at Ashton and said, "Yep, they fire a few rockets and move. They can't stay put and keep firing because British artillery can start shooting back pretty fast."

Ashton looked at Nathan, nodded, rocked forward in his chair, and asked, "Ready?"

The conversation was over, and the SF guys had things to do.

The siren stopped but the all-clear signal had not sounded. The British soldiers were still under the tables.

As Nathan stepped over two pairs of feet extending into the aisle, one of the British soldiers under the table said, "Fuckin' stupid Americans."

Nathan smirked and thought maybe they were right, but he still liked walking past them as they lay on the floor. He thought many of the British protocols were nonsense.

Annie and John followed closely and made their way out of the chow hall. The British soldier checking IDs on the chow hall steps lay between sandbags that were configured to form a two-foot-wide rectangle, ironically about the size of a coffin. A British armored personnel carrier idled on the dirt road. The driver had been under the truck since hearing the explosion. He was waiting for the all-clear announcement over the loudspeakers. Nathan just shook his head as he walked past.

The soldier in the dirt under the truck peered through the dust and grime and said, "Hey dumbass Yanks, you better take some fuckin' cover, you fuckin' idiots."

Nathan went to the edge of the truck, knelt on one knee, craned his neck to look under the truck, and saw a soldier who looked no older than nineteen. The soldier visibly shook. Nathan reached into his cargo pocket and pulled out a bottle of water from the chow hall.

Nathan handed the bottle to the soldier and said, "Here, take this. The all-clear will come up soon."

The soldier eked out a small grin, but the gratitude was in his eyes. "Cheers, mate," he nodded once. His helmet went crooked, and he put the cold bottle of water on the back of his neck.

The British soldier briefly looked up at Nathan and said, "Stay safe, Yank."

"You too, friend," Nathan said, tapping the door of the truck once as he stood.

The others were about ten yards ahead. Nathan caught up, and they walked on the dirt road toward the SF compound.

To stop an armored vehicle in place, get out of the protected cab, and lay in the dirt underneath was not something the Americans could wrap their heads around. For the British though, it was a standing order. British soldiers could be brought up on charges if they failed to obey it.

"*All clear, all clear, all clear*," sounded over some very loud and unseen speakers.

A British ambulance tore across the dirt and gravel about two hundred yards beyond the chow hall. They heard its siren and caught a glimpse before the vehicle raced behind a row of Hesco barriers. The last rocket attack had hit more than just dirt and concrete.

Ashton reached for the mechanical cypher lock to open the door, looked back at Annie and John, and said, "The combination is supposed to be a secret, so I can't tell you the combo." Ashton looked toward Nathan and asked, "Hey, what's the combination again?"

Nathan understood what Ashton was doing and immediately responded. "Three-one-five-four, make sure you press the five and the four at the same time." Nathan looked at Annie and John grinned, "But, don't tell anyone; it's a secret."

Ashton turned to Nathan and asked, "Three-one-five-four, hold the five and the four at the same time, and turn the knob?"

Nathan nodded and, looking at Annie and John, said, "Got it?" Both nodded.

Ashton pulled the heavy steel door open and said, "It's a small base and a small camp; you two will learn where things are quickly. People get around on their own unless they need help or ask for help.

"Let's get you back to your trailers," he added, looking back to Annie and John. "I'll write down the hours the British chow hall is open, so you can come and go as you see fit."

Nathan double-checked their air conditioners and made sure the water worked. Everyone was already drenched in sweat. It was still morning but hotter than in Baghdad. Basra had a moist heat due to different geography.

Nathan said, "By the way, I'm not sure if it will be us, but someone will meet you at 2:00 p.m. to go over your plan."

Annie and John nodded and waved as Ashton and Nathan turned the corner out of sight. Annie and John leaned against their respective metal stoops and looked at each other with blank stares for a moment.

THREE SLATTED STEEL STEPS LED TO THE TRAILER'S square, three-by-three-foot front stoop. The metal stoop, like the three metal steps leading to it, was sturdy and constructed to allow water and debris to pass through.

Annie looked at John and said, "Hey…are you fucking kidding me?"

John shook his head, and walked up, then down the stairs from his trailer, and said, "What in the hell have we walked into?"

John stepped into the gravel as Annie jumped off her stoop and sat down on the uncomfortable steel step.

She looked at John and again asked, "Are you fucking kidding me? Um, I think we found the fuckin' war."

John bent over and stretched his back, there was an audible pop. He stood straight and wiped the grime and sweat from his face with the upper part of his shirt sleeve. It was still early, but the temperature was over 102 degrees, and the sun was relentless. The air conditioning was going to feel great!

"Yeah," said John, rubbing his eyes. "I think we just found ourselves right in the middle of the fucking real war! This is definitely not like the embassy in Baghdad."

John pulled a bottle of water from his cargo pocket, took a gulp, and handed it to Annie, who did the same.

She pushed her little finger into her left ear and said, "Hey, are your ears ringing? That first rocket attack, I had my window open. I felt like the blast mushed my face or something." Annie pulled her hair back, took another swig of water, and handed the bottle back to John. "I think I understand why nobody from HWG ever spent much time down here."

He looked straight ahead and said, "This could be a long couple of days."

Annie nodded. "Yep, I already don't like that damn siren." They both laughed, and John switched legs to stretch. The red-strap flight seats and dehydration left John achy and tight.

John smirked, "I'm sure these guys are wary of us, but they seemed pretty straightforward. I'm thinking our first impression went OK or they wouldn't have given us the combination to the steel door."

Annie picked another rock from the grate and said, "Yep, I think simply not puking or pissing on ourselves during the rocket attacks helped."

She glanced at her watch and said, "Alright, we should be able to shower and get about four hours of sleep. I'd like to be ready when they get here."

John offered her the water bottle again. She took another drink and handed it back. John gulped the last of the water, some of which spilled from the corner of his mouth.

He wiped his sweaty face with his shoulder and said, "Sounds good, let's make sure each other is up and moving?"

"Yeah, good call."

John pointed to Annie's door and said, "How about 1:30 p.m.? If I don't see you, I will bang on your door; if you don't see me, you bang on mine."

Annie walked up the steps to her door. "Good, sounds like a plan."

John walked into his trailer, shut the door, and slid his backpack, helmet, and vest into the corner with his foot. The only sound was the hum of the air conditioner across the room. The interior of the trailer was simple and functional and set up to house two people. The room was about ten feet by fifteen feet, with two single beds on either side. Between the beds against the wall under a window was a desk and a black chair that sat lopsided due to a missing wheel. Opposite the entry door was the bathroom entrance.

The bathroom separated a room identical to John's on the other side of the same trailer. There was one toilet, a sink, and a shower. At least for now, it was all his. The toilet flushed, the knobs on the sink were loose but worked, and the paint on the shower wall was peeling and showing bare wood. He turned on the water, hot and cold. They both worked. Life was good.

John got things together for a shower. At the foot of each bed were neatly folded clean sheets with a towel to the side. The sheets appeared to be children's sheets, and likely counterfeit. One pillowcase showed what looked like a squirrel wearing a batman cowl and floppy bunny ears. John thought it was creepy.

John always traveled with his own sheets and pillowcases. Not everyone was prepared to host overnight visitors. In fact, he had gone to a few places where he got the idea that the accommodations were exceptionally poor on purpose, so people would not come back. It usually worked.

Before this Iraq deployment, John bought two high quality flat sheets and two pillowcases. They weighed almost nothing and could be folded neatly into small squares or rolled up and slipped into the corner of a bag or backpack. He pulled the oversized sheets out of his luggage, tucked the excess under the mattress, and used the pillow on the other mattress as an extra. Sheets with a high thread count and quality feel were not lost on John. After all, about one third of every day, was spent in bed. There is no reason to have bad sheets, even in a war zone. John took a shower, set his clock, and dozed off within thirty seconds.

Annie's room mirrored John's. Annie went into her room, set her alarm clock, brushed her teeth, and took a shower. With the towel wrapped around her, she moved the set of sheets from the bed to the desk and the pillow to the floor to make up the bed, then laid down to test the mattress. Immediately she fell asleep. For the next four hours, Annie slept on the bare mattress without once rolling over.

Hostage Status: 82 Days in Captivity (*continued*)

Surfboy grabbed the index card from under the bathroom bucket and passed it around one last time—they could not be caught with a piece of paper. He scuffed the paper against the concrete wall and poured water over it tearing it into smaller pieces.

Surfboy looked around the room. "Here goes, bros." He put half the contents in his mouth, took a sip of water and swallowed.

Shorebilly held his hand out and asked, "You want help?"

"Nah, I got it. Besides, it's better than this fuckin' food." He managed a faint smile swallowing the other half of the paper.

All the hostages nodded, acknowledging it was a good idea to eat the note.

The mean guards were still on duty—it was time to keep quiet.

CHAPTER 10

ANNIE AND JOHN INTRODUCE THE PROGRAM TO SF ...BINGO...HOT PIZZA

DAY 82 (*CONTINUED*): JULY 6, 2007

John awoke after a three-and-a-half-hour nap, took another shower, and got dressed. He was ready, marginally refreshed, and clean. At 1:30 p.m., he walked down the three metal stairs into the gravel and dirt to Annie's trailer, then up the metal stairs, and tapped on her door.

John called out, "Annie, you there?"

"Yes, come on in," she replied.

Annie had showered again, dressed, and was making her bed. She had just flapped open the flat sheet, and it floated into place on the bed.

John looked at Annie's luggage near the desk that had not been opened yet. She had what she needed for a shower and change of clothes in her backpack; items were strewn about the floor.

"What the hell, didn't you get any sleep yet?"

She tossed the pillow on the bed and replied, "Yep, I slept—I was out before I could even make the bed. I don't think I moved until my alarm jolted me awake." She gestured around the room with her hand, "I'll get my shit together after this first meeting…maybe." They both laughed.

John smiled. "I'll hang out on your metal stoop while you do whatever you gotta do."

She nodded, "I'm good; I just want to make sure I'm ready when the SF guys show up."

John opened the door and stepped onto the stoop for a moment. It was eerily quiet. Hesco barriers had a way of absorbing and compartmentalizing sound. The only sound John heard was the repetitive rhythm of machinery in the distance. He felt a sense of calm and quiet. The heat was more oppressive than any he had ever experienced.

He heard voices nearby and saw three people turn the corner at the Hesco barrier.

John smiled and waved, then called to Annie, whose door was still open. "Hey, Annie, I think we are set."

The trailer door immediately opened wider. Annie looked at John and said, "Hey," then turned and waved to Ashton and the two strangers.

Ryan, the team leader, was the first to lean in and introduce himself, "Hey, I'm Ryan."

Annie and John responded, and Mike introduced himself with first name only.

Everyone shook hands, and Mike said, "The Brit chow hall is closed right now, so we thought we might grab lunch at Echos, a base restaurant. There's one close."

Annie smiled. "You have a restaurant here?"

"Yep, the British have some sort of contract with a company, and there are two of them here on this base. It's not great, but it works," Mike added.

As they walked toward the parking lot, Ryan reiterated, “It isn’t fine dining, but the pizza is OK, and it’s a good place to talk.”

As they turned the corner at the Hesco barrier, Mike pointed to a large dented, mud-caked SUV and said, “We should all be able to fit.”

Ashton had the keys and got into the driver’s seat, Ryan took the front passenger seat, and Mike got in back with John and Annie. John sat in the middle.

Ryan looked toward the backseat and said, “It’s about a five-minute ride after we pass through the camp gate.”

Ashton weaved through the Hesco barriers, the tires grinding through the gravel, and passed a series of T-walls until they reached the chained gate. Annie opened her door at the same time as Mike. Ashton gave Ryan a look that was barely perceptible. Ryan got it. Annie meant to help with opening the gate. The effort showed some heart and that she had paid attention earlier in the day.

Mike looked over at Annie and said, “Nah, don’t worry, I got it. There’s a combination.”

Annie got out, caught up with Mike, and said, “I’ll give you a hand, maybe drag the gate or something. We want to at least try and earn our keep,” she smiled.

Mike appreciated the gesture and said, “If you lift the edge of the gate a little, I can pull the chain around to get to the lock.”

She nodded. “We have the same sort of thing in Baghdad. If someone pulled the chain too tight on one side, you can’t pull the lock around to do the combination.”

Mike nodded. “Yep, same here, and there’s always some idiot who thinks pulling the chain tight makes the camp more secure.”

Annie laughed. The lock was on the other side of the hole in the fence, and the chain was tight.

Mike shook his head as they neared the gate and said, "There it is. Some moron yanked it tight and from the other side. We have a few new guys here, and they haven't figured things out yet."

Sometimes the simplest things could make life difficult in Iraq. Annie kicked her foot into the dirt and gravel underneath the edge of the fence, grabbed the chain link fence at about thigh level, and lifted slightly. That created just enough slack in the chain for Mike to spin the lock around and see the dial showing the numbers.

Mike said the numbers aloud. "Three-one-five-four. It's a secret," he added, smiling as he pulled the chain through the gap in the fence and opened the gate.

Once the SUV was through, they closed the gate and loosely locked the chain.

Mike nodded to Annie and said a simple, "Thanks."

"Sure," Annie said, nodding as she wiped the sweat that had accumulated on her forehead during their moment at the gate. Annie and Mike got back into the SUV. The sharp cold of the SUV reminded her of walking into the liquor store beer cooler in Elkhorn where she would occasionally pick up a thirty pack of Busch Light on summer weekends.

Ashton and Ryan waved to the British soldier standing in the scant shade of the guard shack. The soldier pulled a fist-size chunk of ice out of a cooler and wrapped it in a towel. He returned the wave and sat with the ice on the back of his neck between his helmet and the top of his vest. The soldier had stood at the midafternoon guard post in the Basra summer heat before. He might be killed in a rocket attack, but he was not going to let himself die from heatstroke.

Ryan looked back toward Annie and John, and said, "There's a little store next to where we are going. The British call it NAAFI. If you need anything, we can stop by on the way out. I need a few things, so you two can take a look. It's a little different; everything is British. They use US currency, though."

Ashton pulled up to the edge of an asphalt road, and a British version of a Humvee rolled by with three more just behind. Atop each in a rotating turret, a British soldier manned a loaded machine gun pointed down and to the left. The soldiers in the turrets looked identical: black goggles protected their eyes, bulky earpieces edged under their helmets, tan material wrapped around their faces and necks protected their skin from the sun, dirt, and debris. Their average age was twenty years, five months.

Annie looked out the window to her left and said, "That's weird." Mike leaned forward to see what she had noticed and saw palm trees and greenery along the side of the road. The full and lush fronds were so out of place in the parched and scorched area. The trees were coated with a tan film from dirt constantly wafting in the air.

"Yeah, it is weird," Mike said and shrugged. "Anything will grow here if you can get the water to it."

Ashton slowed slightly and took a hard left across the oncoming lane and into a dirt parking lot. Directly in front of them was a drainage ditch about fifteen feet wide and ten feet deep. He parked next to a homemade armored pickup truck with a machine gun mount welded to the bed. The upright was well constructed and had reinforced struts fused from the truck bed to the machine gun mount post.

Parked on the other side of the SF truck was a commercial-grade armored GMC Yukon SUV. The thick reinforced glass was coated with a dark film on the inside. The vehicle's exterior was dusty; its wheel wells were caked with dirt. The vehicle clearly had taken gunfire. Two bullets had chipped but failed to penetrate the driver's side window. Damage from another bullet spread like a giant spider web across the passenger window behind it, but the glass held.

In front of them across the ditch was the NAAFI, the store Riley had mentioned, and to the right through a Hesco barrier path was the restaurant called Echos. Everyone walked around bumps and holes in the dirt parking lot. The ground was so compacted from heavy vehicle traffic it felt like concrete; dirt even had tire skid marks. Mike led the way around the cars and across the ditch.

Ryan spoke to Annie and John as they walked. "When we get inside there's a place to order; they will give you a little paper ticket with a number." Ryan paused as they stepped onto a makeshift wooden walkway. "Then they will call your number. They actually have real plates and utensils if you want."

Mike opened the door and held it for everyone; civility among those in a war zone was real and necessary.

John tapped Mike on the elbow as he walked by and said, "Thanks." Mike nodded. John had seen how courtesy and a sense of higher comportment emerged among many people in a war zone. It was quite real. For some reason, war nudged people to be better.

Annie and John saw the layout of Echos for the first time. The tables had red and white tablecloths, albeit plastic. The building was constructed with two extra-large double-wide trailers that were set end to end to be four trailers deep and wide.

Three seating areas inside Echos were aggressively cooled by air conditioners about every ten feet. The first area was a ten-by-fifteen-foot cubbyhole with a TV in the middle as a focal point. The other two areas were identical, with five circular tables each seating four to six people. The two larger areas were separated by brown wood balusters and a four-foot-high railing. Windows were every ten feet, but extraordinarily little light came through because the Hesco barriers were above the windows and nearly touched the building.

They walked past the TV seating area and stood in line behind four British soldiers. Their rifles slung over their backs and helmets in hand or strapped to their vests, the soldiers ordered without looking at a menu.

The women behind the counter were TCNs from Bosnia. They were efficient, hardworking, diligent, and friendly. The SF guys were greeted with a warm smile, and a "hello" that included their first names. John received a generous grin.

The five Americans ordered pizza and got their drinks and paper numbers. They sat at a table under an air conditioner, with Annie and John next to each other. The British soldiers sat in the U-shaped TV area and waited for their numbers to be called.

Mike looked at Annie and John, smiled, and said, "So, here we are." He tapped his paper number on the table.

Ryan nodded, grinned, and said, "You've stepped into the hot, loud, and dirty world of Basra."

Annie and John grinned and nodded in agreement. Annie said, "Yes, it's a little different than the US embassy and life in Baghdad." Everyone chuckled lightly.

A few order numbers were called over the loudspeaker, and everyone reflexively looked at their paper numbers—

like looking at a bingo card. Two British soldiers walked to the counter from the TV area and picked up their lunch.

Mike looked at Annie and John and said, "Well, we have some emails going back and forth on the hostage stuff. Just like about every military unit out there, we have a personnel recovery mission that is high priority. It's pretty vague as to what that really means, but we are unconventionally in the conventional hostage rescue game."

Mike glanced briefly across the room as one of the British soldiers tripped over a helmet and vest next to the chair where he was trying to sit. The soldier banged into the wall but managed to keep his tray level, saving his drink and pizza.

Mike looked back and said, "In your emails, we got the impression that you were looking for more than just tactical assistance with a hostage rescue."

Ryan took a sip from an orange drink in a red plastic cup and said, "What do you really want to do, and how do you think you can get there?"

Annie nodded slowly. "Well, we want to shift gears on how we are trying to develop some of this hostage case work. Like a lot of things, what we've been doing and how we have been doing it aren't working." She explained some of the hurdles. "Even before John and I thought about coming here, we knew most of the FBI efforts had been attempted without actually being here in Basra…and were failing. In other words, developing leads, sources, witnesses, and general intelligence had been tried while everyone sat in Baghdad."

They heard order numbers called over the loudspeaker and glanced at their numbered pieces of paper, then tossed them on the table. A British soldier stood and walked from the TV area.

Annie continued. "We have been reinventing the wheel every couple of months with each rotation of personnel, and nothing actually gets developed." She shrugged, tapped her index finger on the table lightly, and said, "Most of what we think can be expanded needs to happen right here in Basra. This is where the event took place on our main hostage case, and there seem to be other kidnappings that took place here in southern Iraq." She shrugged her shoulders, showed the palms of her hands, and said, "We haven't been close enough to the field to say we're really in the game." She tapped the table once with her paper number. "It's like we tied a string to the end of a thirty-foot fishing pole and attempted to thread a needle across the room," Annie paused, then added, "On a windy day, with our eyes closed." She smirked and said, "It just didn't fucking work."

Everyone nodded and chuckled. They understood her analogy and her assessment.

Over the loudspeaker there were three numbers called, then a slight pause, and two more numbers. Everyone at the table reached for their paper number to check. Just barely audible, Annie said, "Bingo." Ashton heard her and grinned.

Everyone brought their pizza to the table on red plastic trays. The pizza was hot. There were beige plastic plates and separate containers with metal utensils by the register. In unison, the group precariously navigated the walk back to the table with trays, plates, utensils, and extra napkins. Annie and John missed the metal utensils but saw the prewrapped plastic ones in a cup on the table next to where they sat. John reached over and took a set for himself and Annie. The SF guys had an idea of what would happen in a moment, and they grinned imperceptibly. The SF operators knew to use metal utensils to cut into the pizza, pull out a piece, and place it on the plate to cool.

First to open his plastic utensils, John turned the metal platter for a better angle to separate a piece onto the plate. He placed the plastic knife between two pieces of pizza and positioned the fork in the middle of a piece to keep the cheese stable. The tines on the fork immediately melted, curled, and left John with the tip of his index finger in the hot cheese.

"What the hell?" John said as he lifted the fork. "Did you see that?" He looked at Annie who immediately put her plastic utensils on the table.

The SF guys grinned slightly. Ashton said, "Yeah, that happens sometimes with hot food here and the chow hall. Nobody is really sure where this plastic crap comes from. Lowest bidder, I suppose."

John got up, walked across the room, and got metal utensils for Annie and him.

Mike shook red pepper flakes on the slice still cooling in front of him and said, "It sounds like this hostage thing is a mess. What do you have in mind?"

Annie tapped the side of a Parmesan cheese shaker, nodded, and said, "John worked up some things with some embassy personnel that work with The Fort." Annie's reference to *The Fort* was a casual way of referring to the National Security Agency, located at Fort Meade, Maryland. Annie decided tapping the shaker was not working and unscrewed the top. "We've looked at some of the efforts in the past, and what we think is there was a lot of missed exploitation and a lot of duplicated effort." Annie poured cheese onto her pizza and continued. "There was a great deal of work, but there wasn't that much understanding as to what the real potential was when it came to drilling into more with The Fort." Annie's pizza cooled enough that she could pick it up at the edge. She nodded to John and said, "Tag."

Annie and John had inadvertently begun their tag-team method about four days earlier when briefing their plans over and over in Baghdad. At first, they cued each other up with a nod. One evening after briefing the same concept three times within five hours and answering the same questions over and over, they spontaneously started saying "tag" during the brief. It worked, and it stuck.

While all ears and eyes were trained on Annie, John had bit into hot pizza, scorching the roof of his mouth. He swallowed a mouthful of water to cool the molten cheese still on his tongue. When Annie suddenly tagged him in to talk, he swallowed without chewing and took over briefing.

"I physically worked at the embassy and met with personnel from The Fort daily on the cluster I was assigned to there." He shrugged. "What I was doing faded away, but I got really familiar with The Fort, their capabilities and reach here." He took another quick drink of water, washed the rest of the cheese down, and said, "Plus, last year when I was deployed in Baghdad, I was able to get some understanding of how things came together, and how some things didn't."

Everyone at the table nodded and grinned while biting into their slices of pizza, which by now had cooled.

John went on. "So, I had some heart-to-heart conversations with two of the guys at the embassy who worked for The Fort, and I think they were pretty candid. What they saw was that the deployment rotation mill was hampering people working hostage cases. Personnel came into the country from one rotation to the next and did the same thing over and over…and may not have realized it." John took a small sip of water and said, "Whether it was FBI, DIA, or anyone who worked at the embassy hostage working group, most people didn't have the big-picture understanding of events; and if they did, they weren't in any real position to put anything into action."

John nudged a piece of pizza cooling in front of him. It was cool enough to pick up.

He shook red pepper flakes over the slice and said, "Also, as Annie said, trying to do something operationally down here while sitting in Baghdad was a joke." He picked up the pizza, and as he brought it to his mouth, he glanced in Annie's direction and said, "Tag."

Annie looked at her pizza, took a sip from her glass, and said, "We would like to try to bring the underutilized resources of The Fort into play and operationally blend it with the HUMINT processes down here. The sources, witnesses, and sub-sources here in Basra haven't been tapped at all."

Ryan swallowed the pizza he was chewing and took a sip of orange drink. "Quick question: What were you getting from the Agency? How has that worked?" Ryan asked, referring to the Central Intelligence *Agency*.

Annie shook her head in disgust. "The Agency doesn't seem to have much going on here; if they do, they aren't telling us. Another huge hurdle to get past is the Agency agenda. Hostage work seems to be pretty far down on their list."

Mike tossed a piece of crust onto his plate and kept his voice low. "Well, how in the hell can that be? How do two agencies with the size, reach, money, and manpower of the FBI and CIA not coordinate and work together on something like finding a goddamn hostage?"

John, shrugged, nodded, and chimed in. "The reality is that even in overseas hostage events, the FBI has the lead and jurisdiction. Once the FBI machine starts moving along, the Agency doesn't want to get near it. They keep the FBI in the dark, even if they develop something on a hostage case." John shrugged again and said, "Some things are supposed to work together, but they just don't."

Ryan tossed a piece of crust onto the plate in front of him and shook his head. "Big egos and bigger agendas. I think I know what you're saying."

Everyone at the table nodded and got quiet for a moment.

Ryan looked at Mike and Ashton with a barely perceptible nod, then looked at Annie and John and asked, "So, what are you thinking, and how can we help?"

Annie took a small bite, chewed quickly, and said, "We'd like to try something a little different, and we want to really lean into blending The Fort detail, the SIGINT, with source development, really push the HUMINT side hard, but coordinate locally. We can't do either by ourselves, and we sure as hell can't do it from Baghdad."

Ryan sat back in his chair, took another bite of pizza, and nodded.

Mike tossed a piece of crust on the tray and said, "Yep, you know we can work with some of that, but down here the technical side is pretty limited."

Annie nodded and shrugged. "Getting that part in motion took some time. That's why we were delayed getting here." She waved toward John with the edge of her pizza crust and said, "We had to lay things out to our hierarchy and work back channels with The Fort for help. It turns out there's a civilian analyst from The Fort working with the British somewhere down here."

John leaned in and said, “He’s at something called GCHQ at the British headquarters building. We have no idea where that is, but we have a meeting set up with him tomorrow.”

Annie sipped her orange drink and said, “We’ve been pitching this as a combined effort across the board, and we wanted everyone to have all the information, so we can make smarter decisions…Can you guys come to the meeting, too?”

“What time is it set for?” Ryan asked.

“1:00 p.m.,” Annie said.

Ryan looked at Mike and Ashton, who both nodded slightly. He said, “Yep, that works.”

Annie crunched down on a piece of crust, looked around the table, and said, “What the hell is a GCHQ, anyway?”

The SF guys at the table sat stoically. They all knew better than to discuss anything regarding GCHQ where they were eating lunch.

Ashton put his hand up in a loose friendly fist, the international sign in Iraq to stop, and said, “We know what GCHQ is…let’s talk about it when we get back to camp.”

All the pizza was finally eaten. All that was left were a few overdone pieces of crust. Everyone picked up their trays, wiped down the table, and stood. Ryan was first to the trash can. He pushed the flap door open, dropped in his trash, set his tray on top of the can, and held the flap open while everyone else deposited their trash and placed their trays on top of the bin.

War could be a polite place.

They made their way back to the SF camp to discuss more details and meet with another SF team operator in a few hours.

Hostage Status: 82 Days in Captivity (*continued*)

The door flew open and slammed against the wall. A barefoot man wearing khakis and a white T-shirt was thrown into their cell. The guards yelled at him in Arabic, and he was yelling back—the door slammed shut. He sat up and put his back in the corner of the cell.

The hostages gathered next to each other sitting on one side of the room.

Surfboy blurted out, "What the fuck is this?"

Everyone shook their head. Tex said, "I don't know, but I don't like it." Nodding toward the new occupant he asked, "Iraqi?"

The man nodded and responded with a one-word question. "Ameriki?"

All four hostages nodded. It was the one Arabic word everyone knew—American.

The door flew open again, and two guards stepped inside holding hoses. They yelled at the Iraqi, who put his hand over his mouth. A guard turned and faced the American hostages. "Shut!" They left and slammed the door.

They understood. Silence prevailed for the next three hours.

CHAPTER 11

MEET KYLE... GREEN BERETS SOLVE PROBLEMS... LEARNING TO GET AROUND

DAY 82 (*CONTINUED*): JULY 6, 2007

John and Annie needed to discuss the meeting at Echos and prepare for the meeting with Kyle, the team intelligence specialist. John made his way out of his trailer; the oppressive heat felt like he was walking in front of a giant blow-dryer from hell. He picked up a small stone and tossed it toward the bottom of Annie's door. She heard the tap and opened the door enough to look out. The air hit her face like she had opened a furnace door.

Blinking from the heat and light, she saw John and said, "Hey, come on in. Let's talk inside. I swear it's hotter here than in Baghdad."

She backed inside and left the door open for John. He came in and sat in a chair that once had wheels; the seat still swiveled.

John leaned back, then forward to stretch his back. "It's good to be inside...and I think you're right," he said, wiping sweat and grime from his forehead. “It is definitely hotter here than Baghdad. This air conditioning saves the day.”

Annie put one boot up on the edge of the bed frame and said, “Yeah, and it’s not a fuckin’ dry heat either…it feels thicker here.”

Annie looked at John and asked, “Well, what did you think of our chat this afternoon at lunch with the guys?”

John shrugged his shoulders, looked up at the ceiling, then back to Annie. “It seemed like it went pretty good to me. They let us pitch the concept and listened to what we had to say.”

She nodded. “Yep, I was thinking the same thing. I don’t think we really said much that surprised them. I think everyone is more frustrated about the lack of interagency coordination than surprised.”

“I think it probably takes a lot to really surprise these guys,” he said, swiveling the chair back and forth as he spoke. “I felt like they understood where we’d like to go with this. My guess is that they were way ahead of us and thinking through the mess we are coming down here with.”

She grinned, swiveled in her chair, and said, “Yeah, we are presenting a pretty big clusterfuck and putting a shitload of work on their already full plate.”

John leaned forward, stretched his back again, and said, “My guess is they probably spent the last couple of hours talking some things through…trying to assess whether or not we are full of shit. I’d like to think they can see we are serious about getting this going and not on the typical sightseeing trip looking for new and exciting war stories.”

They both smiled and shook their heads. Annie said, “This part of the country is a mess…two rocket attacks on our first day…damn…our first morning!”

John shook his head. "Yeah, based on how they handled things it seemed pretty routine."

Annie dropped her foot from the bed frame, straightened both of her legs, looking at the toes of her boots, and let her heels drop to the floor. She pulled her feet back until the soles of her boots were flat on the floor, then looked at John. "You know, if we get everyone down here to bite off on this, it's only the beginning...That's when the long haul starts."

John sat back in his chair. "I know." He looked around the room and back at Annie.

She said, "If we get the SF guys to buy in, as well as the guy we meet tomorrow from The Fort, then the game is really on."

"I know." He also knew where the conversation was headed.

She briefly pressed her eyes shut. "One of us will have to stay."

"I know." John took a long breath.

There was a knock on the door. It was Ashton; he was there to walk Annie and John to the next meeting. John and Annie's conversation would have to wait. The next meeting would be with the SF team's intelligence operator, Kyle.

John walked out and shook hands with Ashton as they stood in gravel by the stoop. Annie waved to Ashton and said, "Hang on a minute—I gotta pee real quick...be right out."

Ashton and John gave a slight wave to confirm they had heard. Ashton leaned on a Hesco barrier, and John picked a piece of gravel out of the metal slat on the stoop.

He looked at Ashton and asked, "So, what did you think of the lunch chat?"

John often found informality disarming—people spoke more when they were comfortable. Avoiding stiff dialogue was best when trying to connect. He called the lunch dialogue a *chat*, not a brief or a meeting. John already picked up that Ashton was an observer—a careful watcher and thinker.

Ashton chose his words cautiously. "There are a lot of moving parts that come into play on something like this."

John nodded in agreement. "Yeah, just the simple logistics of moving around in a war zone can be complicated and take days."

"Yep, people have no idea what real military air transport is like."

John tossed the rock he had pried out of the metal grate, rubbed the back of his calves, and declared, "That shit hurts. I hate to sound like a lightweight, but I think my ass is still a little numb from sitting on the canvas seats on the flight from Baghdad." John was becoming relatable.

Ashton shook his head. "Yeah, I know what you mean. I was on Brit-Air last week coming back from Baghdad; something happened, and we had a really hard landing."

Ashton pulled up his T-shirt sleeve to show a multicolored bruise about two inches wide that started above his elbow and ran up his bicep disappearing under his shirt. The skin was raised in what looked like a cross between a rash and a burn.

"I was asleep. I had myself wedged between the red straps to stay upright. When we hit the runway hard, everyone slammed forward. One of the flight crew guys standing near me was thrown off his feet and landed on top of me."

John's brow furrowed slightly. "Ouch. That hurt. My sore legs don't feel so bad now," he said with a faint laugh.

Ashton grinned. "Yep, it's all relative," he said as he gingerly pulled down his sleeve.

Annie stepped onto the stoop and pulled the door shut behind her. "Hey Ashton."

Ashton nodded and gave her a polite smile. "Hey…we are heading over to the team trailer. It's literally around the corner." We thought we could talk there about a few things then head over to the British chow hall before they shut down, if that works for you two?"

"Sure, sounds great," Annie said. "We just don't want to screw up anything you have going."

John nodded. "Yeah, we don't want to get in the way."

Ashton kept walking and said, "Nah…We're good. This works."

They passed the next double trailer and a small open area with volleyball poles set in concrete inside tires. There was no net, and the area had recently been used as a burn pit. Next to the burn pit was the team trailer.

Ashton manipulated the mechanical cypher lock and said aloud, "Three-one-five-four," then turned to Annie and John with a slight grin and added, "Shhhhhh, it's a secret."

They entered a small foyer with doors left, right, and center. The door on the left was open, and inside the fifteen-by-fifteen-foot room were large commercial drink coolers full of Gatorade, Red Bull, and other soft drinks. Across from the coolers were three boxes containing cartons of potato chips and Pop Tarts. The door on the right was closed. The door in the center was closed and had a cypher lock.

Ashton reached for the cypher lock, clicked the buttons, glanced back at Annie and John, and said, "Sorry, this one actually is secret, for now."

They entered a large open room. To the left was the SF armory, sometimes referred to as the "war room." Three-by-three-foot cubby holes containing helmets, vests, and various munitions stood next to a Ping-Pong table. Occupying the rest of the room were two couches and three chairs, all side by side and facing a blank wall.

Ashton led Annie and John through an open doorway into another large room with three medium sized couches in a U shape with a coffee table in the middle. Ashton invited Annie and John to sit on the couches, then sat across from them. Within a minute Ryan and Mike walked out of the office followed by the SF team intelligence sergeant, Kyle. Ashton slid to the curved section of the U shape couches, and Ryan, Mike, and Kyle sat directly across from Annie and John.

Ryan introduced Kyle and explained that all team intelligence details went through him.

Kyle simply nodded and said nothing. Kyle was about six feet tall, lean, and fit. He wore a mechanic's blue work shirt with the name "Frank" embroidered above the pocket. He had bought the shirt at a Goodwill store before he left the US. His arms were heavily tattooed with ink that started at his wrists and disappeared under his shirt sleeves. He had not shaved in about a week, and his hair hung about three inches past his collar in the back. Kyle had spent more time in a war zone than anyone on the team. He had been in the US only six months of the past four years. He was one of the soldiers who slipped through the cracks when it came to *dwell-time* after deployments.

After his first post-9/11 deployment in Afghanistan as an infantry soldier, Kyle went through the Special Forces Q-course, managed the requisite intelligence schools with ease, and redeployed as events were building toward war in Iraq. His first deployment as a Green Beret with an ODA was in April 2003, one month before the war started. He spent eight months in and around Baghdad. Kyle was comfortable at war, and he was lucky: he came through that first tour unharmed. That did not last.

Midway through his second SF deployment he was wounded and sent back to the US, via Landstuhl, Germany. He lost part of his left heel when his gun truck was destroyed in a roadside bomb explosion. After a month of rehab in Texas, he was back with his unit in North Carolina. He volunteered to go back to Iraq early to set things up for the team.

Each post-deployment break in the US, or dwell-time, was shorter and shorter. Kyle found himself becoming nauseous at night, sleeping for only about two hours at a time at first; after about two weeks, he could not sleep at all. He was better at the war. Kyle understood the war, how things worked and operational concepts that few would ever grasp.

Ryan opened the conversation. "Kyle researched and worked up a few things on the hostage stuff before you guys came down. He went through different databases using the information from the emails you sent when you first reached out to us." Ryan laid a pad of paper on the coffee table. "Over the last hour or so, Mike and I gave Kyle an overview of what we talked about at lunch." Ryan looked toward Kyle, nodded, and said, "I think you had a few questions…What are your thoughts?"

Kyle looked toward Annie and John. "Ryan and Mike gave me the big picture of what you guys would like to do. Basically, you're leaning into blending advanced source development and technical SIGINT, corroborating and exploiting one with the other. Does that sound about right?"

Annie and John looked from Kyle to each other, nodded, then looked back to Kyle without saying anything.

Kyle nodded. "OK, good. Per your emails, it sounds like you have a small collection of sources either in the area, or they can be brought into the area or developed? Is that about right?" Kyle looked around at all the faces in the room.

Everyone nodded.

"OK, I guess one of the bigger moving parts we will be helping with are the logistics and details for source meetings?" Kyle asked. Annie and John nodded again, then looked at Ryan and Mike, who nodded at Kyle.

Ryan picked up the pad of paper from the coffee table. He scanned the page, crossed out a few talking points that had been addressed, then looked at Kyle. "How about tech exploitation?"

Kyle nodded. "Mike and Ryan tell me you have something set up for SIGINT development, and there's some sort of meeting tomorrow?"

John reached into his cargo pocket, extracted a small notebook, and flipped through the pages. "Yes, it's with someone named...," he paused and sorted through more pages, "He's an American...Donny or Don or..."

Kyle stopped him. "Donovan?"

"Yes," Annie and John answered in unison.

Kyle nodded. "Good, if you're having a meeting with him that means he's already interested in your project." He shrugged his shoulders, held his palms up in front of him, and said, "Donovan stays invisible. If he doesn't want a meeting, then it won't happen."

Ryan looked at Kyle and said, "Our direct contact with him and his shop has been limited. Maybe there could be some other benefit."

Kyle nodded. "I know Brit-HQ is having some drama with manpower and logistics, and there might be some give-and-take."

Annie and John stayed stoic. They knew Ryan and Kyle discussed some back-channel interest that was better left unsaid in front of them. Ryan and Kyle recognized the potential benefit of connecting with Donovan. Housing and other logistics had become problematic due to the American surge up north and the increased number of British soldiers in the area, as well. Many aspects of war were developed and furthered through trading favors. The Special Forces ODA often thought several steps ahead, playing mental chess against people who played checkers.

Annie looked at Kyle and said, "Our meeting is tomorrow somewhere at British headquarters at 2:00 p.m."

Kyle nodded and looked around the room. "OK, let's plan on leaving an hour before that, so we have plenty of time to handle security processes and badging. What badges and ID cards are you carrying now?"

Annie and John held up their ID pouches, flipped open the tops, and showed the ID badges issued for sensitive access areas at the embassy in Baghdad. The British recognized the security level and special access areas of the American embassy-issued badges; however, they would have to obtain Brit-HQ badges for sensitive access areas, too.

Kyle recognized the badges and said, "Good, we will be OK to get in the door and get started."

Ryan asked Kyle, "Will those badges get them in?"

Kyle nodded. "Yes, through the front door, and enough for the paperwork to get Brit-HQ badging. The security office is good about access and badge reciprocity, but there are hoops to jump through with picture taking and paperwork. I'll make sure it's wired before we get there; I have a hook in the office."

Relationships and mutual support got things done in a war zone.

Kyle looked at Annie and John and said, "Back to the source development and methodology: We can walk through some of that after the meeting with Donovan. I'm assuming you're ready to hit the ground running?"

Annie tilted her head, looked toward the coffee table for a second, and said, "Well, yes, for the most part…" She paused and looked at Kyle.

None of the SF operators liked the sound of that response. It did not exude much confidence.

"Well," Kyle said, "I've seen part of your potential source development list with their identifying information and details; we can start running right away with source development and tasking…" He paused and let the silence settle, hoping to prod Annie into addressing her obvious reservation. "We have everything logistically set on our side," he added, guessing at the one critical source development logistical variable Annie and John needed to bring with them: money.

Kyle looked at Annie and John, and said, "OK, US currency seems to work everywhere. I'm assuming you brought a few thick envelopes to pay these sources." Kyle meant money to pay sources for incentive, services, and expenses.

Annie and John looked at each other, then sheepishly around the room.

"Well, we aren't as well funded as we'd like to be," Annie said, shrugging her shoulders. "We've been working on things between Baghdad and FBI headquarters, but we've hit a few obstacles."

Kyle nodded and listened without expression, while Ryan responded. "OK, well, what sort of funding do you have for source expense, services, or purchase of phone cards and other possible items, like more phones or something?"

Annie and John looked at each other. Annie shrugged slightly, and her shoulders stayed drooped as they looked back to Ryan.

"None," she said quietly.

Ryan, Mike, and Kyle sat calmly for a moment. Ryan kept his stare directed at Annie and John, but tilted his head slightly toward Mike and asked, "Can we fix the cash flow problem on this, if it comes up?"

Mike kept his eyes on Annie and John, both of whom were trying to shrink into the couch cushions.

Mike nodded. "We can route funding and cash through channels to make it happen." Mike's eyes were fixed on Annie and John as he tilted his head toward Kyle and asked, "Does that work for you?"

Kyle stared directly at John and Annie without blinking and responded with one syllable. "Yeah."

Ashton sat quietly and watched the FBI agents squirm under the heavy weight of SF eyes. He knew how intimidating unblinking stares can be, particularly when followed by silence. Ashton appreciated that Annie and John were smart enough to know when to sit quietly.

If stares and glares had actual weight, Annie and John would have been crushed into the cushions at this point. They both knew how absurd it was to try source development without funding, cash on hand for service, expenses of the source, or other items that might be needed. They had no idea that the issue would come up so early and had assumed they would be able to introduce the shortcoming gently as the relationship with SF developed.

Much of the FBI process in Iraq was in place to supply the FBI machine. Many people in Iraq, both inside and outside the FBI, understood the limited operational ability of the FBI and often compared some aspects to a *self-licking ice cream cone.*

Ryan looked at Annie and John and said, "OK, I think we have enough to run with for now. Ashton, will you make sure you make it over to the chow hall before it closes?"

Ryan nodded toward Annie and John, which they understood was their cue to get up and go. Annie and John walked through the large area with the Ping-Pong table and war room and out into the stifling heat. They knew how to find their trailers without an escort.

Ryan, Mike, Kyle, and Ashton sat on the couches and looked about the room. Ashton got up, walked across the room, shut the door, and came back to the couch area.

Kyle spoke first, calmly, his voice flat. "How seriously is the FBI really taking hostage work? When an ODA has to come up with cash so the FBI can pay and run sources, something is wrong with this picture."

Ryan nodded. "I agree. What I think we are seeing is a top-heavy machine, that being the FBI. And the FBI is being put in check by two of its own."

Mike nodded. "Yep, it sort of appears like two low-level people stepped up to try and pull a rabbit out of a hat, and the FBI can't really say no because it's actually a good idea."

Kyle shrugged. "Yeah, the FBI wants a fuckin' magic trick performed to find hostages. They want to have their agents pull a rabbit out of a hat, but the goddamn FBI doesn't want to pay for what it takes to buy a rabbit…feed a rabbit…or rent a hat."

Ryan looked around the faces of his team members and asked, "Given what we've seen and how things go, can we make this work with this hostage thing and the FBI folks?"

Everyone immediately nodded. Kyle responded first. "Yep, I know it's early, but to tell you the truth I thought they'd be more fucked up than they are. So, yep," he said, smiling for the first time, "I'm good."

Mike laughed. "Yeah, they almost sound a little like us trying to make something happen without the resources to do it and pushing from the bottom up."

Ashton smiled and nodded, and Ryan looked at him. "Can you hand-hold?"

Ryan wanted Ashton to facilitate the care, feeding, maintenance, and logistics of the source development and meetings for Annie and John.

Ashton grinned. "No problem; I'll handle things. I will go check on them now, so they know we are good for tomorrow's meeting at Brit-HQ." He laughed a bit as he stood and said, "Plus, I want to make sure they aren't crying in the corner after their first dose of a Green-Beret-eye-fucking."

Everyone laughed and stood. Ashton left to meet with Annie and John. Ryan, Mike, and Kyle walked into the adjacent office and unlocked their computer screens to check their classified email traffic.

Annie and John arrived at their trailers and stopped at Annie's stoop. She leaned on the edge as John picked up a rock and tossed it at the nearest Hesco barrier.

Annie slid some gravel around with the heel of her foot and said, “Well, here we are...”

John picked up another rock, smirked, and said, “Yep, here we are, and that went...*not well*...but could have gone worse.”

They looked at each other, grinned, nodded, and shrugged. John tossed another rock toward a dirt mark on the side of the Hesco barrier.

Annie bent down, picked up a rock, tapped it on the edge of the metal stoop where she leaned, and said, “I like their mindset and how they don’t seem to dwell on a problem, they come up with a remedy. If they don’t like something, they do a pretty damn good job of making it clear, without even saying a word,” she added.

John nodded and raised his eyebrows. “Yeah, I thought actual knives were going to come out of their eyes and pierce our foreheads.”

They both laughed, while Annie nodded and picked up another rock. John bent over to stretch his back, and they heard a crunch in the gravel. Ashton turned the corner, smiled, and waved. “If you guys are good, we can head over to the chow hall. We should make it in time before they close.”

Annie responded first. “Sure, sounds great.” She looked over at John. “You ready?”

John really needed to use the bathroom but figured he would wait so they could get moving to dinner; he could use the port-a-potty next to the chow hall. “Yep, I’m good.”

They walked down the plastic sidewalk and headed for the chow hall.

“I’m sure you guys could make it to and from on your own, but this way we can talk about timing for tomorrow and any other details.”

The days were still long, the sun was low in the sky, radiating an orange hue and casting long shadows. Annie and John had paid attention earlier in the day. They opened the steel door on the first try and walked down the embankment to the dirt road.

The heat visually distorted a fading horizon. Sound carried better outside of the blast wall and Hesco barriers. Three explosions were clear but distant: toward downtown Basra. Ashton did not seem concerned, so with racing pulses, Annie and John ignored the background noise.

Near the bottom of the incline by the dirt road, a glint of light caught the attention of Annie and John. The sun reflected off the only clean metal in the area: the R2D2 gadget. Ashton had begun talking about the timeline for the next day, so they resisted the urge to ask about the shiny apparatus for now.

Ashton, ever courteous, said, "If it works for you two, we can meet for lunch tomorrow for any last-minute details or issues before we go to Brit-HQ; that way you guys can have the morning to eat, sleep, whatever you need to do. If you need a secure phone line, just come over to the trailer; sometimes cell coverage is bad."

Annie nodded. "Thanks, that sounds great to me. I haven't made any calls, but I checked earlier, and it looks like I have enough bars on my phone for it to work by the trailer. In fact, I need to call into Baghdad when we get back after we eat so they know we got here," she glanced at John, and both cringed slightly.

John looked at Annie, shrugged, and said, "Whoops, I forgot about calling Baghdad, too. I will call them as soon as we get back."

"Yep, this morning was a little busy," Annie said, stifling a slight yawn. "I guess we did have a distraction or two."

Ashton smiled as they neared the chow hall and said, "Yes, you got quite a warm—and loud—welcome to Basra this morning."

They continued along the dirt road. The air was still, and the orange sun highlighted the fine mist of dirt their boots kicked up as they walked. Everything was dirty. The powdery dirt seeped everywhere and coated everything.

To the left of the chow hall on the edge of the dirt road were three port-a-potties, and as they neared, John said, "I gotta pee; I'll meet you guys inside."

Annie and Ashton nodded and walked up the stairs to the British soldier checking identification. He waved them through as they raised the ID pouches around their necks to show their photo identification.

The soldier nodded. "Cheers—and he's with you, right?" he asked Ashton as he pointed to the port-a-potty.

Ashton nodded, stopped at the door, and asked, "Do you need me to wait?"

The British soldier smiled. "No worries, mate, I got it. I'll make sure he doesn't get lost."

He adjusted his helmet and leaned back onto the sandbags stacked to waist level. Ashton and the soldier exchanged knowing nods of common ground and understanding. New people in Basra projected a certain look and feel, and the soldier could tell Annie and John were new. They were too clean. The dust and dirt of Basra had not yet saturated their skin and settled into their bones. Nor did they have the resolved, morose look in their eyes yet. There was a bond between those who spent time in Basra, regardless of rivalries between the Brits and the Yanks. Some things were transcendent. A relationship developed between human beings brought together to live collectively in an untenable situation. Barriers were broken down, and the petty differences separating people back in The World seemed to diminish.

Some Americans thought the British protocols were pointless, and their accents made them sound like they should all be drinking tea with their pinkies extended. Some British thought the Americans were arrogant, irreverent, drooling idiots. But for the next few minutes, the British soldier would make sure the American in the port-a-potty did not get lost and the Americans inside the chow hall stayed safe.

Annie knew the drill from earlier that day. She picked up prepackaged utensils and a plate. The tray shelf was empty. Trays disappeared when the staff tired of rinsing them.

Annie walked to the edge of the serving counter as Ashton came up behind her and said, "The guy out front has an eye on John and will get him through OK." He picked up a plastic plate and utensils and stepped forward.

Annie smiled at Sasha, the same server who had helped her thirteen hours ago.

Annie handed her plate to Sasha, pointed to something that looked like minced pork, and said, "Some of this, please."

Sasha nodded and smiled as she scooped a spoonful of shredded meat onto a plate and looked past Annie to Ashton.

The British Contingency Operating Base, known as COB, was a very small world. It was no secret that the people in civilian clothes at this chow hall were American Special Forces. The predominantly female chow hall staff appreciated their patience and courtesy.

Annie was already through the line and at the table where they had sat earlier that day when John arrived and walked toward the serving line.

Sasha smiled very generously at John. She bent forward at the waist, pushed the edge of her hair back with her left hand, and held the giant spoon in her right hand. She looked down at the minced pork and asked, "Would you like some of this?" She looked up at John. John looked from the spoon to the minced pork and back again—Sasha flirting with her eyes and the tilt of her head.

He simply said, "Um, yes, please..." The women working at the chow hall knew just how to get the attention of the Americans, and still be professional. John's plate was overflowing with food. He joined Annie and Ashton.

Annie, smirked, and said, "I think the ladies are trying to fuckin' starve me." Everyone grinned. John had already heaped some of his overwhelming portions onto her plate.

Ashton slid food from his plate onto hers, too, and said, "Well, yeah, they seem to be comfortable with Americans here."

Annie nodded, looked back and forth between Ashton and John, then back to her plate, and said, "Yeah, no shit, particularly American men." She smirked more and tilted her plate. "Hell, there are no American women around... They fuckin' systematically starved them to death."

Everyone laughed.

Ashton started eating and said, "I think everyone is looking forward to meeting with Donovan tomorrow. If Kyle thinks Donovan is already interested, that's a real good sign." He sipped an orange drink and continued. "Kyle is probably hoping to try to see if Donovan can take a look at some of the programs our unit has going."

John nodded and said, "That would be great if things would work for you guys, too."

"Yeah, I'm not sure how this will play out, but Kyle is usually about two steps ahead of everyone around when it comes to pulling things together through back channels. Down here in Basra anything worthwhile only happens through horse trading and odd alliances and relationships."

Annie sat back slightly and said, "Well, that makes me a little more optimistic. I thought things were about to come to a quick end today when everyone found out we came down here penniless." She shook her head and said, "Just so you know, we realize how fucked-up that is. We've been doing everything we could to handle it, but we thought if we waited until it was fixed, we would delay moving anything forward."

Ashton peeled an orange and said, "No problem, everyone knows there are no perfect plans. A plan is just a place to start." He grinned. "Most things don't really go as planned anyway," he said, pulling off the last of the orange peel, "and the only thing worse than a bad plan, is no plan at all."

Everyone nodded in agreement.

Annie and John grew more relieved as the conversation continued. None of this would be easy. As they stood to leave, Annie took one last bite, as more of an afterthought than anything, and chewed as they walked to the trash can in between the tables near the exit.

They dumped their trays. A piece of Ashton's orange peel bounced off the edge of the trash can to the floor. Annie scooped and tossed it in the can without breaking stride.

John held the door for Ashton and Annie as they left the cool refuge of the chow hall and walked into the haze of grime and heat outside. Annie and John nodded and waved to the British soldier, who leaned on the waist-high sandbags. He had turned to look over his shoulder when the door opened.

Ashton nodded. "Thanks for taking care of things."

The soldier responded with a faint wave and said, "No worries, mate."

The sun had just set. Layers of orange and pink hung on the horizon. In the desert, airborne dirt and dust transformed the light, creating dramatic colors the clear clean sky lacked. Smoke in the atmosphere produced striking hues, too. And there was always smoke here. Something was always burning, or recently exploded.

Annie and John walked on either side of Ashton, who said, "I think we are good for tomorrow. We can grab lunch before we go and make sure we get to Brit-HQ early. There will be some paperwork to handle to keep people happy, and then we can see what Donovan has to say. Does that sound OK?"

Annie and John nodded. "Sounds great," John said.

"Perfect," Annie said with a quick thumbs-up.

Ashton walked them back to their trailer and said, "I will come get you at noon for lunch. If you need anything before then, just walk around the corner to the team house. You haven't met the whole team, but everyone in the camp knows you're here."

Annie and Ashton shook hands first. "Thanks, Ashton, we really appreciate you looking out for us."

"Yeah, very much appreciated, thanks," said John as he shook Ashton's hand, too.

Ashton shook his head slightly and said, "No problem. Hopefully, we can make something happen."

Annie and John nodded.

Ashton turned to walk away, took a few steps, then turned back. He held his hands out, palms up, like he was presenting the area, smiled, and said, "Welcome to Basra."

He turned and disappeared around the Hesco barrier.

Annie and John turned and looked at each other. They walked a few feet to Annie's stoop. She sat on the top square of the metal grate, and John put one foot on the top stair and stretched his back.

He bent over, picked up a rock, and asked, "How long have we been here?"

Without hesitation Annie said, "About a month."

They both laughed, and John remarked, "I was thinking the same damn thing."

"It fuckin' feels like it."

"It hasn't even been twenty-four hours," John said, laughing.

"We are such lightweights," Annie grinned.

John nodded and laughed. "I know…we suck. Hey, speaking of being here, let me shoot that call into the BOC so they know we're here, and make sure we're covered with checking in."

He walked to his trailer, dug his cell phone from his backpack, and came back to Annie's stoop. His government cellular phone barely showed enough bars for a call. As he stepped in a few random directions a bar would add or drop. He stood still once he had three steady signal strength bars and dialed the number for the FBI BOC commercial line.

The phone was answered after the second ring. "FBI BOC, this is Trish," said an unfamiliar voice on the Baghdad end.

John held the phone tight to his ear and said, "Hey I'm just calling to check in and let you know we arrived here at the COB in Basra."

Trish said, "OK, well, who are you, and where did you arrive?"

"This is John and Annie, and we arrived in Basra... no problems."

Trish said as she wrote in a logbook, "OK...logging you into the book, 'John and Annie in Basra.'" Trish paused and curtly asked, "Anything else?"

"No, we are good. Thanks." The call was over—Trish had hung up on *"No,"* the first syllable she heard.

John looked at Annie and said, "Things must be busy at the BOC. No questions, no follow-up."

Sitting near the desk at the BOC in Baghdad, Trish moved her hand from the phone in its cradle to the TV remote and swung her feet back up on the chair in front of her. She pointed the remote toward the TV and switched the movie she had been watching from pause to play. Trish opened a red Gatorade and took a sip. She had never had that flavor before and did not like the taste—screwing the top on tightly, she tossed it into the trash.

Annie and John did not give the lack of FBI BOC interest a second thought. They were logged into the book and covered for checking in.

Annie looked at John. "How about the morning? Does 8:30 work for you?"

"Yep, works great. If you don't see me, bang on my door, and I'll do the same."

"OK, cool," Annie said as she stood up on her stoop, extended her arm, and raised an open palm toward John's face. He tapped it dismissively with the back of his hand. They did not fist-bump, or high-five; shaking hands would be awkward, and hugging would have been just plain weird. The stupid hand-slap worked.

It closed the conversation and ended the day.

Hostage Status: 82 Days in Captivity (*continued*)

The light in the vent was dimming. It would be dark soon.

Surfboy looked around the room and at the Iraqi. "I don't like this dude in here. Should we let him use our bucket?" He was speaking out loud to the group.

CR glanced at the bucket. "Well, not letting him use our bucket will make things worse in here...if that's possible." They all nodded sullenly.

They passed around a half full bottle of water, and each took a small sip—no more water until tomorrow around noon.

Surfboy held up the last of the water—enough for one small sip each. "Hey bros...Karma." He was asking a question—and making a statement—looking from the bottle to his fellow hostages and to the newly arrived Iraqi.

Nobody said anything, but everyone nodded once.

Surfboy put the bottle containing the last of their water on the floor and slid it to the Iraqi, who was still shaking and sweating profusely.

CHAPTER 12

DC ANGST

DAY 83: JULY 7, 2007

John slept soundly through the night. He adapted to the constant buzz of the air conditioner above his bed quickly—the low hum worked to block outside noise. He took a shower, got dressed, and was about to put on his boots when he heard a voice outside. John opened the door to see Annie on her phone, pacing in the gravel.

Annie's voice was direct, calm, and only slightly elevated. She walked back and forth between the trailers, phone jammed to her ear, and sporadically kicked gravel at the Hesco barrier. She was not searching for optimum reception; she was expelling energy and anxiety generated by her conversation.

John sat on the metal stoop and finished putting on his boots. Annie waved as she walked by, pointed to the phone, and mouthed the words, "My boss." The conversation was one-sided.

Annie's side of the call was a series of unfinished statements:

"Yes, I know we are supposed to keep FBI Baghdad briefed and up to speed, but there was nothing to brief, the first day in Basra is..."

"Well, we can't get all the meetings done on the first day because..."

"We haven't met the guy from The Fort yet. That's happening later this afternoon. We have to go to Brit-HQ and work through..."

She stopped pacing, kicked another rock, and after listening for a moment, tried to respond.

"Well, why would DC get so amped up because of..."

Annie walked by John, stopped for a moment, held the phone in front of her, and gave it the middle finger. She brought the phone back to her ear and continued pacing.

"We can't meet with SF, the guy from The Fort, and a source all in one day. Things just don't happen that fast, especially here. We did call in, it should be in the logbook, and John called as soon as the phones were working. Cell coverage is bad here and..."

Annie continued pacing and kicking rocks.

"Well, that guy in DC sounds like a real jerkoff; I think he should..."

Annie was getting an earful.

"OK, I will call after the meeting this afternoon."

"Bye."

John looked at Annie as she pressed the disconnect button and shook her head. She looked at John and said, "Breakfast?"

John nodded.

She turned off her phone completely, slid it into her cargo pocket, and shook her head. "Let's walk and talk. I'll try and explain that ridiculous conversation."

They headed for the British chow hall.

Annie started to explain. "As much as I think this supervisor is pain in the ass, I think he is dealing with someone in DC dumber than these fuckin' rocks. And that says a lot!" The rock Annie angrily kicked into the Hesco barrier flew like a soccer ball tearing through goal netting.

Annie was anxious. She had been on the phone for thirty minutes before John came out of the trailer. She continued kicking at random pieces of gravel on the path. "Apparently, the HWG supervisor didn't check the logbook to see that you called into the BOC to notify and document our arrival in Basra. At the 7:00 a.m. brief, the FBI on-scene commander asked how the two people in Basra were doing, and nobody had an answer. Not good. And apparently the on-scene got an email from some nitwit in DC asking *why* we were in Basra. The guy in DC never read the teletype I sent to him and the HWG supervisor," she said.

John stepped up to the steel door at the blast wall and manipulated the cypher lock. He got the door open on the second try.

"It's the typical chain of miscommunication going full circle with some guy in DC stirring up shit because he was too lazy to read an attachment in his email," Annie said as they descended the slight slope to the dirt road.

John shook his head. "Damn, we haven't even been here long enough to screw things up," he said smiling. "This guy in DC is going to be a problem, isn't he?"

Annie nodded. "I think so. I remembered this is the fucking idiot from the predeployment briefings at Quantico. His name is Ken—I forget his last name. He came off like a pompous know-it-all, and when someone asked him a question, he got his feathers ruffled because he was clueless. It came out he'd never actually been to Iraq. He was one of those guys who spoke as if he'd done everything, when he never actually did anything."

A truck kicked up dust as it passed Annie and John on the road. Annie tasted the grime and dirt it had left in her mouth. She turned, spit, and wiped the sweat from her forehead. It was eight o'clock, and the temperature was already climbing.

She shook her head and gave a disgusted look. "I remember his little brief, as he walked up and down the aisle chewing tobacco and spitting into a cup. He was arrogant and crass." Annie shook her head. "I think this guy in DC is going to be a real pain in the ass."

"Well, you know the players better than I do," John said. "How is the HWG supervisor going to manage things with DC?"

They were getting close to the chow hall. "I think the writing was on the wall from the conversation this morning," Annie said. "My supervisor isn't going to run defense for us. He doesn't like the Basra concept, and he would be fine if we sat in the office and played solitaire on the computer. He expects to promote in the next six months and doesn't need anyone or anything making waves."

John looked at Annie as they started up the stairs of the chow hall. "No problem," he said. "Between the two of us, we can handle this."

"Yep, we got this," Annie said.

They waved to the British soldier leaning on the sandbags and held up their ID pouches. The soldier nodded and waved them through lethargically.

Annie held the door for John, and they entered the chow hall. Twelve British soldiers sat eating breakfast at three different tables. Nobody was in line. Annie looked past John and saw one of the servers stirring eggs in a tray. John picked up two plastic plates and handed one to Annie—there were no serving trays. They moved through the serving line exchanging friendly nods and smiles with the servers who grinned gushingly at John.

Annie and John sat at the same table as yesterday. Annie smirked at John, who had pulled her plate across the table and was sliding eggs and four of his eight sausages onto it. Annie and John adjusted to the oddities of their disparate food portions. John shared heaping piles of food with Annie, and it was already something done without a second thought. They were a seamless team. They had to be.

Annie took her plate as John slid it back across the table. "Thanks, and what the fuck is going on here?" Annie nodded imperceptibly toward the food serving line.

Annie ate two sausages and a forkful of eggs, then held a spoonful of potatoes in the air to cool for a moment. "The meeting this afternoon with Donovan better go OK, or we may as well pack our stuff and leave tomorrow. Bullshit has trickled from DC to Iraq, and the HWG supervisor has been told to brief the on-scene commander twice a day on how things are going here."

John swallowed a mouthful of eggs and said, "Yeah, this jerkoff in DC—what's his name? Ken?—he's going to be a pain in the ass."

She nodded. "We will figure out what we have to do to handle things. We can make it happen, regardless of the inept morons like Ken." She sat back and took a big sip of orange drink.

They both sat quietly for a moment and John looked out the window. "Well, it's a good thing there are two of us," he said, looking back at Annie. She nodded, then leaned forward and raised her plastic cup toward John, who tapped it with his own.

ANNIE AND JOHN FINISHED BREAKFAST, WALKED BACK to their trailers, and spent the next half hour talking in Annie's trailer about their pending meeting with Donovan. They knew getting Donovan on board was critical. Annie and John needed to be ready for the SF guys and lunch at noon. None of this would be easy.

AT 11:55 A.M., ANNIE LIGHTLY TOSSED A ROCK AT JOHN'S trailer door.

John opened the door. "Hey, what's up? Any changes with timing?"

He stepped out; his boots were on but untied. He started sweating immediately as the sun beat down like a sledgehammer.

Annie shook her head. "A little bit…Ashton came by and said we should go to lunch and come back. He will meet us here, and we will ride over to British headquarters. Things are quiet in Baghdad, I think."

Annie and John went to the British chow hall, ate quickly, and made it back to their trailers.

Hostage Status: 83 Days in Captivity

The light in the vent was growing brighter. The dust drifted, and the cell seemed hotter with another person in it. Fortunately, the Iraqi figured out why there was a filthy bucket near the door. He sat in the same corner breathing hard and drenched in sweat. His stomach was slightly over the edge of his pants. He was still clean. He was a new captive.

Surfboy smiled and whispered. "Today's a good day, bro. Shift change."

Everyone nodded. The nice guards should already be on duty.

The door opened—it was time to eat. Everyone nodded toward the guards but said nothing. The Iraqi in the corner received his portion of food, pushing it away as soon as the door shut.

Everyone remained silent for the next four hours.

The door opened, and four guards walked in with hoses. They were the nice guards, but something was wrong today—they began yelling and swinging the hoses at the American hostages. It lasted for a minute. Two guards looked at the Iraqi covering his face and eyes and cowering in the corner. The guards dragged the Iraqi out, slamming the door.

Shorebilly shook his head and in a soft voice, "What the fuck was that? What's wrong with those guys?"

Tex got up and went to the other side of cell. "I don't know. It sure didn't hurt like what those other assholes do." He looked at the welt on his forearm that the mean guards had given him—three days ago.

Surfboy picked up the food left behind by the Iraqi. "It almost seemed like they were doing it for show or something... anyway, we got a snack"

He divided the food into four even portions.

The day was going OK.

CHAPTER 13

TAKE BRITISH SECURITY SERIOUSLY

DAY 83 (*CONTINUED*): JULY 7, 2007

On the short drive to British headquarters, Ryan and Ashton discussed a few last-minute details and relayed a story emphasizing the importance of respecting British security and the world they were about to enter.

Ryan glanced down at his ID pouch and made sure his British ID was showing. "If everything isn't in line on the security side, you won't get the time of day from Donovan or anyone he works with. They need to *see* those ID badges that say you're OK."

"It doesn't matter if The Fort has given the OK for the meeting, or that the US embassy wants the meeting to happen. If the right blocks aren't checked, to his satisfaction, the meeting won't happen. And even if Donovan was directly told to have a meeting, and you did get face-to-face, if things weren't in order, it would be like talking to a brick wall."

Ryan said, "Oh, one last thing: don't take any notes during the meeting. It will make people nervous. Potentially, anything you write in the meeting might be considered classified, even if it really isn't. Until there's trust, it might be better to ease into it."

Ashton looked at Ryan and asked, "Do you remember those two DIA guys?"

Ryan chuckled lightly and said, "Yep, that was a mess."

Annie stopped looking at her notebook in the back seat and asked, "What happened?"

Ryan began the story. "A couple of DIA guys came down from the embassy for a few days trying to do some bullshit assessment or study." Ryan shook his head and continued, "They really didn't have their stuff together when it came to understanding how things worked. I guess they thought they could get around things by throwing their agency weight around. That's usually a bad idea. A multi-agency meeting was held at Brit-HQ with Donovan; we were there representing our unit."

Ryan smirked. "The DIA guys that didn't have their shit together took notes at the meeting with Donovan and one of his British colleagues. It was sort of funny to watch. Donovan and the Brit never really said anything for the whole meeting. Apparently, the DIA guys didn't know about not taking notes. Or maybe they knew and just didn't care. Anyway, at the end of the meeting Donovan asked for the notes and said he would have them sent to them via secure courier. The DIA guys refused to give Donovan their notes. They got indignant and defiantly shoved their notebooks into their cargo pockets."

Ryan continued in a calm even tone.

"We were sitting around the room wondering what was going to happen next. Donovan simply shrugged and sat back in his chair. Donovan and his British colleague sat at the table silently. Donovan leaned back with hands in his pockets, and the Brit looked into space while spinning a pen in circles on the table in front of him. Everyone left the room. Donovan and his British counterpart stayed behind."

Annie and John hung on every word. Ryan shrugged and went on. "I figured that was it, you know, an uncomfortable end to an unproductive meeting…nothing new. We left the room, and everyone made their way through the short maze of corridors to the large foyer near the entrance. Some people needed to pick up their phones or drop off visitor badges at the security desk at the entrance. The DIA guys had checked their phones, so they went to the security desk to pick them up."

Ashton nodded and said, "Here's where the shit really goes bad for the DIA guys."

Ryan nodded, grinned, and said, "There were four British soldiers at the door, and when they got the nod from the soldier behind the desk, the four soldiers approached the two DIA guys. The soldiers politely walked them to the far corner of the foyer. I couldn't hear what was being said, but there was some discussion. I saw one of the DIA guys shake his head, and I heard him raise his voice and say, 'No, fuck you.'"

Ashton snickered as Ryan continued.

"Right about that time I saw two British guys in civilian clothes, you know, dressed like us, come out of a door in the foyer. I'd never seen anyone come in or out of that door. They made a spinning motion with their index fingers at about chest level. Incidentally, these four British soldiers were huge. The four British soldiers grabbed the DIA guys by their shoulders and upper arms, lifted them in the air, and slowly pivoted them around to face the wall, and gently placed their foreheads against the wall."

Ryan continued in a matter-of-fact manner tone. "The guys in civilian clothes walked up to the DIA guys, and pulled everything from their pockets, to include the notes. They made it a point to leave their pockets inside out. The soldiers kept hold of the DIA guys and walked them back to the desk to get their phones. The Brits behind the counter held up two phones in plastic bags. I was close enough to hear the British civilians say, 'Here are your phones. You'll need new SIM cards, batteries, and they may not be all that functional, mate.'"

Ryan glanced at his watch and continued. "The other British civilian nodded to the DIA guys and very politely said, 'Here are your IDs, be on your way now.' Then he nodded to the big British soldiers holding their arms. The soldiers picked up the DIA guys, walked them to just outside the door, and gently let their feet touch the ground."

Ashton looked in the rearview mirror at Annie and John, and said, "So, we left, and on our way out it was still getting ugly. The DIA guys got to their SUV. They had insisted on getting special parking privilege, so they were parked near the Brit-HQ building. Their SUV was now getting *very* special treatment. There were six British soldiers at the vehicle. They had arrived in a gun truck that blocked the back end of the SUV." Ashton shook his head and gestured with his hand. "All of the doors were open, and so was the hood, and the back of the SUV. The British soldiers had punched the door locks on both sides to get in, which set off the alarm. We walked by as they were opening the hood. Since the alarm was so irritating, they cut the wires. It was a mess everything was strewn all over the ground. The two DIA guys saw what was happening and finally got smart. They walked to the side of the building and found an edge of shade and stayed out of the way. We got the hell out of there."

The DIA personnel wanted special parking and handling. No problem. If these Americans did not think the rules applied to them, they would get special treatment.

Hostage Status: 83 Days in Captivity (*continued*)

Midday heat raised the stench in the cell to an insufferable level. The air was thick and rancid.

All four hostages laid flat on the floor breathing slowly.

Without moving and barely audible, Surfboy asked, "Hey CR...thinking about those country roads?"

Quietly CR said, "Yep, always thinking about those country roads...you thinking about them California waves?"

"Yeah bro, I can see them so clearly right now."

Everyone stayed unmoving—mentally seeing and being anyplace but where they were now. Everyone had that country roads song in their head—the *take me home* part.

CHAPTER 14

BRITISH HEADQUARTERS... TRANSLATING ENGLISH TO ENGLISH

DAY 83 (*CONTINUED*): JULY 7, 2007

They arrived at British headquarters and parked on the road near the gate used for vehicle and foot traffic. Brit-HQ, as Americans usually called it, was a two-story building near the airport that the British seized during the invasion. It evolved into its own compound with an entry control checkpoint, a perimeter fence, random work trailers, and generators filling gaps. There were surprisingly few Hesco barriers and no blast walls.

The entry control point was an understated gate at the very least. A ten-by-ten-foot square made of sandbags stood four feet high. Overhead protection for the soldiers was an afterthought of poorly constructed two-by-four boards, and a corrugated plastic roof screwed into the wood.

As they approached the gate Ryan walked in front, followed by Annie and John with Ashton last. The British soldier inside the sandbag square casually watched as they approached. The soldier knew exactly what had happened when Annie and John reached into their pockets, retrieved a small object, then ran back to the SUV. They had forgotten to stash their phones in the SUV.

The soldier recognized Ryan and Ashton and suspected the unfamiliar faces were probably Americans. Ryan slowed his pace and slightly lifted the ID holder dangling from his neck. The soldier gave Ryan a quick nod. Annie had gotten used to walking with John and mirrored the courtesy of removing sunglasses to help with identification and gate passage. The British soldier paused slightly for closer scrutiny and to find the expiration date on the US embassy identification. He had seen US embassy identification before but was more familiar with the layout of British ID. A simple "Thank you" or "Cheers" and nods were exchanged as Ashton followed, keeping stride.

There was a duck-and-cover bunker near the British soldier. Annie had noticed something was different about these concrete structures than the ones in Baghdad. Something was missing, but she could not figure out what. She would ask later.

They continued up the street, walking on pavement, dirt, and part of the curb. Three British soldiers stood near the building's entrance under the small amount of shade it provided, talking about home and smoking cigarettes.

The four Americans passed through the door to a small foyer with a security counter to check in cell phones and recheck identification.

Ryan was first to the counter. He reached into the pouch hanging around his neck and removed his Brit-HQ identification handing it to the soldier. The soldier recognized Ryan but continued the formality of the badge inspection. He held the badge up and looked at the picture on the badge, then at Ryan's face, then back at the badge for comparison. He turned the badge over and looked at the back.

While the soldier examined his ID, Ryan saw Kyle at the far end of the counter just past the inspection point inside the larger main foyer. They exchanged quick nods. Kyle waited there with a folder containing the paperwork necessary to get Annie and John their Brit-HQ badges—just in case there were any problems getting them into the building. Before they arrived, he had also spoken with the British soldiers at the counter, both as a courtesy and to nudge things forward smoothly. Kyle knew how to make things happen.

The British soldier nodded and returned Ryan's identification card. "Thank you, sir. Cheers."

"Thanks very much," Ryan said, smiling as he accepted his ID card.

Instead of putting it back into the pouch around his neck, he clipped the ID to the lanyard about near the middle of chest.

Ryan politely addressed the soldier. "We have a meeting later, and we're trying to get HQ badges for some of our coworkers." He gestured toward Annie and John.

Following Ryan's lead, Annie and John already had their embassy IDs out of their pouches ready for presentation.

"Very well, sir. Let's see what we have here," the soldier said.

He looked to his far right with raised eyebrows toward Kyle. He pointed in the direction of Annie and John, and Kyle nodded and gave a quick thumbs-up.

Kyle prepped the soldier before they arrived. The soldier said in the tone of a question, "I understand we have some American embassy badges to start with?"

Annie and John nodded and smiled and passed their IDs across the counter to the soldier.

"Perfect, very well," said the soldier, returning the smile. "Do we have any mobiles?"

Annie looked to John, then to Ryan, who stayed close at the counter. Annie shrugged, pointed to Ryan, and said, "He drove. It's a big white SUV, but I don't know what kind."

The British soldier tilted his head to one side and gave Annie a quizzical look, then shook his head and looked at Ryan. The soldier leaned to his left and tapped on the sign referencing the prohibition on *mobile* phones in the building.

Ryan translated, "He's asking about cell phones."

The British called handheld cellular phones a "mobile," while Americans used the term "cell." It was a typical case of an American speaking American English and a Briton speaking British English. Occasionally, it took time for translation, regardless of the fact both spoke the same language.

Annie smiled. "Oh no, sorry. No, we left everything in the car."

The soldier nodded toward John, who was already shaking his head and saying, "Same thing—left it in the car."

The soldier nodded and slid two plastic numbered IDs, each with a large black *V* printed on the center, across the counter. "Here we go with your visitor IDs. Return these on your way out to retrieve your American embassy IDs."

The soldier placed their American embassy IDs in a box, filing them alphabetically. The soldier was very polite. Kyle's early arrival and preparation paid off; things ran smoothly.

The soldier motioned toward Kyle and said, "I understand you have an escort to take you directly to the badge-ID-and-security section."

Annie and John clipped the visitor badges onto their pouches, nodded, and thanked the soldier.

The soldier waved them along and said, "No worries. Welcome to Baaasra…"

The soldier recognized Ashton and quickly performed the ID verification ritual.

Kyle nodded to Annie and John, and they shook hands. "Thanks for front-loading things here to keep things moving smoothly," Annie said, smiling and gesturing with her head toward the check-in counter.

John nodded, too, as they walked from the desk. He instinctively knew that over thanking Kyle might come off as disingenuous, so he nodded, shook hands, and kept it simple.

The main foyer was a buzzing hub of activity. Ryan and Ashton had been to Brit-HQ many times and had never been through any of the doors on the right side. That was where the DIA guys had gotten their adjustment. To the left was a busy hallway that was the main artery of the building. In the center of the large foyer, adjacent to a large window, was a coffee, tea, and junk food kiosk. And adjacent to the kiosk were several plastic couches, chairs, and coffee tables arranged in a semicircle.

It was not the grandiose elaborate spectacle of the US embassy in Baghdad, which had literally been a palace. There were no frills, but the area was functional and made for a good place for people to meet. The *show-and-tell* look and the *see-and-be-seen* feel of the US embassy were absent here. Brit-HQ was a place of urgency, and the personnel were not in Basra to pass time and pose for a photo opportunity. Nobody liked how the war was going in the southern part of Iraq, particularly the British.

Kyle led everyone through the large, two-story-tall foyer. "We will head to the security and badging office and get the IDs handled," he said.

Kyle led the group through a maze of hallways to the

badging office, opened the door, and went inside. Ryan held the door for the others. The British soldier seated at one of several desks behind the counter stood when the door opened until he saw it was Kyle. They exchanged nods, and the soldier sat down. Kyle had been in earlier to ensure the necessary paperwork and communications had been coordinated. Kyle went to the edge of the counter by the door, where a stack of clipboards already contained the appropriate forms. A long wooden bench ran the length of the wall. Everyone sat, and Kyle handed clipboards to Annie and John. They diligently filled in the blanks—basic identifiers like date and place of birth.

Kyle had learned that getting through any bureaucracy meant understanding what was expected and simply grinding through it. Months ago, Kyle had met Bradley, the head of British security for the Contingency Operating Base at an unofficial British bar—the previous security officer had vouched for Kyle. Kyle met with Bradley yesterday to grease the skids for today's paperwork.

Paperwork coming from Kyle was expected to be flawless. Kyle looked through the documents twice, then stood and approached the counter.

The office door opened, and in walked Bradley. "Hey Kyle…how we doin', mate?"

Kyle smiled and handed him the clipboards with all the necessary paperwork. "I think we should be OK. See what you think."

Bradley flipped through the documents, gave a thumbs-up, and said, "Very well, mate, indeed all this looks good… Cheers." Bradley had already worked through the British security office at the US embassy to have clearance confirmation sent for the Americans.

The soldier politely asked John to stand on the bright red footprints painted on the floor and remove his ID pouch from around his neck for the photo. The footprints were perpendicular to the wall. Standing on the footprints ensured the backdrop was in the picture; it was the British flag. Although the British soldier was new to Basra, he had already issued HQ identification to a few Americans. None of the Americans ever said anything, but he could see that most bristled at being photographed with the British flag in the background. He found it mildly entertaining.

Annie went through the same process without responding to the background. The soldier took two photos, which were printed onto high quality photo paper used for lamination. The person being photographed picked the photo they liked. Annie and John rolled the dice and deferred to the British soldier to make the selection. Of course, he appreciated the deference, and picked the most flattering photos.

The soldier slid them into the laminating machine, and while the plastic heated and sealed, the soldier walked to a desk drawer and retrieved two metal clips with plastic loops attached. Annie and John sat back on the bench to stay out of the way. Kyle and Bradley discussed another matter, using names and terms so cryptically that only the two of them could follow the conversation.

Ryan focused on a green notebook he carried in his cargo pocket. The small, hard-sided book contained lined pages with dates of meetings and notes. Across Iraq, there were tens of thousands such green books, which US military and some civilian personnel used pervasively. The notes did not concern anything classified and were written to jog the memory of the writer.

Ryan reviewed a few points he wanted to make sure they covered during the meeting with Donovan. Ashton and Ryan shared a few words that were about as cryptic as the conversation between Kyle and Bradley. They used acronyms and slang that only they understood, and Ashton appeared to be asking most of the questions. He was like a human sponge. Annie and John kept quiet and out of the way.

After a moment, the soldier behind the counter retrieved a logbook near the lamination machine, picked up the IDs that had just spilled onto the counter, and inspected the edges to ensure they were sealed correctly.

He smiled at Annie and John sitting quietly on the bench. "Here we go," he said. "Hot off the press. If we could get you both to sign here in the book, you'll be able to get crackin' with your day."

Annie and John stood there with their still-warm Brit-HQ IDs in hand, and the soldier gave additional instructions about how to wear them. His heavily accented message was completely lost on their American ears.

Finally, the soldiers asked, "Any questions?"

He gestured with his hands to his chest area and raised his eyebrows, attempting to prompt a response. Annie and John stood motionless, savoring their warm, fresh badges. After a moment, the soldier took off his ID, held it by the clip, pointed to the IDs in their hands and then to their chests, and clipped his ID back onto his own chest pocket.

Annie and John did the same, and the soldier gave them a thumbs-up. "There we go…perfect."

Annie, John, and the SF operators collected their belongings and walked toward the exit.

The soldier shook his head slightly after they passed through the door. "Daft Americans can't even speak English."

Bradley and the soldier laughed.

Bradley shook his head, smiled, and tossed a ball of paper at the soldier. "English? Is that what you call what comes out of your mouth? You're from the wrong side of London; I can barely understand your barmy chatter." They both laughed, and Bradley admitted, "Indeed, it can be a challenge translating English to English."

RYAN WAS VERY CLEAR AS THEY LEFT THE SECURITY office. "For now, use the clips they gave you and wear those IDs mid-chest or higher. You want them to be easily seen when you're sitting at a table."

ID pouches tended to drop to mid-chest or lower when the wearer was seated.

It was time to meet with Donovan.

Hostage Status: 83 Days in Captivity (*continued*)

Shorebilly woke up lethargically waving his hands over his face and above his head. The wound on his forehead was infected. Sometimes small flies gathering around his face interrupted sleep. He needed a doctor.

These conditions were not survivable for much longer—illness was inevitable.

Surfboy spent more time with the bathroom bucket. "Hey, I don't feel right...I think I'm coming down with something." He needed a doctor, too.

Dysentery was inevitable.

"Here...try and drink more." Shorebilly handed him a

water bottle. The others sat up slightly, handing over their bottles of water, too.

CR looked around the room assessing their dismal existence. Each had sores on their feet that were severely infected. Standing in sewage to empty the bathroom bucket was unavoidable. The unbearable heat was dehydrating them—each hostage had stomach ailments and infected lacerations causing fever.

Tex said, "I sure as shit hope we are worth more alive than dead."

CR looked around the room. "I hope so. We need to try and get these guards to get us some antibiotics or something... we need a doc...these are the guards to talk to. The other ones won't listen."

Water was usually provided in the afternoon. Convincing one of the nice guards they needed a doctor would be difficult, but they had to try.

Surfboy laid down and stopped moving—his breathing was shallow.

CHAPTER 15

MEETING DONOVAN...QUIRKY PEOPLE FROM NSA AND GCHQ

DAY 83 (*CONTINUED*): JULY 7, 2007

Annie and John had their new Brit-HQ badges and were ready to meet with Donovan. They had absolutely no idea where they were going inside Brit-HQ, but at least they were allowed to be there. They were cleared to meet Donovan and enter the secure areas. Fortunately for Annie and John, they were well received and guided by the SF operators. It was far too early to know whether their efforts would be productive, but they were in Basra and would keep pushing.

Kyle stopped near a staircase in a space where several hallways merged. There was room to collect as a group and talk for a moment.

Kyle said, "Bradley told me there are back-to-back meetings scheduled in the room where we're going. We're about ten minutes early, so it might be smarter to wait here before we check into the SCIF."

Everyone nodded.

Ryan looked at Kyle and said, "I'm glad you got things handled with the Brit-HQ IDs; thanks."

Kyle grinned. "Yeah, without those IDs, there's no entering the SCIF. The Brits control things, and they don't give a shit about US embassy badges in some areas. It's a British ID with all the checks done, or nothing."

Kyle pointed to a British soldier sitting at a desk near the edge of a hallway, and as he did the door behind the soldier opened. A stream of people came out of it, and most checked in with the soldier. Two people in civilian clothes did not. They walked toward the foyer and the general area where the Americans stood.

Everyone was required to be logged in and out of the SCIF, or Sensitive Compartmented Information Facilities. The soldier knew these two and signed them out—which meant the upper echelon of British command at headquarters had instructed the soldier to do so.

With his voice low and directed at only the immediate group, Kyle said, "These two are some of Donovan's British colleagues. They usually stay on the other side of HQ, where all Americans need a British escort."

Each of the two men had his own peculiarities. The oddities of the man who had been the first out of the SCIF door were subtle at first. He did not make eye contact with the soldier at the desk, or anyone else for that matter. His head tilted slightly to the left, and he looked toward the ceiling as he walked remarkably close to the wall. He tapped the wall lightly with the fingernails of his right hand and seemed to be counting with his left hand as his thumb touched each fingertip over and over. Each hand had its own rhythm or count.

Annie and John tried to look away as the man walked by but could not. He wore a collared shirt that was inside out. The right side of his collar was stuck under the upper edge by neck. He wore American Chuck Taylor All-Star high-top shoes. One shoe was white and the other black. He continued down the hall, tapped, and counted until he turned the corner to the large foyer and escaped their view.

The second of Donovan's colleagues had idiosyncrasies as well, some visible, but more audible than anything. He also wore civilian clothes and a misbuttoned shirt. Without making eye contact he passed the Americans, and they could hear him talking to himself, speaking an ever-changing series of numbers and words. His hands and eyes moved, and he appeared to be counting the tiles on the floor as he walked. He glanced at Kyle and the group and quickly looked away.

His voice just barely audible, he said, "Five…Americans…three…Special Forces…two…strangers…" He continued past. "Thirty-three…tan tiles left to right…four…vertical concrete seams on wall…twelve…tiles until main foyer."

Kyle looked at the group and tapped his watch once. "OK, it's time. Let's sign in.

KYLE LED THE GROUP TO THE SOLDIER OUTSIDE THE SCIF door. As usual, the soldier was polite and friendly. He looked at everyone's identification, inspected both sides, and verified the number on the back of the identification with the number they wrote next to their printed and signed names in the SCIF logbook. Kyle turned the lever on the SCIF door and pulled. It was like opening an eight-foot vault door and stepping into a giant bank safe.

Everyone stepped up and into the SCIF. It was a large room with fifteen desks. The chamber had been separated into two work areas. Desks were neatly arranged for efficient foot traffic. Two British soldiers sat at two of the desks, typing and looking at computer monitors. Neither soldier looked at Kyle or the group as they walked through. In one corner, two more British soldiers discussed something on a screen in front of them. Several flat-screen TVs mounted on the wall behind the desks displayed live closed-circuit feeds from somewhere.

The other work area to the right had ten desks configured front to front, for seating five people per side. There were small trash cans on both ends of the ten-desk cluster. Each desk had two computer monitors and two telephones—one for calls classified Secret, one for calls classified Top Secret. There were no open or unclassified computers or phones in the SCIF. The desks were not messy, but they were not tidy either.

One person sat at the ten-desk section. He looked a bit out of place given the surroundings. He was an American soldier, who looked back and forth between his computer screen and the rice and chicken he ate from a square Styrofoam container. There was something else odd about the soldier that might be missed at first glance. His Army uniform had no patches for personal or unit identification. No name above the pocket. No current or former unit identifiers on the Velcro square near the shoulder. He was a *no-patch* US soldier. Figuratively, he was invisible and did not exist. The soldier nodded to Kyle as the group walked by, then continued eating and looking at a computer monitor. The no-patch soldier did not acknowledge any of the other Americans.

Often ten or more people were clustered at the desks, and the section was never completely empty. A no-patch soldier always stayed at the desk.

Kyle continued through the large SCIF area toward two offices at the opposite end, each with its own large vault door. They went to the door on the right, which was cracked open. Kyle had confirmed the meeting location earlier. Voices escaped the open door, which Kyle gently nudged as he knocked.

A voice called out, "Come in…it's open." Another voice in the room could be faintly heard.

The room was simple with a rectangular table for eight, plus six chairs around the perimeter of the wall for overflow. Kyle and the group entered, and the two men at the far end of the table stood to greet them. One of the men walked around the table. He stood six feet five inches tall, weighed 250 pounds, and wore a full beard that made him look like a lumberjack. His hair was long and spilled down the sides of his face to his shoulders. It was long enough to put into a ponytail but kept defiantly free. He wore boots, jeans, and a loose-fitting unbuttoned shirt over a black T-shirt with the word *NERD* printed across the chest in white letters.

He approached the fresh faces with a broad smile, his right hand extended, and said, "Hi, I'm Donovan."

Annie and John exchanged pleasantries with Donovan, and he greeted the SF guys more familiarly. Donovan knew Kyle, and he had seen Ryan and Ashton around Brit-HQ and the COB.

Donovan introduced the other person in the room. "Everyone, this is Jensen." Handshakes and head nods were exchanged. Jensen said nothing.

Donovan looked around the room, then asked Kyle, "Are we expecting anyone else?"

Kyle looked at Annie and John, and said, "No, I think we are good."

Everyone paused for the awkward moment when seating. Donovan maneuvered to the side opposite Annie and John and sat down. There was not going to be a status grab for the head of the table. Instead, Ashton, the most junior person in the room, ended up there. Jensen waited until everyone was seated, then took a chair in the corner against the wall behind Annie and John. From there, Jensen could observe their profiles while sitting silently, seeing and hearing everything.

Jensen was with the General Communications Headquarters, the Brits' NSA, simply referred to as GCHQ. Like his counterparts from NSA, Jensen exercised great discretion and preferred to be unnoticed like background noise.

NSA and GCHQ personnel owned *background noise.*

Jensen said nothing—not the agency where he worked, not why he was there, nothing. It really did not matter. If the meeting did not go well, neither Donovan nor Jensen would ever see Annie or John again. Annie and John would somehow lose access to the Brit-HQ, and their badges would no longer be accepted by the British soldier just outside the SCIF door.

Donovan rubbed his palms together briefly, looked directly at Annie and John, set his hands palms-down on the table, and said, "So, you have a project."

It was as much a question as a statement.

Annie spoke first. "Well, yes, we think the hostage work would be more productive if the operational focus were down here. Here, meaning Basra," she tapped the table with both hands as she emphasized the location.

Donovan looked at Annie and said, "And?"

Annie explained that she was speaking candidly. "Hostage casework in Iraq has been a mess. In fact, hostage casework outside of the United States has been a grueling, confusing maze under the FBI extraterritorial process at the Counterterrorism Division. John and I are *not* here to say we can fix all of it…or any of it, but maybe we can lean into *one* small piece of it."

Donovan listened and nodded; Jensen leaned forward slightly in his chair. Annie explained the timeline of past efforts for fifteen minutes.

She nodded at John, tapped his shoulder, and said, "Tag."

John looked directly at Donovan and picked up the thread. "Baghdad is absurdly far from where things need to be actioned. Sitting in Baghdad trying to work a kidnap case that happened in Basra is like trying to thread a needle with string tied to the end of a thirty-foot fishing pole. And doing it with your eyes closed. It doesn't work."

Annie and John liked that analogy.

Donovan shrugged and looked back and forth between Annie and John. "Well…The Fort has people in Baghdad. They have the same reach I do."

"OK," John said, "the concept is to develop human intelligence more aggressively. We simply have not been talking to witnesses or people who might be able to provide information, especially if they are given specific direction. In fact, the HUMINT side of the program has not really been worked at all. We know the FBI simply doesn't have the reach and the means to develop that end of it. Connecting with the SF guys is critical to that part moving forward."

John looked around the table and gestured with both hands toward the SF operators.

Donovan asked the obvious question first. "What about the Agency? That's their world…you're in their backyard…how's that going?"

John shook his head. "It's a completely dysfunctional relationship. The CIA does not want anything to do with the FBI on anything if they can avoid it. Hostage work isn't a priority for them." John shrugged and went on. "FBI has the jurisdictional lead on hostage work even in the Agency's back yard or war zone. They want nothing to do with us, even when we are really trying to make it work."

Donovan shrugged slightly, and with a pained smile, he said, "Enough said...I get it...There's a chance we might have seen some of that here."

John shook his head. "It isn't pretty but at least acknowledging the realities can be half the battle in trying to move forward. We aren't going to get CIA help on source development, and we—being FBI—don't have anything for in-country SIGINT development or exploitation."

Annie chimed in. "We have no reach into the signal intelligence world without The Fort. Realistically, FBI Baghdad and people assigned to look for hostages have been doing the same thing over and over with SIGINT. There hasn't been any real coordinated effort...nothing cohesive or long-term, either."

Donovan sat back in his chair, scratched the back of his neck, looked at them, and said, "So, these guys have been gone about three months. How close are you to finding any hostages?"

Annie shook her head. "Not very close."

Donovan shrugged. "I think in numbers. On a scale of one to ten, and with one being the same as the day they were captured, ten being found in the next month...how close are you?"

John said, "Zero...maybe less than zero. Things haven't always gone well. Too often the Hostage Working Group has spun its wheels, duplicated effort, and even discontinued ideas that might have been productive…such as HUMINT development."

Annie did not blink and nodded her head slightly as John talked. Donovan nodded, too.

John went on. "The Fort analysis requests were the same over and over. There hasn't been any sustained process or effort to cohesively blend HUMINT and SIGINT." He glanced at Annie, tapped the table in front of her, and said, "Tag."

Annie leaned forward slightly. "And that's why we are here," she said without missing a beat. "Nobody had a better idea. Right now, we are just trying to pull the players together, and see if we can make anything work."

"Take this however you want, but you're not painting a very flattering picture of US government hostage recovery," Donovan said, shaking his head in disgust. "I'm glad I'm not a hostage."

John looked around the room, and said, "No, it's not a pretty picture, but we thought being candid with everyone was the thing to do…blowing smoke up anyone's ass on this would just make it worse…you know…less than zero."

Everyone briefly smiled, and the tension dipped slightly.

Donovan grinned and nodded. "When I heard you were coming down from Baghdad with an idea of sorts, I took a look at the old requests from your people to mine and saw what's been written up over the last six months." Donovan stopped nodding and started shaking his head. "How you described things sounds about right. So, at least we are all on the same page…and at the same starting point…that would be zero."

He smiled as did everyone else in the room.

Donovan looked at Annie and John, and said, "Well, I guess we will do what we can. I have a lot of latitude, but my agency is asking for me to relocate to Baghdad, and they aren't going to bother to shift things around unless there's a good reason. I would rather be in Basra, but they don't necessarily care about that, and they won't connect with anyone down here for my care and feeding." Donovan shrugged. "I like your project, so we will see what we can pull together over the next couple of weeks before I leave."

Kyle gave Ryan a quick glance when Donovan said "care and feeding." Ryan knew he would have to work this angle quickly.

Annie nodded and said, "We are trying to line up a source meeting in the next day, probably tomorrow afternoon. Do you think we could get together before and get you the details?"

Donovan nodded. "Nice approach on the methodology. The proactive tactic is smart...and way overdue." He looked around and said, "How about 11 a.m.?"

The SF guys looked at one another quickly and nodded.

Annie shrugged and said, "Well, we are trying to cram a lot into a short period of time. We were hoping to meet at 8:00 or 9:00 a.m. Would that work?"

Annie was not trying to push as hard as it appeared; she was doing her best to keep the supervisor in Baghdad and the guy in DC off her back.

Donovan looked at Annie without blinking and simply said, "No."

He offered no explanation. The room sat uncomfortably silent for a moment, and the SF operators exchanged quick micro-glances. Donovan established boundaries, and the FBI was stepping into his realm. The FBI needed

Donovan and the dark, wall-tapping, odd-shoe-wearing-number-mumbling world he brought to the table. They were not going to come in and move his furniture, figuratively or otherwise.

Another variable Annie and John had not observed or digested was the nocturnal lean for functioning activity in Basra. Much of the operational movement took place at night, and everyone's sleep cycle was upside down, and inside out. In addition to the nighttime rocketing and random artillery periodically fired by the British, the pace was brutal. Donovan was already booked in the morning, but he did not owe them an explanation. Capture/kill operations were on a twenty-four-hour cycle, seven days a week.

John looked around and cut through the silence. "Eleven o'clock sounds great. We have a few logistical details to work through, and we want to make sure we aren't getting in the way of what everyone has going on."

He gestured with a slight and respectful wave of his hand around the room and nodded toward Donovan.

Donovan smiled and said, "Great, that will give me a little time to push some recent things through my system before we meet, and we can go from there."

Donovan placed both palms on the table and leaned forward slightly as his chair slid back—signifying the end of the meeting. Everyone stood. Annie and John were particularly gracious, thanking Donovan for the meeting and his interest in the program. Jensen stayed in the corner and waved as the group filed out of the SCIF conference room. Ashton led the crowd with Kyle and Ryan was the last to leave.

As Ryan passed the large block of desks and neared the SCIF exit, he turned to Donovan and said, "I think Kyle and

I will finally get to the HQ command briefing this evening. Maybe I will see you there."

Without any facial expression, Donovan nodded.

Ryan asked, "Is it still at 7:00 p.m. right here?"

"Yep, right here, seven o'clock, on the dot," Donovan said as he followed them to the door of the SCIF. When he had seen them leave and shut the door, he returned to the conference table, where Jensen joined him.

Donovan nodded to where Annie and John had sat, and said, "Well, what do you think of all of this?"

Jensen shrugged. "Ambitious."

Jensen sometimes went with curt British understatement. Donovan grinned at the profound level of dryness.

Jensen spun the pen on the tabletop momentarily, then stopped the pen's motion with his index finger, looked directly at Donovan, and said, "Working these hostage things jointly is way overdue. I know your American friends are simply trying to get Americans to talk to Americans, but…" Jensen sat back in his chair, looked up at the ceiling and back to Donovan, then added, "The real coup would be getting all of us talking to each other… US and UK."

As Jensen said the last few words, he moved his thumb back and forth, gesturing between himself and Donovan. Jensen's reference was meant for the big-picture concept—the US and the UK and all the layers of agencies and entities and commands not communicating or collaborating with one another.

Donovan leaned back in his chair, nodded, and said, "Yeah, I like the way they are thinking." Donovan was one of the few Americans in Basra. He understood the need to coordinate with the British.

Jensen spun the pen on the table again, then gently laid the palm of his hand on the pen to stop it, and said, "And as you know, there were several Britons taken about two months ago." He spun the pen, shrugged, and said, "Maybe there's a chance to coordinate amongst ourselves instead of relying on those wankers, yours and mine, in Baghdad."

Jensen rarely voiced his disdain for the hierarchy in Baghdad—and only in extraordinarily trusted company. Donovan had recognized the labyrinth of competing interests and turf battles he was potentially walking into before Annie and John even sat down.

He nodded. "Yep, working this hostage stuff has a potential to get really complicated and is a serious uphill battle." Donovan shrugged and said, "I may be hauled out of here before we can even take a step forward into this clusterfuck."

They both laughed.

Donovan pulled his hair back out of his eyes again, straight back over his head, and asked, "Do we take on this hostage thing, or not?" He held his hands up and said, "If you're in, I'm in; otherwise, we are just pissing in the wind."

Jensen grinned at that Americanism. The British did not really have an equivalent, which was probably good. The thought process was complete for now. Jensen stopped the spinning pen with his palm and placed it in his shirt pocket; like putting a period on the end of a sentence. Everyone from GCHQ and NSA had quirks.

Jensen looked at his hands momentarily, then back to Donovan and said, "I'm in, mate. We should do this—at least give it a go."

Donovan shook his head, nudged a chair with his size fourteen boot, and said, "One big issue is the barmy embassy fucks in Baghdad trying to pull me up north. Two weeks isn't enough time to do much on a project like this."

Donovan blended British slang with American insults. Jensen pulled the pen from his pocket. He spun it on the table again. There was a shift in topics, and he needed the pen spinning to keep tempo.

He looked at the pen spin on the table and over to Donovan, and said, "Look mate, I don't want to see you leave. Truth be told, we could use more help here in Baaasra." He smiled, and said, "As you know, I have the British brains, but we could use a little of your American brawn."

Donovan leaned back in chair and said, "Thanks…I really don't want to go to Baghdad. Basra is a mess, but I really don't want to be around all those berk embassy fucks doing nothing."

Jensen stopped the pen from spinning with the palm of his hand, picked it up, placed it in his pocket, tapped the table once with his index finger, and said, "No worries, mate. We will figure that part out. I don't know how yet, but we will put our heads together and come up with something."

They both stood, and as an afterthought Jensen asked, "What's with a command briefing at 7:00 p.m.? I thought you were coming over to the compound for a pint or two, or three?"

Donovan shook his head, rubbed his eyes with his palms, pulled the front of his chin-length hair out of his eyes and back from his face, and said, "There is no HQ command meeting. That was Ryan's way of letting me know he needed to meet with me without telling everyone around."

Jensen grinned. "Oh bravo, how fucking covert of you, and from a SIGINT chap like yourself. Well, aren't you daring!"

They both laughed.

"I don't know what he wants," Donovan said, "but I will head over to your compound for a pint or two right after."

Donovan grinned at Jensen and said, "You're such a tosser."

"And you're such an asshole!" Jensen immediately fired back.

They laughed.

They had learned to speak to each other's language… English.

Hostage Status: 83 Days in Captivity (*continued*)

The cell door opened, and CR returned from emptying the bathroom bucket. He did his best to communicate the need for a doctor. He was not sure if the guard understood all his pointing and miming.

Surfboy was not moving, and his breathing was labored.

Tex sat up when CR came through the door and asked, "Well, how did it go?

"OK, I think. Good thing we have the nice guards right now. Hard to say. I think they know how fucked up this is."

"Well...at least you didn't get knocked around for talking to them," he added.

CR sat the bucket in the corner glancing at the door to make sure it was tightly shut. "And I heard something out at the trench...the guards were yelling at someone."

Sluggishly shrugging his shoulders Tex said, "So..."

"The guards were yelling one-word commands. In English."

CHAPTER 16

HOT CHAINS... SF FACILITATE A MEETING

DAY 83 (*CONTINUED*): JULY 7, 2007

After meeting with Donovan, Kyle led the group back to the busy foyer to retrieve their embassy badges; couches and chairs were full.

John whispered just loud enough to Annie, "Teatime?"

Annie grinned, leaned toward John, kept her voice low, and said, "No shit, I was thinking the same thing. I just didn't want to say anything."

John leaned toward Annie and said, "I just heard part of a conversation, and the guy actually said, 'Crikey.'"

Annie grinned, leaned toward John, and said just above a whisper, "No fuckin' way…is 'crikey' really a thing? I thought it was just some word Americans made up when they were imitating a British accent."

John shrugged. "I guess it is real. I can't wait to find out what it means."

Kyle led the group from the front of Brit-HQ along the haphazard walkway to the fence line. The British soldier stood under the corrugated roof in his sandbag pen, joined by another soldier who arrived with a cooler of ice and a jug of water. The soldiers wrapped wet towels with ice chunks around their necks and shoulders—the sweltering afternoon heat was unrelenting.

Kyle acknowledged the soldiers with a wave and said, "Thanks, guys."

The two British soldiers nodded, and one said, "No worries, mate. See you soon."

The heat was oppressive, and the sun was brutal. There was no shade at the outer edge of Brit-HQ perimeter. When they reached their vehicles, Kyle said, "How about we meet back at the team house to talk?"

Everyone nodded in agreement, and Kyle slid into a rickety pickup truck while the others got into the white SUV.

Kyle followed close behind the SUV. Both vehicles had FM radios tuned to the British armed forces station. Only one station was available, and it aired miscellaneous news reports about events in the United Kingdom, as well as scores for sports that none of the Americans followed. In fact, most Americans in Basra were unable to determine what sport was being discussed. They waved as they passed the British soldier standing his post near the edge of the perimeter gate.

The soldier nodded and waved as he adjusted the ice melting in the towel on the back of his neck. He was in the process of a shift change with another soldier who was just putting a small block of ice into a towel for his neck. The soldier being relieved had only been in Basra about a week.

He asked the other soldier, "Who are those Americans?"

"Dunno, but they seem nice enough. They wave. They always come to the fence line and check on whoever is here standing at this post after we get slammed with a bloody rocket."

"Well, that's good of them," he said in a British understated tone.

ASHTON NEARED THE FENCE OF THE SF COMPOUND AND slowed. Annie and John already pulled the handles of their doors to get out and open the gate for both vehicles to drive through.

Ryan did the same with his door, but as he opened it John said, "Ryan, we got it."

Ryan nodded and said, "Thanks."

He shut the door quickly without argument. The heat was severe. When Annie and John reached the gate, clearly one of the newer SF operators had entered and secured it earlier. The lock faced the inside, and the chain was tight. Annie lifted the left side of the gate with both hands and kicked her boot under the edge for a little leverage. It created just enough slack in the chain for John to slowly spin it around, so the lock was on their side.

"Ow, motherfucker!" he let go of the chain, and it clanged against the fence pole.

It was too hot to grip and hold for more than a second.

Once Annie realized he was alright, she said, "Be careful, dumbass, that metal chain sitting in the sun all day may be hot."

The large dose of sarcasm was evident in her tone. The sun had super-heated the dark metal chain.

John nodded as he let the chain swing and hang in the square hole of the fence, and said, "No shit, that chain is straight out of hell…fuck, that thing is hot." He had to spin and drop the chain over and over a few links at a time.

Annie pushed the gate open, and John walked around the side of the gate just a few steps. He shook his hands unconsciously and blew on his fingers.

Annie smirked as she dragged the gate. "You better not let the boys see you hurt your little wussy hands," she said with a rhythmic, playful taunting tone in her voice.

John blew on his fingers again, grinned, and said, "Shut the fuck up…these are man-hands," and he licked his thumb and touched the chain lightly as if to prove it—then turned his head to spit out the dirt he just licked off his thumb.

Annie laughed out loud. They locked the gate and got back in the SUV.

Kyle led the way to the team house.

Nathan, the team weapons specialist, was inside the team house at a table near the couches. He smiled politely toward Annie and John and made quick eye contact with Ashton. He was still skeptical of the Feds. He scooped his machine gun parts into a towel and left.

Everyone took a seat in the U-shaped couch arrangement, leaned back, and silently embraced the air conditioning for a moment. Annie and John sat in the center of the U while Ryan and Kyle sat on either side. Ashton pulled up a chair and completed a circle by sitting in the opening of the U. Mike, the team sergeant, came out of the adjacent office, and looked around the room.

He pulled a chair next to Ashton and asked, "So, how did it go?"

The question was not directed at anyone, but Kyle spoke first. "Well, there are a few moving parts. What did you two think?" Kyle asked, nodding toward Annie and John.

Annie looked at John, then to Kyle, and said, "It's hard to say, but I got the impression he is a no bullshit kind of guy." She paused, looked up at the ceiling, then back to Kyle, and said, "I think if he really wasn't interested, he never would have agreed to meet tomorrow." Ryan and Ashton nodded at that, and Annie went on. "But...he seemed a bit concerned about the timeline."

John nodded. "Yeah, I can't say that I blame him either. Two weeks just doesn't cut it for this sort of thing."

Kyle sat his water bottle on the coffee table, and said, "Yep, you're right. Two weeks is a joke, but it might be enough time to determine if what you're trying to do is viable. Plus, you never know, things change." He looked at the ceiling and avoided looking in Ryan's direction.

Ryan nodded. "Yeah, that he said he would run with things for a couple weeks is really good. And Kyle is right, things do change. We will have to run with what we have and adapt to what happens in two weeks."

Mike looked around the room, stopping at Annie and John, and said, "Hell, you're here, you may as well throw things against the wall and see if anything sticks. How is that going to work with your timing?"

Mike remembered that Annie and John were only scheduled to be in Basra for four days. Getting anything done quickly in a war zone was difficult, particularly in Basra. They technically left the FBI BOC in Baghdad three days ago. Their clock for departure was ticking fast.

Annie rubbed her eyes briefly and said, "Good point, I'm glad you brought that up. Going to and from Baghdad is really time-consuming and would probably stop the forward movement of anything being done down here. Does that make sense?"

Everyone nodded but kept quiet—Annie was thinking out loud.

She smiled and continued. "OK, work with me as I think this through...I'm trying to get my speech together for the call I'm going to have to make to pitch what we do next." She took a quick sip of water. Everyone sat back and listened intently as Annie went on. "Getting down here for four days and planning a source meeting, coordinating with you"—she moved both hands in front of herself, gesturing to everyone in the circle—"and meeting with Donovan was something some of the idiots in Baghdad thought we could do in a day."

Kyle blurted, "Thinking American."

Annie looked at Kyle and said, "Huh…thinking what?"

"I call it thinking American," Kyle said. "People come here thinking this world works the way it does in the US. It doesn't. They either can't or won't adjust—I don't know which. I just know some will never adapt or be able to do anything over here. The only way to get things done over here is to *stop thinking American*."

John nodded. "Yeah, you're right. They have unrealistic expectations about how things get handled, particularly how long things take to get done."

All heads nodded.

"So, here's where we are," Annie continued. "We have a two-week window to try and see if we can prove this concept…actively and aggressively blending HUMINT and SIGINT…is even viable. And worth developing long term, right?" she asked rhetorically.

Everyone nodded.

She held her water bottle in front of herself, and spun the water in it momentarily as she thought through the next words, then she said, "We aren't even sure if we can pull a source meeting off tomorrow, but even if we did, it would be one of many that would be necessary, right?"

Everyone nodded.

"Our SIGINT guy from The Fort is likely leaving in two weeks, right?"

Everyone nodded. Ryan and Kyle took a sip of water and glanced at each other. Ashton picked up the eye movement. There was something communicated. Ryan and Kyle were conjuring up a plan of sorts.

"...And," Annie went on, "I have to make a call in the next thirty minutes to a supervisor in Baghdad and convince him to give us the OK to stay here for the next two weeks solid—and expect him to explain that to the FBI on-scene commander and a clueless, do-nothing clown in DC?"—she paused, swirled her water once, then added—"all of whom would just as soon, and probably prefer, we failed or gave up and flew back to Baghdad."

She looked around at everyone in the room and said, "So, we essentially have little or no chance of success?"

Everyone nodded and appreciated her clear and candid assessment.

Annie looked around the room again, saw John nod once, and said, "OK, fuck 'em, I'm in."

Everyone laughed out loud.

Kyle grinned. "I really wasn't sure which way you would go after all of that."

Annie nodded and said, "Fuck 'em. Game on," she grinned and rubbed the bridge of her nose with her thumb and forefingers. "Now I need to get my best bullshit going for the call I'm about to make."

Everyone stood at the same time. Ryan looked to Ashton and asked, "Are you going to give them the schooling on how the gates work and source meeting protocols?"

Ashton smiled. "Yes, I will handle things, get them through their communications with Baghdad, calls to handle source timing, protocols, and logistics, and whatever else comes up."

Ryan grinned, nodded, and said, "Thanks for handling."

Annie stood straight with her hands on her hips, resolved. The group fed off her energy.

Kyle walked toward the office, looked from Annie to John and back, and said, "Welcome to the hapless, hopeless, haphazardous world of Special Forces. We can do this."

Annie sat down and put the edge of the water bottle on her neck. She wanted to puke. She knew she had to keep it together. John and Kyle walked over to the corner of the room opposite the office for a moment until she looked up.

John knew there were occasions when less was more. "Good?" he asked.

Annie nodded, took a sip of water, and stood.

John said, "OK, how about me, you, and Ashton head over to your trailer and work out how to handle the call to Baghdad?"

Annie nodded and said, "Good, that works." She looked at them as she slowly transitioned from her semi-haggard-self-beat-down, and quietly said, "We got this."

Ashton nodded, and John said, "Let's go get our shit together for your call to Baghdad."

Kyle, Mike, and Ryan gathered on the U shaped couches to discuss their next move. The first concern was figuring out a way to keep Donovan in Basra.

Mike looked at Ryan and said, "If there's no Donovan, there's a lot less chance for success in the hostage project, right?"

Ryan nodded and unlaced the tops of his boots to let his feet breathe and cool. "I think you're exactly right," he said. "Assuming Donovan even really wants to stay down here, he's going to be critical to the FBI's hostage program, and we will just be spinning our wheels if we don't get a real SIGINT guy to work with." He nodded toward Mike, "Oh, by the way, we pulled a meeting out of our ass with Donovan for this evening."

Kyle grinned at Ryan and said, "Yeah, nice job on sliding that one in at the last minute. Donovan did a great job of going along with your pretend command briefing for this evening." Kyle looked at Mike and said jokingly, "The HUMINT team leader went all covert and talked in code to the SIGINT guy and set up a meeting!" Everyone smiled, and Kyle said, "Seriously though, I think the timing for that was perfect, particularly after what Donovan said about nobody giving a shit about his care and feeding. It was almost like he was setting us up to offer to help."

Ryan shrugged, smiled, and said, "Well, maybe he was… Who cares? One hand washes the other, especially down here."

Ryan looked to Mike and asked, "If Donovan wants to stay in Basra, and we can pull off some way to make that happen, can we come up with a trailer where he can live?"

Mike grinned. "No problem. Done."

Ryan stood and said, "Thanks."

Kyle looked at Mike, nodded, and said, "Thanks. We have the potential to do a lot if we can get some of Donovan's time for us. Donovan is directly dialed in with the British intelligence community. We would all benefit from talking to each other a little more."

Everyone nodded.

Hostage Status: 83 Days in Captivity (*continued*)

The afternoon heat crushing the hostages made breathing difficult. Surfboy was motionless—each of the other hostages hoped to be selected to empty the bathroom bucket—anything to get out of the room for a moment.

Tex stared up at the ceiling. "Hey...Country Roads... someone is looking for us, right?"

CR gave a lifeless thumbs-up. "Yep...they're looking... probably got thousands of troops close...rescue us any day now."

Shorebilly waived the flies from his face and lethargically chimed in. "Yep...real soon...I'm sure of it." He drifted back into a semi-conscious haze—his mind's eye seeing the light reflecting off the Bay Bridge at sunset from Kent Island.

Looking up at the ceiling Tex murmured, "OK...good."

Losing hope meant death.

CHAPTER 17

PLANNING FOR COMPROMISE... SF AND DONOVAN

DAY 83 (*CONTINUED*): JULY 7, 2007

Back at her trailer, Annie, John, and Ashton discussed how she should handle the call with her HWG supervisor in Baghdad. Annie and John wanted Ashton around to answer questions that might come up during the call. Annie and John were also savvy enough to know that an extra set of eyes and ears on an issue could help.

Annie rubbed her eyes and said, "Well, we have a few minutes to figure out where to go with the conversation and how we try to move forward. I don't think the chat will go well. He's going to want us back in Baghdad in two days."

John nodded. "I think you're right. After the last conversation you had, it sounded like he was looking for a reason to pull the plug on this. I know he didn't like the idea in the first place, so he's looking to yank us both up to Baghdad any way he can."

Annie grinned. "What was it Kyle said with the American thing?"

John rubbed the back of his neck and said, "Stop thinking American." He propped his foot onto the rail of the bed and said, "That's the problem. We are talking with people in Baghdad and DC who can't think outside the boxes they built around their own heads." John interlaced his fingers, leaned back in his chair, and put his hands behind his head. "We are going to have to come up with some sort of compromise to keep Baghdad and the guy in DC happy." He looked at Annie and paused. "We saw this coming."

Annie nodded. "Yeah, I know. I guess I was hoping we would be able to spend more time down here."

Ashton saw the writing on the wall: compromise would mean someone stayed in Basra and someone returned to Baghdad. He straightened his legs, crossed his ankles, and said, "So, the real question right now is who stays and who goes?"

Annie and John both looked at Ashton. They were impressed with how quickly he had assessed the situation. The room was quiet except for the constant hum of the air conditioner.

Annie was much better equipped organizationally and administratively to handle the bureaucracy in Baghdad. They both anticipated that someone besides the HWG supervisor would have to take the lead in dealing with Ken the know-it-all in DC, and ultimately, Annie would be better and ironically more patient than John.

John adapted quickly to new environments. He had adjusted well during his first rotation in Iraq the year before, and he had taken to the HWG work with Annie quickly, too. John had honed source handling skills through years of field work on several FBI drug squads. John was a "fit" in Basra and could make it work.

Annie looked at John. "Me there…you here?

He nodded.

Annie would return to Baghdad.

John would stay in Basra.

Annie looked at Ashton and John, and said, "I will go with the tempo of the conversation. I want to make sure I don't push so hard that I completely fuck things up."

Everyone smiled briefly.

John nodded and said, "Perhaps push hard for both of us to stay for the next two weeks, and when it sounds like he's about to either shut it down or blow a fuse, back off, and maybe give the appearance that you're compromising?"

John gave his suggestion in the tone and form of a question. It was how he and Annie communicated. Thoughts and ideas evolved better.

Annie said, "Yeah…OK. Let me pee, and then I'll call Baghdad."

Annie returned to the room. Ashton said, "If it works for you two, after the phone call I can give a quick tour of some of the gates and a few perimeter details so we can get things going with the source meeting tomorrow."

Annie nodded and said, "That sounds great."

John grinned. "Terrific, assuming Annie and I are still here after she calls the HWG supervisor."

Everyone laughed. It was a good tension reliever, and Annie needed to be composed for the conversation. She leaned back on to the desk, removed her cell phone from her cargo pocket, and pressed the buttons to speed dial FBI BOC. The call failed: not enough bars. Cellular connectivity and signal strength varied throughout the day in Basra. Nobody really knew why, and it did not matter, it was just something to work around.

Annie nodded toward the door. "So much for making the call in the comfort of air conditioning. Besides, I'll probably do better pacing when I talk to this guy." As she walked out of the trailer and down the metal slatted steps, she said, "Can you guys stay close in case I need to shout out a question or miss something?" She shrugged as she continued redialing and said, "Plus, that way you'll have an idea how the conversation is going."

Ashton and John nodded, and Ashton said, "Good luck."

John kicked a rock toward the Hesco barrier and said, "Yeah, good luck…We got this."

Annie looked over at John, grinned, and nodded. The call connected, and the phone was ringing. Ashton and John leaned against the edge of Annie's metal stoop and casually nudged gravel with their heels. The person who answered the phone at the FBI BOC command center had only been in Iraq for two days and did not know Annie or the HWG supervisor. Annie patiently explained to the person who she was and where to find the supervisor so he could come to the phone. The person was anxious to help. Ashton and John listened to Annie's side of the conversation as she paced. She intermittently strode on the plastic walkway, crunched through the gravel, or sometimes did both at the same time.

"Hey, just checking in. Things are moving along about as well as they can."

She paused slightly to listen.

"No, we're not on our way back yet. We still have a few more days down here and…"

The HWG supervisor was already talking over her.

Annie shook her head. "Well, yes, the source meeting was…is a priority. But there are things to be put in place.

First, we had to connect with the guy for numbers, work out the logistics with the people we are staying with, and…"

Annie tried to gently remind her supervisor of the moving parts that came into play when trying to get anything done. She avoided the use of specific organization names like NSA or Special Forces. She was on an unclassified phone line, which probably did not matter, but she would adhere to security protocols. She also did not want to give her boss any reason to take a run at her for security violations.

"No, we haven't done that yet, we anticipate the first source meeting tomorrow. It really wasn't possible to make that happen without getting the logistics together and coordinating with the guy we need to…"

She paused and listened, kicking a rock off the walkway into the gravel.

"Yes, John is handling the communication with the source. He talks to him on the phone he was issued in Baghdad."

Annie stopped pacing, stood near her stoop in front of Ashton, and shrugged. She had a confused look in her eyes as she looked at John.

"Well, yes, I know John's phone is a US number…but… how else would he be able to call the source if he…"

Annie shook her head and looked disgusted.

"How does that matter? And why would the guy in DC care about the calls an agent is making to a source and…"

Annie looked at John, her brow furrowed, and she shook her head.

"Well, about getting back up there in two days. Here's the timing with our numbers guy, he's leaving in two weeks, so we have a short period of time to see if any of this concept is viable. If we stay for a solid two weeks, I think we will be able to…"

Annie was cut off immediately from the other end.

"But if we come back in two days, we won't have anything to brief and..."

She listened, pacing to the end of the trailer and back to Ashton and John.

"Well, it's just two weeks, and we are getting buy-in from everyone down here. If we just..."

She paused, held her hand out in front of her like a symphony director, and looked at John who nodded. They were both on the same page. The time was right in the conversation for Annie to work the locational split for her and John. He could tell by her tone there were other issues. He would have to wait for the details.

"Yes, I know you are between a rock and a hard place, but if we..."

She paused and paced.

"This phone thing is a really bad idea. I mean a *really* bad idea. That guy Ken in DC sounds about like the dumbest motherfucker I have ever..."

She paused momentarily, smiling as a small chuckle emerged.

"Good, we agree on..."

She listened and walked slowly and stopped again in front of Ashton and John.

"OK, how about this...we split the difference. I will come up to Baghdad in two days, handle the write-ups, emails, briefings, and bullshit meetings. We keep John here, running the source meetings, coordinating numbers, and connecting with whoever he can? That way we can at least say we gave the concept a legitimate try, and I can scrape some of the crap off your plate onto mine?"

Everyone was motionless.

"Yep, they're good. They will take care of him."

She grinned slightly and looked back and forth between Ashton and John.

"OK...thanks...I'll call you tomorrow morning... Thanks again."

She nodded her head and smiled toward Ashton and John.

"Oh yeah, we will figure out the phone thing."

She dramatically raised the phone above her head, looked at the button pad, pushed the "off" button, and brought her hand down in front of her in a theatrical stage bow.

Ashton and John grinned, and John asked, "OK, now what the fuck is going on?!"

Annie pulled a bottle of water out of her other cargo pocket, took a big drink, and said, "OK, here's what's up. First, here's the good news. The HWG supervisor went with the two-week plan where you stay here, and I go back up to Baghdad."

Everyone nodded, grinned, and stood still. Nobody noticed the sweat dripping from their own chins.

Annie shook her head, took another drink, and said, "I don't know what will happen after that. We will have to work out how to extend that as we move along."

John tossed a rock he had been holding toward the Hesco barrier, raised his eyebrows slightly, and asked, "And the bad news?"

Annie shook her head. "At the direction of the FBI in DC—specifically, our little friend Ken—your cell phone is being shut off by the end of the day."

That piece of information caught Ashton and John by surprise.

She went on to quickly explain. "According to the HWG supervisor, Ken handles part of the budget for deployment expenses, and your phone bill is higher than what was budgeted, so it got flagged."

John looked at Annie, shrugged, reached into his cargo pocket, and pulled out his phone. "Well, of course my bill is high. I'm calling Iraqi sources on their Iraqi phones using a US phone and phone number. Every call is technically international."

Annie nodded, "I know, and I get it, and *fortunately* so does the boss. Oddly enough, he's on our side on this one. DC-dildo-Ken sent an email to the supervisor, and all the other supervisors in Iraq on this rotation, including the on-scene commander, and said your phone will be shut off."

Annie held her hand up with her palm forward and made a fist, a universal sign used in Iraq to stop when driving, and she said, "Hang on, hang on, hang on, there's more. What pissed off the HWG supervisor more than anything is that the email didn't list any other high-use phones, and it didn't just indicate the phone number." Annie took another sip of water, wiped her forehead with the back of her hand, and said, "According to the boss, Ken went to the trouble to research the rotation deployment website in FBI-net, tracked down prior emails, determined who had what phone, and attached your name to the phone and the phone number." Annie shook her head, kicked at the gravel, and said, "The HWG supervisor met with the big boss, who already had made up his list of high-use phone users, and you were not even in the top five."

Ashton rattled a few pieces of gravel in his hand, he tossed one randomly into the sea of gravel, and asked, "Well, why would the guy in DC do what he's doing, and why would the FBI on-scene commander do that, and what does it matter?"

Holding the water bottle by the cap, Annie swirled the water in it and said, "That's what stirred things up. Everyone knows that emails last forever. The FBI in Baghdad doesn't really give a damn if anything we do here in Basra is actually successful. A lot of these fuckers don't care if *anything* over here in Iraq is ever successful. But it must always *appear* that they are trying…even if it's a half-assed try. A lot of what rotations have done over here was simply done to keep the big FBI machine living and breathing."

Annie was sweating and angry, but she was also elated. The phone call went well. Annie bent over, picked up a piece of gravel, and tossed it where the two nearest Hesco barriers met.

She looked back to Ashton and John and continued. "As the HWG supervisor noted, and rightly so, shutting off the phone of a guy who is actively working sources in a war zone gives the impression that the FBI is actually trying to fail. The mistake Dildo-Ken made was putting it into an email to all the FBI supervisors in Baghdad. That pushed them into a collective corner. At the very least, they have to rally around themselves."

She wiped the sweat from her forehead with the edge of her thumb and said, "They don't give a damn if this hostage thing is successful."

John nodded, looked from Annie to Ashton, and said, "It boils down to pushing, pushback, and ego. The FBI BOC doesn't exactly like what we are doing, but it doesn't want the FBI DC trying to tell them what to do or control things in Iraq. So, we accidentally end up being better supported by our own here in Iraq."

Ashton nodded and stood up straight—he had sat on the steel grate stoop long enough. "Pitiful," he said. "And I hate to say it, but I've seen it before."

John stood up as well and nodded. "Yep, me too. We just have to make sure we work it to our benefit and push the hostage program here in Basra."

Annie shrugged and said, "I will have to give the HWG supervisor a little credit, though. He actually did recognize how ridiculous it is for them to cut off John's phone. He couldn't do anything about it, but he knows how fucked up turning off a phone undermines the effort so overtly. It makes everyone look so bad. I think he's afraid someone might go public with it."

The HWG supervisor knew he had to at least give the appearance of supporting the program that Annie and John proposed. Like many things at the FBI, appearance and perception played a big role. It was why the HWG supervisor relented so quickly and let John stay in Basra for the next two weeks. The perception that management was being supportive was often considered to be as relevant as actual productivity. In fact, everything was a success on paper, regardless of actual achievement. A self-licking ice cream cone…

Annie and John knew a chess game was better played using your brain, not your ego.

Now it was time to get moving. They needed to check out gate protocols and the process to bring sources through the COB perimeter. Ashton led the way to the parking lot. Annie, right behind him, held the lukewarm water bottle against the back of her neck as they plodded in the stifling heat.

John kicked an errant rock off the path and said, "Annie, any idea how to handle the phone situation?"

Annie shook her head. "I'm thinking."

Ashton turned slightly around at the waist, looked back, and said, "We got it...we'll work out the details when we come back. SF can come up with a phone."

Annie and John let out audible breaths and sighs of relief.

THEY CLIMBED INTO THE LARGE BLACK SUV, SO ASHTON could show Annie and John the gates and how to get an Iraqi through the perimeter. The SUV was in good shape, with only a few surface scratches and a severe dent in the front bumper. It had been used to push a smaller truck stuck in a fresh gravel pile about two weeks earlier. The inside was as dirty as the outside, but nobody minded or even noticed.

Ashton took the driver seat, Annie jumped up front on the passenger side, and John sat in the back, right in the middle so he could see through the windshield. Ashton talked through the logistics of contacting a source, bringing the source to and through the gate, the meeting itself, and getting the source back out of the perimeter. It may not sound difficult, but nothing was simple in a war zone.

As they headed out of the gravel parking lot, Ashton glanced in the mirror, made quick eye contact with John, and said, "It sounds like we are working against the clock when it comes to your phone being shut down. Have you talked to your guy today?"

Ashton meant the source they were planning to meet the next day.

John shook his head. "No, not yet. I tried earlier but didn't have enough bars to connect."

Ashton nodded and glanced in the mirror again. "Well, I don't know how good you know your guy, but if we are going to reach out to him with a new phone, he might get a little nervous unless he knows a number change is coming. Some of these guys just won't answer their phone if they don't recognize the number."

"Good point," said John, as he reached into his cargo pocket and pulled out his cell phone. "You're right about not picking up…It was hard enough to get word to him that it was OK to answer the phone when he saw my current number."

John took out the small notebook from his other cargo pocket and flipped through the pages to the source number. He checked the bars on the phone for reception: there were three, which was plenty for a call. He carefully dialed the number, and within a moment heard the unusual busy signal. The call was not connecting. Ashton pulled over near the fence with the torn tennis court netting so everyone could focus on the call. John tried connecting two more times without success.

He looked at Ashton in the mirror, shrugged, and said, "Hell if I know. It shows plenty of bars but won't go through."

Ashton nodded. "Maybe it might be worth sending him a text, so he expects a new number tomorrow."

John nodded. "Good idea…what's a *text*?"

Ashton turned around, looked at John, then at the phone John held, then back to John.

John held up the phone and asked, "Is that the same thing as a *message*?" He looked at Ashton and then to Annie, who had turned around in her seat.

Ashton nodded, "That's usually what we end up using down here because the cell system is such a mess. A text message will go through when a call won't."

John looked at Annie and asked, "Do you know how to do that?"

Annie shrugged, looked at Ashton and back to John, and said, "Sort of. I've seen someone do it a couple of times."

Ashton nodded, turning back around to continue to the gate. "No problem, we will work that out when we get back."

Ashton stopped at the gate. As Annie and John stepped out of the SUV to open the gate, Ashton turned the volume of the radio down, grinned, and said, "Careful, that chain gets pretty hot."

John nodded and smirked as he turned his head to say, "Yeah, no shit."

Annie and John approached the gate. The chain was slack. John gently touched it and turned the lock around to where it was accessible.

Annie nudged the fence with her foot and said, "How dumb are we that we don't know how to use our damn phones." She was mildly embarrassed but laughed it off.

John nodded. "Well, I guess we are reasonably dumb, but not so dumb I'm going to walk up and grab this hot fuckin' chain again."

They both laughed and handled the gate movement.

Everyone burns their hands once on that chain. Some do it over and over. It was like tripping on the same misshapen steps in the FBI BOC stairwell in Baghdad. You either adapted and stopped falling on your face—or burning your hands—or you did not.

Annie and John got back into the SUV. Ashton grinned. "How was that chain?" The hot chain incident would follow John throughout his time in Basra.

Annie laughed. John turned to Ashton and gave an exaggerated nod, then turned and chuckled with Annie. "Those fuckers," he said. "I'm going to hear about my singed fingers on this chain forever."

Ashton's good-natured razzing was healthy. It brought them together. The giant mess that Annie and John had stepped into was slowly coming together.

NO PLAN WAS PERFECT. IT WAS USUALLY JUST A PLACE TO start. The only bad plan was no plan at all.

Ryan came out of the team office, nodded to Kyle, and said, "Well, how does our timing look? Are you ready to have a chat with Donovan?"

Kyle smiled. "I think so. Are you ready for your Donovan recruitment?"

Ryan grinned. "I think so…How do you want to play this?"

Kyle shut the computer off. "Based on what I know of Donovan, I think simple and straightforward would be the best route. You know, this is something that could actually work for everyone."

Kyle stood and pushed the chair under the desk. Ryan held up a set of keys. He had just signed out the white SUV from the whiteboard near the door. There was only one set of keys on the series of hooks screwed into the wall under the board. The team was busy, and most vehicles were used regularly. Ryan knew taking on more people with the team would strain resources, but they would adjust.

Ryan and Kyle headed from the team house to the SUV and drove out to the main road. As they passed the NAAFI store, they waved to Ashton as he drove past in the opposite direction with Annie and John for a walk-through of the main gate, perimeter lot, and fence line.

Kyle and Ryan made their way to Brit-HQ.

Ashton, Annie, and John made their way to the gate.

Everything was going according to plan…for now.

Hostage Status: 83 Days in Captivity (*continued*)

The hostages were sick. Shorebilly tried pouring a small amount of water into Surfboy's mouth. He did not swallow. He was barely breathing.

The door of the cell opened. A guard with a man they had never seen walked in—he held a rag up to his face looking around, turned, and left the cell.

The door shut.

CHAPTER 18

MEETING BETWEEN DONOVAN, KYLE AND RYAN

DAY 83 (*CONTINUED*): JULY 7, 2007

Kyle parked on the Brit-HQ perimeter road. He and Ryan walked past the duck-and-cover bunker near the sandbag square where the British soldier stood.

The guard had seen them before. He gave their IDs a cursory look, nodded, and said, "Cheers."

Upon entering the Brit-HQ building, they saw the security check-in counter was quiet. Most people were between meetings or at the chow hall. Ryan and Kyle took their British headquarter IDs out of their pouches to present to the British soldier, who knew their faces well.

The soldier held up his thumb and gave it one quick spin in a tight circle. Kyle understood what he meant and turned his Brit-ID to show the other side. It was a courtesy to expedite check-ins for regulars. Ryan did the same, and the soldier quickly glanced at each ID.

Kyle looked at the soldier and said, "No mobiles," gesturing with his thumb to Ryan and back to himself to show he was speaking for both.

The soldier smiled. "No worries, mate. Have a good

evening," he said and went about replacing the broken clips on the visitor badges.

Kyle and Ryan walked through the large quiet foyer past the coffee kiosk. One British soldier drank tea and read a magazine.

The British soldier at the SCIF sign-in desk recognized them. They signed in the logbook and went through the main SCIF entry into the large room, where several conversations could be heard. The previously vacant desks to the right were occupied by British soldiers and civilians. There was a different American soldier seated behind the far-right desk, and like the soldier earlier in the day, he had no unit patches or name on his uniform. One British soldier sat next to him and pointed to the American soldier's monitor with his index finger like he was tracing something.

Kyle and Ryan passed mostly unnoticed by everyone in the room. The exception was the American in the no-patch uniform. He nodded to Kyle, who responded with a quick, subtle wave.

As they approached the conference room, the door was open, and Kyle saw Donovan sitting at the far end of the meeting table. He leaned back in his chair and looked up at the ceiling with both hands above his head in the sight line of what he saw on the ceiling. Donovan held a piece of notebook paper that had been tightly and meticulously folded into a small triangle. He held the triangle in his left hand between his thumb and forefinger, with the tall side facing toward him and the pointy end of the triangle facing the ceiling. Just as Kyle and Ryan were about to step through the door Donovan moved his right hand toward the triangular piece of paper and flicked his middle finger off his thumb, striking the back edge of the triangle with a snapping sound. The triangle shot toward the ceiling.

It was not until Kyle and Ryan walked all the way into the room that they could see someone had taken two pencils and shoved the sharp ends into the ceiling tiles and tied a six-inch length of string from the eraser of one pencil to the eraser of the other. It was a makeshift field goal. Kyle and Ryan entered just as the triangle deflected off the ceiling, hit the edge of one of the pencils, went through the goal, bounced off the wall, and onto the floor.

Donovan bent down and picked up the paper triangle as Kyle and Ryan made their way farther into the room, and said, "Hey guys, come on in, grab a chair."

Donovan smiled because he had been attempting that shot on goal for fifteen minutes. This was the first one he had made. He walked over and shook hands with Kyle and Ryan. Again, he sat on one side of the table, and they sat on the other. Donovan was still not going to play the head of the table game.

As Ryan sat, he said, "Hey, thanks for taking the unplanned meeting."

Donovan turned the paper triangle slowly between his thumb and forefinger on the table and said, "Sure, no problem. You caught me a little off-guard when you said something about a command meeting, but I got it." He looked down at the spinning triangle and added, "I guess I figured it was the company you were keeping…you with the FBI, or maybe it was the company I was keeping…me with my British colleague." He smiled broadly.

Kyle and Ryan smiled, too, and Ryan said, "Well, maybe it was a little of both."

Everyone chuckled and relaxed.

Donovan looked back and forth between the two SF operators and said, "Well, I would imagine you might be able to keep something away from the FBI—actually that's pretty easy—but it's unlikely to stay hidden from my brothers and sisters at GCHQ."

Donovan pulled his hair back from his face and paused. He tilted his head slightly forward, and leaned back in his chair, smiled, then adjusted his back and legs so his two-hundred-fifty-pound frame settled better into the chair.

Donovan tossed the little paper triangle on the table in front of him and said, "So, what's up?"

Ryan leaned forward slightly with his hands folded on the table. "Well, a couple of things. We wanted to see what you really thought regarding this hostage thing. And we wanted to see where your head was regarding Basra and being here compared to Baghdad."

Kyle nodded as Ryan spoke. There was a slight pause, and Kyle said, "We wanted to see if we might leverage influence from our side if you want to stay in Basra. Or try other back channels, to make things work…We could use some help in our shop, if you're interested."

Donovan liked Ryan's directness and appreciated Kyle's back-channel thinking, which was as specific as it was broad. Kyle and Ryan sat back in their chairs. Donovan nodded and scratched his neck under his beard. He brought his forefinger up to the bridge of his nose and rubbed it twice. He was counting his own hand movements but had long ago adapted to doing so subtly in public, without people really noticing.

Then he said, "Well, I've drilled into the FBI hostage thing. I think what they're describing is a good idea, and the best way forward. How the USG has handled hostage shit over here is a joke. Based on everything I've seen and the conversations I've had, these two FBI ding-dongs are on the right path."

Donovan looked to Ryan, then to Kyle and back to Ryan, and said, "And I believe I'm speaking for my British colleagues, as well." Several British citizens were still being held hostage, and kidnap threat was high.

Kyle nodded and sat back. Ryan continued, "Well, it sounds like there might be something here that could work for everyone. Our ODA needs some help on a few things. Directly connecting with you would make a difference."

Donovan nodded and said, "Yeah, maybe, but my people are pulling me back to Baghdad in two weeks. I don't have much say in that. The bean counters at my main headquarters in Maryland are making personnel placement decisions for some reason...simple things get complicated here."

Kyle nodded and folded his hands on the table in front of him. "Before we did anything, we wanted to check and see what worked for you. Do you want to be in Baghdad or Basra?"

Donovan did not blink or hesitate. "Basra. Yeah, I would rather be here. I'm not interested in camping at the embassy in Baghdad. I will be in-country for three more months, and have the option of extending, if what I'm working on is real." He shrugged, pulled his hair back like he was putting it in a ponytail, then let it go, and said, "I don't seem to blend in too well in Baghdad, for some reason."

Kyle said, "Maybe we can help...we will have to balance all of the agendas and show it benefits everyone... The Fort, FBI hostage project, Army Special Forces Ops, and the British."

Donovan smiled. "You mean that *one team, one fight bullshit* that the hierarchy preaches but never practices?"

Everyone laughed, and Ryan said, "Ironically that might be what we are actually doing. We have to be smart about it. We will be playing chess with people playing checkers."

Kyle nodded, then leaned forward slightly. "We poke and prod and work back channels from as many angles as possible and see if we can get the system to do the right thing." Kyle paused, then added, "We will make it clear nobody has to really do anything, except say yes. We will take care of housing and logistics for your care and feeding through our team."

Donovan grinned and said, "OK…we'll see…As I see it, one of the biggest variables in play is something we don't control at all." He leaned back in the chair and pulled his hair away from his face again. "The FBI…and the FBI fighting with itself."

They all laughed and shook their heads in comedic disgust.

Donovan spun the paper triangle on the table and watched it until it stopped, then said, "OK, I'm in." He looked back and forth between Ryan and Kyle and said, "I will connect with my British guys and see if they want to try and leverage any influence. If they do, they will be subtle. They're smart like that." Donovan shrugged his shoulders, put both palms on the table, and said, "Oh, by the way, would you guys be able to drop me off at a British compound by the range?"

Ryan and Kyle nodded. "Sure, no problem," Ryan said.

They all stood and made their way from the SCIF to the SUV.

Hostage Status: 83 Days in Captivity (*continued*)

The cell door opened, slamming into the wall. Four nice guards walked in and appeared agitated—they yelled one-word commands, pointed to the door and two had hoses. "Up...Out...Up...Out..."

Shorebilly and CR were grabbed by the neck and pushed toward Surfboy, who was unconscious and unmoving on the floor. The guards kicked the bathroom bucket toward Tex yelling, "Up...Out...Up...Out..." The guards pointed to the door.

Shorebilly and CR carried Surfboy to the courtyard. Tex trailed behind with the bucket.

All the hostages made it to the courtyard near the trench.

Two guards they had never seen stood with rifles. "Down!... Down!...Down!..." The guards pointed at the hostages gesturing toward the ground. The hostages were quickly pushed face first onto the concrete slab, and everything got quiet.

Explosions in the distance faintly echoing in the courtyard gave way to guards murmuring and lightly laughing. The guards smiling at the explosion meant the British or the Americans were on the receiving end.

The hostages were trying to digest what was happening—perhaps this is how executions were done.

It was dusk, and they could see more guards standing around the courtyard near the trench.

The hostages were face down with hands at their sides.

Without warning the hostages heard an extraordinarily loud bang and saw a blindingly white light. This must be what it is like to die—they did not move.

Surfboy remained unconscious. The other three dared to turn their heads slightly. The bright light was shockingly vivid.

The guards looked up in the sky laughing among themselves.

Tex looked straight ahead and quietly said, "What the fuck? Are we dead?"

Shorebilly stayed flat and quiet. "No. Not yet. Illumination rounds."

The British periodically fired illumination rounds from artillery batteries. The rounds exploded hundreds of feet in the air and provided light for several minutes over a large area.

"Shut mouth," hollered one of new rifle-carrying guards.

The hostages were still alive...for now.

CHAPTER 19

ONE ATTACK . . . TWO ROCKETS . . . THREE DIFFERENT PERSPECTIVES

DAY 83 (*CONTINUED*): JULY 7, 2007

The Donovan Perspective...

Donovan waved as Kyle and Ryan drove away. He stood in front of a large steel door, the entrance to the living area for many of the British personnel working at the British Headquarters. The compound was hastily built as the British moved out of the downtown Basra Palace, turning it over to the Iraqis. Donovan stood at the threshold to a place where few Americans would ever be invited—the British Bar.

Donovan paused at the perimeter of the Hesco barrier where metal framing supported an eight-foot steel door. He reached near the steel door and opened a small, scarred metal box containing a phone. It looked like something left over from World War II and even had a hand crank attached. The irony of such a simple communication device utilized by one of the world's most technically advanced intelligence and communication agencies was not lost on Donovan. He lifted the phone from the cradle and pushed a one-inch-square green button that had a mechanical feel. The button clicked when he pushed it.

A voice said, "Hello."

"Hey, this is Donovan."

The voice on the other end said, "OK, someone will be right there."

Donovan hung up the phone. In about thirty seconds the door swung open, and Jensen said, "Come in, mate." Jensen glanced at his watch, then looked up to Donovan, and said, "I presume your meeting with your American Special Forces was rather timely?"

Donovan nodded. "Yeah…I will tell you all about it."

He followed Jensen through the winding dirt path between eight-foot-high Hesco barriers. Donovan had been to the British Bar Compound several times before and was one of the few Americans ever welcomed. Donovan unconsciously counted the steps and pivots as they walked. They zigzagged through the Hesco barriers, came to the common area of the compound, and stepped onto a makeshift wood walkway.

Donovan and Jensen continued past the white plastic chairs and walked up two steps to a fifteen-by-fifteen-foot wooden deck connected to a three-by-fifteen-foot makeshift plywood bar. Under the bar were waist-high coolers, and behind the bar were two six-foot-high commercial-grade coolers with clear doors. On either side of the bar were several stacks of red cups. The hard liquor sat on shelves under the bar. Jensen looked at a chalkboard with an ever-changing list of available beer and booze. A tan retractable awning shaded the deck. About ten people stood at the edge of the bar. Everyone was holding a red cup or drinking from one.

Behind the bar stood a British soldier in his early fifties. He was known only as Mr. Ethan—his military rank was not used, and he was always addressed as Mr. Ethan. He was one of the senior enlisted command soldiers assigned to GCHQ. He was extraordinarily well respected and was shown great deference by all. He kept personnel at the bar in order and managed anyone who had too much to drink without saying a word. He simply looked at the friends of the misbehaving patron and guided them with his eyes to address their over-imbibed mate. Mr. Ethan was a career infantryman who had been in the twilight of his career just before the war began in 2003. The commanding general recognized his seemingly effortless ability to get things done. The general promoted Mr. Ethan to be his senior enlisted aid.

Two months before the Iraq war began, Mr. Ethan was politely invited to tea at Vauxhall Cross overlooking the River Thames. Also at tea were two other generals and two men in well-tailored suits. Mr. Ethan's reputation for fixing things was widely known. The well-dressed men were from GCHQ and kept their mouths shut. Mr. Ethan was asked to lead liaison between GCHQ and US intelligence agencies—war in Iraq was inevitable. Mr. Ethan was assured by the senior general that he would have immediate support at raised levels anytime needed. Mr. Ethan liked the idea and agreed to the challenge.

Mr. Ethan's influence might be compared to the mastery of a US military chief warrant officer (CW-04). A person at that level could be invisible when it came to some command structures, yet they could wield enormous influence, and sometimes directly connect with raised echelons at the White House or Pentagon. It was a mistake to underestimate the sway of a US military CW-04, and it was an extraordinary blunder to underestimate Mr. Ethan.

Mr. Ethan greeted Donovan with a cold can of Guinness, a firm handshake, and a disarmingly warm smile. He handed Jensen two cans of Strongbow. They exchanged pleasantries until Mr. Ethan excused himself to greet others. Donovan and Jensen walked back down a step to the chairs on the wooden pallets and sat.

They looked at each other, tapped cans, and nodded. "Cheers," they said and took a sip.

They sat back, saying nothing and surveying the bar for a moment. Near the edge of the bar, a young woman talked with a circle of men around her. She wore civilian clothes—a plain white shirt, jeans, and boots. She held a half-consumed can of Strongbow in one hand and a cold unopened can in the other. Donovan had never acquired a taste for that hard cider; in fact, he'd had several gut-wrenching puke sessions in the parking lot of this very compound because of it.

Five men surrounded the woman, hanging on every word she said. She talked about the weather and how she thought it was so hot in Basra, as compared to England. The men could care less what she said. They were simply getting a chance to talk to a woman.

Jensen took a gulp, exhaled, and said, "So how did the meeting go with your SF mates?"

Donovan nodded, took a sip from his cold Guinness, and said, "OK, I think…They wanted another opinion on the FBI hostage thing, and they know I don't want to go to Baghdad, so they wanted to see if they might be able to work something out to keep me here in Basra."

Jensen nodded and listened while he took two large gulps from his Strongbow, then said, "As you know, we could use the help down here, and connecting on this hostage thing might work. Nobody seems to talk to each other in Baghdad. Hell, both the US and the UK are missing people."

Jensen sat the empty can of Strongbow by his feet. "Well, mate," he continued. "I don't know what your SF friends can pull together, but we may be able to get this adjusted right here."

Jensen popped open the other can of Strongbow and looked at Donovan. While taking a sip, he raised his eyebrows, tilted his head, and subtly pointed in the direction of Mr. Ethan.

Just then an explosion went off close enough to stop conversation, but far enough to keep everyone standing. There was no incoming audible alarm. It was some distance across the base. Everyone looked around momentarily, a few heads shook, and a quiet expletive or two was uttered. The conversation and ogling resumed.

Donovan took another sip and asked, "Mr. Ethan?"

Jensen responded with a nod and a shrug, sipped his Strongbow, and said, "Your call, mate. Do you want to stay here in Basra?"

Donovan leaned back in the chair momentarily with the front legs up, came back forward as he nodded, and said, "Yeah, I'm in." He took the last sip from his can of Guinness and gently squeezed the can together in the middle.

Jensen grinned and said, "Cheers…thought so…Let me get you another Guinness and have a moment with Mr. Ethan."

Jensen stood, picked up the empty cans, and tossed them in the trash as he neared the bar. He leaned over the center of the bar, and Mr. Ethan did the same. Their faces were only a few inches apart as Jensen spoke. Donovan looked down at his dusty, size fourteen boots, then back to the bar, and saw Jensen motion for Donovan to come over. The conversation between Jensen and Mr. Ethan took less than ten seconds.

Donovan stood and walked up the step to the bar patio. Another explosion quieted conversation again. It sounded about the same distance as the first blast. A few people glanced at the sky and edges of the Hesco barriers.

Donovan's fate in Basra was already sealed. The SF operators, the FBI agents, the magic unicorns in the sky were simply going through the motions. The back-channel bar chat between Jensen and Mr. Ethan was all that was needed. It was done. Donovan would stay in Basra. Mr. Ethan would see to it. Mr. Ethan poured three shots of Jameson whiskey. The special tumbler glasses were under the counter. He rarely brought them up to the bar counter.

Mr. Ethan looked to Donovan and said, "So, I understand you're inclined to keep us company here in Baaasra for a bit?"

Donovan nodded.

"Very well," Mr. Ethan said. "We'll see what we can do."

Donovan, Jensen, and Mr. Ethan clinked glasses, brought them back to their noses for a brief sniff, tapped the edge of the glass on the surface of the bar at the same time, and then drank the whiskey with one gulp. Mr. Ethan looked at Donovan and Jensen, nodded, and they all placed their glasses on the bar. They stood quietly at the makeshift wooden bar. Donovan looked at the edge of the sky over the Hesco barriers and briefly wondered about the two rocket blasts.

The Ashton, Annie, and John Perspective...

Ashton turned from the main road toward a gate on the COB perimeter and said, "All the gates have phonetic alphabet designators, like Alpha, Bravo, Charlie, but we never use those names. We go by description of where the gate is and what it looks like at the entry point. Basically, we come up with a gate nickname."

Annie nodded, turned the radio down slightly, and said, "I guess that's probably pretty good for security. That way your sources don't know which gate has what designator, right?"

John leaned forward and nodded in agreement from the back. "Yeah, that's smart."

Ashton grinned, glanced in the rearview mirror to John, then over to Annie, and said, "Nah…that's not it. Nobody can remember which gate is A, B, or C. We mess it up among ourselves and get confused."

Everyone laughed. Nicknames for the gates had nothing to do with security—they were done purely out of necessity. Ashton stopped along the roadside to explain what they were about to see.

"It's sort of like up in Baghdad when you come in and out of gates. There are different layers for security. Those guys up ahead are Czech. I don't really know why they are here; they all have uniforms and seem to have a military structure, but for all I know they are contractors. Anyway, their English is really limited."

Ashton pointed to the orange high-impact plastic barriers that were dented, scratched, and had a brown dirt tint. The barriers were four feet high, three feet wide, and ten feet long. There were six barriers set up in a manner that required a vehicle to zigzag to get through. It was a method used at almost all gate entry control points to force vehicles to slow in order to negotiate the turns and show identification.

Ashton pointed in the direction of the first barrier, where a helmeted Czech with a machine gun stood. "Sometimes they are good about just waving us through if they recognize us," he shrugged, "sometimes not. We just go with it. They may open your door and look around the floor. Have your ID ready. If they stop us, just nod, point past the last barricade, and smile a lot."

Ashton started driving forward. The Czech guard at the edge of the serpentine barricade recognized Ashton and started to wave him forward. The guard quickly held his hand up in a fist for Ashton to stop and called to another guard, who was sitting on a stool near a small five-foot-by-five-foot makeshift sandbag bunker. The Czech guard saw a new face. The new face belonged to Annie. She was with the American in the SUV, maybe an American woman. There were not many American women in Basra, and most of the guards had never spoken with an American woman. The Czechs needed to see IDs.

The guard came to the driver's side door. Ashton pushed the button and lowered the window. The Czech guard looked past Ashton and smiled from ear to ear at Annie. Annie and John were looking at the grinning guard standing at Ashton's door when Annie's door opened. It was the guard who had been sitting on the stool next to the bunker. He had to do a quick visual inspection of the inside contents of the vehicle, specifically Annie.

In his absolute best English, the guard at Annie's door said, "Good evening, IDs please.

Though Ashton had warned of the door potentially being opened, Annie instinctively raised her hands in a defensive posture. She was quick to turn her defensive hand gesture into an awkward two-handed wave.

She accompanied the wave with a smile and said, "Hello, good evening. How are you?" She tilted her head slightly, touched her hair, and continued the smile.

"Good, very good," said the Czech at Annie's door. He did the best he could to look around the floor, and then said in the form of a question to Annie, "American?"

Annie nodded. "Yes, American." She held up her ID in the pouch around her neck.

The Czech did not care about seeing her ID, but nodded in acknowledgment and asked, "You go where?"

Annie smiled and pointed past the orange serpentine barricade where they were sitting, and said, "Over there."

That was good enough for him. He did not care. As far as he was concerned, she could go wherever she wanted. The Czech guard at Annie's door was beyond enamored. He would later savor the fact that she not only waved at him but smiled and touched her hair. As his story would progress later to his friends, the American woman flirted with him, and he might end up marrying her. The stories men told each other when they were bored got real absurd, real fast.

In their best English, both Czech guards said, "Thank you," and motioned for Ashton to move through the entry of the serpentine barricade. They continued waving.

Ashton kept his eye on the orange barricades as he made the tight turns and said, "I think our little visit, or should I say Annie's little visit, is the best thing that has happened to those guys in weeks."

Everyone laughed, and Annie wiped her forehead with the back of her hand and said, "That guy opening the door scared the shit out of me."

John leaned forward to the edge of the front seat and said, "Me too, and I was even expecting it after Ashton's warning."

Ashton smiled, glanced at Annie, and said, "Well, for the time you're here, we will either get through the Czech checkpoint easier than usual or harder than usual."

Everyone snickered for a moment.

Ashton passed the last of the serpentine barriers, took a hard left, and parked the SUV next to a four-foot gap in the Hesco barriers. The gap led to the two-room building that British security forces occupied and used as the entry control point command center.

Ashton turned off the engine. "Here's where we go to check in with the Brits," he said. "It's a good idea to do this before we go down the road. They will give us a heads-up if anything is going on, or if anything at the perimeter checkpoint has changed."

Ashton led the way through the opening in the Hesco barriers and across a ten-foot length of wood planking over a drainage ditch. Near the end of the wooden walkway was the door of the single-story two-room building. From inside the building a British soldier saw Ashton and the two unfamiliar faces as they turned the corner. He opened the door and gestured for them to enter.

The soldier had never met Ashton but had seen him come through the gate on numerous occasions and knew he was an American. The soldier had seen Ashton and other Americans bring Iraqis through the gate for what they called *meetings*. The British soldiers did not know or care what the *meetings* were about. They were simply directed to facilitate the Americans and some British civilians with their passage for *meetings*.

"Come in, mate. Get in the air," the soldier said.

The room was twenty by twenty feet and sparsely furnished. Its three chairs all had broken wheels, a wood bench ran the length of one wall, and a two-foot-wide makeshift shelf ran ten feet across the adjacent wall. On the shelf sat a myriad of handheld radios, battery chargers, and empty water bottles. Everything had a thin layer of the Iraqi-powder-dirt.

The soldier smiled and nodded, and asked Ashton, "What can we do for you, mate?"

Ashton said, "Well, we are going to try and have some *meetings* over the next few days, and we need to bring some people through, so we wanted to check with you and then take a look around...you know...see if anything has changed."

The soldier nodded. "No worries, have a look around. I assume they are with you," he said, gesturing with his thumb toward Annie and John.

Ashton nodded. "Yes, they will be down here working these *meetings* with me and some of our guys."

Ashton nodded in the direction of Annie and John, both of whom started edging toward the soldier with their ID pouches raised and taking out their recently issued British IDs.

The soldier saw them trying to slide their fingers into their ID pouches and held his hand up. "No worries. There with you—good enough, mate," he said, looking back at Ashton.

"Will the person you're meeting use the car park...or park outside the gate...or be on foot...or do you know?" the soldier continued.

Ashton shrugged, shook his head, and said, "I don't know yet; we're still figuring it out."

The soldier walked over to a door opposite the one they had entered and said, "Well, have at it. Be sure to check the entry into the car park again, some things have changed, and do be sure to let us know if you need anything."

Ashton nodded. "OK, sounds good. We'll just be a few minutes."

The soldier nodded and opened the door for them to proceed toward the perimeter. Ashton led the way with Annie next and John last. They zigzagged through Hesco barriers, walking on mostly compacted soil with minimal gravel. Above their heads, tan camouflage netting covered the walkway. It looked like something from an old war movie or surplus from World War II. The netting was incredibly effective in creating shade.

Annie got one step closer to Ashton and kept her voice low. "What the hell is a car park?"

Without breaking stride, Ashton tilted his head slightly to the left and said out of the side of his mouth, "That's British English for parking lot."

"Oh," she said, and wiped her forehead with the back of her left hand, then scratched her right elbow. She stayed within a step of Ashton. Just above a whisper, she said, "Well, I could have figured that out, and actually, a car park makes more sense than a parking lot, huh?"

Ashton glanced over his shoulder and grinned. He stopped walking to face John and Annie. "Are you ready to walk into your car park?"

They looked from the edge of the Hesco barriers and stayed in the shade. The car park's surface was an uneven forty-by-forty-yard moonscape of compacted soil. A ten-foot-high chain link perimeter fence capped with concertina wire surrounded it. About forty yards from where they were standing was the gate for the lot. It was the outer edge of the perimeter. The area was where the supposedly *safe* inside merged with the *dangerous* outside.

The chain link gate was usually kept open during daylight

hours. Traffic stopped at a simple two-inch steel pole welded to a gear attached to a four-foot vertical post. The rudimentary barrier was manually raised and lowered by hand.

About forty feet from the gate sat a guard tower. A wooden stairway zigzagged from the ground up twenty feet to the tower's entrance. John briefly looked up at the tower and quietly said to Annie, "This sure as shit doesn't look like Baghdad." The plywood guard tower had a plastic roof and was not enclosed.

Annie leaned toward John and quietly said, "No shit. That fuckin' guard tower looks like a Kentucky tree fort where I grew up!"

Two British soldiers occupied the tower. The soldier with a rifle over his shoulder gave a faint wave to Ashton. The other soldier sat behind a heavy machine gun and kept his eyes and barrel pointed toward the horizon.

Ashton walked toward the guard post, with Annie and John on either side. "This time of day things aren't very busy. Most Iraqis who needed to do anything at the base have already come and gone," he explained. "There isn't much movement here from about now until it gets light in the morning. The Brits search cars as they come up…then let them park where they can."

Ashton pointed to the edge of the lot about thirty yards to their left. Two picnic tables and a single-wide trailer sat underneath camouflage netting for shade. Annie and John kept quiet as they meandered across the uneven compacted dirt lot. The parking lot contained four sedans randomly parked.

Ashton continued looking at the tables and said, "They do another personal search, recheck gensiya, and confirm escorts or business papers over there by that trailer."

Annie looked to where Ashton pointed and asked, "What's *gensiya*?"

"A gensiya is an ID card for Iraqis. They have a national ID card system here," he said.

Once at the fence, Ashton pointed to the road on lower ground. "That is the main road everyone travels on to get to and from Basra. During the day it's full of people milling around. Cars are picking people up and dropping people off...Others are just watching the gate to see who comes in and out." He pointed to a flat area down the embankment—there were two cars parked.

"That's another spot where Iraqis will park and just walk up to the checkpoint. That way they don't have to get their cars inspected. And sometimes the lot we're standing in gets full of people. They will end up parking up and down the road that way." He pointed farther to the right, slightly north and east. Ashton stood with his hands on his hips, looked toward the horizon, then pointed just above the same northeasterly direction, and said, "And right there about two miles from where we are standing is downtown Basra."

John looked at the horizon, then turned and looked at the lot where they stood. He kept his voice low so only Ashton and Annie heard. "This looks and sort of feels dangerous as shit. You would think the British would do something for a better buffer against a car bomb...or a suicide bomber...or even just some dumbass shooting."

Annie slowly turned in a circle as she looked at her surroundings. The area had an uncomfortable openness, and she felt exposed. She noticed the randomly strewn water bottles scattered near the picnic tables. A slight breeze baked her skin like air from a blow-dryer set on high heat. Every few feet along the perimeter fence, shredded plastic bags fluttered in the concertina wire. Things could go bad very quickly in this area.

Ashton shrugged, took one last look in the direction of Basra, his gaze fixed, and said, "Yeah, this is a very dangerous place, and a lot could happen. I suppose people are doing what they can to minimize the risk. At some point there's an outer edge to a perimeter, where the safety area is behind you. I guess you could say this is where the edge of the perimeter begins…or ends…it depends on your perspective."

He smiled, looked at Annie and John, then turned around to face the parking lot and the entrance to the path between the Hesco barriers. Annie and John nodded, took one last look at the horizon, and turned to survey the lot one more time.

Ashton nodded. "We should get going. The sun is setting, and it will be dark before long. How about we head back to the compound, get the phone set up, and get to the chow hall."

They meandered across the lot, waved to the soldiers in the tower, then weaved through the Hesco barriers and into the British control room. Ashton knocked on the door before entering. They thanked the British soldier and left, walking back through the zigzagged Hesco barriers to their SUV parked on the roadside.

They climbed in, and Ashton started the engine. He did a U-turn at the end and was directed through the end of the barricades by the two Czech guards from earlier. The guards waved and grinned from ear to ear. Ashton and John smiled, nodded, and gave a quick thumbs-up. Annie smiled, nodded, and did her best parade wave.

Once they passed the Czech guards they came to a seemingly random intersection, and on the corner to their right Annie noticed a duck-and-cover bunker. It finally came to her why the Basra duck-and-cover bunkers looked different from the ones in Baghdad.

She pointed, tapped her thumb nail on the window, and said, "The bunkers here don't have the square concrete caps on the end." She turned to get a better look at the bunker and said, "I knew something was different…How come they don't have concrete ends?"

In Baghdad, the four-foot-square end caps of a duck-and-cover bunker were positioned on either side of the upside-down U-shaped bunker, about two feet from the entrance. To enter the bunker a person slid between the edge of the bunker and the end cap, ducked their head under the four-foot-high top, and stepped inside. The configuration allowed entry from either end and blast protection from nearly 360 degrees, as well as from above.

Ashton glanced over to the bunker as they passed it. "I don't know. That's how they all are here. It's fucked up." He shrugged. "It is what it is…"

Annie and John nodded and shrugged.

Annie said, "Hey, can we make a quick stop at the NAAFI? I need a couple of things?"

"Sure, no problem. We're coming up on it," Ashton said.

The parking lot was about fifty yards ahead. Ashton took a right into the compacted dirt lot and parked in the corner next to the drainage ditch, and they went inside. Annie picked up toothpaste and a small box of powder laundry detergent. John and Ashton randomly perused British tabloid magazines as Annie paid at the counter. No sooner did she receive her receipt than an explosion rattled the walls and windows of the one-story building. Ashton knew from experience that it was a rocket impact and was not immediately close.

Per protocol, four British soldiers who had been shopping and the British contractors behind the counter all dove to the floor. Ashton wanted to get an idea where the rocket had hit. Annie and John followed him as he headed to the door, stepping over two British contractors prone on the floor in the foyer. Just as they reached the door, another impact rattled the building. There was no siren or anti-rocket fire.

They cautiously walked out of the store and crossed the drainage ditch. They climbed into the SUV, and Ashton backed out of the parking spot, drove toward the main road, and weaved around a small pickup truck stopped in the middle of the lot. The doors were open, and two British soldiers were lying on the dirt near the rear tires. They were fine—just following base protocols.

Ashton took a right onto the main road and saw a fading plume of smoke to the left of the road in the distance. About one hundred yards down the road, he saw SUVs and trucks stopped in the middle of the road on both sides. As he got closer, he saw two British security force gun trucks blocking both lanes, and a soldier was out of the gun truck standing in front of the traffic. The soldiers had been nearby on another matter, and they immediately sealed the area for safety, post-blast investigation and documentation, and most importantly, to expedite emergency personnel if necessary.

Ashton swerved to the right and slammed on the brakes. There was no going around the recently stopped traffic or the gun trucks. There were steep drainage ditches on either side. Everyone would have to sit and wait.

The Ryan and Kyle Perspective...

After Kyle and Ryan dropped off Donovan at what appeared to be some arbitrary British compound, they headed toward the SF compound. As they passed the parking lot at Echos and the NAAFI, an earsplitting explosion brought their conversation to a halt. About a quarter of a mile in front of them and thirty yards to the right of the main road, they saw a flash of light and a plume of smoke. It was the first rocket attack in two days.

Kyle continued driving and pushed harder on the accelerator. As far as Kyle was concerned, driving in the direction of a rocket impact was not necessarily as risky as it seemed. Kyle had a counterintuitive perspective of rocket attacks. He knew how insurgent rocketing worked, and their limitations. The chances that the next rocket would hit in the exact location as the prior rocket were slim. The next rocket, if there was one, could be in front of them, behind them, or perhaps on top of them. Besides, getting hit was random.

They heard another thunderous crash as a second rocket impacted. This time it was about one hundred yards in front of them, and to the left of the main road. The impact was close to their compound. Kyle hit the gas even harder. The priority was to get to the compound and assess the situation.

They neared the turn off the main road to the gravel road. Over the left edge of the road, a plume of smoke lingered from the second rocket explosion. The impact was a near miss of the SF compound. It was close: another fifty yards and it would have hit their team house.

Ryan looked at Kyle and said, "That was pretty close; it would be fucking nice if the anti-rocket shit would work every once in a while."

Kyle nodded. “Yeah, they are coming in too low for the radar to pick it up, I guess.”

Kyle was calm but hyper-aware. Ryan was calm but pissed off. They were both composed as Kyle made the turn from the main road onto the gravel and compacted dirt. The smoke had almost completely cleared, but a thick haze of dust lingered. Any rocket impact you could actually see was too close. Kyle knew from experience that the dirt and dust meant they were near the impact area.

Kyle turned the corner and drove to the fork in the road where the guard post for the British soldier was set against the Hesco barriers. The SF compound gate was just across from it. The cloud of dust was thick. Something looked different as he turned to pull up in front of the gate. Dust raised from the blast and unmoving air obscured his vision just enough to make it difficult to see sharp details. He stopped. Kyle did not see the British soldier at his post, and he assumed the soldier who usually stood in the sandbag hut was lying in the sandbag bunker or had dived into the nearby duck-and-cover bunker.

Kyle looked at Ryan and said, “Something is off.” He paused and squinted, trying to see through the dust-filled air. “I think we are really close to the impact area.”

Ryan leaned forward and looked up through the windshield. “Yeah, you’re right…The dirt in the air is thick.”

Kyle rolled his window down and focused on the area toward the post where the British soldier usually stood. The recently arrived duck-and-cover bunker had been placed right next to the square sandbag post. Something was wrong. Kyle looked in the direction of the SF fence, then back to the sandbag post, and the duck-and-cover bunker.

He glanced at Ryan, then back to the Hesco barriers behind the guard post, and said, “Hey Ryan, that looks like fresh damage to those Hesco barriers near the hut…and on the duck-and-cover."

The concrete on the duck-and-cover bunker had ten gouges on the side, which were easier to see as the dust started to settle. The now pockmarked concrete had new cavities that were a different color. The sun had set, but there was still enough light to make out details.

Kyle left his window down and turned off the engine. He heard a faint hissing. The sound came from the area of the guard post. Kyle and Ryan opened their doors at the same time and got out of the SUV. They both walked toward the sandbag guard post. Kyle peered into the sandbag square and saw a cooler, empty water bottles, a first aid kit with a red cross, and a hand-held radio sitting at the edge of a makeshift bench.

Kyle heard the hissing sound again and looked toward the duck-and-cover bunker. It was darker inside and hard to see, but he saw something move.

Kyle called out toward the bunker, "Hey, is someone in there?"

There was no response. Kyle walked a little closer and tilted his body forward at the waist to better see inside. It was a typical Basra duck-and-cover: no concrete end caps. It was just a concrete upside-down U about twelve feet long, four feet high, and four feet wide.

"Ryan, I see movement in the duck-and-cover." Kyle took three more steps and was at the edge of the bunker. He kept his eyes forward and yelled, "Ryan, grab the med-kit out of the sandbag bunker…open it and dump everything right over here." Kyle pointed to the ground at the edge of the duck-and-cover bunker.

Kyle bent further at the waist, stooped a little more,

and went inside.

The British soldier was inside on the ground. After the first rocket impact, he dove into the duck-and-cover bunker. He thought he was safe. After all, he was in a concrete bunker that had a top. It had to be better than lying in the dirt pressed up against sandbags with nothing but a plastic roof overhead. A person in the bunker was safe from a blast on the left and right, as well as on top, but not front and back.

Kyle visually assessed the British soldier. He heard the hiss again. His eyes adjusted to the lower light, and he kneeled next to the soldier. The soldier was conscious and trying to control his breathing. The hissing sound was made as the soldier exhaled through pursed lips and gritted teeth.

Kyle looked at the British soldier who seemingly stared into space. "Hey, we're here…We're gonna get you help." Kyle started taking off the soldier's helmet.

The soldier looked up at Kyle and asked, "Yanks?"

Kyle nodded. "Yeah, Yanks. Let me see what we have going on here." Kyle's eyes adjusted to the lower light in the bunker. He could see that the soldier clutched his left thigh, and his hands were bloody.

Kyle heard Ryan dump the contents of the first aid kit at the edge of the bunker, and he called over his shoulder, "Ryan, throw me a few pressure bandages. There's a radio where you got the med-kit; see what you can do." Kyle changed his tone and said the next word a little louder for emphasis, "Medevac." Ryan quickly found three pressure bandages, tossed them next to Kyle, and went back for the radio.

"Good to see you, mate," said the soldier, whose voice had a strained gurgling sound. He squeezed his left thigh with both hands. He was struggling to control his breathing with the hissing exhale.

Kyle nodded. "Let me see what we have," he said, pulling at the soldier's fingers so he could check the wound, but his fingers kept slipping off the soldier's hands. Kyle's hands were drenched in blood. The soldier's leg was severed just above the knee. He had been holding his leg to stanch the bleeding.

Kyle grabbed the soldier's hands, placed them midthigh, and said, "Squeeze...Hold tight." Kyle took off his own belt and slid the end under the soldier's hands, so it looped completely around the soldier's thigh, then he threaded the end through the buckle. He quickly pulled the belt tight and held it in place with his left hand.

Kyle yelled over his shoulder to Ryan, "*Nine line*!" Then he reached down, picked up a pressure bandage with his right hand, and held the belt tight with the other.

The belt was slippery...the soldier twisted slightly, gritted his teeth harder, but stayed composed. The hissing was louder, and so was the gurgle that came with it. Kyle brought the end of the now blood-soaked packaging of the pressure bandage up to his mouth, bit and held the corner of the pressure bandage package with his teeth, and tore the plastic open with his free hand. He shook out the bandage and used the pressure bandage ties to secure the belt tightly.

Kyle used the term "*Nine Line*" to express extreme urgency without panicking the soldier. A Nine Line medevac order is performed when a severely wounded soldier is to be flown to a medical facility for treatment. Ryan understood what Kyle meant, and he knew it was bad.

Kyle heard Ryan talking on the radio. He was giving someone directions to their location. The bleeding pulsed just below the belt. The soldier twisted back and forth. Kyle held the belt tight, opened the new pressure bandage beside him, and tied it tighter over the belt. The bleeding continued but stopped pulsing.

"I gotta grab some stuff. Keep pressure here," Kyle said as he pushed the soldier's hand onto the soldier's femoral artery near his hip to try to slow the bleeding. Kyle saw another bleeding wound near the soldier's neck that would require pressure and clotting powder to stop the blood flowing. It was pulsing.

Kyle bumped his head and scraped his back on the bunker ceiling as he stepped toward the opening where he could see the first aid supplies. He knelt next to the edge of the bunker and picked out two packages of clotting powder. He looked up to see Ryan talking into the radio, and their eyes locked. For an instant, Kyle saw a look of horror flash through Ryan's eyes.

Ryan walked toward Kyle and said calmly into the radio, "We will get him as stable as we can here. If you're not here by then, we will transport." He slid the radio into his cargo pocket and came over to help Kyle.

Kyle said, "I don't think I have the bleeding stopped. Let's check before we try and move him. See if you can find any more clotting powder."

Ryan nodded, dropped to one knee, and sorted through the rest of the contents of the medical kit. Kyle stepped inside the bunker and knelt beside the British soldier. Ryan found more pressure bandages and two more packets of clotting powder. He crouched, took two large steps into the bunker, and knelt on the other side of the soldier. The soldier made the hissing sound again, but there was a strong gurgling overtone. He was still conscious, but his eyes looked sleepy.

The soldier looked at Ryan and back to Kyle. "Another Yank?" The pressure the soldier was putting on his own femoral artery weakened—it was useless. Kyle's belt tourniquet held, for now.

Kyle replied, "Yep, another Yank. We're going see what else we have here. We're going to open your vest."

Kyle reached for the Velcro tab on the side by the soldier's waist, and again his hand was soaked in blood. He remembered that the standard British vests zip and Velcro in the front, not like the SF vests with Velcro straps on the sides. Kyle unzipped the vest as Ryan eased it open as much as possible while keeping the soldier lying flat. The shrapnel and debris had blown through and ricocheted off the inside of the bunker. The vest was torn and shredded. The soldier hissed as he tried to keep air moving. He began to make an almost constant gurgling sound. Kyle and Ryan opened the front of the vest.

Kyle lifted what was left of the soldier's shirt and saw a wound that made the severed leg look like a scratch. The soldier had been eviscerated and was open with a two-inch gap from the left side of his hip to his right shoulder. He was alive on sheer willpower and youth. He was all of nineteen years old.

The soldier's breathing was a steady hiss now. He was barely conscious. Kyle and Ryan did their best to hold his chest and stomach together and to dump clotting powder on the neck wounds that pulsed blood. The soldier looked up to Kyle and Ryan, then back to Kyle.

Through sluggish fading eyes, in a barely audible whisper, the soldier said, "Hey, Yanks…I need to ring me mum."

His breathing was a steady gurgling hiss when he inhaled and exhaled. His eyes were shut, he lost consciousness, and blood ran from the corners of his mouth. Kyle and Ryan knew they had done what they could with what they had, and it was time to move him to a hospital.

Kyle looked at Ryan and said, "Let's get him in the back seat. You drive, and I will keep holding him together."

Ryan nodded. "OK, let's go."

As Kyle and Ryan were about to move the soldier, they heard a loud crush of gravel.

Just then, Mike slammed on the brakes of the black SF pickup truck, which slid to a stop near the sandbag hut at the edge of the bunker. Nathan was in the passenger seat, and they were doing their post-blast perimeter check. This always included a check of the British soldier who stood guard here. They knew something was wrong as soon as they got to the gate and saw the SF SUV with the doors open.

Mike and Nathan got out of the truck as the British ambulance turned the corner from the other direction. Kyle and Ryan had already decided to get the soldier out of the bunker—either to transport him themselves or to give the medics space to work. The soldier had stopped breathing—but they would keep trying.

Ryan heard the ambulance arriving, looked out of the bunker, and saw Mike and Nathan. "One bad casualty in here. Let's get him out so they can transport or work on him." Nathan and Mike nodded. Ryan said, "Kyle and I will get bottom, you guys get shoulders." Nathan and Mike moved forward and nodded to Ryan at the same time.

The British medic driving the ambulance slammed on the brakes, and his tires mashed into the gravel near the far end of the bunker. He knew there was a casualty, and that it was bad. There were two medics in the back of the truck-like ambulance, and another in the passenger seat. The two medics in the back were out with a wheeled gurney within seconds of the ambulance stopping. They dragged the gurney through the gravel toward the other end of the duck-and-cover bunker where they saw Nathan and Mike enter.

Nathan and Mike backed out of the bunker, stooped over, supported the soldier with the back of his vest, and held his arms across his chest. Ryan held the soldier's right leg and supported his lower back, while Kyle held the soldier at the upper thigh where his belt was tied.

The British medic who drove the ambulance ran to the side of the bunker and guided them to the wheeled gurney. The fourth medic began assessing and working on the mortally wounded soldier as they dragged the gurney through the gravel to the back of the ambulance.

The ambulance driver was about to get in the vehicle when he paused to look at the four SF operators, and asked, "Any other injured?"

He looked at the four from right to left. He glanced at Nathan and Mike, his scan slowed when he looked at Ryan, and then stopped completely at Kyle. His brow furrowed, and he rubbed his forehead with the middle of his right forearm for a second.

The British medic looked Kyle up and down again. "How 'bout you…you OK?"

Kyle nodded. "Yeah, I'm good." He raised his hands to waist level, shook his head slightly, gestured with his open palms toward the ambulance, and said, "We did what we could."

The medic nodded. "Thanks, I know…"

He ran to the ambulance, got behind the wheel, and drove down the gravel road, disappearing behind the wall of Hesco barriers.

Nathan and Mike were coated in blood from their shoulders to their hands.

Ryan was blood-soaked from midchest to his shins and all the way up his arms to his shoulders.

Kyle was saturated beyond imagination. The back of his shirt, his neck, and his head were drenched in blood. As Kyle had moved around inside the bunker, he had inadvertently brushed his back and shoulders against the blood-coated ceiling and walls. When the British soldier had been hit, blood and tissue had burst and sprayed from his artery until he had grabbed his leg to slow the bleeding. Blood spatter covered Kyle's face and neck from tying off the soldier's leg with the belt tourniquet. Kyle was spitting blood—he had used his teeth to open a blood-drenched package for a pressure bandage. Kyle was blood-soaked from the bottom of his boots to the top of his head. He had been sweating profusely, and the British soldier's blood mixed with Kyle's perspiration to give the front and back of his neck, as well as his face, an eerie pink hue.

If the British soldier standing his post had laid down in the sandbag square with the flimsy plastic roof, instead of diving into the protective concrete bunker, he would have been unscathed.

This was the randomness of a rocket attack…and death.

Hostage Status: 83 Days in Captivity (*continued*)

Without warning the hostages felt something hitting them on their backs and heads—taking their breath away: the unfamiliar feeling of water and being sprayed with a water hose. After about twenty seconds, the guard tired of holding the hose and threw it next to CR saying, "Use…Wash…"

He motioned toward the other hostages.

Surfboy was taken care of first. He was still unconscious. A half hour passed as they cleaned themselves, their clothes, and the bathroom bucket, while the bored guards smoked cigarettes and talked among themselves.

Unknown to any hostages, the guards had been directed to clean them up. The hostages were supposed to be kept alive and reasonably healthy.

A guard took the hose from CR and pointed it at Shorebilly, gesturing for both men to follow him; they walked to the cell. The guard dropped the running hose on the cell floor. "Clean." The stench was horrendous, but this was their chance to make life a little better.

"Let's get this dump cleaned up as much as possible," said Shorebilly, picking up the hose and starting to systematically spray from the corner to the door.

CR moved water and filth with his feet toward the door. The guard returned throwing a broom into the cell. "Clean."

They did not know if or when this would happen again—they were energized and cleaned as fast as they could.

CHAPTER 20

CLEANUP

DAY 83 (*CONTINUED*): JULY 7, 2007

Ashton saw several emergency vehicles and units from British Explosive Ordnance Disposal wind through the traffic, and almost push a small SUV over the edge of the embankment. Ashton, Annie, and John sat in the unmoving traffic for a few minutes. Whatever had happened was going to take awhile to clean up and document. Ashton made the decision to turn around and return to the parking lot at the NAAFI and get pizza at Echos. They would wait it out at the restaurant and eat since it was unlikely they would make it back to the chow hall near the SF compound any time soon.

RYAN, KYLE, NATHAN, AND MIKE LOOKED AT ONE another momentarily and decided they would leave their vehicles where they were. The wounded soldier's blood was everywhere. There was no need to saturate the inside of the trucks with blood as well. It was a decision made easier when the first British security forces arrived. One gun truck with four British soldiers parked across from the bunker. They got out of the truck, and the British soldiers slowly walked toward the four SF operators. They tried to process what they were seeing. One soldier looked at Kyle and asked if he needed an ambulance or first aid. The blood-drenched SF operators all shook their heads. Everyone stood and silently looked at one another for a moment.

Kyle looked at the British soldiers, pointed at the bunker, and said, "Everything happened there. I think the soldier moved from the sandbag post and entered the bunker on one side, and the impact was on the other."

The British soldiers stood motionless and looked from the blood-soaked men to where Kyle pointed, then back at the ghastly SF operators.

Finally, Ryan gestured with a slight wave to the SF compound gate and said, "We are going to our compound through that gate and clean up some. We will come back in an hour if you have more detailed questions or need anything else. We will leave the trucks where they are."

The British soldiers did not respond. They were still trying to process what had happened to these four stoic, dreadful, crimson creatures in front of them. The soldiers stood momentarily still as the SF operators walked toward the compound gate. Then they started to assess the area where Kyle had pointed a moment earlier. Two of the soldiers got to the edge of the bunker about the same time Nathan was securing the lock on the gate. Kyle, Ryan, and Mike watched the British soldiers through the fence.

The first soldier to the bunker uttered in a panicked voice, "Oh, fuck-sake." The second soldier bent over and retched near the side of the sandbag post.

It was just past dusk, but the dimming sky still threw enough light to see. The four macabre SF operators walked slowly and silently along the gravel and dirt road to the opening at the Hesco barriers and into their parking lot. The crunch of gravel under their boots was the only sound they made. Just before the entrance to the compound, the gravel gave way to compacted dirt, and the crunch of rocks quieted. Kyle's feet made a wet squishing sound, audible for only a few steps until he stepped back into gravel. Nobody blinked, but for all four men the sound gave new meaning to the phrase *blood-soaked*. Nothing needed to be said.

They turned the corner, stepped onto the plastic path, and walked to the volleyball court that had become a burn pit. Two team members came out of the team house, stepped down the stairs to the walkway, and saw the four blood-drenched men.

It was obvious something really bad had happened. One of the SF operators looked at Ryan and asked, "What do you need?"

Ryan calmly said, "Drag the water hose from the team house over to the edge of the burn pit and grab some plastic bags and towels."

The two team members nodded, and quickly brought the hose and turned on the water, while the four bloody SF operators sat on cinder blocks, taking off their clothes and boots. Ryan started with Nathan and Mike; they would clean up quickly and could then help with Kyle.

Everyone knew what to do without being told. Their ID pouches and pocket contents were set aside with their boots and hosed off first. All of their clothes were tossed in a heap on top of a partially burned wood pallet. Their clothes had to be burned. Trying to clean or wash them in a machine would be impossible. Kyle's boots were tossed on the pile, too.

Ryan looked at the two team members and said, "Find some gas and torch the burn pit, and the area where we were hosing off, too."

They nodded, and Ryan stood in wet boots and a towel for a moment. Everyone went to take a shower and put on clean clothes and shoes. They had to go back to the impact site, get the vehicles, and talk with the British soldiers for the post-blast report. The soldiers would have questions.

Hostage Status: 83 Days in Captivity (*continued*)

The hostages had carried Surfboy to the cell and gently set him on the floor. The man with the cloth on his face earlier in the day was already in the cell, with an open backpack. He was sitting in a chair.

Starting with Shorebilly, he gave each hostage an antibiotic shot. He poured peroxide on infected cuts, taking his time cleaning Shorebilly's forehead gash, and bandaged any open wound.

Before leaving he reached in his backpack and pulled out several pill bottles—antibiotics—the directions were in English. The doctor remained stoic when tossing the containers across the room to each hostage. He gave two peroxide bottles a quick glance while placing them in a corner.

The Iraqi doctor calmy picked up his backpack, looked around the room once, and in perfect English said, "Try not to die."

CHAPTER 21

NOKIA RINGTONES... QUIET RESPECT...HUMILITY

DAY 84: JULY 8, 2007

The next day, at 8:29 a.m., Annie tossed a small piece of gravel at John's trailer. John opened the door with one hand and held his new SF-provided Nokia cell phone in the other. He focused on the screen and tried to complete a text message he had worked on for the last fifteen minutes. The phone Ashton had given him had an Iraqi telephone number, which made things a little easier, but he was still very new at texting. The autocorrect feature changed his wording, and he already inadvertently sent the source a message that made no sense. He had not realized the error until he hit send. Adjusting the screen for sending a text took John ten minutes to figure out because he had accidentally changed the language from English to Arabic. He was finally back to the English setting.

"Hey, ready for breakfast? How's it going?" she asked.

John nodded and stepped onto the stoop. "Yep, I'm ready to eat. I'm starving," he said, still focused on the small phone screen. "How's it going, you ask? It's going a little fucked up...but still OK." He looked at Annie, smiled, and walked down the step. "I'm still playing catch-up on this phone crap," he mumbled, keeping his eyes on the keys of his phone as he followed Annie on the path to the chow hall. "How about you? How did your Baghdad call go?"

Annie looked straight ahead as she walked along the plastic footpath to the giant steel door. "What a clusterfuck. It wasn't just a Baghdad call. It turned into a conference call with Dildo-Ken from DC." She shook her head. "For some reason this jag-bag thought we were going to find hostages who have been missing for months immediately following this source meeting today. The guy has no concept of the real-fuckin'-world!"

Annie stepped up to the giant steel door and manipulated the cypher lock, then nudged the mass of metal open with her hip like she had been doing it her whole life. "I had to explain the concept is for long-term development and big-picture exploitation through The Fort."

She held the door for John, who pressed buttons on his new Nokia, then she said, "I didn't even try to explain that we were not working this hostage shit in a vacuum, and the British are in the game, too…Fuck, who knows how much we could all benefit from talking to each other?" Dust coated her recently brushed teeth; she turned to spit, then continued. "The guys in Baghdad left me flapping in the wind. Our hierarchy in Baghdad knew what this was about, and this fuck-stick Ken, who is dumber than a box of rocks, had not grasped the basics. Baghdad was silent on the call and left me to explain. That's why those fuckers want us, or at least me, back up there…They don't want to deal with DC."

"Yeah, well, we saw that part coming. This will get worse before it gets better."

His new Nokia rang for the first time—default ringtone. Almost everyone who spent a significant amount of time in Iraq can identify the Nokia ringtone.

John attempted to answer, but the call dropped. They were approaching the chow hall, and the British soldier checking IDs looked in their direction. John knew it was not a good idea to walk up to a guard post with a cellular telephone. He slid the phone into his cargo pocket. They showed their Brit-HQ IDs and went inside.

Annie walked directly to the serving counter, received a courteous head tilt from Sasha, who took Annie's plate and put a scoopful of eggs in the middle. Sasha already looked at John as she handed the plate back to Annie. Annie took her plate and moved left.

Sasha served John several helpings of potatoes and fresh cut fruit. Annie and John sat at the same table under the window, as usual.

Annie scooted her plate across the table as John did the same, and he slid half of his food to her plate. John tilted his head down slightly and looked up at Annie while he filled her plate. He smiled for a moment. She shook her head and pulled the clear wrap off her plastic utensils. John smiled with his eyes.

Annie took a bite then nodded her head toward the chow hall entrance as she saw Ashton come through the door.

He nodded back at Annie and John, went through the serving line, and received more than his fair share of smiles and food.

Ashton sat down next to John and asked, "Hey, how are things? Sleep OK?"

Ashton had fallen back to sleep after the 4 a.m. rocket attack but figured Annie and John might have trouble. He was right. They would not admit it though, and they commented on the comfort of their bed and nice air conditioning. The rocket attack had consisted of three impacts that rattled the camp but were not urgently close. Ashton figured they probably hit near the airport. Annie had stayed up and done her laundry at a trailer in the SF compound.

She took a sip of orange drink and asked, "What the hell happened yesterday? Things at the gate seemed sort of tense."

Ashton shoveled a quick forkful of eggs into his mouth, swallowed without chewing, and said, "One of those rockets that hit when we were at the NAAFI landed near the British soldier at the post near our gate." He took a bite of potatoes, chewed a couple of times, and swallowed. "Kyle and Ryan came off the main road right after the impact, found the soldier, and worked on him some."

Annie and John were just about finished. They listened and scraped the last bit of potatoes off their plates.

Annie peeled an orange and tossed the peel in the nearby trash can. "So, how's the British soldier who was hit at the post?"

Ashton, looked down at his plate as he finished chewing, then to Annie and John. "Dead. He bled-out while Ryan and Kyle were working on him."

Annie brought her napkin up to her mouth and subtly spit the chewed orange slice into the napkin, while John stopped the movement of his fork midway between his plate and mouth. He put the forkful of eggs back on the plate.

Breakfast was over.

Ashton, Annie, and John strode from the chow hall to Annie's trailer to discuss details regarding the source meeting. The pending pre-meet with Donovan at 11:00 a.m. was as important as the source meeting, maybe more. Ashton went over the anticipated movement at the gate and how to handle communications. He expected the gate activity to be busy and more chaotic.

IT WAS TIME TO MEET WITH DONOVAN AND DISCUSS THE source meeting. Ashton, Annie, and John moved from the SF compound to Brit-HQ without any problems. Kyle was waiting in the foyer near the kiosk. "How's everything? Are you ready for this chat with Donovan?"

Annie said, "Yes, we are good. I have some paperwork with numbers here for Donovan." She held up the folder and tapped it with the index finger of her other hand.

"Good, I'm sure he will appreciate that. How about this afternoon?" Kyle asked.

John nodded. "We are set for 2:00 p.m. We just confirmed again about a half hour ago."

"Great, it sounds like things are moving along." He looked past John briefly to Ashton, who flashed a quick thumbs-up.

They signed in at the SCIF desk and went inside. They passed through the first door of the SCIF and into the large open area and heard the usual level of conversation. All the desks to the right were occupied. The same no-patch US Army soldier from yesterday was sitting at the desk on the far right.

Kyle led the way through the room. As they turned the corner around the bank of tables the no-patch soldier saw Kyle, subtly stood, and looked toward Kyle. The no-patch soldier slowly and gently raised his right hand to the left-center of his chest, tapped slightly twice, kept his eyes on

Kyle, and tipped his head slightly forward. This was a sign of thanks and respect among many cultures, particularly in the Middle East. The movement of the no-patch American soldier was not missed by the British soldiers and civilians around the desks. Anyone sitting at the desks in this area had a particular affinity for situational awareness.

The loss of a British soldier last night was still uppermost in the minds of many. British HQ staff were briefed by the British Medical Corps regarding the response for the blast incident and the casualty. These circumstances were taken very seriously by the British military and Foreign Office out of profound respect for expeditious briefing of the decedent's family.

The British Medical Corps brought the ambulance driver to Brit-HQ to brief command leadership within an hour of the soldier being declared dead. The ambulance driver was the senior medical responder-on-scene. The senior medic described how they were automatically and immediately dispatched to the area of the first rocket, via the COB impact direction system. While there, he received word that there was an injury at the second rocket impact and exact directions had been provided by an American who identified himself as "*SF*," used the name "*Ryan*," and spoke with another American named "*Kyle*."

The British medic described what he saw when he arrived at the impact site. "The Americans in civilian clothes were drenched in the soldier's blood. One American had taken his belt off and used it as a tourniquet. The explosion appeared to have taken place at one end of the bunker and blown through the bunker where our soldier was tucked in."

The medic was asked his opinion of the American effort, and he said, "I saw the Americans and transported the wounded soldier from the scene through the emergency medical process. The Americans provided first aid and moved the soldier to the gurney. They used the clotting packages, pressure bandages, and all means available to save our soldier. They even used improvised means, such as the self-made tourniquet. I don't believe the Americans, or anyone for that matter, could have done more. The soldier was essentially dead when the rocket hit at the edge of the bunker. The Americans were absolutely the most bloody and horrific sight I have ever seen...yet, they appeared unfazed."

Questioned further, the medic said, "Once in the ambulance, all attempts to resuscitate the soldier were unsuccessful. It is my opinion that the soldier's injuries were catastrophic and that he was mortally wounded on the scene."

The no-patch American soldier and others around the desk area were present at the briefing the evening before. As Kyle led the way through the SCIF open area to the SCIF conference room, the conversation around the desks quickly diminished until there was complete silence. The British soldiers and civilians stood up from their chairs deftly as Kyle passed. He nodded his head once and slowly brought his right hand to about chest level. It was not so much a wave, but a hand gesture of acknowledgment and thanks. He looked across the faces, continued past the silent standing group, and walked into the SCIF conference room.

Annie and John saw the deference given to Kyle but still did not know the details. They surmised something terrible had happened, and Kyle's response was clearly held in extraordinary regard. Donovan waited inside the SCIF meeting room and leaned on the edge of the conference table as Kyle walked through the door with Ashton,

Annie, and John following. Everyone exchanged subdued greetings. Earlier that morning Jensen gave Donovan an overview of the events surrounding the death of the British soldier the prior evening. He even provided a copy of the summary of the command briefing along with a transcript with the exact wording of the British medic. Donovan had an eerie feeling as he read the briefing because he knew exactly where he was when the rocket hit. He had just met with Mr. Ethan and sealed his own fate to stay in one of the most rocketed places in Iraq.

Donovan looked around the room as they came in and said, "Late night, huh?"

Everyone nodded. The events early in the evening shook some, and the 4:00 a.m. rocket attack shook others.

Annie placed a folder on the table, opened it, and said, "So here are some of the numbers that we have worked with over the past few weeks that might be new to The Fort. We were interested in getting your take on the best way to move forward with how to handle the exploitation." Annie turned the folder 180 degrees so Donovan could see the numbers and the associated narrative.

Donovan asked, "Are you still on for meeting your source this afternoon?"

John nodded. "Yes, I've been in touch with him this morning to confirm…so far, so good. I think we are good with the other moving parts." He looked to Ashton and Kyle, who both nodded.

Donovan spoke for the next twenty minutes and gave an overview of how he exploited numbers and patterns regarding hostage-related SIGINT over the last week. Annie and John nodded politely but did not really understand a great deal of what he said. Ashton generally understood, and Kyle comprehended everything Donovan said, including the somewhat obscure acronyms used only in the SIGINT world.

Donovan leaned back in his chair, looked at the ceiling momentarily, then leaned forward again, and glanced at the folder. "OK, that's enough for me to get going," he said. "What's the phone number you are using to contact your source?"

John reached into his cargo pocket and pulled out a small notebook. "It's a new phone. Ashton hooked us up with it." He flipped through the pages, found the phone number, and gave it to Donovan.

John looked up from his notebook. "Do you need the source's number?"

Donovan shrugged. "No, not really. Does your source have more than one phone?"

"No, not that I know of," John replied.

Donovan nodded, looked around the room, and said, "OK, sounds good. Do you want to meet later this evening so we can go over the source meeting…That will give me time to work things, and we can start to compare SIGINT and HUMINT notes?" He looked around the room. "Would 7:00 p.m. here work?"

Everyone nodded. The group stood to leave.

Ashton, Annie, and John were already out the meeting room door when Kyle halted and turned. "Hey, Donovan, regarding that thing we talked about… I've nudged things a little from our side," he said, referring to finessing relationships to keep Donovan in Basra. "Let me know if you're hearing anything."

Donovan nodded. "Thanks, will do…I've nudged a little bit from my direction, too. I will let you know what I hear, if anything."

Kyle raised his hand with a subtle thumbs-up. "OK, see you this evening…unless things go to shit again," he added with a quick, faint smile.

Donovan nodded and said, "Yeah, well, stay safe."

Kyle walked out of the conference room, and the busy outer office quieted as he passed, and people acknowledged him with head nods. Getting back to normal quickly was often the way some tragedy and grief were handled. Ashton led the way back to the coffee kiosk, where they decided to have a cup of coffee and discuss the process for that afternoon's source meeting. Ashton and Kyle confirmed the movement timing, and Kyle left for another meeting somewhere at Brit-HQ.

Ashton, Annie, and John had pizza at Echos. The conversation centered on the source meeting and how they might be able to direct the source activity. Today was all business.

Hostage Status: 84 Days in Captivity

The light in the vent was growing brighter. The cell was hot, the air stale—but not like it had been yesterday. Surfboy was still unconscious but breathing better.

Shorebilly dabbed peroxide on a cut. "I thought we were dead last night. I really thought I died...you know...eaten my last Maryland blue crab!" He kept his voice low.

CR looked at a pill bottle and said, "Yep, me too."

Tex grinned, holding a cotton swab he found on the floor. "What the fuck was that? I thought I was shot and zooming to the bright light of the pearly gates or some shit."

CR nodded and said, "The British shoot those illumination rounds sometimes after they've been rocketed."

The three hostages laid flat, quietly waiting for food.

"Hey fuckers...wake up, you lazy bastards...what happened...I gotta pee." Surfboy was finally conscious.

"I had the weirdest dream, bro. I dreamed I died and was dragged through a car wash toward a bright light...like I ate a rotten fish taco and rode a really bad wave...Weird bro."

CHAPTER 22

CREATION OF CRICKET... BLENDING AGENDAS

DAY 84 (*CONTINUED*): JULY 8, 2007

Ashton, Annie, and John stood near the main gate in the searing heat, soaking in sweat. The meeting with the source was set for 2:00 p.m.; it was now 2:45, and there was no sign of him. John had instructed the source to park his car along the road outside the gate and enter the COB gate on foot. The source described what he would be wearing, so he could be seen in a crowd. Ashton, Annie, and John were thankful for the shade of the camouflage netting.

The parking lot did not look like yesterday's vacant moonscape. The area was now a convoluted collection of humanity and cars. People came and went, others stood in the baking sun and waited for a base escort. Still others seemingly milled around doing nothing. There were at least thirty cars in the lot and sixty Iraqis. Fifteen Iraqis stood in the scorching sun at the edge of the outer perimeter gate, where two British soldiers checked the Iraqi national identification gensiya and conducted a pat-down search of each person before they walked into the lot.

John walked from the shade of the netting within the footpath and the relative safety of the Hesco barriers. He nodded to the guards as he passed the guard tower, moved to the edge of the chain link fence perimeter and looked over the boundary. The makeshift parking lot below was full of cars that came in as fast as they left, and the road that led to the gate was busy with cars coming and going. It was controlled chaos.

John still saw no sign of his source. He walked back to the shade at the edge of the Hesco barrier where Annie and Ashton stood and checked his phone. There were no bars for reception on the cell phone screen. Cell phones did not work at the gate.

John looked at Ashton and said, "Well, what do you think?"

Ashton adjusted his sunglasses, took a sip of water, leaned against the barrier, and said, "Let's give it a little time."

Ashton did not appear stressed at all. Annie was anxious but kept quiet, just gently grinding the toe of her boot into the gravel.

Ashton said, "How about you go jump in the SUV and drive down the street to where the phone will work. Annie and I will stay here in case he shows up." Ashton tossed John the keys to the SUV.

John nodded. "OK, sounds good. Thanks. I will be back in about twenty minutes." He disappeared around the Hesco barriers.

Ashton adjusted the position of his hat, crossed his arms, looked perfectly relaxed, and said, "Don't worry, this is normal…It's about how these things go, especially the first couple of times."

Annie looked at Ashton as she lightly prodded gravel with the toe of her boot, and said, "It's never easy, is it?"

Ashton wiped the sweat from his chin with the back of his hand, shook his head once, looked at Annie, and simply said, "No."

ANNIE LOOKED AT HER WATCH, THEN OVER TO ASHTON. She scanned the parking lot and glanced again at her watch. John had been gone about forty-five minutes. Ashton and Annie constantly watched the lot and the makeshift gate at the edge of the outer perimeter. The British soldiers appeared undaunted as they checked each vehicle arriving to the pole at the gate. One soldier raised the pole while two others checked IDs of the occupants. The soldiers in the tower kept a sharp eye on their fellow soldiers at the gate and constantly scanned the area just beyond the perimeter fence line.

Annie's attention was focused on the gate, and she had not heard John come up from behind.

He wiped the sweat from his face with the shoulder of his shirt and said, "He should be walking though there in about another twenty minutes or so."

Annie's shoulders tensed momentarily. She had not expected his voice. She felt the stress of the day and the dread of the potential conversation she would have to endure with Baghdad and DC, if the source never arrived.

She was relieved to see John and said, "Good, what the fuck…where was he…and don't sneak up on me like that, fucker." She said the last few words with a smile and lightly backhanded the side of his shoulder.

John glanced at this watch and said, "I was able to talk to him for about thirty seconds before the call dropped, then we had to send messages." He reached into his cargo pocket and pulled out his cell phone. As he expected, there were no bars, no signal. “The short story is this. He drove up the road to the parking area outside the gate…tried to call when he couldn’t find parking…phone didn’t work…he left to get another battery at home…came back and didn’t like the people below the gate…left…and now he’s coming back.”

Annie and Ashton were facing John with their backs toward the parking lot while they listened to the summary of why the source was late. John was just about finished with the broad details and looking at the perimeter gate when he paused, nodded his head once, and said, “Oh shit, there he is…Right there—third in line at the gate.”

Ashton and Annie slowly turned around, and both let out a barely audible chuckle. The source was easy to pick out of a crowd. He was the same height and build as those next to him in line, but he wore a hat. And not just any hat: he wore a cricket helmet.

Ashton looked at the source who was now second in line to be searched by the British soldiers, then back to John. “He is wearing a cricket helmet. Tell me again why this fucking guy is wearing a cricket helmet?”

John had thought the source would be wearing a cricket *hat*. He figured there was something missed in translation and assumed the source would wear a cricket ball cap. The source actually wore a cricket batters’ helmet with the face mask removed.

John said, “I thought this nimrod was going to wear a hat with a cricket insignia or something, not a real helmet. Anyway, he mentioned the British soldiers liked him better when he wore it.”

The source was now at the front of the line, and it was his turn to have his ID checked and clothes searched. The

British soldier who stood in front of the source with his hands on his hips called another soldier over. They gave the source a very brief pat-down, and the soldiers stepped back and put their hands on their hips and called a third soldier over. The three soldiers looked at the source's ID very briefly and returned it to the source. The source looked at the three soldiers, grinned, and looked down toward his own feet.

John said, "Uh, son of a bitch, he was right."

John watched the three soldiers each give a light three-tap knock on the source's cricket helmet and smile.

Ashton nodded and said, "Yep, it looks like the Brits like that fuckin' hat, or helmet, whatever the hell it is. Let's move and get him through here."

Separating the source from other Iraqis had to be finessed and coordinated with the British soldiers in the area and done without garnering the attention of other Iraqis. The source grinned at the British soldiers, who smiled and waved as they let him pass. Ashton walked toward the trailers in the expected path of the source. The source saw Ashton, who nodded and subtly pointed to John, who stood near the guard tower. The source slowly adjusted his direction toward John. When the source was about thirty feet from the tower, John motioned with his head for the source to follow, and John walked toward the Hesco barriers where Annie waited. John walked several paces in front of the source, while Ashton followed him. One of the soldiers in the tower kept a close eye on the process, while the other watched the lot and perimeter for any indication that the source movement might have been noticed. Everything went well. Hasty introductions were done while they walked through the zigzag Hesco barriers to the SUV.

Once they were in the SUV, John said, "We will go to a trailer inside another secure area to talk. It's more comfortable, and we can take our time."

The source nodded, removed his cricket helmet, wiped his face with his forearm, put his cricket helmet back on, and said, "OK, sounds good."

As Ashton drove, moving through the Hesco barriers near the weapons range, Annie turned to the source and broke the quiet. "Thanks for coming in. I really like your hat."

A broad smile came across the face of the source, and with strongly accented English, he said, "Thank you. It's my cricket hat. It brings me good luck," and he tapped it lightly with his knuckles. He took the helmet off and held it in both hands gingerly. "It brings me good luck especially when around the British." He was beaming and nodded his head once slowly. He said to Annie, "It is yours. My gift to you."

Ashton had cringed slightly as soon as he heard Annie's compliment of the source's hat. He knew what was coming regarding custom and cultural issues. Annie was not used to dealing with Iraqis and some of the cultural considerations, particularly when it came to the compliment of the possession of another. In Iraqi culture if one receives a compliment on an item such as a watch, pen, or glasses, it would be practiced etiquette to offer the item as a gift to the person providing the compliment.

Annie was taken aback, she was not sure how to respond, but thanked him profusely, and said, "It is better that you keep it so we can see you easily."

The source held the cricket helmet in front of him, a mildly disappointed look on his face. John recognized the potential for the source to be offended with the perception that his gift was not considered worthy.

John looked to the source and said, "In fact, it would be important and help us greatly if you did keep the hat. That would help with the gate, the British, and *your code name*."

The source nodded, and his eyebrows raised. He liked the idea. He said, "Code name? Why code name?"

Ashton watched the road but was just as focused on the conversation, wondering what John might say next.

Annie smiled, looked at John, and said, "Yes, John will explain the *code name*." She had no idea what was going to fly out of John's mouth next.

John looked at the source and said, "We want to keep you confidential, protected, safe, and a secret, so we will have a *code name* for you."

The source liked what he heard, particularly being kept safe. John paused, squared his shoulders to the source, and gestured to his helmet with both palms open.

John looked the source right in the eye and said, "It would be best if you hold onto the helmet for now, because your new code name is…*Cricket*."

Annie smiled and bit her lower lip. Ashton nodded, grinned, and watched in the mirror as Cricket raised his cricket helmet and with slow reverence placed it on his head. He took a moment to adjust it slightly with both hands on the brim.

Once in place, he looked at John, held out his right hand, gave John a strong handshake, and said, "Very well, I am Cricket."

Cricket glowed. He now had his own code name, he could keep his hat, and all cultural sensitivities were intact. Everyone saved face.

Ashton was impressed at how quickly John had handled a potentially prickly situation, and Annie was pleased the potential for offending Cricket had been mitigated. She also recognized that Cricket's connection with John was important for building trust. John's real-world source handling was finally being utilized.

Source code names were somewhat common. They were not truly secret code names; they were nicknames that made the source easily identifiable in open conversation and simply made handling multiple sources less confusing. Nicknaming a source also allowed people to discuss the source without using his or her real name. The nickname for a source usually had something to do with an easily recognized physical attribute or eccentricity associated with the source—such as Smelly, Shorty, One-eye, Scarface, Buzz-cut. The source usually did not know his or her nickname because sometimes less than flattering characteristics were what resulted in the name. Naming Cricket was easy. It not only worked for Ashton, Annie, and John, but it also worked for Cricket.

Ashton parked in front of a trailer surrounded by Hesco barriers. Everyone moved from the SUV to the trailer; the air conditioner was blasting.

At one end of the trailer was a conference table with six comfortable armchairs. Next to the table sat a couch and three comfortable recliners. Two small refrigerators next to the table were stocked with water and soft drinks. At the opposite end of the trailer was a bathroom, complete with a shower. All the windows had blue nondescript drapes, and four three-by-five-foot whiteboards hung on walls around the room where they could easily be seen from the couches or conference table. Each board had its own set of multicolored markers and erasers.

Ashton made sure everyone was inside, closed the door, and gave a brief tour. The presentation was for the benefit of Annie and John, as much as Cricket. The quick walk-through ended near the small refrigerator, and Ashton opened the door to show what was available. Cricket took off his hat and placed it reverently on the conference table.

Everyone picked their preferred beverage. Cricket chose a can of Coke and a can of Fresca. Once each person had drinks in hand, Ashton passed control of the meeting to Annie and John with a simple nod.

Ashton gestured toward the conference table, then to the couch area, and said, "Wherever you'd like to sit. We have the place for the next two hours, if we need that much time."

John said, "Great place, I think I would be comfortable in either area." He looked to Cricket and said, "And for you, our guest?"

John was careful with words. He used short phrases, plain language, and no slang. He was still assessing Cricket's level of English comprehension. Cricket was quick to gesture toward the couch area with a head nod, an open hand, and raised eyebrows. "This is good," he said.

It was as much a question as a compliment to the room.

Courtesy was the rule of the day.

Cricket's English was exceptionally good. John took a sip of his Fresca and said, "Your English is excellent. Why is it so good?"

Cricket was absolutely elated, and a broad smile flashed across his face. Being complimented on his English by an American was something he held in high regard. Cricket explained that he had spent several years in Toronto, Canada, and had worked for a relative who managed maintenance contracts for several apartment buildings. He was immersed in the predominant language spoken in Toronto, which was English.

Cricket took a sip from his Fresca and said, "My work visa expired... I missed my family here in Basra...so I came back."

Ashton and John listened intently. Out of the corner of his eye, John could see Annie drumming her fingers on her thigh. She was not good at small talk and did not like it, but she knew to let John run with this part of the process.

John crossed his legs, ankle to ankle, careful to keep the soles of his feet parallel to the floor, and asked, "Then what happened?" John paced Cricket up to the discussion of hostage issues and built rapport at the same time.

Cricket smiled, took a sip of his Fresca, and said, "I worked in the Basra oil fields for a British company...as a laborer at first, until they found out my English. Then they gave me a raise and a different shirt with my name on it, and I became a translator."

Annie took a few notes for the report she would have to do later. It gave her something to do with her fidgety hands, and Cricket could have cared less—he talked to the men anyway. Annie knew to just let things flow. She noticed the way John was sitting; it seemed unusual. John usually crossed his legs to try and stretch his back.

Cricket slowed his tempo, and his voice lowered. "In 2003 the war came, and everyone was killing each other. Then the insurgents came. I like the Americans and British. I don't hurt anyone...everything is good...but when militia came to my house, they already controlled both ends of the street where I live. I have no choice but to do what they say."

John nodded and said, "You have to take care of your family." John validated the course of dialogue to keep Cricket speaking freely.

Cricket briefly squeezed the bridge of his nose with his thumb and forefinger. "So, I have no job because the oil field is too dangerous to work for British…The Americans, British, and the rest of the coalition shut down all major traffic unless controlled by the coalition. Electricity is not working… Everything like stores and refrigeration runs with generators."

Ashton did not say anything. He had heard the evolution of events from numerous Iraqi sources. In many respects, as Iraq devolved, the emergence of an insurgency or militia was inevitable. The success of the militia depended on the health and welfare of its population. As the centralized government degraded, lost legitimacy and relevance, the ensuing chaos was counterbalanced by regional control that nurtured the growth of an insurgency. Taking care of the poor and disenfranchised produced popular support. For those citizens who did not accept the legitimacy and righteousness of the insurgency, the lethality kept them in check.

Cricket drank the last of his Fresca and put the can on the coffee table. "So, because I stayed in my neighborhood, and know who to talk with to make the generators work, and my English, I am valuable to the coalition *and* militia."

Nobody said a word for a moment, and Ashton asked, "Do you know people who make bombs that blow up on the road?"

Cricket tilted his head and asked, "You mean the improvised explosive devices? The IEDs?" Cricket also prided himself on knowing the latest military acronyms and used them when he could.

Ashton stayed stoic and said, "Correct, the IEDs. Do you know anyone doing that?"

Cricket was more assured and leaned forward. "No, I do not…but I do know people that know them."

"OK, thanks, I'm sure we will talk more about that." Ashton simply needed Cricket to say something about IEDs.

Cricket's comment on the subject helped legitimize interest, and particularly SF funding and working with Cricket. It would make the money flow easier. And that was important, because clearly the FBI was not prepared to handle the logistics or the expense of working sources.

Over the next hour the conversation centered on who Cricket thought was involved in the American and British kidnap events, what neighborhoods used the most fuel, and tasking Cricket to take photos. Cricket was extremely willing to assist and believed he knew others in Basra that he could recruit. Cricket said he was very comfortable approaching people he considered militia and thought they might be the best assets. The meeting ended, Cricket put on his cricket helmet, and everyone walked out of the trailer into the blistering heat for the ride back to the gate.

John handed Cricket a bottle of water. "Send me a message when you get through the gate, so I know you got out of car park OK."

Cricket nodded. "OK, I will send right away after I get to the main road."

John asked Cricket for the message so he could evaluate his responsiveness to directions and follow-through. Ashton drove to the edge of the Hesco barriers by the main gate and dropped off Cricket. He walked nonchalantly through the lot and out of the gate.

On the way to meet Donovan at British Headquarters, they stopped at the NAAFI and picked up prepackaged sandwiches. They sat in the SUV and ate in the parking lot. John's cell phone gave a beep. A new text message had arrived. Cricket had made it onto the main road. He clearly embraced his code name, signing the text message "Sincerely, Cricket." John let Ashton and Annie know, and both nodded and mumbled something positive while devouring their sandwiches with the SUV running. Annie peeled an orange that came with the lunch and tossed the peel into the lunch box on the floor—she quickly ate the orange as they arrived at Brit-HQ for the meeting with Donovan.

Hostage Status: 84 Days in Captivity (*continued*)

Surfboy was awake and talkative. "How much longer before the mean guards are back?"

Collectively they said, "Tomorrow."

"Too bad—today has been good."

Along with the meager daily food rations, the guards included two oranges. The hostages split the oranges four ways, devouring and savoring them at the same time.

"Look at all this food." Surfboy was elated.

Everyone nodded while eating the last of the orange peels.

CHAPTER 23

CONNECTING HUMINT AND SIGINT... DC ARROGANCE...ANNIE TO BRIT AIR

DAY 84 (*CONTINUED*): JULY 8, 2007

Ashton, Annie, and John arrived at Brit-HQ at 6:55 p.m. for the 7:00 p.m. meeting with Donovan. The day was long for everyone, and it was not quite over yet. Annie still needed to call her supervisor after this meeting and pack to return to Baghdad. They moved quickly through Brit-HQ security, signed into the SCIF logbook, and entered the large SCIF area. A no-patch American soldier at the far-right desk glanced up from his screen to Ashton, Annie, and John. He knew they were Americans but did not know them—they were ignored.

Ashton entered the conference room first and saw Donovan at the far edge of the table watching a neatly folded triangular piece of paper spin. Donovan stood as they entered, stepped forward with a comfortable smile, and shook hands.

Ashton said, "Hey, I hope we aren't late. Timing on some of this is a bitch."

Donovan shook his head, grinned, and said, "No problem, I know how things work, and it's never easy in Basra."

Donovan gestured toward chairs for everyone to sit. He

picked up the small triangular piece of paper between his thumb and forefinger, took a seat, and leaned back in his chair. Everyone took a collective breath and sat for a moment.

Donovan smiled and said, "In fact, you're not late at all, you're right on time. Hell, if you got here an hour from now, that'd still count as on time given the nature of source meetings…and Basra."

Donovan's relaxed demeanor took the hurried edge off everyone. Donovan watched as Ashton wiped the sweat from his forehead, John tied his boot, and Annie dug into her cargo pocket to pull out the notes she had taken during the source meeting. Donovan had been working his magic for the past eight hours.

Donovan sat forward in his chair, folded his hands, and asked, "So, how was the meeting with our new best friend, Cricket?"

Everyone stopped moving. Donovan was the right guy from The Fort to find hostages.

ANNIE FINISHED UNFOLDING THE MEETING NOTES SHE had pulled from her cargo pocket. During the meeting with Cricket, she had placed a D with a circle around it next to a couple notes. She did not want to leave anything important out of her overview. She summarized Cricket's biography, including his language ability and years in Canada.

Annie thumbed through her papers and said, "Fortunately, his English is excellent, so we won't have to go through a translator to communicate."

Direct communication would be far less time-consuming. Donovan listened attentively as she continued with a chronological list of objective details.

After the summary, Annie sat back in the chair.

"Why Cricket?" Donovan asked, cocking his head slightly and leaning forward. "How did he get the name?"

Annie was surprised; she had expected that if Donovan knew the name Cricket, he would know its origin. This was a perfect example of how and why blending signal intelligence (SIGINT) and human intelligence (HUMINT) was so critically necessary. Far too often, people placed an uninformed and misadvised reliance on one over the other.

People like Donovan who worked in the world of signal intelligence were often called SIGINTers. Signal Intelligence told Donovan part of the story, while HUMINT gave Ashton, Annie, and John other insights. Merging the two disciplines developed the big picture. Decision-making was better because it was more informed. SIGINT and HUMINT complemented each other. Unfortunately, intergovernmental relationships were not readily encouraged when it came to hostage events. When it came to career development, it was safer to do nothing. Pushing through the managed apathy of an organization was a tiresome and often unrewarded pursuit.

Annie looked at John briefly and started laughing before telling the story. Everyone immediately smiled, the mood was lighter and more relaxed, and Annie was animated. Her hands moved by her head like she was putting on and taking off a hat.

Annie smiled, her enthusiasm telling the story was evident, and she sat straighter in her chair, and said, "We were looking for someone wearing a hat…so, this guy finally shows up at the gate." She paused momentarily and said, "He's the only Iraqi wearing anything on his head, and it's a fuckin' cricket helmet."

Everyone laughed. Donovan sat back in his chair, shook his head, tossed the little paper triangle into the air, and caught it with two hands. Annie was excited and grew more animated. She brought both hands up to her head and gestured as though she was gently grasping the bill of a cap and smoothing the brim.

"So, then we had this really awkward conversation on the ride from the gate to the trailer. He wanted to give me this hat, or helmet thing, as a gift." She brought her hands up to her face, laughed, and shook her head. "Believe it or not, *I* was at a loss for words."

Annie's joke at her own expense was well received, and everyone laughed.

"So, John, thankfully, stepped in to bail me out of this strange corner I'd painted myself into. He came up with this absurd code name concept and pulled this line of bullshit straight out of his ass that was so good even I started to believe it."

Annie shook her head as laughter continued to fill the room. She laughed so hard her eyes teared.

She wiped her eyes with the back of her hand and said, "And it worked…The guy got to keep his hat, and John created *Cricket*!"

After a moment everyone composed themselves, and the room quieted.

Donovan, still smiling, said, "Well, it sounds like progress. Anything else?"

Annie looked to Ashton. "What else? What did I miss? Tag…you guys are in."

Ashton shook his head. "Nah, I think you've covered it."

John leaned back in his chair and looked up at the ceiling, going over the earlier conversation with Cricket in his head. He scratched his neck and crossed his leg, ankle over knee.

Annie tagged herself back into the conversation, pointed at John's foot, and said, "Hey that's what was different. I knew there was something different at the meeting. You were sitting weird." She moved her index finger in a circle, pointing at his foot and knee.

John furrowed his brow, looked puzzled for a moment, and looked at his boot, then the tread of his boot.

He realized what she was talking about, nodded, and said, "Sitting with my foot like this and showing the sole of my boot would have been a cultural faux pas. It would have appeared I was showing him disrespect personally or projecting it culturally."

Everyone nodded and listened. Ashton was thoughtful and aware but realized he still occasionally missed some subtleties in the culture. Donovan and Annie had been briefed on cultural differences before coming to Iraq, but never had the real-world experience.

John added just one thought to Annie's overview. "Based on how Cricket answered a few questions, and how the militia and insurgency blend into the mainstream population, it makes for a very broad gray area to work with. Cricket is probably playing both sides, and that's the kind of guy we need."

Annie nodded, shrugged her shoulders as she held her palms up, and said, "Well, the cultural foot thing…the bullshit code-name thing…the straddling-the-fence thing… and how that game is played—that is why you're leading the dance with the sources."

John grinned. "And the hierarchy in Baghdad…and the DC-Ken thing…and how you juggle the managers… is why we can all keep moving forward." He gestured around the room and held his hand up. Annie shook her head and nonchalantly backhanded John's palm.

Everyone laughed again, and Donovan said, "OK, how about we meet tomorrow midmorning to see where this might go with your other sources and what I can drill into on my side?"

Donovan and Ashton pushed back slowly from the table as John helped Annie collect her papers.

The group stood, and John asked, "Would 11 a.m. work again?"

Ashton and Donovan nodded. Annie would be in Baghdad by then.

Donovan walked with everyone to the edge of the SCIF conference room and leaned against the door frame as he watched the others walk through the large SCIF area and depart. He stared into space for a moment, then shifted his weight to one side as he leaned against the other side of the door frame and scratched his eyebrow with the corner of the folded triangle paper. He wondered what was next, how long it would take to find out if Mr. Ethan had the influence to keep him in Basra, and he hoped they might nudge something forward in a hostage case sooner rather than later.

He walked across the conference room, sat in the chair, faced the makeshift pencil-and-string field goal on the ceiling, and leaned back. The chair creaked and shifted slightly under his weight. Donovan looked at the goal, gave careful aim along with a concerted flick of the right middle finger off his thumb to the long edge of the triangle. The triangle flew, tapped the ceiling, went through the goal, bounced off the wall, and landed on the floor. He scored a goal on the first try. He hoped it was a positive omen. It was time to get back to work.

On the way back to the SF compound, Ashton, Annie, and John rehashed the meetings with Cricket and Donovan. Though fatigued, everyone had a renewed sense of optimism, and the atmosphere was light. It was all part of the roller-coaster ride endured by anyone who has ever truly been immersed in a real-world hostage event.

Ashton turned off the main road onto the gravel toward the SF compound and drove through several puddles of water. Everyone in the SUV quieted when they heard the first splash of water. It was a sound not expected. They turned the corner to the SF gate, drove through more puddles and saw a new duck-and-cover bunker in place of the old bunker. It had a bright gold two-foot horizontal stripe painted on the side, and two bright gold four-by-four-foot concrete end caps. Ashton focused for a moment on the new duck-and-cover bunker and its brightly painted end caps as he turned toward the SF compound gate.

Just audibly, Ashton uttered, "Finally…end caps…too fuckin' little…too fuckin' late."

Puddles were everywhere. It took three tanker trucks to thoroughly wash the blood spatter from the blast walls, Hesco barriers, sandbag square, and gravel. The ground was too compacted to absorb water, so it would sit until it evaporated.

A British soldier leaned against the edge of the sandbag square and waved his hand once and nodded as they drove by. All the British soldiers who stood—or had the potential to stand—that post knew of the Green Berets' efforts to save the mortally wounded British soldier.

Ashton, Annie, and John waved to the British soldier standing in the square sandbag post. They went directly to the team house for flight information. Annie needed to be at the British Air Terminal for the flight to Baghdad. It was different every day. The "show time" for check-in was usually hours before the actual flight. Passengers had to be there for what was referred to as "show" or "show time" to get on the passenger manifest for the flight. Annie had to be at the terminal at 11 p.m. for a flight that departed at some unknown time thereafter. The British only flew in or out of Basra under cover of darkness. It was going to be a long night for Annie.

Ashton and John agreed to meet for breakfast at 8:30. Annie and John walked to their trailers, so Annie could make another dreaded call to Baghdad. She hoped it would not be a conference call with DC. She was afraid she might try to actually choke the idiot Ken through the phone.

Once they were back at their trailers, Annie prepared for the call. She took out her notes from the Cricket interview and summarized the meeting with Donovan in her head. She knew she could not go into detail regarding Donovan's concepts until she was in Baghdad unless she utilized secure communication systems.

Annie assumed her pacing posture while John sat on her stoop. He knew he was not going to add anything to the call, but his moral support and presence had a particular relevance. It took eight attempts and ten minutes for Annie to get a voice connection with her cell phone. The duty agent at the BOC found the HWG supervisor, who came to the command center and immediately put the call on speaker. The supervisor sent the duty agent to track down the on-scene commander and the deputy on-scene commander.

Annie put the phone behind her back and whispered to John, "It's a full-court press with the FBI BOC hierarchy." John nodded, while Annie shook her head and whispered, "Clusterfuck…"

John slid off the stoop, picked up a handful of gravel, and leaned against the edge of the stoop to stretch his back.

Annie paced and talked, then stopped, pulled the phone in front of her face, then back to her ear, and said, "Standing by…"

Annie walked toward John quickly, held the phone behind her back, and whispered, "Yeah, they are connecting a conference call with Dildo-Ken in DC. Apparently, he has questions and wants in on the conversation."

John looked at Annie and shook his head. Annie put the phone back to her ear and walked to where she was in front of the stoop next to John. She took the phone from her ear, held it at chest level, and put it on speaker, so John could hear the other side of the call. There was momentary silence.

Finally, a voice said, "This is Ken. How's everything in Iraq."

Over the speaker they heard a peculiar yet familiar rhythmic sound: beep…beep…beep. It was the timer on the microwave at Ken's house in northern Virginia. He could technically start his day with the phone call, and then go home early. Ken sat in shorts and a T-shirt, drinking a cup of coffee that he audibly slurped during the call.

Annie and everyone from the FBI BOC responded curtly to Ken's question, "Fine."

Ken asked, "So, how was the source meeting? Do we have the location of the hostages?"

Everyone listening at the BOC shook their heads. They were incredulous. She looked at John, tilted her head slightly, and squinted. She was not sure if that was really a serious question. She thought maybe it was a joke.

Annie held the phone in front of her mouth. "Well, not quite, but we hope to have the source lean into some things and connect with interested parties."

"Well, do you have a position on the hostages? We need to launch an operation or something."

A steady clanking sound followed by three quick taps came through the telephone connection. Ken slurped and exhaled. "Ahhh…so…when will we find these hostages?"

Someone at the BOC said, "Ken, this could take a little while. Our people just got there and connected with the source."

Annie looked at John, shook her head, and tipped the phone to ensure he could hear the conversation. John nodded and looked at Annie. They grinned because the FBI BOC was about to push back on the FBI DC.

Ken audibly slurped another sip of coffee and said, "Well, I have the victims' families calling *Hoover* and asking what we are doing. They are threatening to go to the press or launch their own rescue or something. The families are a pain in the ass." "Hoover" was agent-slang for FBI headquarters in Washington, DC.

Annie and John heard another slurp. Clearly, Ken did not care what people heard from his side of the call. Annie and John stood perfectly still for a moment. John jiggled a few pieces of gravel in his hand. Annie decided to stay quiet for a moment and see what the FBI BOC had to say. She held her other hand out, palm up toward John, who dropped several pieces of gravel into it. She kept the phone steady in one place and tossed pieces of gravel one at a time at a Hesco barrier.

Annie leaned toward John and whispered, "We are getting traction because the FBI BOC wants to say 'fuck you' to FBI headquarters."

Annie and John heard Ken say, "Well, I need a little more detail here. I'm going to be out of the area the day after tomorrow, and I have to push some information in a teletype."

Ken was going on vacation in three days and planned to forget his cell phone at his desk for a week. He did not want to be bothered.

Annie and John then heard someone from the BOC say, "Fine, this is the on-scene commander. We will have a video teleconference after Annie gets back from Basra. Have your supervisor there, and your supervisor's supervisor."

There was silence on the call.

Annie and John heard a very audible slurp as Ken said, "OK," sipped his coffee, and hung up.

Annie and John heard a stern voice on the line. "Annie, hang up, and call right back."

Continuing a conversation after a conference call was a bad idea. Talking about someone who might still inadvertently be on the line ended friendships and sometimes careers.

Annie called the FBI BOC after ending the conference call. Her call was immediately answered and placed on speaker. Annie did the same with her speaker so John could hear.

The sound stuttered at first, and she was afraid of losing the connection. A voice said, "Annie, this is the FBI BOC on-scene commander. As I understand things, you are returning to Baghdad, and we are leaving somebody there to work this source concept, correct?"

John raised his hands and whispered to Annie, "Yay, I'm the 'somebody.'"

Annie grinned at John and said into the phone, "Yes sir, John will be staying and working with partners. I leave in about an hour—it's an all-night event to go from here to Baghdad."

The on-scene commander was curt and to the point. "Fine. Get here, get everyone together, brief them. Everyone, get your shit together, have a mother-fucking plan, brief me, then we talk to this jerkoff Ken and his supervisors at Hoover tomorrow evening."

Annie's eyes widened. The FBI pissing contest and shit-storm was going to get worse. Annie and John could use this to their benefit, but right now she had to keep composed.

Annie said, "Yes sir, I am being picked up here within the hour to start the trip north and will lock into things when I get there." Annie's composure was noted by everyone on the other end of the call.

The on-scene-commander asked, "Can you and the fuckin' guy that's staying down there handle this?"

"Yes sir, we are good, and he's got this," Annie said.

Annie and John looked at each other and waited. All they heard was, "Good," and the line went dead.

Annie pressed the end button on her phone again to confirm the call had ended and slid the device into her cargo pocket. John grinned and tossed a rock at the Hesco barrier. "Finally, I've been recognized and promoted to the position of *that-fuckin'-guy*."

They both laughed.

Annie looked at John and said, "This is crazy. The only way the FBI has a chance at being successful is if the FBI wins a fight with itself!"

"OK, what a clusterfuck," John said. "We can do this… Now you have forty-five minutes to pack. What do you need help with?"

Annie shook her head. "Shit, you're right. It's getting late. Let me jump in the shower real quick. I will bang on your door in ten or fifteen minutes."

Annie quickly walked up the stairs and into her trailer, while John meandered to his trailer, walked up the step, and stood on the stoop for a moment. He realized that the better he and Annie did their jobs, the longer he might be here.

AT 10:30 P.M., JOHN HEARD THE TAP OF A SMALL PIECE of gravel bouncing off his door. He quickly slid his boots on, got up from his chair, and walked outside. He would accompany Annie and her bags as far as the parking lot beyond the Hesco barrier. The SF support team on duty handled the airport movement to the flight line. They did not transport people for airport good-byes.

Annie stood near the bottom of the stairs, near John's trailer, pulled her wet hair into a ponytail, and said, "Come on, we can go over last-minute details while I get my shit together."

She motioned with her hand for John to come over as she returned to her trailer. John went inside and watched as Annie stuffed the clothes she had worn that day into a plastic bag. She had already poured soap powder into another plastic bag and shoved it inside the dirty clothes bag.

Annie sat on the edge of her bed, retied her boots, and said, "We will have to work out some secure communications. I think the SF guys have a secure phone line in the office."

John nodded. "Yeah, I think you're right. I will work that out in the next day or so and see what I can do about getting access to a secure computer for email, too."

John sat across from her on the opposite bed. She had stripped down her bed to the mattress. He would wash the sheets she had used and clean the room for the next person. Annie stood, dragged her backpack across the floor, and sat on the edge of the bed again. She checked the backpack compartments, making sure everything was zipped and in place. Her protective vest and helmet were stacked next to the door and connected to each other with a metal link. The drag strap was up so the gear could be carried easily.

Annie picked up her backpack, looked at John, and said, "It's time…We can do this…" John nodded silently.

Annie carried her backpack and protective gear, while John dragged her rolling bag until he hit gravel. A large pickup truck with an extended cab idled at the edge of the lot. Two SF operators sat in the back, and one stood next to the driver side. The two men in the back were traveling to Baghdad, as well. They would look out for each other, as well as for Annie. John eased her rolling bag over the sidewall and into the pickup bed, then stowed her protective gear alongside it.

As she was about to step into the passenger side of the truck, she said, "Hey, by the way, I left something under your stoop, so you don't forget what I'm dealing with in Baghdad."

Annie grinned slightly, and John nodded. He held the palm of his hand up about chest level, and she backhanded it indifferently as she stepped up into the cab of the truck. John shut the door and heard the truck go into gear as the headlights came on. It was time to go. Annie turned to meet her fellow travelers, and the truck departed.

John stood in the parking lot for a moment—all he heard was a generator in the distance. The temperature was still ninety degrees, but compared with the heat of the day, it was quite comfortable. John looked around the lot and briefly wondered how long this would be his home. As he walked down the plastic path in near darkness, he hoped he would find whatever Annie left under his stoop.

When he reached the edge of his trailer, John saw the outline of a small box just under the edge of the stoop. The box was surprisingly heavy. It was the soap powder box Annie had bought the day before at the NAAFI. She was getting her receipt when the first rocket impacted. The second rocket hit—killing a British soldier.

John momentarily wondered why Annie left him laundry detergent, and then why the box was so heavy. A quick picture of Annie packing flashed through his mind; Annie put a plastic bag of soap powder into her backpack.

John walked up the stairs, struggled with the keys to unlock the trailer in the darkness, opened the door, and went inside. He placed the box on the desk and looked down. Annie had taken off the top of the box and filled it with rocks. He sat in the chair at the desk so he could better inspect this peculiar box of rocks. On the front of the box Annie had drawn a circular smiley face in a frown and written the name "KEN" under the drawing. He turned the box slowly and looked at the other side. Annie drew the same picture, but underneath she wrote "FBI PAPERWORK." John would not forget what Annie was dealing with in Baghdad. He knew Ken was probably going to be the most difficult variable and might even be dumber than this box of rocks sitting on the desk.

Annie and the two SF operators arrived at the Brit-Air terminal and went through the check-in procedures. The outgoing terminal was next to the incoming area, but instead of a large block warehouse it was like a giant canvas circus tent. The tent had air conditioning, a raised composite floor, electricity, and even a large television.

Annie followed the lead of the SF operators.

A very polite British soldier with a clipboard asked, "Any torches?"

"No." She shook her head.

They sat in hard metal chairs that were connected in rows of five, like at a civilian airport but less comfortable. Annie sat in one of the uncomfortable metal chairs, and knew it was still better than the canvas seats on the C-130 to Baghdad. Annie leaned back in her chair. Their show-time was 11:00 p.m., but their departure, or go-time, was 3:00 a.m.

She sat across from the SF operators who were about to doze off, and asked them, "Why do the Brits want to know if I have a torch? Did somebody really try and carry a torch onto one of their planes?"

The SF guys looked at each other, and then back to Annie, and one of them said, "Torch is British for flashlight."

Annie folded her arms, grinned slightly, and said, "Oh, well, I guess that makes sense. A flashlight doesn't really flash, I suppose."

One SF operator fell asleep, the other dozed. Annie looked up momentarily, put her head back on the edge of the chair, and gazed at the tent roof. For a moment she thought of the difference between *torch* and *flashlight* and wondered why Americans did not use the term torch. It actually made more sense. Within thirty seconds, she was asleep.

Hostage Status: 84 Days in Captivity (*continued*)

The light in the vent had been dark for hours. The cell still smelled, but the stench was lighter. The hostages were awake but dozing.

Surfboy whispered, "Hey jarhead, you awake?"

Shorebilly responded, "Shut up...go to sleep."

"I'm feeling better...I'm ready to be rescued. How about sending some positive mental energy to your Marine Bros and have them come get us...I've seen it on TV...this rescue shit looks pretty easy."

"Shut up...go to sleep. Hostage rescue is complicated."

"Nuh-uh...not on TV."

"Shut up...go to sleep."

Surfboy smiled in the dark. "Bro, you're harshing my orange-peal-buzz."

"OK...OK...OK...I will send some positive fuckin' Chi and shiny Chakras their way and see what I can do...Now shut the fuck up and go to sleep"

Surfboy smiled as his voice trailed off into the darkness. "Thanks bro."

CHAPTER 24

STAR WARS R2D2...JOY OF MILITARY AIR TRAVEL IN WAR... MR. ETHAN HAS INFLUENCE

DAY 85: JULY 9, 2007

At 8:30 a.m., Ashton tapped on John's trailer door. John came out, and they walked toward the chow hall and discussed communication and logistics. Ashton knew John needed to communicate securely with Baghdad. "We will get you onto the team house computers between users. We'll just have to figure it out. And we can see if Donovan has any connections at Brit-HQ for a computer over there."

John nodded. "Thanks, there are a lot of things we will probably shift and change, I guess."

They heard the clatter and clank of metal on metal and saw a truck near the fence surrounding the R2D2 device. A ladder leaned near the pole with the constantly spinning radar dish next to it.

John pointed to the small complex and asked, "By the way, what the hell is that?" Contractors were performing maintenance on the components, and they had part of the shiny metal cap of the R2D2 section removed. The dish slowly stopped spinning as they reached the dirt road.

Ashton glanced where John was pointing and said, "That's a C-RAM."

John looked at the contraption over his shoulder as they walked, and asked, "Well what the hell is a C-RAM? Does it stand for something?"

Ashton kept walking, glanced over his shoulder briefly as he thought, and slowly said, "Um, yeah…Counter-rocket, artillery, and mortar. Damn, I had to think for a minute—we get so used to using acronyms I don't think about what the long names are anymore."

They both nodded and laughed.

As they walked on, Ashton said, "It's designed to detect incoming stuff like a rocket or mortar and shoot it out of the sky. It sends a barrage of munitions into the air. It looks like fireworks when it goes off."

John asked, "Does it work?"

Ashton shrugged his shoulders. "I suppose. The rocket, or whatever, has to be detected early enough, and that R2D2 thing goes off automatically." Ashton paused, looked at the shiny space object, and said, "You'll know when it goes off. There's no other sound like it."

John looked back at the C-RAM once more, then walked up the chow hall stairs with Ashton. The British soldier picked himself up from leaning on the sandbags, stood straight, and nodded toward Ashton. The British soldiers who stood the posts nearby knew who was SF. They knew it was SF who had stepped into the blood-soaked bunker to try to save one of their own. The SF efforts and the dreadful appearance of Kyle and the other Green Berets had become legend within a day.

At 8:45 a.m., Annie stood at the edge of the tarmac at the Baghdad International Airport with her phone to her ear. She spoke with the BOC duty agent and said, "I'm at BIAP about to get on a helo. I should be at the airfield by the embassy in about ten minutes." The duty agent would have to come pick her up.

Helicopter travel was a necessity because ground movement was hazardous. The road from BIAP to the Green Zone was not long. The highway was named Route Irish and touted by many as the most dangerous highway in the world. Flying in a British Puma or an American Blackhawk was safer than driving.

Earlier in the morning the British Puma helicopters originally scheduled for the seven-minute flight from BIAP to FOB Washington, adjacent to the US embassy, had been canceled. One of the two helicopters had a mechanical issue and was grounded. Helicopters in Iraq always flew in pairs for safety. The next scheduled flight to the Green Zone was on US Blackhawks.

Annie was three hours late getting back to the Green Zone. She had been bumped from her second scheduled flight. A civilian or military member at a higher grade than Annie took her seat. It was automatic. Not negotiable.

The reason for missing the third flight was different—the helicopters were "re-missioned." She inadvertently overheard part of a conversation between flight line personnel while she sat on the tarmac. "Some two-star general just decided he wants to fly to Kirkuk for breakfast and take his fuckin' entourage."

The general and his troupe got both helicopters for his

breakfast travel while Annie and the sixteen would-be passengers sat on the tarmac.

Annie recognized that anyone who thought military air movement was smooth and easy had never been in a real war zone. The only people who traveled around Iraq conveniently, particularly with military air transport, had stars on their uniforms. Everyone else sat on the tarmac, in the dirt, on their luggage, or stood around looking for shade. Most people carried energy bars and shared food with one another.

ASHTON AND JOHN FINISHED BREAKFAST, CONSUMING A plate and a half of food each. Annie was not around to feed. They sat at their usual table near the window and discussed how to handle the logistics of source meetings, and whether Donovan would be in Basra much longer.

Ashton tossed his fork onto his plate and said, "As I see things, you and Donovan may be able to work and coordinate at Brit-HQ. You and I can work out the logistics for the source meetings. I will still be operational on the hostage side, as well as the SF mission side. What do you think?"

John nodded. "That sounds good. I'm hoping Donovan can lean into this early and figure out some way to stick around. Anyway, I know there are going to be tons of moving parts, and everything will change as we go." John stared out the window momentarily then back to Ashton. "This is pretty fucked up down here, and I think we are walking into a shitstorm."

Ashton nodded. "Yeah…but, it beats having a real job."

Both men laughed, stood, picked up their plates, dumped them in the trash, and left the chow hall. They were on the same page. They recognized they were involved with something that most people who worked regular nine-to-five jobs in the US only imagined, or perhaps read about. In fact, what they were doing was what most SF operators and FBI agents only read about. What they were putting together was not the norm, and they were embarking upon a process and a project bigger than themselves. They knew it.

Ashton looked over at John. "Yeah, this clusterfuck of looking for hostages might be hard to explain to other people someday, huh?'

John nodded as they walked along the dirt road toward the C-RAM. "Yep…maybe…when that day comes…why bother…nobody would believe it."

They walked silently to the giant steel door at the blast wall, then onto the plastic walkway to the team house. They had a meeting with Donovan at 11:00 a.m.

DONOVAN SAT AT HIS DESK INSIDE THE SMALL WINDOW-less room. It was only large enough to fit two desks, a chair for each, and two extra desk chairs in the corner. One desk was used for eating or sitting. There were no file cabinets or files lying about. Anything to do with paper was kept to a minimum. The area had an institutional or prison-like feel, which led Donovan and others to refer to the workspace as *Donovan's cell.*

Donovan had three computer screens giving him five feet of 180-degree workspace. He could expand, move, and research different systems simultaneously. There were no pictures, personal effects, or calendars on his desktop.

Donovan had spent the last hour in front of the screens, looking at the relationships between the telephone number associated with Cricket and numbers linked with suspected members of the insurgency. He was just about to push a complicated search of pattern and association and decided to check his email first. He had one unopened email. It was from the NSA director of operations in Fort Meade, Maryland. The email contained three short paragraphs.

The first paragraph read, "Donovan, operational considerations have been reassessed. It has been determined the most productive place for you to be located for the rest of your deployment in Iraq will be Basra." Donovan's eyes widened as he completed reading the first paragraph, and his jaw dropped as he read the second.

The second paragraph read, "If you or anyone in the cc line has any questions on this matter, please feel free to contact me directly."

The third paragraph left Donovan shaking his head, it read, "I understand you are engaging in raised-level processes and working hand-in-hand with our British partners concerning hostage events. As you know, our relationship with the United Kingdom and continued cooperative initiatives are paramount to success. There is a strong interest in advanced targeting, and our British partners have a great appreciation for the mutually beneficial relationships forged in Basra."

Clearly, the conversation with Mr. Ethan at the British bar two days ago had been productive. Mr. Ethan had the influence and back-channel muscle to make things happen. He had reached the top of a US government agency, had the concept expeditiously directed downward, and cut through the bureaucracy of indecision and second-guessing. Donovan picked up the secure telephone next to his desk and dialed a four-digit in-house Brit-HQ extension.

The phone was answered on the first ring. "Good day, Donovan," said Jensen.

The secure telephone lines had caller identification, and Jensen knew it was Donovan as the number flashed on the phone.

Donovan said, "Hey, when you get a minute, can you come by?"

"No worries, mate. On my way."

Jensen was in an exclusively British SCIF across the large foyer. Donovan stared at the screen for a moment and double-checked the email distribution line. His entire supervisory chain was on it, along with others he did not know. Donovan stood, pushed the hair from his face straight back over his head with his palms, and pondered his next logistical steps.

Jensen tapped on the door as he nudged it open and said, "Hey mate, have we something on fire?"

Donovan shrugged then gestured with upturned palms to the chair in front of the computer. It was common for Donovan and Jensen to take turns in the chair. They had full access to each other's computer systems. Jensen saw the email and immediately tried to scroll down to the bottom to read chronologically through the email chain. There was no email chain to read; it was a very brief narrative. Jensen handled the computer mouse skillfully with his right hand and spun a pen in circles with his left as he read the email.

He read through it once and looked up at Donovan, who rubbed his hands together and grinned like a mad scientist in an old movie. Jensen had seen this look before, usually when Donovan had made critical connections and merged complicated SIGINT patterns. Jensen looked back to the email and reread it to make sure he was absolutely clear.

He looked up at Donovan and said, "Well, I suppose you will be here in beautiful Baaasra for the foreseeable future."

Donovan nodded. "Yeah, Mr. Ethan sure didn't waste any time, and he does have juice."

Jensen stayed seated and stoic, crossed his arms, and said, "It's rather odd it took this long. I mean, two days... He's losing his touch."

Jensen looked up at Donovan, and they both broke into raucous laughter.

Jensen glanced back at the email on the computer screen, then up to Donovan, and said, "Indeed, Mr. Ethan does appear to have some influence."

"No shit, *indeed*." Donovan grinned at Jensen, knowing that he had completely misused the word "indeed" to make the phrase sound anachronistically American.

They both laughed, Jensen placed his index finger beside his forehead, and said, "Perhaps this is worthy of a pint later as we inform Mr. Ethan of the news. We might persuade Mr. Ethan to pop the bar open for a special occasion...you know, US and UK special relationship, kinship, and all that."

They both grinned, and Donovan said, "Great, I'm in." He paused for a moment, glanced at the email, and said, "It's interesting the hostage thing was emphasized. Do you think there is more to that...you know, more going on here than we know?"

Jensen scratched his head, looked at the screen, and said, "Maybe that's a question for Mr. Ethan. I will nose around a bit myself, as well." Then he stood and walked toward the door, adding, "I'm glad you're going to be around, mate. We could use the help, and things are getting more complicated, not less here in Baaasra."

Donovan nodded. He had to get his head together logistically, let Ashton, the SF team, and John know he would be staying in Basra, move into the SF compound… and stay focused.

Hostage Status: 85 Days in Captivity

Morning light through the vent reflected off the specs of slow-moving dust—the hostage world was momentarily calm.

Without warning the door flew open and crashed against the inside wall.

The mean guards were on duty.

Today nobody would get hung by their wrists from the rebar in the ceiling, but everyone would receive the obligatory beating with the hoses. The mean guards were aware of the doctor visit and cleaning. They were vicious for sake of being vicious.

The beating lasted about a minute, and the hostages had the usual welts on their forearms and backs. A few recently closed cuts opened.

The mean guards knew about medicine and peroxide. They made sure to stomp the medicine bottles and the two peroxide bottles during the melee.

The beating ended as soon as it began; the guards left, and the door slammed shut.

The hostages sat against the wall, checking their cuts and new welts, staying silent. The mean guards might be outside the door listening to see if they talked—hence, another beating. Broken plastic pill containers and water bottles littered the area.

Oddly, the four hostages looked at the mess of crushed plastic and grinned—each letting out a silent laugh. They quietly waited for another ten minutes—listening for the guards.

Surfboy nodded at Shorebilly and said, "I got the door." He sat against the door—it would slow the guards if they came back.

Shorebilly walked to the edge of the bathroom bucket—and reached inside. It was putrid but not as bad as before. He retrieved a pill container as Tex came over with a rag he had found the day before and wiped the bottle.

CR gathered the broken plastic and peroxide bottles, putting the mess in the bathroom bucket. It would be dumped later.

Surfboy grabbed a half full water bottle—it was half full of peroxide. "Hey bro, your forehead opened up a little... stay still." He blotted Shorebilly's head with the peroxide.

The mean guards were so concerned with breaking and beating that they never noticed there were no pills in the containers. The hostages knew the evil nature of the mean guards and had come up with a plan. The pills were consolidated into one container and hidden in the one place the guards would not go near—the bathroom bucket. The peroxide was hidden in plain view—empty water bottles.

The hostages kept quiet and embraced the small victory.

CHAPTER 25

COMMUNICATION IMPROVED... DONOVAN TO SF...JOHN MEETS JENSEN...MR. ETHAN EXPLAINS

DAY 86: JULY 10, 2007

Ashton and John walked from the team house to the parking lot on their way to British headquarters. The sun was intense. The heat pushed down from the sky and up from the superheated ground. John remembered not to grab the chain when moving the gate.

John noticed the British soldier standing the post near the improved duck-and-cover bunker seemed to stand a little straighter as they drove past. The eye contact was more prevalent, and the nonverbal cues had a more reverent tone as the soldier ceased leaning on the sandbags, tipped his helmet, and nodded.

Ashton and John arrived at Brit-HQ, moved through the perimeter checkpoint with a nod and flash of ID, and into the building to the security desk. They both received the expedited treatment and visual hand-flip from the soldier at the security desk. Since they were about fifteen minutes early for the meeting with Donovan, they decided to have a cup of coffee at the kiosk in the large open area. Several couches were open, as well as a few moderately comfortable casual chairs in the corner. They got coffee and sat at a table with two chairs and sipped the incredibly hot beverage.

Ryan and Kyle came down the stairs, went to the kiosk, and got coffee. Everyone moved to a corner where there was an open couch and two chairs. The coffee table was full of empty cups.

Ryan looked at John, then Ashton, and asked, "Are we OK if Kyle sits in on your meeting?"

Ryan was being courteous. He did not need to ask, but things always worked better with courtesy. Ryan also made sure Kyle stayed in the loop on hostage developments and linked with Donovan.

RYAN TOOK THE LAST DRINK OF HIS COFFEE, STOOD TO leave, and said, "OK, everyone, I will see you back at the team house. Let me know how it all goes."

The group nodded and glanced at their watches. They all leaned forward slightly and drank the rest of their coffee. It was time to meet with Donovan. Kyle led the way, and all signed into the SCIF entry desk quickly. They entered the SCIF and passed the collection of desks. The no-patch soldier gave a barely perceptible nod. Kyle responded with the same. The no-patch soldier did not know Ashton, so Ashton was not acknowledged. The no-patch soldier had heard that John was with the FBI and wanted nothing to do with him. John was summarily ignored.

Kyle tapped lightly on the conference room door and entered. The room was empty. Donovan stepped up behind them as they walked into the conference room. He had been immersed in pattern development in his cell. Donovan greeted everyone, and all sat randomly around the table. The formality of handshakes already shifted to the informality of smiles, head nods, and a casual wave.

Donovan leaned forward in his chair, pulled the hair from his face, and could hardly contain himself as he started the conversation. "Well, you're not going to believe this, but the word has already come back regarding my timing here in Basra."

Ashton and John leaned forward and nodded slightly to prod the details from Donovan more quickly. Kyle stayed placid and composed.

Donovan held his palms up, rocked back in the chair, leaned forward again, and said, "I'm not really sure how things went, but I got an email from a guy in the upper echelon at The Fort that said I'm staying in Basra."

Ashton and John smiled and waited for more.

"I'm still looking into exactly how that happened…I think the Brits leaned into it. And there was a reference to working hostage events…and working with the British…you know…partnerships, and all of that." Donovan grinned, looked toward Kyle, and said, "So, I guess I'm going to be looking for a place to live while we crank things up."

Ashton and John looked around the room, and at each other. They were not aware of Kyle and Ryan's previous conversation with Donovan about living arrangements. John had no idea what to do, and Ashton had already considered a few potential remedies. Fortunately for all, Kyle had come to the meeting.

Kyle nodded, folded his hands with his fingers interlaced on the table, and said, "Sounds good. We just happen to have an open trailer right next to John. When do you want to move in?"

Donovan scratched his head, smiled, and nodded appreciatively. "Wow, thanks. I was hoping you'd say something like that. How about this afternoon? I know it's probably asking a lot, but when I got the word I was leaving, they moved me to temporary quarters for transient personnel. The place sucks…so the sooner, the better."

Kyle looked at Ashton and John, nodded with raised eyebrows as if to ask a question. Ashton and John understood the nonverbal question, and both immediately nodded in reply. This afternoon worked fine.

Ashton said, "Let's work out the timing, and we will come get you and your stuff and make it happen."

John gave a thumbs-up. "Absolutely. That sounds like a plan," He smiled at Donovan, then looked toward Kyle, and added, "Thanks for green-lighting the housing thing so fast."

Kyle nodded his head slightly. "Yeah, no problem. If you guys are good with getting Donovan moved and settled, then we are all good."

Everyone nodded; it was done. The stress of obtaining housing added immensely to the day-to-day weight of life in a war zone. Arduous living arrangements in any environment make the rest of life difficult; onerous living arrangements in Iraq made life untenable. Soldiers were often stacked four to a room better fit for two, or even one. The transient quarters and temporary housing for military and government personnel in a war zone added a level of hardship that only those who spent time in a war zone understood. The housing challenge would never be fixed because those in a position to address such unpleasant conditions rarely experienced the hardship. They were the same people who thought everything was fine and had a great affinity for things like war zone military air travel. In other words, they were people higher up in the government or who had stars on their uniforms, and they moved and lived in a bubble that was perpetually inflated and padded by the people who surrounded them and kissed their asses.

The SF operators handled things for themselves and made sure they took care of their own, and those around them. John and Donovan were being absorbed into the SF fold.

Donovan grinned from ear to ear. "OK, let's go take a look at my computer screens, and I will tell you what I think I'm seeing."

Donovan led the way to his cell. Once inside the room Ashton and John found chairs, while Kyle sat on the desk adjacent to Donovan's desk. He sized up the room as he came in and knew that would probably be the best vantage point to see the screens over Donovan's shoulder. Donovan rubbed his hands together and bent his fingers with either hand. A faint pop could be heard as he cracked his knuckles, then seated himself in front of the screens like a concert pianist in front of a grand piano. For the next forty-five minutes Donovan explained the various databases and systems he utilized and spoke about the patterns he had evaluated and associated with Cricket's telephone number.

Ashton and John were quickly lost in the blur of details and new acronyms. Sitting quietly and listening was the smart option. Kyle followed and understood everything Donovan said, and he had numerous questions. Donovan welcomed the questions and explained details in terms that Ashton and John almost understood.

Finally, Donovan said, "I need more numbers from Cricket, and for you guys to get more sources using phones."

John peered at the screens, which had become a blur of graphs and charts, and said, "We are meeting with Cricket in two days and hope to have another source coming in by the end of the week."

Donovan nodded. "OK, sounds good. I am waiting to run a few other programs in different systems, but I want to make sure I'm plugging in everything."

Donovan opened the top left drawer of his desk. Inside the drawer was the file he received from Annie with telephone numbers associated with hostage events.

Donovan held up the file, looked at John, and said, "I could tell there were a lot of numbers in some of these reports that aren't making it into the intelligence community databases. Why?" Donovan had his suspicions but thought he would keep things positive.

John shrugged. "Well, I'm not sure, but my best guess is that people are hoarding information. I hate to say it, but we've had a few FBI people come through the rotations who refuse to share information. They won't talk with other agencies, and sometimes won't even share relevant shit with the agent sitting next to them at the BOC in Baghdad." John shook his head and said, "Small thinkers who are afraid of someone else taking the credit."

Everyone nodded and understood. Ashton and Kyle had seen it before, and for Donovan it was always one of the great hurdles to get past.

Donovan nodded, tapped the folder, and said, "OK, no problem...actually, that's about what I thought."

John shrugged. "I know that sucks, but that's why I'm here…you know, to try and fix that sort of bullshit, and connect the dots."

Donovan turned, glanced at his screen for a moment, and looked up at the ceiling.

He spun back around in his chair to face everyone, looked at the ceiling, and said, "Can you get up with Annie, and see if she might be able to pull any numbers associated with any other hostage events in Iraq the FBI is working?"

John nodded. "Yes, great idea. In fact, we just worked out how to get my email working over the Secret browser. That will help in getting information like the numbers and the reports to me here in Basra."

Donovan nodded. "Yeah, that will help. It will be time-consuming with communication because what you're talking about won't sync with my stuff." Donovan waved his hand toward the screens on his desk and said, "Everything here is on Top Secret lines. It's the same in the outer SCIF, too."

"I guess I can print things at the SF compound and run it over as things come through and develop," said John, trying to stay optimistic.

Donovan rubbed his neck for a moment and looked at the ceiling.

Donovan looked at Kyle. "I think there might be a terminal in the command center next door." He looked at Kyle because he had seen Kyle periodically in the British command center next to the main SCIF over the last month.

Kyle nodded. "Yeah, I think you're right. I know I've seen an American dickin' around with email on a computer terminal. It had a Secret screen, so there must at least be a line or connection. That would save a lot of time to be able to just walk next door."

Donovan thought of the next move. "Yep, being able to walk to the next room would streamline things..." Donovan smiled, looked at the ceiling and back to Kyle, and said, "How about I email my British GCHQ guy and see if he can help with that one."

Kyle grinned. "Yeah, good call. They seem to be pretty good at making things happen."

Donovan nodded, turned toward his computer keyboard, and said, "Give me one minute...Let me send a quick email and see if we can make this happen."

He clicked the computer mouse a few times, typed an extraordinarily brief message to Jensen, and sent it. Ashton and John stared at the maze of charts and graphs on the screens as Donovan turned around, placed his palms flat on his thighs, and asked a one-word question. "Lunch?"

Everyone smiled, nodded, and stood.

As they edged out of Donovan's cell, Ashton asked, "Hey Donovan, do you want to move your shit to your new home after lunch?"

With a large grin and a laugh, not even trying to restrain his elation, Donovan said, "I'd love to. I thought you'd never ask."

The group laughed as they headed out of the cell.

As they left, Jensen's reply arrived in Donovan's email queue. He had been at his desk when Donovan sent the inquiry about computer access for John in the British command center. Donovan had already locked his screens and would not see Jensen's response until later. It read:

"D, regarding a computer for Secret level access in the command center. Done. Access will be handled by noon tomorrow. Assume we are still on for a pint or two with Mr. Ethan this evening. Cheers...J"

Things were coming together.

THEY WENT FOR LUNCH AT THE CLOSEST CHOW HALL, across the main road between a junkyard, British operational offices, and a dirt parking lot ringed in barbed wire. Donovan was the only American who ate there regularly. They parked in the dirt lot, walked to an entry control point staffed by a British soldier who glanced at the IDs of hungry soldiers and contractors. The chow hall was a series of interlocking freight shipping containers designed to fit together into a uniform prefabricated building.

Donovan pointed to the edge of the structure. "We enter the chow hall around there," he said. "This is a pretty good arrangement here…I guess wars are easier to set up if you bring your own buildings."

Entering the chow hall involved passing through a set of four-inch-wide plastic strips that hung from the top of the doorframe and reached the floor—like at the entrance to a walk-in freezer. Behind the plastic freezer strips hung lengths of lightweight chain about a quarter-inch thick, which formed a curtain easily parted by hand. The idea, as far as anyone knew, was to keep hot air out, air-conditioned air in, and prevent bugs from entering, particularly flies.

Inside the chow hall the pace was brisk and energetic. Staff behind the counter and in the kitchen were third-country nationals from Nepal. They worked long hours, tirelessly and without complaint. The food was available, and the service was fast and efficient.

Just after they passed through the serving line, Kyle received a call from Ryan, who needed Kyle to return to the team house for a meeting. Kyle was used to interrupted plans; he did not mind eating quickly and returning to the compound early. He would be able to give Ryan some notice that Donovan would be moving into the SF compound and likely be in Basra for the rest of his tour.

Ashton and John handled the move with Donovan. Like most people deployed to Iraq, Donovan traveled light. However, as with any move, a few extra hands made an enormous difference. When they arrived at the SF compound gate, John got out of the SUV to unlock the gate. Without prompting, Donovan got out to help. He knew he needed to learn how things worked, and he had a positive attitude to pull together.

John pointed at the chain securing the gate and said, "Careful! That motherfucker gets hot during the day," and they both grinned.

"Something tells me you learned the hard way," Donovan said.

John nodded enthusiastically, and they both laughed. He told Donovan the "secret" four-digit combination. Donovan simply nodded and said, "OK, got it."

Donovan did not need to write it down or repeat it to himself. He immediately remembered three- and four-digit sets of numbers and how they associated with something else; he had complete recall of even the most complicated numeric relationships. People at the NSA had odd and very necessary skills. While Ashton and John were getting Donovan settled in, Ashton was called to the team house for a meeting.

Ashton tossed the keys to John and said, "I gotta go. If you need anything, just get up with someone at the team house, and they can find me. I will be around for the meeting with Cricket the day after tomorrow."

Donovan and John sat for a moment. John had an unnerving feeling of déjà vu as he sat in the chair by the bed. Donovan sat in the chair by the desk and put his size fourteen boot on the edge of his bed frame. It was only yesterday that John had sat in the same place and spoken with Annie, who sat in the same chair as Donovan. To John, that conversation already seemed a lifetime ago. He knew he needed to contact Annie and let her know the good news about Donovan's confirmed and continued presence in Basra.

John considered the task of hostage casework as sort of a coin, a penny haphazardly discarded on the street. He knew he dealt with the best side of a scraped, scratched, run over, usually ignored, coin. He had the side of the penny with the dangerous operational absurdity of Basra. Annie had to contend with the worse side of the penny—the ridiculous, ego-driven minefield of FBI Baghdad and DC. John knew he had gotten the better side of the ugly, beat-up, discarded, and neglected penny.

They left Donovan's trailer and walked across the plastic path to the parking lot. Donovan looked comfortable in his surroundings already. He, too, adapted quickly to environs. John had the keys for the white SUV and noticed it was the only vehicle in the lot.

He said, "I think we're good for now, but there may come a time when the guys are short of vehicles."

Donovan shrugged, nodded, and slapped his stomach. "No problem. I think I could use the exercise anyway."

Donovan secured the lock, chain, and gate, and got back in the truck. He noticed the duck-and-cover bunker with the gold horizontal strip and end caps. It was the first duck-and-cover bunker he had seen with end caps in Basra. He surmised this was where the British soldier had been killed the other day. The British soldier standing in the square sandbag bunker stopped leaning on the sandbags as they drove by, stood straight, and waved. Donovan waved and nodded. They were quiet for a moment as John turned from the gravel and dirt road to the main asphalt street. Donovan watched either side of the road and assessed the best way to walk in case they had to go on foot in the future.

On the left side of the road, he saw a line of palm trees. The fronds were coated in dirt, but they were full and healthy. He pointed toward them and said, "That's odd. Who would expect a bunch of lush trees right there?"

John laughed momentarily. "Yeah, I noticed that too. There's nothing alive anywhere, then all of sudden there's a set of healthy trees and overgrown weeds…weird."

John parked the SUV on the Brit-HQ perimeter road. Donovan led the way to the British soldier at the perimeter post. He noticed the duck-and-cover bunker there still did not have end caps. The guard recognized Donovan's large frame at a distance and had already begun to lean back on the sandbags and wave him through. Donovan was a fixture at Brit-HQ and was well liked by the soldiers. He smiled, held up his ID in the pouch, and thanked the soldier as he walked by. The soldier nodded and waved John through before he had even lifted his ID pouch. John was with Donovan.

Once inside Brit-HQ they breezed through the security check-in desk with the quick-flip check of the ID that was a courtesy only regulars received. It was common knowledge to avoid being rude or in a proverbial American-hurry. The security check-in desk and any ID post could make one's life a nightmare. John was pleased to see that he and Donovan were on the same page.

They walked through the large open space and passed the coffee kiosk to the SCIF check-in desk. The guard greeted Donovan by first name and turned the book around so he could sign in. John still had to produce his ID, but it was given the expeditious scrutiny of a quick glance, and he signed in promptly.

There were hushed conversations between different sets of people—some on the telephone, some looking at computer screens. Quiet dialogue continued as they moved through the large SCIF area. Donovan led the way and passed the set of desks. The no-patch US soldier at his usual desk in the corner nodded to Donovan, who nodded back and gave a quick wave. John was ignored. They passed the SCIF conference room and entered Donovan's cell. Donovan ran his hands across his keyboard and opened his email on one of the screens as John sat on top of the desk behind him.

Donovan slid his chair back slightly and said, "Holy shit, read this email…It looks like you're in."

John pushed a chair next to Donovan, sat down, and scooted up to the screen to read. Donovan's hands flashed over the keyboard, and the email tripled in size so they could both read it as they sat back. John read Jensen's email confirming he would have access to a computer terminal in the British command center.

"Wow, that was fast. It looks like you have some juice here," John said.

Donovan said, "Yeah, that really was fast. They get things done when they want to."

John nodded, pointed to the bottom of the email and asked, "So, who is Jensen?"

Donovan sat back and said, "Do you remember the guy who sat in the corner during our first meeting? That's

Jensen. He's my connecting point to GCHQ here. He's linked across the British intelligence community and works well with everyone."

John nodded, leaned back in the chair, and said, "Well, he sounds like a great guy."

"Yeah, he is. If he can't make something happen, he knows someone who can. I will email him back and see if he wants to catch up. I want to show him what we have going. Talking and working with Jensen and his GCHQ guys could make a big difference in how some of this goes." Donovan paused for a moment. "I hope you're OK with it… This guy is smart," he added, then emailed Jensen to see if he might be available.

Jensen responded immediately. He welcomed the opportunity to come to Donovan's cell. He would be there momentarily.

John nodded and said, "Hell yes, keep them in the loop. Make them part of the loop. Share any and all information. I'm so tired of this bullshit that goes on with people not working with each other."

John was shaking his head. Territorial games played by so many were mind-numbing. The absurdity of it all was beyond comprehension.

Donovan looked from his screens to John and said in a very casual tone, "By the way, Jensen is the smartest guy I've ever met."

JENSEN TAPPED ON THE DOORFRAME OF DONOVAN'S CELL as he entered and greeted Donovan with a wave and John with a more formal handshake. There was little small talk. Jensen pulled up a chair on Donovan's left and was immediately immersed in the details on the screens. Just as Jensen sat down, Donovan passed the computer mouse from his right hand to his left. He worked the mouse as easily with his left hand as with his right—he had moved the device so Jensen could also use it. John sat on the desk behind them and watched the screens over their shoulders. Donovan spoke for the next half hour, and the computer mouse passed effortlessly between Donovan and Jensen. For a while John assumed they had forgotten he was there. They asked each other questions and slid the computer mouse back and forth in seamless conversation. John absorbed more of the details as he heard the overview for the second time, but he got lost as they traded questions and answers. Donovan and Jensen used acronyms and spoke a language familiar only to those in the world of SIGINT.

While John's attention was focused on the chart that looked like a tangled multilayered spider web, Jensen looked to Donovan and made a gesture with his hand as though he was holding a glass. He raised his eyebrows as one might when asking a question, pointed to John with the other, and brought his hand up like he was taking a drink. Donovan understood: Jensen was asking if Donovan thought it was OK to bring John over for a drink. Donovan nodded and gave a thumbs-up.

Jensen nodded and said, "Well, moving right along, aren't we?" He spun his pen on the desk, looked at Donovan and John, and said, "We need more numbers, mates."

They both nodded.

Jensen smiled, stopped his pen from spinning with the palm of his hand, and said, "To that end, are we all up for a pint or two in a bit?"

Jensen and Donovan looked at John, who raised his eyebrows slightly, and said, "Oh yeah, I'm in…I'm overdue for a pint, if you will."

Everyone chuckled at John's failed attempt to be formal and sound British with the invitation acceptance. Jensen led John and Donovan through the command center and showed them where the terminal for John would be installed later that night. They agreed to meet at the Brit-bar in about fifteen minutes. Donovan and John departed Brit-HQ and walked to the SUV. John drove as Donovan gave directions. John had never been to the part of the base near the range.

Donovan was slowly nodding his head. "I don't know for sure, but something's going on. Jensen may not have all the details, or they are still coming together, but something's up…"

Jensen, Donovan, and John had a lengthy and enlightening chat with Mr. Ethan at the bar. Mr. Ethan spelled out the big-picture hostage process and how the US and UK relationship would work. By the end of the evening Donovan and John were a little tipsy, and Mr. Ethan had a British soldier drive them to their compound. Things were coming together.

Hostage Status: 86 Days in Captivity

The day was long, hot and quiet.

Surfboy whispered, "Hey bro, when we get out of here, I want to go kayaking in your state." He was bored and wanted to talk.

Shorebilly nodded and shook his head. He placed his left index finger over his mouth and with his right index finger he pointed to the cut on his head. He gently shook his head and looked toward the door. "Shhhhhh......Nice guards tomorrow."

Surfboy nodded, lying flat and going to the beach in his head.

CHAPTER 26

TIME PASSED...THE FOREIGN OFFICE ...RELATIONSHIPS DEVELOP

DAY 86 TO DAY 236: JULY 10, 2007 TO DECEMBER 7, 2007

For the next month Donovan and John walked to Brit-HQ daily. The next month turned into the next month, and so on, for the next five months. The shortage of SF vehicles became severe, and they grew comfortable with the walk from the SF compound to Brit-HQ. They established a routine. Donovan was usually up about an hour before John and went to the team house. He met with Kyle to discuss SF operations, and received or developed a plan for that day's technical research. Then Donovan played Ping-Pong with Nathan, who took a break from his myriad daily weapons duties.

While Donovan played Ping-Pong, John checked into the team house and grabbed two Red Bulls from the fridge and two packages of Pop Tarts. He got a general idea of SF availability for the next few days to better coordinate source meeting plans. John gave Kyle and Ryan a daily overview of hostage development, and he used the SF secure phone to call Annie in Baghdad. Donovan and John did not eat breakfast anymore at the chow hall, to the dismay of Sasha. Their daily routine and timing were not consistent with the chow hall's morning hours. Besides, they had Red Bull and Pop Tarts.

Donovan and John had full access to the team house, including the combination to the cypher lock. They could enter its inner sanctum like any SF team member. About a week after Donovan moved to the compound, they learned why the team house chairs and couches were arranged so oddly. The seating area faced a blank wall; the wall doubled as a movie screen. If time allowed, the team came together for *movie night*. Donovan and John had an open invitation to *movie night*, and even input regarding the movie selection. They had been brought into the fold.

Relationships at Brit-HQ in the command center developed for John. His time each day at the computer that Jensen and the GCHQ technical staff had installed for him proved invaluable. John became commonly known for being in Basra for one thing: trying to find hostages. More than anything, John's presence was noted for consistency. The British finally saw an American with operational longevity. John's protracted presence caught the attention of the British Foreign and Commonwealth Office. The Foreign Office, as it was commonly called, had an undisclosed number of people in Basra from its numerous branches, including the Secret Intelligence Service, the British version of the US Central Intelligence Agency otherwise known as MI6. Foreign Office personnel appreciated John's sustained presence.

One day while John sat at the computer in the British command center working on an email summarizing for Annie his latest meeting with Cricket, he felt a tap on his back. He turned to see a woman in civilian clothes, dressed like everyone else; boots, cargo pants, and collared shirt with three buttons. She introduced herself as Amelia and said she was from the Foreign Office.

Amelia briefly smiled and said, "I work on the other side of the foyer…you know, to the right as you come in the front door."

John knew the area was for British personnel only. Americans had to be escorted even if they had Brit-HQ identification. He had never been to that section of the building.

John stood and shook hands and briefly described why he was in Basra. She nodded politely. Amelia already knew who John was and why he was there. She offered no specific assistance but said to let her know if he needed anything. She mentioned her supervisor might also stop by sometime to say hello. Two weeks later, John was diligently typing at his desk when he felt a tap on his shoulder and turned around. John had seen the face before at the Brit-bar but had never met the person.

The stranger said, "Hello, I'm Quinn…I'm with the Foreign Office."

John stood, shook hands with Quinn, and introduced himself. He described why he was there in much the same way he explained it to Amelia.

Quinn nodded politely. "You have a difficult job. How long are you scheduled to be here?"

John shrugged. "It's hard to say. I've extended twice, and as long as I'm making progress, I'll stay."

"Very well," said Quinn. "I do hope you have continued progress."

They shook hands, and Quinn walked away. John sat down and finished his email to Annie, who'd had a particularly bad stint of run-ins with Ken as he sat on his ass in DC. Two days later, Quinn walked through the command center and nodded to John as he passed. Two days after that, Quinn stopped by John's workstation and perched on the edge of the table near his computer monitor. Quinn made small talk about the command center and how the fine, floury dirt seemed to coat everything, even indoors. John took the opportunity to take a break from emails and have a light conversation.

Quinn said, "I just met with your mate Donovan. Nice fellow. It's good to see Donovan and Jensen from our GCHQ get on so well."

John nodded in agreement, sat back in his chair slightly, and had the curious feeling there was more to the conversation. Quinn's casual chats were now daily, and the conversations were longer.

John said, "Yes, it's great when people start actually talking with each other. Sometimes it works for everyone." They both chuckled.

Quinn handed John a piece of paper with his name, number, and email on it, and said, "Let me know if you need anything, mate. I would imagine we might have some common ground to work with. Cheers."

John slid the note with Quinn's information into his pocket. John and Quinn connected on the classified computer system just to confirm email addresses. Two weeks passed. Quinn continued to cut through the command center en route to the SCIF, often stopping to perch on the edge of a desk or pull up a chair and chat briefly with John. Quinn took a greater interest in the human source expansion and SIGINT exploitation John and Donovan developed.

One afternoon, after a particularly lengthy conversation with Quinn, John and Donovan decided to get pizza for lunch at Echos. They ordered, found a table in the corner, and sat quietly for a moment. A rocket attack had interrupted their sleep, and they were fatigued and distracted. A food order number was called, and both picked up their numbered slip of paper, looked at it, and tossed it back on the table. It was far too soon for their order to be ready but picking up the paper and looking at it when a number was called had become a standard lunchtime tic. John looked at Donovan, who rubbed his bloodshot eyes and swept his hair off his face.

John briefly peered around to see how close people were before speaking, then said, "Quinn sure has been talkative with me lately. Do you think there's some overlap with the US hostages and the British hostages?"

Donovan continued to rub his eyes as he shrugged his shoulders and said, "Well, I don't know. It wouldn't surprise me if there was some sort of relationship or association. I haven't seen it." He sat back in his chair and said, "But, then again, I haven't looked for it."

John nodded, and they both picked up their paper slips to check the latest number called. It was someone else's order. They tossed the slips back onto the table.

Donovan looked at John, stretched his neck, and said, "It might be one of those things where it's HUMINT driven, but SIGINT verified."

John thought he understood but wanted to make sure he grasped Donovan's real meaning. "I think I know what you mean…but, what *do* you mean?" They both chuckled at how that sounded.

Donovan leaned forward in his chair and said, "Well,

the hostage processes the British could be working may be HUMINT driven and not necessarily coordinated with the US. So, if they compartmentalize their reporting, I wouldn't have the reference points to determine what should be exploited."

John nodded, shook the Parmesan cheese in the clogged shaker, and said, "OK, I'm on the same page…that's why it's so important to have the HUMINT people from the US and the UK talking with each other."

Donovan nodded. "Right, if people collecting from sources aren't sharing the information with other people collecting from sources, then people like me, and other SIGINT guys like Jensen, are still only seeing part of the picture…sort of working in the dark."

They both heard several numbers called, picked up their paper numbers from the table, looked at each other, and said, "Bingo."

Hostage Status: 236 Days in Captivity

The hostages had a routine, and they were managing.

They were able to hose off every month. The air was bad, and it was hot, but nobody was sick—no fever.

Shorebilly came back to the cell with the bathroom bucket. It was cleaner than usual. He had almost two minutes to clean it. The nice guards were on duty.

He was escorted by a new guard who securely shut and locked the door and could be heard walking away.

"Hey, I heard the guards yelling at someone across the courtyard. It was in English again." Shorebilly put the bucket in the corner and sat against the wall.

CR lying prone was somewhere else in his mind and lightly humming the West Virginia song they all played over and over in their heads.

Tex looked around the room. Nobody acknowledged Shorebilly's observation. He quietly said, "So, they have some other Americans. Nothing we can do. I hope they are OK."

It was getting dark. Another hour passed.

Surfboy was bored. "Hey, what day are we on?"

"Right around 236 or 237, I think," Shorebilly said while staring at the ceiling.

"Long time..."

"Yep..."

Surfboy felt like talking. "They wouldn't forget about us, would they?"

"Shut up."

Surfboy flicked a pebble toward Shorebilly. "Hey, what's the name of that place where you live?"

"Kent Island. Maryland's Eastern Shore."

"I didn't know Maryland had islands. I thought you were next to West Virginia or Kentucky or something," Surfboy joked.

"Shhhhhh...."

"Bro, how do you get food? Do you have a boat?"

Shorebilly was lightly shaking his head and said, "There's a bridge you fuckin' moron."

"Oh, it would be cooler if you had to take a boat there," Surfboy added.

"I can take a boat there, but there's a bridge...shut up... talk quieter."

"A boat? OK bro, you're cool again." Surfboy tossed a pebble up and caught it.

"Shut the fuck up."

They grinned at each other.

The door crashed open—the nice guards AND the mean guards. The guards placed burlap bags on the head of each hostage, and they were led to the courtyard. This had never happened before.

The American hostages would never see their cell again.

CHAPTER 27

DEVELOPED TRUST...BRITISH CANDOR

DAY 237: DECEMBER 8, 2007

Quinn passed through the command center from the SCIF. Instead of perching on the edge of the desk near John, he pulled up a chair to chat. John appreciated the break and the chance to talk. Conversations with Quinn had gotten much more detailed. Quinn shared different big-picture interests, and John gave overviews of source meetings and summaries of how the SIGINT was advancing with Donovan. During the prior week, Quinn even invited John for a break at the kiosk. Ironically, John had tea, and Quinn had coffee.

John was in the middle of an email to Annie, who had fought with Ken about whether this project should be terminated or continued. Annie put together a comprehensive overview of events and the expected steps forward on US hostage events in Iraq. Annie and John knew that the basic premise and attention only on *US hostages* missed the mark. An overemphasized focus *exclusively* on US hostages illustrated that Ken and his DC Band-of-Bureaucrats had no real-world understanding of hostage events in Iraq.

Quinn and John discussed the difference in US and UK hostage event processes. Americans looked for hostages and were extraordinarily obsessed with "proof of life." Governments usually wait for the heart-wrenching and sensational video of a hostage pleading for their life or a picture of the hostage holding a recently dated newspaper. John considered proof of life, by itself, only marginally relevant. It was only part of what he called "proof of status." For John, the focus was not necessarily the proof that a hostage was alive, but that a source who provided the proof had the status and ability to get close enough to a hostage and the hostage holders to obtain proof of anything.

Obtaining proof of status meant that a source could obtain an item directly associated with a hostage, which confirmed that the source was someone to work with. The British understood the concept and committed to developing long-term sources.

John leaned back slightly in his chair, interlaced his fingers, placed his hands behind his head, looked directly at Quinn, and asked, "What's your take on this hostage work… Do you think we will get any of them back?"

Quinn nodded and said, "It's all very complicated, as you know. Sorting out who to even talk to—you know… who is actually relevant—is difficult."

John asked, "Well, how about the Americans? Do you think they are alive?"

Without blinking or hesitating, Quinn said, "No, not now…It has been too long since anyone heard anything."

John nodded, scratched the back of his head with his thumbs, and said, "Well, what do you think happened, and what do you think we should do?"

Quinn leaned forward in his chair, momentarily paused, and with a lowered voice said, "Good question…Well…the hostage holders have the same problem we do."

"What do you mean?" asked John, as he sat up and leaned forward closer to Quinn.

Quinn leaned forward with his elbows on his knees. He looked down and interlocked his fingers.

He paused for a moment, looked back up to John, and said, "The hostage holders don't know who they are supposed to talk to either…particularly, in the American maze of people out there looking for hostages."

John sat quietly and listened.

Quinn shrugged and said, "The American structure for handling hostage events is awkward and really unworkable. American politicians jump up and down, scream and shout, and say, 'We Americans refuse to negotiate with terrorists.'…Many Americans, including US government personnel running hostage repatriation efforts, take that as a signal to shut down dialogue with anyone. Essentially, people are hoping hostages will simply show up on their doorstep someday, magically."

John continued to sit silently and listen. The candid opinion from Quinn was invaluable.

Quinn shook his head and said, "You know as well as I do. If you want to catch people that are bad, you have to talk to bad people…or at least someone who knows bad people."

John listened intently. Quinn had become blunter over the past four months and provided John with a developed perspective most Americans never received. He nodded for Quinn to continue. Quinn was quietly incredulous, with his shoulders shrugged and his palms raised to chest level. He said, "People who take and hold hostages are bad and evil people. They are the devil incarnate…but, you can't dance with the devil if you only talk to angels."

Quinn's next questions made his point. "What else are the hostage holders supposed to do…so what do they do next?"

John shook his head and held up his palms in bewilderment. "I have no fuckin' idea."

Quinn shook his head slowly and said, "And neither do the hostage holders, nor those who are in charge of the hostage holders." Quinn shrugged and stared at John, and said, "They don't know what to do next, so…that's when they just do it."

John's eyebrows furrowed. "Well, what?" he asked. "Just do what? What will they just do?"

Quinn shook his head. Then, with his elbows still resting on his knees, he settled his chin atop his interlaced fingers, paused, and said: "They…*just kill the hostages.*"

THAT EVENING DONOVAN AND JOHN MET WITH ASHTON at the British chow hall near headquarters. John recounted his conversation with Quinn. They had all seen the potential of where the project might lead, both good and bad. Everyone needed to start preparing for the worst. Nobody came into the hostage event process to simply recover bodies. Everyone working to return a hostage hoped for the dynamic rescue, with an eventual parade, a pat on the back, and a hearty handshake with the proverbial thanks of the American people. Maybe even a hurried cup of coffee and a photo op with a midlevel staffer on the south side of the White House, perhaps even in the Rose Garden.

That was just not reality. Most American hostages came back to the US after being brutally murdered, if at all.

No midlevel staffer would ever come to the US mortuary in Dover and have their picture taken with someone who brought home the body of a hostage. The tears at Dover were shed for different reasons than the tears in the White House Rose Garden…and for good reason.

Nobody celebrates grief.

They pushed the remnants of chicken and rice around their plates, and John said, "All of the information we have indicates the Americans are dead. And we have been leaning into this hard since we all came together five months ago. But…we also think the hostage holders use rumors of death as a ploy to keep us from asking questions and aggressively looking around."

Donovan looked back and forth between Ashton and John. "Well, didn't you say Cricket thinks they're alive?"

John sat back in his chair. "Yep…but Cricket always tries to spin things positively. We need to find a source with real influence."

To get someone who had influence with the hostage holders to walk through the gate and talk was difficult. They simply did not trust the Americans.

Hostage Status: 237 Days in Captivity

Nothing to report.

CHAPTER 28

BIG ASK . . . KEEPING QUIET

DAY 267: JANUARY 7, 2008

A month had passed since John had gained the insightful perspective from Quinn. Donovan and John regularly sat at a couch and table near the coffee kiosk at Brit-HQ. They drank tea and met informally with Jensen and others. Sitting in the high traffic foyer promoted and nudged interaction. Quinn walked to the kiosk to get his usual cup of coffee. He made eye contact with Donovan and John, who nodded. John slid a chair next to the couch where they sat. Quinn joined them after getting his coffee.

The conversation was light and friendly, and Quinn said to John, "Those digits you slid to me last week were helpful…Cheers," and he tipped his coffee slightly as he blew over the top. "In fact, I was just coming to see you both, and visit with Jensen."

Quinn was referring to telephone numbers and source reports John had provided after a meeting with Cricket and a sub-source. Quinn worked with sources and had begun gathering information regarding the British hostages. Particularly in Baghdad, the British efforts were kept from the Americans, and for good reason. The British thought their hostages were still alive. Quinn and the cadre of British operators feared the inroads they made with Iraqi intermediaries would be stomped upon by brutish, shortsighted, embassy-bound Americans looking for a quick and convenient fix. The British wisely thought long term.

John sat his lukewarm, half empty cup of tea on the table, looked at Quinn, and bluntly asked, "Do you think you might have anyone to help find out about my guys?"

Of course, John was referring to the American hostages.

Quinn nodded, sipped at the edge of the cup, and simply said, "Maybe…I'm meeting with someone today. I will see. However, if you don't mind, might we keep what I find out between us?"

John nodded and said, "Done, no problem."

Quinn looked to Donovan, who also nodded. Quinn said, "Very well…talk soon…I'm sure."

Quinn got up from the chair, sipped his coffee, and walked to the exclusively British side of the large foyer. He touched the buttons of an electronic cypher lock and entered a door that neither Donovan nor John had been through. Donovan looked at John, took a deep breath, and slowly exhaled. John did the same as he rubbed his forehead with the back of his hand and looked at his cup of tea.

He glanced at Donovan and said, "I really can't tell if that fuckin' cup of tea right there in front of us is half full or half empty."

DONOVAN AND JOHN WENT BACK TO THE TEAM HOUSE. Movie night was early. Donovan and the SF team crammed into the chairs and couches, while John rested flat on the floor with a pillow under his head. His back felt better lying flat. They watched *Caddyshack* for the fifth time.

THE NIGHT WAS INTERRUPTED BY TWO ROCKET ATTACKS, with three impacts each. Nobody was hurt. The ground shook and alarms sounded, but the impacts were far enough away to ignore. Neither Donovan nor John got up—they simply covered their heads with their pillows to quiet the siren. Along with the SF operators, they adopted the absurd notion that their pillows were ballistic and maintained some sort of magic rocket protection. John had embraced the SF thinking of "random" when it came to getting killed by a rocket.

Neither slept well. They feared what they might hear from Quinn.

Hostage Status: 267 Days in Captivity

Nothing to report.

CHAPTER 29

NOTE FROM QUINN

DAY 268: JANUARY 8, 2008

On their walk from the SF compound to Brit-HQ, John sipped a Red Bull and ate a Pop Tart while Donovan kicked at miscellaneous rocks along the road. They usually crossed the main road near the grove of palm trees and oddly overgrown grass. The road widened there, and the stench from the aboveground hookup where septic trucks emptied was less pungent. Near the edge of the road where they crossed stood a concrete pedestal that before the war had held a statue.

Donovan and John passed the trees to a sidewalk near the fence line. Some time ago they had determined why the trees were lush and the weeds were flourishing. A water pipe had broken in several places and kept the palm grove puddled. Nobody knew or cared where the water came from.

John usually split the second package of Pop Tarts with Donovan by the time they arrived at the Brit-HQ perimeter fence line, and today was no different. They walked on the sidewalk around the edge of the perimeter fence line and were waved through without raising their IDs. They passed between the sandbag post and the duck-and-cover bunker, still without end caps.

Donovan and John had become fixtures at Brit-HQ. They were always well received and entered the command center without issue. Typically, Donovan continued to his cell, started his computer, and logged in to the secure system. Then he would return to the command center to see what's John's latest emails showed.

Today, when Donovan arrived at John's desk, he was standing over his terminal, waiting for his email to download and holding a yellow sticky note in his hand. "I found this on my keyboard," he said, handing the note to Donovan, who read it. It said, "John, please come by when you have a moment. Quinn."

"It's weird. This is the first time he has ever left a note. And the first time he ever asked me to come by."

Donovan put his hand on his hip, handed the note back, and said, "Well, whatever he wants to talk about, he doesn't want to put in an email."

John nodded. "Yeah, no shit."

Donovan pulled his hair from his face and back into a ponytail briefly, as he eagerly said, "Well, fuckin' go find out what the fuck is up."

They both grinned at each other.

John nodded, folded the note once, and said, "Yeah, OK, got it. I will come find you when I'm done."

Donovan hurried back to his cell, and John walked out of the command center. John quickly passed the coffee kiosk to the side of the large foyer and arrived at the door where he had seen Quinn pass through almost daily. He looked at the electronic cypher lock, unfolded the note in his hands, and gently knocked on the door.

A fit man in his early thirties wearing civilian clothes opened the door. He was rather nondescript, except for the fact he wore a clear plastic radio earpiece and a sling across his chest that held the machine pistol resting comfortably at his hip.

He smiled and quite pleasantly asked, "Hello, how may I help you, sir?"

The gentleman was a member of the Special Air Service, or SAS. Like the rest of the security detail in this part of the building, he was battle hardened, extraordinarily bright, and had been handpicked for security in the Foreign Office. His talents were presently underutilized, but it was recognized as a certain honor to be selected.

John nodded, smiled, and said, "Hello, I'm looking for Quinn."

"Quinn?" asked the SAS operator.

John held up the yellow sticky note, and said, "Um, yes, I have a note."

With dry sarcasm, the SAS operator said, "Oh, a note? But of course, you do, mate," he smiled briefly and said, "One moment, be right back."

They both grinned at each other, and the door shut. John stood patiently outside the door. He looked at his note from Quinn. Unknown to John, the SAS operator was not quizzing John on who he wanted to visit. The SAS operator took a moment to process John's American accent and sized him up. The SAS operator had an uncanny ability to quickly assess where an American was from based on accent.

After a minute, the door opened, and Quinn stepped out into the foyer. His brow was furrowed, and he said, "Hey mate, I see you found my note." They both smiled briefly. "The security guys just love it when we have Americans come to the door with a note."

They both chuckled.

John looked at the floor, then up to Quinn, and asked "So, how was your meeting yesterday?"

"Productive and dismal, all at the same time, I'm afraid," said Quinn.

John expected bad news. He could tell by the tone of Quinn's voice, and the way his head dropped.

John said, "OK…well, I'm getting used to bad news. Something tells me coming from you…it's really bad."

Quinn nodded. "Afraid so, mate. Your guys are dead. I don't have any more detail than that."

John rubbed the back of his neck and asked, "Well, what do you think? Can we get them back…you know… the bodies?…Are we even talking to the right people to make that happen?"

Quinn nodded slowly. "Good question. I think so. I should know more this afternoon. We can talk later this evening."

"OK…thanks. Can I keep Donovan in the loop on this?"

Quinn's eyes widened, he nodded, and said, "Absolutely, it will be because of Donovan and Jensen that we will know anything, really."

Quinn re-entered the British lair, passing the SAS operator at the door, and John returned to brief Donovan in his secure vault-like cell.

John weaved through the command center and into the large SCIF area. He passed the collection of desks where voices murmured about the operations of war. The no-patch US soldier in the corner typing at his keyboard glanced at John and said nothing.

John turned the corner to Donovan's cell and tapped on the partially open door as he entered the room. Donovan seemed to have the cursor on all three screens at once as he ran different programs and searches simultaneously. He heard John at the door but needed to complete the current pattern searches, so he sat and clicked. John had once before interrupted Donovan when he was at this level of intensity, and it had thrown him off for hours.

Donovan tapped the computer mouse on the desk three times, which was something he did unconsciously at the very end of a complicated series of queries. John knew Donovan would finish the program within the next ten seconds. John had been around the SIGINT people like Donovan and Jensen so much now that even he had taken on some odd counting quirks. When John saw Donovan tap the computer mouse three times, he started counting backwards from ten, in his head. He did this as he laid flat on the desk behind Donovan to stretch his back.

He heard Donovan push the keyboard forward, slide his chair back, and stand. Donovan knew John was behind him stretching his back on the desk. Donovan walked across the small room and shook out his hands and wrists while John sat up on the desk.

Donovan looked at him, continued to shake his fingers and forearms with his arms at his side, and impatiently asked, "OK, what the fuck…What did Quinn say?"

"They're dead," said John. He shrugged his shoulders and shook his head slightly.

Donovan stopped shaking his forearms and fingers, and said, "OK…that's not good…What do we do next?"

John summarized the conversation with Quinn. "I asked if he was sure, and if he was talking with the people who could get the bodies back. First, I think he's pretty damn sure. Second, I think Quinn is going to need you and Jensen and your magic in order to confirm he's talking with the right people to get bodies back."

Donovan nodded. "This is a critical and sensitive time."

John nodded. "You're exactly right. We can't fuck this up, and the British have to keep trusting you and me." He stood up from the desk and said, "How about we walk and talk, go to lunch early...I think it could be a long afternoon."

"Echos?" Donovan asked.

"Perfect," John said, watching Donovan rub his hands together and raise his shoulders like a mad scientist. They both acknowledged the moment with brief anguished smiles.

Hostage Status: 268 Days in Captivity

Nothing to report.

CHAPTER 30

ROCKETS AGAIN...JOHN AND DONOVAN BRAINSTORM

DAY 268 (*CONTINUED*): JANUARY 8, 2008

Echos was only a fifteen-minute walk from Brit-HQ for Donovan and John, who were immersed in conversation, discussing how various scenarios might develop. As they headed from the front door of Brit-HQ toward the soldier at the sandbag post, a deafening explosion thundered behind them. A rocket impacted fifty yards to their left in a field. Donovan and John reflexively brought their hands to their ears as they felt the force from the blast wash over them.

John turned in the direction of the sound and yelled, "Fuck, that was loud!"

They walked and cupped their hands over their ears despite the ringing already in their heads. In the distance the alarm began to sound, warning of an incoming rocket. The British soldier posted at the perimeter fence hurdled the ten yards to the duck-and-cover bunker in two strides and was flat on the ground.

With a short buzzsaw groan, a C-RAM fired a barrage of munitions into the sky, trying to shoot down another incoming rocket. Donovan and John raced for the duck-and-cover bunker. As they neared it, they heard the second impact but kept focused on the bunker and stepped inside. They stood stooped on one side of the bunker, and the British soldier now sat on the ground, leaning against the concrete wall with his fingers in his ears. He was the smart one. The soldier looked up at Donovan and John and nodded.

There were no end caps on the bunker. Donovan looked out past John at the smoke and dust hovering over the first impact area, and said, "That was way too fuckin' close. Damn, these fuckin' rockets are loud."

They heard the third impact but could not see where it landed. It was not as close as the first or second rockets. They looked out toward the junkyard across the main road, and just then the fourth rocket slammed to the earth one hundred yards to their left. They saw a flash and an immediate plume of black smoke, and they heard a piercing burst of thunder.

Stooped over with their hands on their thighs, Donovan and John looked out either end of the bunker. They looked to the right and watched the plume of smoke and particulate waft across the open space between Brit-HQ and the Basra airport. They looked to the left and contemplated the dark smoke one hundred yards away at the junkyard.

Donovan looked at John, and simply said, "This isn't good."

Being caught in a rocket attack was common. What was unusual was being caught in a rocket attack in a risky position and actually seeing the impact of another rocket. That they were in a duck-and-cover bunker without concrete end caps with rockets exploding on either side was surreal.

The incoming warning siren continued in the distance. As soon as the attack started, it was over. Within two minutes the all-clear signal sounded.

Donovan and John stepped out of the duck-and-cover bunker. The British soldier stepped out with them and brushed the dirt from his uniform. Nobody said anything at first.

Donovan and John stood at the edge of the bunker for a moment, then shook hands with the soldier, who said, "Alright…Alright?" It was first a statement, then a question.

Donovan nodded. "Yep, OK."

John nodded, straightened his ID pouch, and said, "Yeah, OK, thanks…You?"

The British soldier nodded, gave the front of his uniform one last swipe, and said, "Indeed…I am…Cheers, mate."

The soldier turned and walked back to his sandbag post. Donovan and John continued their walk toward Echos.

Donovan looked toward the junkyard and said, "That was really fucked up. How do we ever explain what just happened?"

"Why bother? Nobody would believe us anyway," John said.

At Echos, Donovan and John ordered pizza. Their usual table was open. They were focused and needed to be smart about how they handled things. They both agreed that if they strayed from their agreement with Quinn to keep their mouths shut, they would never be trusted by the British again. They had to be smart.

John knew he needed to update Annie to keep DC off her back. Ken in DC had actually proved that he was dumber than the box of rocks Annie had left for John. John would have to be vague and talk about Cricket and meetings pending with sub-sources. Donovan would be able to keep Baghdad and The Fort satisfied with vague summaries of analysis and patterns he was exploiting. If Donovan got pressed on specifics, he would refer anyone who asked over to John and the FBI. That would create a circular pattern of queries that would confuse most people and frustrate others into lethargic head-scratching.

Donovan and John planned to provide just enough smoke and mirrors to buy time to see if Quinn could pull things together. Quinn was making operational decisions based on historical information Donovan and John had provided and other variables they did not know he was managing. Donovan and John had to do what they were doing and do it quietly.

At the end of their pizza brainstorming session, Donovan grinned and said, "Well…it's a plan…not a great plan, but still a plan…"

John nodded. "Yep…and the only thing worse than a bad plan…is no plan at all…"

They laughed and shook their heads at the absurd reality in which they found themselves.

Hostage Status: 268 Days in Captivity (*continued*)

Nothing to report.

CHAPTER 31

ANOTHER NOTE… SCIF COLLABORATION

DAY 268 (*CONTINUED*): JANUARY 8, 2008

After lunch, Donovan and John talked on the way from Echos to Brit-HQ. It was quiet, no rockets. Inside the command center they stopped at John's computer. On the keyboard was another yellow note. It read, "John, when you have a moment, could you and Donovan stop by?" and was signed "Quinn."

Donovan and John looked at each other, nodded without saying a word, and walked out of the command center. They crossed the large foyer past the coffee kiosk where people urgently discussed the damage from the earlier rocket attack. They stopped at Quinn's door, and this time Donovan knocked. The door opened immediately.

The same SAS operator from earlier in the day greeted them. "I assume you have a note, mate?" he said, grinning and holding the door.

He motioned for Donovan and John to follow him. They passed through the doorway and stood in a nondescript hall that looked like any other at Brit-HQ.

The SAS operator said, "One moment, I'll get Quinn.

Be right back."

John whispered to Donovan, "Well, we've made progress. We're finally through the door."

Donovan grinned and nodded as they stood looking at each other's feet. The SAS operator emerged from a doorway about forty feet away followed by Quinn, who gestured for Donovan and John to come down the hallway. They walked to meet Quinn as he stood at the doorway. They stood in the hall. Behind Quinn at a desk in the SCIF sat Amelia. She smiled, waved, and said hello.

Quinn was hurried and said, "Gentlemen, thanks for stopping by. I do believe we may get some movement in that effort we discussed regarding body delivery of your American hostages."

Donovan and John nodded and listened.

Quinn looked at Donovan and said, "As this developed, I've provided reporting to Jensen, who just received it. I believe it might be most productive if you both reviewed it and worked through the verification process. Do you have time for that?"

Quinn and his group were the consummate polite professionals, even under great stress. Donovan and John stood silently, nodded, and shrugged.

Quinn said, "Very well, gents. Jensen will be over to see you in five minutes." He turned toward Amelia and added, "Amelia will be over in…"

"Three minutes," she finished his sentence and smiled.

Quinn turned and walked into the SCIF while Donovan and John walked toward the door.

After they took a few steps, Quinn leaned out the door and said, "Gents, this all needs to stay between us, for now." It was as much a question as it was a statement.

Donovan and John nodded, waved, and continued to the door, which the polite SAS operator opened for them.

"See you soon, gentlemen, and don't worry about needing a note anymore, mates." He grinned as they nodded and walked through the door.

Donovan and John did a great deal of staying quiet and nodding.

Within ten minutes Donovan's cell was full. Jensen and Donovan sat at the desk in front of the monitors. Amelia and Quinn stood behind Jensen and Donovan and looked over their shoulders. John stood near the door out of the way. The pace of the computer work was beyond what John could process. A constant flow of questions and answers streamed among the four. The back and forth was urgent. Answers were curt and precise. John was asked several seemingly innocuous questions by Quinn and Amelia. Fortunately, he had the immediate answers, and the movement on the three screens continued to race. The ad hoc meeting went for three hours.

Finally, Quinn leaned back on the desk and said, "OK, everyone please keep the day after tomorrow open between 2:00 p.m. and 6:00 p.m. . . . We may have a delivery."

Everyone agreed, and as Quinn was leaving the room, he looked back to Donovan and John, brought the first knuckle of his extended index finger to his lips, and raised his eyebrows. His message was clear: hush. Donovan and John nodded.

Hostage Status: 268 Days in Captivity (*continued*)

Nothing to report.

CHAPTER 32

BRITISH INNER SANCTUM

DAY 269: JANUARY 9, 2008

The following morning, John arrived to find another note from Quinn on his keyboard. Just in case he needed to show the note, he folded it in half and placed it in his pocket.

Donovan and John walked to Quinn's door and were met by a different SAS operator, who asked, "Are you here for Quinn?"

They both nodded and followed their escort to the SCIF door. Amelia noticed them immediately and invited them into the SCIF working area with the wave of her hand. Donovan and John were trusted. If they had alerted their US colleagues in Baghdad about the pending delivery, Amelia and Quinn would have known by now.

Quinn came from around the corner of a room divider and said, "Morning, gents. Moving right along, I'd say. Let's expect something tomorrow afternoon. I'm not sure how many…As you might expect, we may get everyone or just a partial delivery. This process could take some time. We take what we get and keep our hands off the delivery person. No matter how much we want to grab him. Are we OK with that?"

They both nodded. Quinn smiled, shrugged his shoulders, and nodded. He was satisfied with their ability to keep their word.

Hostage Status: 269 Days in Captivity

Nothing to report.

CHAPTER 33

STAYING CRYPTIC WITH ANNIE ...HEADS UP TO SF

DAY 270: JANUARY 10, 2008

The next morning, John called Annie from the Special Forces team house while Donovan finished his second game of Ping-Pong with Nathan. Using the SF secure phone, he gave her an overview of what he expected during the next meeting with Cricket and a sub-source of Cricket's. Annie asked how Donovan was doing, and if there was any more detail she could put in the overview she was assembling for Hoover—the FBI headquarters in DC.

John was cautious on the phone. He knew he could trust Annie, but he did not want her in a position where she could be put on the spot by the FBI BOC hierarchy or the idiot Ken in DC, who was looking for a reason to get someone in Iraq in trouble.

John said, "Well, I think it might be fair to say that US exploitation efforts, coupled with coalition partner interests, are yielding extraordinary technical targeting benefits."

Annie shot back, "OK...What the fuck does that mean? That means nothing. That's a bunch of bullshit gibberish... what the fuck?"

"Well, that's what I have right now," he replied.

"You don't want to tell me *something* right now, huh?" she said.

"Correct."

"I have to trust you on this, don't I?"

"Yep."

"OK. Got it…I will come up with some bullshit to put in the overview for Hoover," Annie said.

She knew John was shielding whatever process he was developing—and protecting her.

"Don't go anyplace where your phone won't work for the next day," he added.

"OK…understood. Be careful, dumbass," Annie said.

"OK…no problem…Talk soon."

John went out to the U-shaped couches, where Ashton, Ryan, and Kyle sat. They had just finished in the gym and were discussing a plan for a meeting with a new source.

John looked at the edge of the coffee table and said, "Hey, this is really close-hold…goes nowhere." The SF operators nodded. "The British have something going with hostage stuff. I really don't know the details, but I think we might have something coming in…maybe today."

Donovan, John, and the SF team had spoken several weeks earlier and knew they needed to start planning for the worst: recovery of remains—or in layman's terms, pick up body bags. This morning it did not even need to be said. They could tell by John's demeanor that they would *not* be conducting a live rescue or hostage debriefing.

Ashton, Ryan, and Kyle nodded, and Kyle said, "No problem. Let us know when and where."

Everyone understood the compartmentalization of information, and the reality that John probably really did not know what the hell the British were up to.

Ashton said, “Do you need me anywhere?”

“I really don’t know,” John replied. “Donovan and I are going to Brit-HQ now to see what’s happening, if anything.”

Ashton said, “OK, I will take a shower and meet you there in a bit.”

John nodded. “OK, good idea. Thanks. If I’m not there, I will leave a note on my keyboard in the command center.”

Ashton gave a thumbs-up as he took a big swig of water.

John got up from the couch and waved to Donovan. He was finished playing Ping-Pong with Nathan and was bouncing the ball on the paddle and counting the taps. John stopped in the junk-food room and grabbed two Red Bulls and Pop-Tarts. They made their way to Brit-HQ on foot.

Hostage Status: 270 Days in Captivity

Nothing to report.

CHAPTER 34

AND ANOTHER NOTE...THE DELIVERY

DAY 270 (*CONTINUED*): JANUARY 10, 2008

Another note appeared on John's computer terminal: "John, we are moving along for today. You and D come by when you get a chance. Regards, Quinn."

John handed the note to Donovan, who read it and nodded. They left the command center, crossed the foyer, and knocked on the hallway door, which a polite SAS operator promptly answered. He held the door for Donovan and John and gestured toward the SCIF entrance. They were not escorted or announced. At the SCIF, Amelia waved them in and walked them around the divider to the coffee and tea counter. Quinn would be right back, she explained; they should make themselves at home and have a seat on the couch or chair. The two Americans made tea, and Amelia had coffee. They sat on the couch and chatted for a moment until Quinn arrived.

Quinn looked at Donovan and John and quickly said, "Hey Amelia...Morning, gents. We should get to the gate at the far end by the airport...right now." It was not a request.

Amelia opened her bottom desk drawer, grabbed a submachine gun, and put the harness on as they left the SCIF.

On their way out of Brit-HQ, they ran into Ashton at the front security desk.

John looked from Ashton to Quinn. "Do we need an extra car or gun or anything?"

Quinn nodded, shook Ashton's hand, and said, "One of your Special Forces chaps, I presume. I have SAS for cover and security...Let's have your friend jump in with the SAS gents, and he can start working communications on your side." Quinn was a pro. He never ignored an asset and knew how to capitalize on an operational opportunity.

Ashton called the team house and explained where they were headed. Kyle called out to Ryan and Nathan, and they snatched their machine guns as they passed the war room and ran to an SUV. When they pulled onto the main road, they could see the SAS operators and an ambulance ahead in the distance and were able to catch up. The SF operators coordinated and communicated directly with the SAS operators over secure radios. SAS made sure the SF operators knew the ambulance was driven by an SAS operator with five others inside it to provide security.

John rode with Amelia and Quinn, who drove. They headed down the main road, passing the SF compound turnoff and continuing with the airport on the right. A gate at one side of the COB was rarely used. It was down a long empty stretch of road, and the location was simply inconvenient, and not well secured. They drove past the Iraqi gate guard and parked about fifty yards from the outside the fence line.

A car was parked on the side of the road, and a white panel truck was parked about thirty yards behind the car on the same side. The Iraqi driver was out of the car, leaning against the hood and smoking a cigarette. Quinn got out of the SUV, walked toward the driver, and nodded. The SAS vehicle with Ashton and the Green Beret SUV drove past and parked near the truck. The ambulance full of SAS operators parked next to the rear of the truck. There was no truck driver.

Quinn called out to the SAS operators poised near the back of the truck, "I'm going to the trunk."

John followed Quinn to the car. The driver tossed the keys to Quinn, who went toward the trunk. Quinn watched the driver, who did not flinch. He was not a suicide bomber and was comfortable with what he was doing.

Quinn neared the trunk, with John following closely. Suddenly hit with the unmistakable smell of death, neither flinched. A dead body had a certain smell. It was hard to mask. Quinn opened the trunk to see a misshapen roll of plastic. He put on the gloves he had stashed in his pocket. Quinn was prepared; he had done this before. He tugged at the edge of the plastic, pulling it farther and gesturing for John to look. John saw the upper shoulder of the body.

THUMP!

Just then a loud thump came from inside the white panel truck. Quinn let go of the plastic turning with John toward the truck—SAS and SF tactically aligning themselves toward the back of the truck. The pounding grew louder and aggressive—a sort of double thump.

THUMP-thump!

Quinn had not told John every detail of what was anticipated today. Along with what they had seen in the trunk, Quinn expected another delivery. The British hostages—alive.

Quinn pushed the plastic back in place and stepped back from the trunk. The sound had a double-thump like a heartbeat. The pounding in the truck grew louder and weightier. John had a ridiculously fleeting thought of Edgar Allen Poe's "The Tell-Tale Heart" flash through his head. The double-thump got louder.

The SAS operators opened the back of the white panel truck. They had been briefed and expected at least one of the four British hostages. No immediate threat was seen, but there were four rolls of carpet lying side by side.

A pair of bare feet protruded from each roll.

The senior SAS operator called to Quinn and described what he was seeing. And just then the other three pair of feet began moving—his voice was a trigger. The carpet rolls were taped shut. One roll of carpet had loosened enough for the hostage inside to bend his knees, pushing and kicking at the side of the truck when he heard Quinn's voice earlier.

…thump-thump!…thump-thump!…thump-thump!…thump-thump!

The hostage's knees struck the side of the truck before his feet—producing the sound of a loud eerie heartbeat.

The five SAS operators from the ambulance climbed into the truck.

Quinn ran to the back of the truck and yelled, "Cut the tape…get that fuckin' carpet off them!"

Three sets of feet protruding from the carpet began moving and twisting faster. And the one set continued the double-thump. Muffled voices were heard—the hostages were trying to talk. Ashton and Ryan climbed into the back of the truck, helping unroll the carpet and removing scarves covering the hostages' eyes and mouths.

Quinn and John stood near the back of the truck as blindfolds and gags came off. The hostages were unrecognizable—filthy, incredibly thin, unshaven, and unshorn for 270 days.

Quinn yelled to any of the hostages who might respond. "Say your name so we know who we have!"

The four hostages sat dazed, guzzling water provided by the SAS, and panting while catching their breath. The hostage who had been kicking the wall of the van slowly looked up—he had an infected four-inch scar on his forehead.

He said, "Hey, it sure is nice to see you guys…Thanks for the water."

He was speaking English. American English.

John knew who he was right away—he pronounced "water" with a Maryland accent.

All four BWH hostages were safe.

CHAPTER 35

HOSTAGE MOVEMENT… AND WTF HAPPENED

AFTER 270 DAYS IN CAPTIVITY: APRIL 15, 2007, TO JANUARY 10, 2008

The American hostages were brought to the British hospital for immediate medical care. A US military transport plane was sent from Baghdad, and they were flown to a US base in Landstuhl, Germany. Then to Texas, where they would voluntarily undergo debriefing, medical treatment, and set up long term counseling, if desired.

The body in the back of the car was an actual hostage—an Iraqi hostage. He had been kidnapped and held for ransom. A criminal element among the hostage holders tried to make money on the side. The Iraqi hostage did not have much money. Nobody would pay the ransom. So, he was killed. His body was later released to Iraqi authorities by the British.

The British hostages were still alive. Quinn had SIGINT verification of that earlier in the day. The confusion in communication was due to messages passing through layers and layers of people. Someone in the chain misunderstood that Quinn was looking for the *English* hostages. Instead, they produced hostages who *spoke* English—the Americans.

The search for the British hostages would continue.

CHAPTER 36

WHAT'S NEXT...UHOH

AFTER 30 DAYS IN THE US: MARCH 12, 2008

One month after returning from Iraq, John took the vacation leave he had saved up during his prolonged stay in the Middle East. He was two beers into the afternoon and a thirty pack of Busch Light when his cell phone rang. John had rented a house on the water in North Carolina—in a small town called Duck in an area known as the Outer Banks. He was sitting on the deck overlooking the ocean. He had already ignored his phone for several days, particularly when he saw a seven-zero-three area code and knew it was FBI Quantico. He glanced at the phone, and the caller ID showed Annie's cell phone number, so he answered.

"Hey dumbass, it's me," she said. "Are you shit-faced, yet?"

John popped a new beer near the phone so she could hear it and said, "Not yet."

Annie laughed. "Ha, you idiot… Hey, here's what's up. Some ding-dongs at FBI Quantico want to know what you did and how you did it…you know, in Basra."

John paused for a moment, then said, "Uh-oh."

Annie laughed. "Yeah, no shit. I said fuckin' 'Uh-oh,' too." She paused for a moment, then said, "I told these fuckers that you and I had not discussed some details, and that I wrote the paperwork in Baghdad based on your emails… that's why they don't see your reports."

John took a large sip from his beer, burped into the phone, and said, "Uh-oh."

Annie snickered. "Yeah, that's a no-shit-uh-oh. Here's the thing. They don't know about all the other moving parts. I think we will be fine with whatever weird shit you might have done to make things happen down there."

John nodded, cringed slightly, paused, and looked at the beer he had just opened, then said, "Well, that's good, because some people aren't gonna like how some of this came together."

After a pause, Annie said, "I know…All good…and here's why…What they really want to see is if you can do it again. Some British guy named Mr. Ethan bumped a request up to the directors of the FBI and NSA somehow."

John finished the beer and opened another. "Uh-oh," he said. "…And?"

Annie continued, "The British are still missing their hostages…They want you and Donovan back as a team. You both know the territory and how shit works in Basra. You can say no, but…I'm thinking you won't."

There was a long pause on both ends.

Annie broke the silence. "Well, are you in? You got this?"

"Maybe…," he said. "How about you? You got this?"

"No dumbass…*WE* got this."

The End

ACKNOWLEDGMENTS

WOMEN OF LAW ENFORCEMENT AND THE INTELLIGENCE COMMUNITY (US AND UK)

First, my sincerest thanks to so many of you in various agencies for your patience and tolerance and allowing me to be part of your lives. You fixed what I broke, cleared paths for me to operate, and led the way when I was hopelessly spinning my wheels and going nowhere.

If not for the women leading the fight from the shadows with grace, commitment, and character, the bodies of some of those kidnapped and murdered would not have come back when they did. Other measures of justice would not have been exacted.

Countless aggressive, forward-leaning actions and deeds happened because of you. Whether you are still on the job or have retired, you are owed a great debt of gratitude by so many who will never know your names or how you made a difference.

Thank you for your intelligent, back-channel operational thinking and self-sacrifice resulting in real progress in an environment often dominated by small-thinking, egotistic, and self-centered careerists.

From the time I came on with DoD and for the next 30-plus years, through numerous agencies, and around the world, I was fortunate to be surrounded by consummate professionals…most of the time…well, some of the time.

When something broke and came off the rails, it was frequently and professionally “fixed” by a woman on the job. Some of these remedies were seemingly disconnected actions, episodes, and circumstances. Often these women did not know one another, yet they all leaned forward in the same daunting, thankless, uphill direction to do what was right and bring solutions to a problem set. And frequently there was no precedent, no template, and no playbook. They adjusted, adapted, and overcame the hurdles in front of them. They persevered.

The women I worked with in law enforcement and the intelligence community produced results through grace, finesse, savvy, and selfless commitment. And periodically, they got up in someone’s face and adjusted things.

Thank you.

Critical women of courage: JG, LW, NC, ML, JJ, A?, PL, H and A, JR, LS, TK, DK, NR, VR, AJ, PN, BF, DN, JN, BO, MW, SK and KK, DN, AK, and so many more.

And a respectful nod to Green Berets (ODAs): ’07, ’08, ’09, ’10, and ’11; and SEALS ’10.

And to Lieutenant Colonel JG, US Army, Retired (Baghdad): ’08 and ‘09

And to “The Fort”: 2*2.437/23.0.+?=f(x).√?=4.47214.0

I would also like to express my gratitude to Chris Frisella for his patient and thoughtful editing of the manuscript and to the team at Luminare Press for their skill and expertise throughout each of step to publication.

AFTERWORD

What the reader should know is that hostage events are complicated.

Writing a book about hostage events, even fictionally, takes time and can be complicated.

Opinions vary greatly on whether former government personnel should write and publish. Some people think anyone who worked for the US government should be prohibited from ever writing. Others suggest writing can enhance government practices in the future and prevent the bureaucracy from keeping its head buried in the sand.

My assignment to the FBI's Counterterrorism Division was considered by many to be worthwhile at the time. We were productive, and since the FBI paid the tab, I was allowed to continue with operational development—for years.

Countless people strive to exist in a clearly defined world; I found myself in a blurry, gray, murky reality of uncertainty. And I liked it.

What we collectively moved forward was out of the ordinary—an extended operational team lasting for years.

Soldiers and some government folks I worked with wanted to hear about my promotion and awards I received. People assumed that I was offered a "choice position" after spending five evolutions in a war zone and years away from home—maybe promoted.

None of that happened, and I seemed to be the only one not surprised. Soldiers and others appeared dismayed. Almost by definition, I was supposed to be invisible. I had disappeared so efficiently, I was unseen to my own agency.

The FBI arranged for a letter from the director and mounted it on a plaque. Nice. Thank you.

After some closure at FBI, I put in for a position at the National Counterterrorism Center (NCTC) to start the twilight of my government career. I thought I had earned the support of my agency hierarchy—I was mistaken. Perhaps the fear of mission creep by one of my own at NCTC, or maybe big egos with myopic vision. Feasibly I had not merited the opportunity. Likely, a multifaceted combination. I was denied the chance to serve in the position after being selected by NCTC. It really was the first stage of the end of my career.

A few months later, I was part of a videoconference with headquarters regarding new hostage response concepts. Some agency headquarters staff had agendas I considered to be unrealistic. Further, they wanted nothing to do with anyone who had real-world-operational-boots-on-the-ground experience with hostage events in denied areas—that is, in war zones. I was embarrassed for them. I voiced my thoughts—at and to raised levels in the agency.

It was time for me to retire. I did.

Just after retiring, I collaborated with a former hostage to develop and launch a big-picture concept on hostage events with real international impact that went nowhere. Too bad.

Some people said, "You should write a book." So, I did. It took years. I walked around Washington, DC, with different concepts, story lines and multi-sided conversations in my head. Finally, the abstract thinking turned into action, and thoughts morphed into writing. After a lot of starting, stopping, and starting again, and after various government agency prepublication reviews, my first book was finally finished.

POSTSCRIPT

One last thought…

To current and future government employees: strive to never get hurt on the job. Nobody will care. And soon after the injury you will be on your own to deal with the process.

During the fall of 2007, I got hurt in Baghdad; I made the trek from Basra on British military air. The Puma helicopter landed at the airfield adjacent to the American embassy (FOB Washington). The landing zone was dark, loud, and rotor wash blindingly filled the air with dirt. I was the only American on the helicopter.

When we landed, I slid out of the helicopter over the edge of the floor and awkwardly got my feet on the ground. I turned and grabbed my pack from the floor then pulled it from the helicopter. I could feel my shoulder "pop."

I was injured but functional. The moving parts we had in play took priority over a comparatively minor injury in a war zone. I managed and pressed on for some time until I got back to the US and put in the paperwork to get medical follow-up care.

A claim for treatment/care was denied. I did not have a witness for the injury. I explained I was the only American on a helicopter flight in a war zone on a non-US aircraft.

The claim for treatment/care was denied again later because I was past the thirty-day limit for submitting the paperwork. Getting medical care after injury on the job, even in a war zone, was nobody's priority or interest but mine.

I decided to continue the ongoing hostage work that I believed was bigger than me and my sore shoulder. I was not being valiant or tough. I just decided to focus my energy elsewhere—perhaps I was looking after myself more than I thought.

I was staying part of something that I feared I would not be able to get back into if I stepped out of the game and off the field. I was afraid of becoming a spectator, not a player. I did not want to become part of the crowd in the bleachers instead of on the field—one of the few truly in the game.

Ironically, not getting medical treatment was selfish on my part. I was driven to stay entrenched in a complicated operational setting that few government or military people will ever glimpse in a career. Along with a near constant infusion of adrenalin-generating situations, I got extremely comfortable where others could not, or even have the chance to try…war zones…and, I had a long leash…

As I explained in the Introduction of this book, I brought this upon myself. I stepped into something bigger, and far beyond any one person. I am good with it.

To that end, stay in the arena. Avoid getting hurt. And as one character in this book said: "Try not to die."

GLOSSARY

Agency – Informal way of referring to the Central Intelligence Agency (CIA)

Baaasra – Exaggerated British pronunciation of Basra; spelling is the writer's emphasis

Badge – Identification, usually with a photo, expiration date, and issued by and for a particular facility or entity

BOC – Abbreviation for the FBI's Baghdad Operation Center; pronounced "bock"

Brits – Informal way many Americans refer to British citizens or personnel

Brit-Air – Informal American term for British military air support; usually Lockheed C-130 transport plane or Puma helicopter

Brit-HQ – Informal American reference to the location of British command and control in Basra

Car park – British English for parking lot

Chemlight – Six-inch plastic tube containing chemicals that react when mixed and create light

Clotting powder – Substance that when applied to an open wound causes blood to rapidly coagulate

COB – Abbreviation for Contingency Operating Base; same as American FOB, or Forward Operating Base in a war zone; COB Basra; pronounced "Cob"

C-RAM – Abbreviation for Counter-Rocket, Artillery, and Mortar system; utilized to detect and destroy incoming fire

BWH hostage event – Broken Wheel Hostages; kidnap event 2007

Down range – Phrase used to reference a war zone

Duck and cover bunker – A blast resistant concrete structure that stood four feet high, four feet wide, and approximately twelve feet long; open on either end; sometimes had concrete end caps, or barriers, at either side

Dwell time – Time American military personnel spent in the US between deployments

Echos – British contracted restaurant on Basra; sold pizza; casual dining

ECP – Abbreviation for Entry Control Point; usually a gate or guarded entry/exit

FOB – Forward Operating Base; fortified area where the military lived and functioned; pronounced "Fob"

FOB Washington – Forward Operating Base; airfield adjacent to the US embassy in Baghdad

Foreign and Commonwealth Office – Comparable to the US State Department, however, more pervasive and inclusive; often referred to as the Foreign Office

FM – Fuckin' magic; reference made when something happened that was unexplained

GCHQ – General Communications Headquarters; British equivalent to the NSA; per Wikipedia: The Government Communications Headquarters is a British intelligence and security organisation responsible for providing signals intelligence and information assurance to the British government and armed forces

Gensiya – Iraqi national identification card

Green Zone – Area in and about Baghdad with concentric

perimeters usually considered safe; also reference to any area within the perimeter of the US or UK forces

Hesco barrier – Protective barrier against blast; reinforced metal mesh squares with thick material like felt paper lining the metal box frames filled with dirt; size ranges upward from four feet by four feet by four feet

Hoover – FBI Headquarters; informal way of referring to FBI DC; name of the structure is the J. Edgar Hoover Building

HUMINT – Informal and professional way of saying Human Intelligence; per Wikipedia: category of intelligence derived from information collected and provided by human sources

HWG – Hostage Working Group; usually reference to FBI Hostage Working Group; also a reference to numerous entities that developed to attempt to address hostage events

ID – Informal way of referring to identification; see Badge

IED – Improvised Explosive Device

NAAFI – Navy, Army, and Air Force Institutes; British equivalent to the US military system for shopping and convenience stores

Nine Line – Method and procedure for the US military to call in a medical air evacuation

NSA – National Security Agency; per NSA website: The National Security Agency/Central Security Service (NSA/CSS) leads the US Government in cryptology that encompasses both Signals Intelligence (SIGINT) and Information Assurance (IA) products and services and enables Computer Network Operations (CNO) in order to gain a decision advantage for the Nation and our allies under all circumstances.

ODA – Operational Detachment Alpha; Green Beret operational team; per US Army website: Special Forces Soldiers rely on stealth to complete their missions. Special Forces teams are generally organized into small, versatile groups, called Operational Detachment Alphas

Red Zone – Any area outside the protected perimeter; dangerous

Rotation – Phrase utilized to describe a personnel deployment; early FBI deployments lasted three months

Route Irish – Strip of highway from the Baghdad International Airport to the Green Zone; once touted to be the most dangerous length of highway in the world; "highway of death," TIME 2010

SAS – Special Air Service; elite cadre of British military

SCIF – Abbreviation for Sensitive Compartmented Information Facilities; an area, room, or building where sources and methods, including Sensitive Compartmented Information (SCI), is stored, used, processed, or discussed.

Self-licking ice cream cone – An entity that produced little and whose main function centered on sustaining itself

SF – Informal way of referring to Special Forces

SF designators – See names in characters section

SIGINT – See NSA; informal and professional way of saying signals intelligence

SIM card – Subscriber Identification Module; small hardware item within cellular telephone used to identify a subscriber

T-wall – Multiton prefabricated concrete wall about six feet wide, two feet thick and ranging in height from eight to fifteen feet. Each section required a crane for movement, and when set side by side the T-walls made a barrier that was blast resistant and later moveable, making the concept more desirable than a poured concrete wall.

TCN – Abbreviation for Third-Country National; contract worker brought to Iraq and employed

That-guy – Vaguely defined as someone with undesired traits and who could be described by antics, personality, or other characteristics without using a name

The Fort – Informal way of referring to the National Security Agency; physically located at Fort Meade, Maryland; hence the Fort reference

The World – Informal way personnel in Iraq would refer to the US, life outside of Iraq

Torch – British English for flashlight

USG – Informal way of referring to the US government

Wanker – British English for idiot

Made in the USA
Monee, IL
01 May 2023